PRAISE FOR AMY GAIL HANSEN'S
HAPPIER HERE WITH YOU

"*Happier Here With You* is a warm, hygge-shaped hug for the burned-out reader who wishes life would just slow down . . . As Maggie learns more about her family's history at the farm, stretching back to World War II and the Women's Land Army, she will find out what she truly wants for herself and her future. Amy Gail Hansen will make you crave a slower-paced life, a farmhouse kitchen, and homemade scones, in that order!"
—Kate Quinn, *New York Times* bestselling author of *The Briar Club*

"*Happier Here With You* has all the ingredients of a novel you can escape into. Hansen combines the perfect blend of mouthwatering foodie fiction with a generous helping of historical fiction and a dash of romance. Touching and heartfelt, this story speaks of loss, tempered by the restorative powers of love and family bonds. It was a delight from start to finish!"
—Renée Rosen, *USA Today* bestselling author of *Let's Call Her Barbie*

"*Happier Here With You* is the kind of book you want to settle down with and just bask in its warmth! Amy Gail Hansen has created a main character, Maggie Brodbeck, whose journey to find herself after being widowed reconnects her with a great-aunt she never knew, as well as her family's long-buried history in a small town in Wisconsin. Best of all, Maggie rediscovers the pleasures of cooking and the joy of food, as she works to save her great-aunt's legacy. I adored this deeply satisfying story."
—Maddie Dawson, bestselling author of *Matchmaking for Beginners*

"Heartfelt and immersive, *Happier Here With You* by Amy Gail Hansen is the kind of book that feels like eating a warm chocolate chip cookie. Hansen has woven a beautiful tale of found family, community, romance, and the healing power of food. I savored every page!"
—Laura Barrow, author of *Call the Canaries Home* and *The Marriage Slip*

"With warmth, charm, and a perfect hint of nostalgia, this novel pulls you in from the first page and delivers a deeply satisfying story about love rediscovered in unexpected places. Treat yourself to this delicious read!"
—Liz Fenton and Lisa Steinke, authors of *The Naysayers*

"What a scrumptious treat of a story! Delightful, delicious, and heartwarming, get ready to curl up and savor every page!"
—Rachel Linden, author of *The Secret of Orange Blossom Cake*

"Escape to Wisconsin in this sweet tale of overcoming loss and finding sustenance, love, and home."
—Ellen Baker, author of *Summerland Cove*

"A tender, deeply reassuring novel about a woman who discovers how wide the world can become when she reconnects with her instincts. Maggie's move to her great-aunt's Midwestern home sets in motion a cascade of small, brave choices that open her to new possibility. Her journey from burnout to renewal, from disconnection to love and community, comes alive through the vivid celebration of cooking and the sensory richness of food, as well as the steady generosity of the people who welcome her in. As past and present intertwine through the home that shaped generations of her family, long-buried stories rise to the surface and draw her back to the roots she thought she'd lost. The result is a quiet kind of magic: finding where and with whom you truly belong, and remembering that opening your heart can lead to a life you never imagined."
—Therese Walsh, author of *The Last Will of Moira Leahy* and *The Moon Sisters*, and cofounder of Writer Unboxed

"Amy Gail Hansen's *Happier Here With You* celebrates the landscape, food, and good-hearted people of Wisconsin—all while tugging at readers' heartstrings. Whether you have a connection to the Midwest or not, her charming and deeply moving story will make you feel right at home in the rolling green hills of the Driftless Area. (Also, it will make you very hungry, so have snacks handy.)"

—Laura Anne Bird, author of *Marvelous Jackson* and *Crossing the Pressure Line*, and cofounder of the Great Midwest Book Group

PRAISE FOR AMY GAIL HANSEN'S
THE BUTTERFLY SISTER

"That rare thing, a dark mystery that also works on your heart, *The Butterfly Sister* is a beguiling, terrifying story and Amy Gail Hansen a true find."

—Jacquelyn Mitchard, author of *The Deep End of the Ocean*

"*The Butterfly Sister* begins with the arrival of a mysterious suitcase, but that is only the first of a series of surprises Amy Gail Hansen has in store for readers. Just when we think we have a handle on the latest plot twist, here comes another—and the suspense builds again, all resting in the hands of Ruby Rousseau, a spirited young woman who has great taste in literature but not in men. Hansen's first novel is heartfelt, suspenseful and very, very satisfying!"

—Nancy Woodruff, author of *My Wife's Affair*

"I LOVED IT. That book is the perfect beach read . . . girls who like dishy romantic thrillers are going to go nuts for it this summer. I myself couldn't put it down 'til I was done, like it was a big fat piña colada."

—Meg Cabot, *New York Times* bestselling author of
The Princess Diaries

"Rewarding reading."

—Publishers Weekly

"Hansen's debut cleverly entwines these literary ghosts into a suspenseful and swiftly paced light mystery."

—Kirkus Reviews

"*The Butterfly Sister* offers an intimate and fluidly told tale of one young woman's seeming to find love, nearly losing her mind, and slowly uncovering a complex history of betrayal . . . finding out what has happened to Beth leads Ruby to find out, in a satisfying and well-constructed conclusion, what happened to herself."

—Barbara Hoffert, Library Journal

"Hansen's debut tale of madness, mystery, revenge, betrayal, love, and literature will keep you guessing until the surprise ending."
 —Karen Briggs, Great Northern Books & Hobbies, Oscoda, Michigan

"Hansen creates a multilayered mystery that hooks the reader from the very beginning . . . One hopes for more offerings from Amy Gail Hansen."

—New York Journal of Books

"Ruby proves to be a smart, complex, and very engaging character. An agreeable mix of suspense and literary fiction."

—Heather Paulson, Booklist

Happier Here With You

ALSO BY AMY GAIL HANSEN

The Butterfly Sister

Happier Here With You

A Novel

Amy Gail Hansen

This is a work of fiction. Names, characters, organizations, places, events, and incidents are either products of the author's imagination or are used fictitiously.

Text copyright © 2026 by Amy Gail Hansen
All rights reserved.

No part of this book may be reproduced, or stored in a retrieval system, or transmitted in any form or by any means, electronic, mechanical, photocopying, recording, or otherwise, without express written permission of the publisher.

Published by Lake Union Publishing, Seattle

www.apub.com

Amazon, the Amazon logo, and Lake Union Publishing are trademarks of Amazon.com, Inc., or its affiliates.

EU product safety contact:
Amazon Media EU S. à r.l.
38, avenue John F. Kennedy, L-1855 Luxembourg
amazonpublishing-gpsr@amazon.com

ISBN-13: 9781662538230 (paperback)
ISBN-13: 9781662538247 (digital)

Cover design by Emily Mahon
Cover image: © Raymond Forbes LLC / Stocksy; © Roc Canals / Getty; © Orhan Cam / Shutterstock

Printed in the United States of America

For my children—Andrew, Luke, and Amelia—
for inspiring me to become
the best, most authentic version of myself

This above all: to thine own self be true.
—William Shakespeare, *Hamlet*, act 1, scene 3

1

The exhibit opens to clinking champagne flutes, but all I hear is the ghost of Charles Dickens, whispering from his grave:

It was the best of times, it was the worst of times.

It *is* the best of times. For my career. As a food anthropologist and curator at the Midwest Natural History Museum at Lakeside University, where I'm also an assistant professor, this exhibit is my tour de force. It highlights the most influential American female cookbook authors over the span of two-hundred-plus years. From Amelia Simmons and her 1796 masterpiece *American Cookery* to Julia Child, and beyond, it reveals the private lives of these women, their original handwritten recipes, and historical re-creations of their kitchens.

And yet, it feels like the worst of times—for my motherhood report card, at least.

Tonight, while I rub elbows with some of Chicagoland's finest female chefs and field questions from journalists, my five-year-old daughter, Hannah, will graduate from kindergarten. She will walk across an adorable kid-size wooden bridge in her school gymnasium and receive her diploma. After, she will look into the audience to see not her mother waving from her seat, but her longtime babysitter, April, who graciously agreed to take Hannah in my absence. April promised to film the biggest ten seconds of my daughter's young life and text me the clip.

If ever a person wanted to be in two places at once . . .

The opening gala date was set the moment we miraculously booked Ruth Rivers, the only living cookbook author featured in the exhibit, and extremely hard to pin down. She literally had one night available in late spring to fly in for the festivities—a Wednesday evening—the same night as Hannah's graduation ceremony, set by the school board a year ago.

There was nothing I could do.

When I told Hannah, she didn't seem fazed. "It's okay, Mom," she said. "April can just put it on YouTube."

It probably is okay with Hannah. It just isn't okay with me.

This isn't the kind of parent I want to be.

I know it's one hundred percent acceptable and financially necessary for today's working parents, mothers *and* fathers, to miss their children's soccer games and ballet recitals and science fair presentations. And because I'm a widow—my husband, Sean, passed just two months before Hannah was born—I likely receive a double get-out-of-jail-free card. But just because I *can* do it, and I *have* to do it to support us, doesn't mean I *want* to.

The truth is, I am in two places tonight. My body and brain are here at the museum, but my heart is in that stuffy school gymnasium, where Hannah will step toward another version of herself. And if I'm really being honest, it isn't just tonight. For the past six weeks, as I've been preparing for the opening, there's been too much screen time, for both of us, and lots of fast-food takeout. We used to read three picture books together every night, but lately, we rush through only one or two on the weekend. When I do make time for Hannah, I'm hardly in the moment. Despite my best efforts, my mind always wanders to work.

Tonight, I try to put Hannah's graduation out of my mind. I mingle and shake hands and snap photos and answer questions and laugh at a food-pun joke and smile. And I remind myself to actually celebrate this accomplishment. It's exhilarating when something that was once just an idea transforms into something tangible—an event, no less—and I revel in seeing guests stop at various points of the exhibit to study an artifact or read a placard. The pièces de résistance, in my opinion, are the kitchen replicas. We curated every detail to whisk museum visitors back in time, to a specific place. The countertops in Julia Child's Cambridge kitchen, for example, were taller than standard to account for her six-foot-three stature, and our replica reflects this difference. It also boasts her blue pegboard with hanging brass pots and pans, painted black refrigerator, and yellow oil-clothed dining table.

When I feel my phone buzz inside the pocket of my black dress pants, I immediately head to my office. I want to watch Hannah's graduation clip in private.

Because I already know I'm going to cry.

On the tiny phone screen, I watch Hannah bounce across the bridge, her brown curls grazing her shoulders. She smiles at her kindergarten teacher as she accepts the roll of white paper that is her graduation certificate. In reality, the whole ceremony is silly. Hannah's school is K–6, so next year, she isn't even changing buildings. She is literally moving one classroom down the hall. There is no *need* for a graduation. And yet, it seems so important to encourage her education, to celebrate her first full year of school. But this isn't why I'm crying. The tears are because I know that while I get to see Hannah graduate, thanks to April's cell phone camera skills, Hannah will not see me watching her graduate. There is no one capturing the love and pride on my face now for her to view another time.

The phone screen is a one-sided mirror.

I can see her, but she can't see me.

By the time I arrive home and relieve April, it's almost 11:00 p.m. Hannah is fast asleep, but I sit at the edge of her bed for a few minutes. Her chest rises and falls in a steady rhythm—the epitome of peace. Her graduation cap, crafted out of black cardstock, sits askew on her pillow. She must have gone to bed wearing it. I move it safely to her nightstand.

I'm bursting to tell her about my night, how I finally met—in person, at least—one of my all-time heroes. Ruth Rivers is a chef extraordinaire, entrepreneur, food-industry icon, and editor in chief of *Mirepoix*, a gourmet cooking magazine to which I've long subscribed. She's a goddess in the foodie world. My head still feels light, floating above me like a balloon, from actually being in her presence tonight. While I've conducted several phone interviews with her over the past two years—exhilarating on their own—actually seeing her in the flesh, hearing her iconic Minnesotan accent without the buffer of a television screen, felt surreal. She was everything I thought she would be, and also, so humble. I expected a well-earned air of importance, but I caught her more than once serving drinks to guests, rearranging appetizers on platters, and clearing crumbs, as if she were more comfortable being in the back of the house than the front. She called me Ms. Brodbeck several times, even though I asked her to call me Maggie. Of course, this only reminded me of Sean. I was resolute in keeping my own name when we married, but after he passed, I questioned that choice. Sometimes, I still do. Not that it could have possibly made a difference. But somehow it feels like more of a loss, more of a severing, without this shared name forever binding us. Now, I recall my conversations with Ruth this evening and wonder if I made an equally good impression, or if I seemed distracted, which I was.

I kiss Hannah's forehead, then head to the kitchen and peek inside the fridge. The food served tonight was catered and gourmet, but feeling anxious, I didn't eat a bite. Now, I'm suddenly starving. There are no leftovers because I asked April to treat Hannah to her favorite fast-food kids' meal tonight. Plus, I need to go grocery shopping. Dinners have been haphazard as of late, with the opening of the exhibit, the end-of-school-year vibe, the warmer temperatures and longer days. Once late May arrives in Chicagoland, everyone heads outdoors—where cutting, chopping, roasting, or sautéing go by the wayside. Grabbing cold subs and eating a picnic dinner at the park feels right. Or a bowl of cereal with ice-cold milk. *Easy* and *quick* seem to be the core requirements of any meal since losing Sean. Once upon a time, I lingered at the stove, constantly stirring a roux for gumbo or pitting fresh-picked Montmorency cherries for a cobbler. Unfortunately, cooking seems to be a gift of time and contentment—neither of which I have much of these days.

After looking into my near-empty fridge, I grab what's left of the bread—two ends—and slather on some peanut butter and cherry jelly. A cup of herbal rooibos tea completes my meal, and I sit at the kitchen table and sort through the mail April brought in earlier. It's a lot of junk. Most of it will end up in the recycling bin or shredder. I see there's another issue of *Mirepoix*, and I wince. I have yet to look at the last issue. Has a month passed already? I should probably cancel my subscription.

But that would be like canceling who I used to be, the hope of rebecoming that person.

At the bottom of the pile, there's a long white envelope with curvy scripted handwriting and a return address in St. John's Ferry, Wisconsin. The trifold letter inside is typed—as in, on a typewriter—the corners of each letter nostalgically pooled with black ink. I start reading, but it's late and my eyes blur. I blink and begin again:

```
The time has come, Magpie.

Spend the summer here on Rosehill Farm.
You and Hannah. Anytime is fine.
But I should warn you, they say
the cell reception is "spotty." No
internet. And there will be work.
But I promise, it will be the best
summer of your life.
The time to grow like wild.

Alice
```

And then a phone number typed below her name.

I read the letter again, and then once more, trying to process.

I've never even met my Great-Aunt Alice, and yet, she is asking—no, practically *telling*—me to come to her Wisconsin farm for the summer. *There will be work.* Like what? Milking cows? Repairing fences? As if I could just drop everything—work, life—and do that.

As if I could live three months without internet.

And why did she call me *Magpie*? No one has ever called me that in my life. My full name is Magnolia—like the flower—but everyone calls me Maggie. Could it be a typo? I wonder if she's almost blind or going senile, typing fragmented letters on some dusty typewriter and mailing them to estranged family members. Her tone is too casual, almost patronizing.

The time has come.

What does that even mean?

I glance at the clock. It's half past eleven, which means it's only 9:30 p.m. on the West Coast. My mother, a math professor at UCLA, is probably still awake, grading papers. My impulse is to call her, read her the letter from Alice. Gossip. But the idea sours my stomach. For some reason, it feels like breaking a trust with Alice.

But how can I have a trust with someone I've never even met?

I know very little about Alice. She's my late grandfather Albert Jr.'s much younger—by eleven years—sister, my mother's aunt, and the family outcast. Last I knew, she lived alone—no husband, no children. In addition to her "wild" hair, curly and unruly, *wild* has also referred to the berry jam she makes and sells on the side of the road and the turkeys she eats. Throughout my childhood, Alice was a whisper at Independence Day picnics, a murmur over Thanksgiving pie, a heavy sigh between sips of Christmas eggnog, and a cleared throat after Easter Sunday ham. I knew her only through stories, which made her a mythical enigma. My juvenile brain placed her somewhere between Paul Bunyan and a unicorn.

My mind travels back to the Brodbeck family Fourth of July picnic, the summer I turned seven. I remember my mother baked cupcakes, frosted them white, topped them with blue or red sprinkles, and arranged them on a platter to resemble the American flag. She carried that platter to the picnic table like an overfilled fish tank.

"Diane, did you make these?" my aunts—all three—asked.

My mom nodded and beamed at their oohs and aahs. "Homemade," she said.

When my cousins peeled off the cupcake liners and bit into them like cheeseburgers, I dabbed my fingertip into the frosting and tasted, then ran my tongue over the roof of my mouth, noting the heavy film. I didn't know then about hydrogenated fats; they don't dissolve in your mouth because their melting point is higher than the human body temp of 98.6 degrees. Instead, the commercially made frosting coats your mouth in blubber.

All I knew was I didn't like it.

"Watch out, Mags. You better eat that cupcake, or I'm going to," joked my Uncle Tony. He was always chiming in with something instructional as if to make up for me not having a dad. "Those are homemade cupcakes."

"No, they aren't," I blurted. The table chatter came to a deafening silence. "My mom made them *at home*. But it was from a box," I corrected. "From the store. And the frosting was also from the store."

I held my breath. Had I just told one of my mother's deepest, darkest secrets? Would she ever forgive me?

"Well, of course it was," Tony said, while the rest of the aunts and cousins chuckled at my naivete. "That's how you make homemade cupcakes."

"Actually, it's not," I said, barely audible over their snickers.

I had never baked a cake from scratch, but I knew that truly homemade versions didn't come from a box or a tub. You could make them by combining a list of ingredients and following steps in a recipe, something I had recently figured out after perusing the cookbook section at the public library. In the limited food vernacular of a seven-year-old, I attempted to explain all of this, until my cousin Tommy cut me off.

"Your cupcakes are the best, Aunt Diane!" he announced. Then the kids all grabbed a second one as if to prove me wrong and shut me up.

Which they did.

Later, I could barely hear my mother and her sisters while they packed up for the night. But I knew they were talking about me, their voices hushed, side glances in my direction. I sat alone on a flannel blanket studying the constellations instead of the fireworks.

I couldn't make out what they said, except a single phrase.

"She's just like Alice," one of them said.

"Alice," I whispered into the darkness, the name tingling the tip of my tongue like pickle juice. As the ground shook below me, I wondered who this Alice was. If my mother disowned me after tonight, maybe I could go live with her.

And we could be just like each other, together.

My mind snaps back to the present. I set the letter down and begin to tidy up, run through the muscle memory of my nighttime routine, all while a barrage of questions floods my brain: Why did Alice write me? How did she get my address? How does she know about Hannah? Why does she want me to come to her farm this summer?

Why does she think I need to *grow, like wild*?

And, what if she's right?

2

I call my mom from work Thursday morning. Alice's letter sits open on my desk.

"How's the weather?" she asks as soon as we exchange greetings.

"Well, it's late May," I say. "So it's as nice as California right now. But don't worry, the heat and humidity will ruin everything in a month."

"Ugh, and that god-awful cold and snow," she laments. "I seriously do not know how you live there."

She means *why* I live here. I moved to Eastridge, an urban college town just north of Chicago, when I married Sean. When we met, he lived here and worked at Lakeside University as a professor of mathematics—an occupation he had in common with my mother, and the only reason she ever tolerated him. But after he passed, suddenly and tragically, my whole family expected me to return to Los Angeles. I couldn't possibly raise my daughter alone in the Midwest. My mother had raised me alone—I never even knew my father; I was the product of a very short-lived romance, something longer than a one-night stand but too short to be called a relationship—but she did it with the support system of her parents, three sisters, their husbands, and an army of cousins. The truth was, after Sean died, I couldn't bring myself to leave. That's why I also said no to Sean's parents, who live in a retirement community in Orlando, when they offered to pay for our relocation to Florida. Because I saw Sean—at least, I saw the memory of him—all over Eastridge, standing on every street corner, eating at every restaurant, sipping coffee in the window of every bookstore.

At first, learning to live without him every day felt like acquiring a new and challenging skill, something that would take me years to master: playing the violin, becoming fluent in Mandarin, or baking perfect macarons. I fumbled daily. In the morning, still half asleep, I would roll over to Sean's side of the bed, my arm free-falling to the cold comforter instead of landing on his warm chest. At breakfast, I would instinctively pull out Tabasco when I made scrambled eggs, even though I never shared Sean's affection for spice. I still signed his name on birthday cards. And at night, just before bed, I would mindlessly measure enough coffee grounds and completely fill the water reservoir to brew a full pot in the morning.

Over the past five years, I honed the skill of living in a world where he didn't physically exist, a world he left. But if I leave Chicagoland, the Midwest, then I leave Sean.

Forever.

"Are you teaching over the summer?" my mother presses.

"No, I decided not to, so I can spend more time with Hannah. You know, movies in the park, waterslides, roast marshmallows on the patio."

"Then book a flight to LA," she insists.

I cringe. "I'm not sure I can take the time off from the museum."

"You must have months of vacation stockpiled by now," she argues.

I do. But while I took personal days without any regard before Sean passed, using them now is something I can't get myself to do. A day here or there is fine. But a week? Two weeks? What if something happens, an emergency—I get sick, Hannah gets sick—and I don't have enough days banked because I've squandered them on empty visits with my family or expensive, unnecessary jaunts to Disney World? It feels better, safer, to leave them untouched. An insurance policy. Plus, my boss, Elena, who is about the same age as my mother, is retiring from her position as museum director in the fall. I'm the number one candidate to fill her spot, which includes a pay raise and better job security. I don't want to do anything that makes me appear undedicated.

I change the subject. "Did you watch the video of Hannah's graduation ceremony?"

"Oh. Not yet, but I will," she says. I hear water running and dishes clanking in the background. "So what activities is Hannah signed up for this summer?"

None. By the time I remembered to sign her up, all of the day camps and swim lessons and craft workshops had waiting lists.

"Her babysitter, April, will keep her busy," I say instead. "Today they're at the beach, then probably the library for story time." Before she can comment about Hannah's mind "turning to mush" over the summer, I add, "So you'll never believe what I got in the mail yesterday. A very weird letter from your Aunt Alice."

A sudden silence. "Really?" she finally says. "What did it say?"

I clear my throat and read the letter.

"That's random," she says. "And audacious, really. It's like she's telling you to come, not asking. No one has heard from Alice in decades. And now, all of a sudden, she sends you this letter?"

She sounds more angry than curious.

I think of my first cousins. "No one else got a letter, did they?"

"I don't think so. I just saw half the family last weekend at Becky's baby shower. Trust me, they would have mentioned it."

I know she's right. "What do you make of it?" I ask.

My mother sighs. "Oh, she's a bit eccentric, Maggie. Always has been, but she's getting up there in years. She's probably developing dementia or the like."

I thought the same thing last night, and yet my first impulse is to defend Alice. I bite my tongue, thinking back to the day I finally got the nerve to ask my mother about Alice point-blank.

I was in sixth grade, and for a history assignment, we had to research our surname and design a family coat of arms. Hunched over library books, I was shocked to learn that my last name, Brodbeck, means *bread baker*.

As in, I—and everyone in the Brodbeck family—was destined to bake bread.

By the time my mom arrived home from work, the kitchen was a village in a snow globe, coated white with a heavy dusting of flour.

"What in heaven's name are you doing?" she asked in horror.

"Baking bread," I said.

"There is perfectly good bread here." She pointed to the loaf of soft white slices inside the yellow, red, and blue plastic bag on the counter.

"But did you know our last name means *bread baker*?" I charged.

"It does?" She rubbed her temples in tiny circles with the tips of her fingers. "Well, I guess it's a good thing our last name doesn't mean something else, like *fire starter*." She laughed to herself. "But, Maggie, really, this is a disaster. You're going to need to clean it up. Later. Right now, I'm hungry. Let's go grab a slice of pizza first."

"Don't you want to try it?" I asked.

"What?"

"The bread." I reached for the mound cooling on the counter. We didn't own a loaf pan, so I'd formed it by hand into the shape of bread. There were a lot of steps and a lot of time waiting for the dough to rise, but I ended up with something that looked and smelled and hopefully tasted like bread.

My mom looked surprised—she hadn't seen the loaf of bread, just the messy kitchen. I tore off a piece, and she took it with apprehension. I popped a morsel in my mouth at the same time. The two of us chewed and stared into each other's eyes, watching for the other's reaction.

"Maggie, it's . . ." She chewed more and swallowed. "It's actually very good. Very good," she repeated.

"It's a little tough. I may have overworked the dough," I explained.

She shook her head. "I've only known one other person who made bread like this, from scratch," she said.

"Alice?" I blurted.

Her eyes grew wide. "Well, yes . . . you know about Alice?"

"I've heard you talk about her, sometimes," I said.

She cocked her head as if trying to remember what she might have said, and when I might have been listening.

"Why do you and your sisters whisper about her?" I asked. "Like she's a secret?"

"Alice is . . . different. Than us. She marches to the beat of her own drum."

"What does that mean?" I asked.

"She's just kind of old-fashioned."

That's not enough of a reason, I thought. It must be more than that. But just as I prepared a follow-up question, my mother clapped her hands once loudly, which meant she was switching gears, and I'd better be ready to follow.

"We'll talk about this later," she said.

But—and I remember because I tried to bring Aunt Alice into our conversation three more times that night—we never did. Like my father, my Great-Aunt Alice seemed a topic my mother did not want to broach.

Now, my mother picks up on my silent hesitation.

"You're not thinking of going, are you?" Her tone is accusatory. "You just said you can't take any time off work anyway," she adds.

"No," I protest. "Of course not."

My stomach churns, a lump forming in my throat, like it's a blatant lie, despite the fact that I never once considered going to Alice's farm.

"Well, good," she says. "You really don't want to get mixed up with Alice."

My mother's words, *mixed up with,* seem dramatic, like Alice is a cocaine addict or a religious cult leader. She's just a woman who lives on a farm in Wisconsin. *What is so bad about her?* I want to ask my mom, but she cuts me off.

"Look, Mags, I've got to run. I've got breakfast with a colleague and an afternoon class," she says. "But keep me posted, if you get more letters or anything. And I'll ask the family."

I suddenly wish I hadn't told my mom about the letter. It's just fodder. She'll ask the family, and they'll all have a field day speculating about Alice and her mental state. Again, I feel protective of Alice. Why do I want to shield her from this ridicule? Is it because being different than my mother was also my downfall? Like Alice, I marched to the beat of my own drum, never falling in line with my mother's carefully laid plans. Or is it because Alice's banishment never seemed fair, her crimes never matching her punishment?

This sense of loyalty to Alice is almost as big a mystery as why she sent me the letter in the first place.

By afternoon, the grilled cheese sandwich I grabbed from the museum cafeteria isn't sitting well. I'd only had time—and bandwidth—to pack a bag of peanuts for lunch. The "butter" must actually be some hydrogenated vegetable spread. I chew a piece of mint gum to ease my digestion and check my phone. I quickly notice I haven't heard back from April all morning. I sent her an early text about buying sunscreen on the way to the beach, and another asking for a photo of their sandcastle. It's been several hours and nothing.

Agreeing to let Hannah go to the beach today was difficult. When April asked, my gut reaction was a hard no. But Hannah begged, and I rationalized away my hesitation; April is an excellent swimmer and CPR certified. Lake Michigan is still rather cold in late May, so they would likely only go in to their knees. They'd spend most of the time in the sand surrounded by buckets and shovels. Still, the whole idea didn't sit well—six years ago in May, Sean drowned in that lake; we marked the anniversary of that fateful day earlier this month. And while I've had to pass the lake, even watch the sun rise over it, just the sight of it throws me, if only momentarily, into fight or flight. Either my fists clench or I stop breathing, or both. But fueled by the guilt of missing Hannah's graduation, and spoiling a fun start to her summer vacation, I said yes.

I call April instead, but her phone goes immediately to voicemail. I leave a message, trying to sound more relaxed than I feel.

A half hour passes, and still no calls or texts.

I try to focus on work, but can't. I keep checking my phone, and then double- and triple-checking it, assuring myself that it isn't on silent mode.

Worst-case scenarios flood my mind, hijacking all bodily functions. My breath turns shallow, and my heart pounds in my chest, in my throat. I stand and start to pace, stomach acids creeping up my esophagus. I begin to sweat everywhere—my armpits, my forehead, my upper lip. *I can't stay here.* I have to leave. I have to drive to the beach right now and find them. I have to make sure Hannah is alive and okay.

As I try to dash out, I run into Elena. My boss takes one look at me and stops me with a firm grip on my upper arm. "Maggie, what's wrong?"

"I can't breathe," I say.

"You can't *breathe*?" Elena repeats in the soothing, grandmotherly tone I wish belonged to my own mother.

"And my heart is . . ." I try to take in a full breath but seem to hit a wall inside my lungs. "It's pounding. I can feel it in my head. It's in my throat."

I suddenly feel woozy, and Elena instinctively leads me to a chair and has me sit.

"I knew it was a bad idea," I protest as she takes my pulse. "I should never have let Hannah go swimming with April. I'm going to the beach now to find them."

Elena tightens her grip on my wrist. "Maggie, I can't let you drive in this condition," she says. "Of course, we need to make sure Hannah is safe. But first, I think we better go to the hospital."

"Hospital?" I barely get the word out.

"Do you have shortness of breath?" she asks.

I nod.

"Are you sweating? Nauseous?"

I nod again.

She remains quiet as she counts my heartbeats under her fingertips.

"Your pulse is 180," she says. "Maggie, I'm calling an ambulance."

April finally texts a few minutes after we arrive at the hospital. Because I'm hooked up to monitors, Elena reads April's note. It's all very benign. April forgot to charge her phone the night before, and the battery died early. She didn't notice until they were at the beach, and she had no way to charge it there. As soon as they returned to my house, she plugged her cell back in and received my messages. They had a wonderful time at the beach. Hannah even made up a story about a mermaid and is now busy writing it all down with illustrations.

But even as I let relief wash over me, my heart rate sits at 150 beats per minute. It's dropping, but slowly. The ER staff has run every test imaginable—blood tests, EKG, an x-ray of my lungs—and can't find anything wrong.

When my heart rate drops to 120, the doctor returns to my bedside, her head cocked and soft eyes filled with pity. "When your pulse is below 100, I'll let you go home," she says.

"So I didn't have a heart attack?" I ask.

She shakes her head. "You had a panic attack. The symptoms are very similar. And you're not alone. I can't count the number of women around your age, mid- to late thirties, who come in feeling exactly like you did. But it's likely stress and anxiety based."

I nod.

"So the question is, Maggie, why does a perfectly healthy thirty-five-year-old woman have a resting pulse over 100?" she asks, gesturing to the beeping monitor.

I let her question linger between us.

"She was worried about her daughter," Elena chimes in from her bedside chair, quickly taking an advocate role.

"Your daughter?" the doctor repeats.

"She was at the beach with her babysitter, and I couldn't get ahold of them," I explain. "My imagination got the best of me. That might sound very irrational—and I guess it is—but my husband died in . . ." I pause, the word is still so bitter in my mouth. "My husband *drowned* in the lake," I say instead.

The doctor nods. "And did you see someone, a professional, about that?"

"Yes, for a whole year but . . ." I pause, then shrug. "Maybe that wasn't enough."

"Maybe not," she says. "So that's also why, while I'm not sending you home with any prescriptions, I'm giving you a referral for a therapist. And it would be a good idea to take it easy for the next few days. Try to do activities you find relaxing. Meditation, yoga, reading?"

I nod again, agreeing to her terms, and thank her.

When the doctor leaves, I lock eyes with Elena. "I guess I'm taking the rest of the afternoon off," I say. "Doctor's orders."

"The afternoon?" Elena arches her eyebrow. "More like a week. *Boss's* orders."

"A week?"

Elena scoots her chair closer. "Maggie, you just had a panic attack that landed you in the hospital. You've been burning the candle at both ends. Sleeping less, eating less. Doing too much. I don't think you realize what a toll it's taking."

She's right. I haven't slept more than three to four hours at a time. My meals the past month have mostly consisted of French fries or packaged protein bars pretending to be nutritious. Not the diet you'd expect a gourmand food anthropologist to follow.

Elena lays her hand on mine. "I think your body is trying to tell you something."

"Like what?"

"Slow down," she offers. "You haven't taken more than a day or two off since I took this position three years ago."

"You're going to make me take a vacation? Is that legal?"

She shakes her head, but her coiffed hair, streaked with gray, doesn't budge. "I can't make you, but I can *highly advise* you. Things are definitely slower now that the exhibit opened. Summer is always calmer than the school year. And I'm still here full-time until the fall. This is actually an opportune time to take a week off before everything that's ahead of you."

She's talking about the job promotion, taking on her role as museum director, without actually talking about it. Nothing is official yet, though I know she wants me for the position.

When I don't seem convinced, she adds, "You heard the doctor. Why does a perfectly healthy thirty-five-year-old woman have a resting pulse over 100? It's a valid question and worth a week to ponder. Don't you think?"

It is a good question. I'd like to blame it on the greasy sandwich, or April and Hannah's trip to the beach, or April's phone dying, but I wonder if it's more than that. Once upon a time—when Sean was still alive, when I was younger—I was different. Calmer. Easygoing. Fun. But being a single mom, knowing I am the sole breadwinner—that the balance of our life rests fully on my shoulders—has changed me. How many times since Sean passed have I thought, *Stop the world, I want to get off*. It's as if every day I'm opening a new business, but before I can set everything up the way it needs to be, someone opens the front doors and lets all the customers in. And they just keep coming, so I have to keep the business going. But everything behind the counter is still a mess, and all I really want to do is push all the customers out the door, lock it behind them, and post a sign that says "Closed for Renovation."

The problem is, I don't run a business. I run a home. I run a family. I run a life. And you can't close a home or a family.

You can't *close* a life.

But you can *vacate* it.

"Okay," I finally say to Elena, so soft, it's almost a whisper.

"Okay?" she repeats.

"I'll take some time off."

"Good. Because I was already planning to lock you out of your office if you tried to show up tomorrow." She laughs, and I do too.

I feel my pulse slow down a few beats.

"And think about actually *going somewhere*," Elena goes on. "Take Hannah on a little trip. It's good to get away. Is there anywhere you've wanted to go? Somewhere you'd like to show her?"

On my long list of travel destinations are New York City, the Outer Banks, and Key West. But oddly, none of those places come to mind. I turn to Elena and say, "St. John's Ferry, Wisconsin."

3

I wake Friday morning determined to make the most of this unexpected break from work, the gift of more time with Hannah. We never really celebrated her kindergarten graduation, so I envision making her celebratory French toast, the fluffy kind dripping with real maple syrup. But then I remember I used up the remaining two end pieces of bread on the PB&J the other night. I could *bake* a loaf—I haven't done that in years—but it will take too long for a double rise, and I want to go to the first farmers market of the season, which runs until noon. The ER doctor told me to take it easy, to do things that relax me, and walking around the market always makes my heart feel light, though I rarely go these days.

Pancakes would be an equally special breakfast for my new kindergarten graduate, but a quick look at the flour canister reveals a scant tablespoon or two. I ran out a month ago and obviously haven't baked anything since.

And I thought I could bake bread?

I definitely need groceries.

I think back to how Sean and I used to go to the grocery store every Friday night after work. I'd plan all the meals—including a few new recipes—and write the list, but Sean was the muscle. He could reach the high items and lift the heavy ones. He maneuvered the cart through crowds and determined the most efficient path through the store. We were a symbiotic team, wending our way toward a weekend of relaxed kitchen experimentation and quality time.

Nowadays, I'm too tired to shop; instead, I order online and get virtually the same groceries delivered every week.

"Want to get doughnuts at the farmers market?" I ask Hannah.

Her eyes grow wide. She squeals at the mention of the *D* word, and now I don't feel like such a terrible mom after all.

At the market, we eat our warm rings of cinnamon sugar as we stroll past the delicious, colorful offerings of late May. There's a smell of potential in the morning spring air, the promise of sun and summer and bounty and harvest. Anything is possible. The future is bright. At least, that's how it feels at the first farmers market of the year. I'm relaxing already.

Hannah points to a table ahead. "Is that celery *pink*?" she asks.

I see a familiar but forgotten sight, a table loaded with crisp crimson stalks. "That's not pink celery. That's rhubarb."

I show Hannah the gorgeous color up close. "You can eat only the stalk," I tell her. "The leaves are actually poisonous."

"Oh no." Her lips twist in concern.

"Don't worry," I say. "The farmer cut that off already. See?"

Her shoulders relax.

The woman selling the rhubarb asks how much we want.

"Want to bake a pie today?" I ask Hannah, as I pay the woman for two bundles. "A strawberry-rhubarb pie? With whipped cream?"

"With ice cream?" she asks.

"I mean, with ice cream?" I correct.

She gives me the doughnut eyes again and licks her lips.

"This is the best day ever," she says.

By afternoon, Hannah sits in a carbohydrate-induced coma in front of her iPad. The doughnuts for breakfast and boxed mac and cheese for lunch have hit her hard. Forget the strawberry-rhubarb pie. While I may have time to make a pie, I don't have the energy. I haven't made dough in years. It's only five ingredients—flour, butter, sugar, salt, and water—but I feel a bit rusty. I decide to just cut and freeze the rhubarb for another day. Besides, watching Hannah's zombie stare at the screen prompts me to suggest a walk to the playground this afternoon.

While Hannah pumps her legs on the swings, I sit on a nearby bench with a slew of other parents about my age. Most seem more interested in checking Instagram or playing Candy Crush than talking to each other. However, I note one mom and dad talking on an adjacent bench—can even overhear their banter about weekend errands and calling someone about the dead tree in the front yard, their debate about whether their oldest is responsible enough to get a cell phone. The exchange makes me pause. Would Sean and I be discussing these types of things if he were with me on this bench? Brainstorming venues for Hannah's sixth birthday party? Buying a newer, safer car? Planning our next date night?

I shake this thought away, and instead take the quiet opportunity to open the Maps application on my phone. I type in the address of Great-Aunt Alice's farm in St. John's Ferry. I just can't stop thinking about her letter, about her invitation to visit. And as I do with most things that won't leave my mind, I begin to obsess and search the internet.

St. John's Ferry, I learn, is a small town of about three thousand people located in southwestern Wisconsin. It sits on the banks of the mighty Mississippi River, and thus, just over the border from Minnesota. It's at the very heart of the Driftless Area, a region of the Midwest characterized by steep bluffs and dramatic valleys caused by a lack of glacial drift, hence the name "driftless." The rest of the Midwest is flat because glaciers essentially plowed through them ages ago. The photos are breathtaking—this part of the Midwest could double for somewhere like Ireland or Scotland—at least, that's how it looks on my phone. From an aerial view, Alice's farm appears fairly large. I see a pond, walking path, barn, henhouse, small orchard, garden, and main house just from the map image. The street view doesn't reveal much, though. Her farmhouse is significantly set back from the road and not visible. All I see is a black mailbox and a gravel driveway lined with oaks and maples.

I do a quick Google search using my aunt's name and address, but it seems she has no digital footprint, which makes sense given she doesn't have internet service. I don't know why I even bothered looking her up. But there's something at the bottom of the list that catches my eye. A recipe from over thirty years ago archived in the *St. John's Ferry Gazette*:

Magpie's Zucchini Bread, submitted by Alice Brodbeck.

I peruse the recipe and find it interesting. Orange marmalade is one of the primary ingredients. But that's not the most intriguing part. At the bottom of the recipe is a postscript in italics.

My three-year-old great-niece, who I call Magpie, can't get enough of this bread, especially if it's slathered with orange honey butter.

I wait until after Hannah's bedtime to call my mother, and I cut right to the chase.

"There's something you aren't telling me about Alice," I say.

I hear everything she hasn't told me in her silence.

"What do you mean?" Her voice is high and tight.

"Mom. Please."

"Please what?"

I take a deep breath. She isn't going to budge unless I back her into a corner. While I feel my blood pressure rising, and know I shouldn't get myself upset or angry, this is important.

"I spent time with her when I was kid," I say matter-of-factly, because it's all I can infer from Alice's recipe. My great-aunt nicknamed me *Magpie*. She made me zucchini bread and slathered it with orange honey butter because she knew I loved it that way. These are things you do when you *know* someone, when you interact with them on a regular basis, not once.

Another silence.

And then, "You remember?" she asks.

I don't. My only memories of Alice aren't really memories at all, more like stories or anecdotes I heard growing up. But my mom's reply tells me I'm getting closer to the truth.

"Did we stay with her?" I ask hesitantly. "On her farm in Wisconsin?"

"For a short time," she finally says.

"When?"

"When you were very young," she says brusquely, as if clearing off crumbs from the conversation. "So young, I didn't think you could possibly remember."

I wonder if I do. My first childhood memory, at least what I have long thought to be my first childhood memory, is biting into a tomato like an apple, and the warm, sweet juice dripping down my chin onto my hands and down my forearms to my elbows. The midday sun hits the top of my head, and I feel my scalp burn. I'm barefoot and the summer grass sears my feet. When I shared this memory in the past, my mother told me I was around three, and it was likely the summer months, when tomato plants are ready for harvest.

Except my mother doesn't garden.

"When *exactly* did we stay with her?" I push. "And for how long?"

My mother lets out a loud huff. "Oh, you were just a baby. I don't really remember exactly, Maggie. It's been so long."

"Give me a ballpark figure."

"A month or so?"

I think back to the zucchini bread recipe printed in the local newspaper, the note in italics. Alice called me her *three-year-old* great-niece. That isn't *just a baby*. We had to have been there more than a few months.

"It was longer than that," I say with certainty, although I am far from certain.

She clears her throat. "Did she write that in her letter?"

"Mom," I snap. "I'm going to be thirty-six years old this summer. Whatever it is you're dancing around, afraid to tell me, just let it out. I can handle it."

I hear my mother exhale, but this time it isn't in defense. It's in resignation. "You went to live with her when you were about three months old," she finally says.

My stomach drops. Because she said *you*. Not *we*.

"I was finishing my master's." My mother's voice cracks. "I didn't know how to build a career and be a mom, a good mom, at the same time."

I can empathize, juggling motherhood with a career, because I do it every day. Every time I act in my own best interest for time or sanity—staying late at the museum, working on weekends, grabbing takeout, prodding Hannah to get to the point of a story instead of listening to the beautiful cadence of her five-year-old voice—feels like a point deducted from my daughter's childhood. Sometimes, since Sean's passing, I think back to moments growing up and see them from my mother's point of view. But right now, I can't let her off the hook.

"What about my father?" I ask. "Couldn't he have cared for me?"

"Maggie, you know he wasn't in the picture. He didn't even know you existed, and I've told you this before, I didn't even know how to find him. I had nothing to go on. I didn't even know his last name."

This was how the story went: My mother met a very handsome European man during her first year of graduate school. He was visiting the States for some sort of conference, though she didn't know what kind. Because they believed they would never see each other again, they decided to only share their first names—she was Diane and he was Chris—and no real personal details from their lives. It was mysterious, thrilling, and made sense from a logical point of view. If they didn't get to really know each other, there would be no hard feelings, no attachment.

I stop pressing the subject of my father. It's a game we've played my whole life—me asking questions, Mom deflecting them, claiming how little she ever knew or remembers. But I do question how my mother left her infant in the care of someone else for so long. Didn't her heart, her arms, ache for me? I think back to that first year with Hannah; my daughter's sweet milky scent would start to fade by the end of the workday, a siren's call home. How could my mother give up that time with me?

"So you let Alice *raise* me?" I ask instead.

"No, *I* raised you," she argues. "You lived with her until you were only three years old, when I was finished with school and able to get a good job and make money and support you as a single mother. I came to visit every few months. I called every week. And she mailed me pictures and updates on how you were doing in between. It was *temporary*."

I have no words, except, "I can't believe you never told me this."

She sighs. "Maybe I should have, looking back. But I didn't want you to think I didn't love you or that I abandoned you in any way. I didn't see what good could come from telling you. I could see only the downside. So I decided it was best not to say anything."

"So *this* is why you made Alice out to be such a pariah?" I say.

"I regret that now." My mother's voice grows soft. "But I was always afraid of you finding out the truth, so I . . ."

"Defamed her," I blurt.

She sighs. "Looking back, yes, I guess I painted her in a negative light."

"But it wasn't only you," I push. "It was Aunt Cathy. All of your sisters."

"Well, they had their own bone to pick with Alice," she divulges. "Alice inherited that farmhouse from our great-grandmother, Rose."

I digest this information. My mother always acted so detached about where Alice lived, as if it was just some place she picked at random, in the obscure, rural Midwest. She never let on that it was a family home. "And they were jealous?" I prompt.

"They wanted their cut. There were developers who tried to purchase the land for an obnoxious amount of money, the kind of money that could truly change lives. But Alice wouldn't sell. My sisters felt shortchanged."

"So they were more than happy to join your smear campaign?" I press. I'm being spiteful, but I can't help myself.

"No, Maggie, it wasn't like that. At least, not intentionally." She pauses. "You know how it is, when Hannah asks questions about things you don't want her to fully know, at least not yet. You protect your children. And sometimes, you overreact. Go a little too far. I really felt like I was protecting you from something that might hurt you."

She pauses, waiting for me to absolve her. But I don't.

"It was hard," she goes on. "Not being able to take care of you and be your mother and go to school and care for myself at the same time. You can understand that, right?"

I could, in a way, but I also couldn't imagine leaving Hannah like that. Ever. Leaving Hannah's side longer than absolutely necessary, especially in those first cherished years, would have felt like leaving my lungs behind. But I wasn't my mother. I knew that for sure now.

Still, I soften. "Why Alice?"

"She didn't have children of her own," she explains. "And I knew her farm would be a safe place for you, away from the craziness of the world. I thought it was the best place."

I imagine myself as a toddler running through a field of flowers on a sunny afternoon, holding a bouquet of dandelions. Carefree. But this image is quickly replaced by reality.

"So then one day, you took me home, and we never saw her again?" I ask.

Another heavy breath. "Well, I started working, teaching at the community college. And we lived in California, and it was hard to travel back to the Midwest on a regular basis. And you started school. And . . . life happened. We lost touch. And to be honest, that's what felt right."

It felt right to you. But maybe not to Alice. She took care of me for almost three years, and then never saw me again. "She never called or even wrote? All that time? All those years?"

My mother's silence is again incriminating.

"She did, but you didn't tell me," I say.

"I acted in your best interest," my mother offers.

And now more than thirty years later, my great-aunt has written again. But why?

We hang up, and I sit for a long time with my thoughts, wondering what the first three years of my life were like. Could the early moments I shared with Alice on her Wisconsin farm explain the divide between my mother and me, why we are so dissimilar, why we value different things?

Did my love of food come from Alice? It certainly didn't come from my mother. She always saw my affection for cooking as a strange obsession.

I remember a particular night when I was in high school. She'd just come home from work.

"What's for dinner?" she asked. She slid off her black leather loafers, and her toes looked misshapen through the feet of her pantyhose, a hole developing in the big toe.

"Shrimp pasta," I said. "The one with the spinach and the Dijon mustard?"

She smiled. "These dinners you come up with. I don't know how you do it." She kissed my forehead, then sat. "Thank you for doing the dirty work."

"Oh, I don't mind," I said, setting the Parmesan cheese shaker on the table. "I love it."

"Well, that makes one of us." She fussed with her napkin. "I could just never get the timing right. And the thinking ahead, the planning."

I sat and watched my mother take a bite. "Do you taste anything different?" I asked.

My mother looked dreamily above her as if trying to conjure a deep thought. But she seemed to come up short. "It tastes the same to me."

"Really?" I quickly twirled my fork through the spaghetti noodles. The fresh lemon juice I added instantly zapped my taste buds. "I taste it."

My mother shrugged. "Well, you have a more refined palate than me." She kept chewing in silence.

"It's lemon juice," I said after too much time passed. "That's what I added this time."

She shrugged. "Maggie, you could put coffee in this, and I'd still eat it."

Coffee? I thought. Lemon juice or coffee. Apparently to my mom, it didn't really matter.

Toward the end of the meal, I built up the courage to ask if I could take a culinary class called Foods the following semester instead of study hall.

Her eyes narrowed. "Foods? As in *Home Economics*?"

"No, it's called Foods. It would actually be Foods 2. The teacher gave me a placement test, and I tested out of Foods 1. That's really basic stuff like scrambled eggs and chocolate chip cookies. But Foods 2 is an advanced cooking and baking class. You learn to make some really cool stuff."

I could see my mother biting her tongue, or rather, her inner cheek, a sure sign of her disapproval. "Uh-huh? Like what?"

"Like sponge cake. That's the kind of cake where you use whipped egg whites, instead of baking soda or baking powder, to make it really light and spongy. And I'll get to make spaghetti sauce from scratch from tomatoes they actually grow in the garden outside the Foods room."

The corners of her lips turned. "Maggie, I appreciate that you like to cook, but these are exactly the kinds of classes women my age fought to *get out* of taking." She shook her head. "You have to think about your future, your career, and someday supporting yourself financially. And to be honest, colleges are going to be impressed with academic courses, with a 4.0," she added. "Not whether you can make a cake that resembles a sponge."

If my heart had been a piece of paper, she had crumpled it into a ball and tossed it in the trash can. I wanted to correct her, to tell her she hadn't listened. The cake didn't *resemble* a sponge; it was airy and light *like a sponge*. But I knew it was no use.

The answer was no.

Now, I compare this interchange with the recipe for Alice's zucchini bread I found online. In the list of ingredients, the careful description of steps, the postscript, I sense Alice's strong attachment to food. Her recipe reads like a diary entry, and I know, even without meeting her again, that we both see food for what it really is.

Love.

I have no idea how Alice found me or exactly why she wrote, but I do know one thing for sure: I still hold a sacred place in her heart. And this time, I'm not going to let my mother keep me from following what feels right in my bones.

Not again.

4

After a restless night's sleep, I have a headache Saturday morning that two cups of strong coffee do not cure. I'm having trouble concentrating, so I pour myself a Hail Mary third cup. I am still sorting everything my mother told me last night like items in a junk drawer, and by the time Hannah wakes, I'm jittery. I need to leave the house.

So we spend the day following whims. We catch the Metra train to the city and try on wide-brimmed hats and cat-eye sunglasses reminiscent of Audrey Hepburn at Macy's. We eat Garrett's popcorn for lunch, then head to the Art Institute, where we stare at the dots of a Seurat painting until our vision blurs. After, we grab a gelato, and I let Hannah run around barefoot with countless other children in the Crown Fountain.

I successfully escape.

But when we arrive home late in the day, legs rubbery from miles of city walking, we find a package on the stoop of our brownstone three-flat. I don't remember buying anything online. After a closer look at the small brown box, I realize it's from my mother in California. From the amount of postage, I can tell she overnighted it. I take it inside, wondering what it is.

Once Hannah runs off to play on her iPad—I tell her she can have one hour of device time before dinner—I take the box to the kitchen and slice it open with a paring knife. Under the flaps, the first thing I see is a piece of notebook paper that reads:

I'm sorry.
—Mom

And below that, the box is full of unopened envelopes. I grab a stack and slide through them like a deck of cards. Every single one is addressed to me, at my childhood home in California.

Every single one has a return address in St. John's Ferry, Wisconsin.

Every single one is from Alice Brodbeck.

I feel a sting at the corners of my eyes. Receiving one letter in the mail in the days of texts and emails is beautiful, but taking in decades of them at once is overwhelming. One after another, I open each envelope to see Alice's scripty handwriting, sending me birthday wishes and good fortune. She had sent me a birthday card every year from the time I turned four until I turned eighteen, plus Christmas and Valentine's Day cards and other intermittent letters. I count thirty-nine total. My mother had not given me a single one of them.

Until now.

I look again at my mother's note. *I'm sorry.* She's a woman of few words when she's wrong. I know those two words mean so much more. *I'm sorry for never giving you these cards and letters. I'm sorry for never telling you about your childhood.*

I'm sorry for keeping Alice out of your life.

It takes me a good hour to read each card and letter in detail, a crash course in the history of my relationship with my great-aunt. I notice her word choices change as I age. She calls me her "baby girl" at first, then "sweetheart," and eventually, "my dear." But her dedication never waivers, even as the years pass, even when she doesn't hear back from me. Her faith remains. "The world is at your fingertips, my dear," she wrote in my high school graduation card, one of the last in the lot. "Just reach." By the end, my eyes burn dry and my wrists ache. And while I feel content—like I've been tucked into bed after a long, hard day—I also feel insatiable, like there's still so much I need to know.

Hannah finally comes out of her screen cave and finds me sitting silently on the couch.

"Are you okay, Mom?" she asks.

"Yes, honey." I pat the cushion next to me. "Just thinking."

She sits. "About what?"

I'm not sure how to explain the situation, or whether I should. My daughter is precocious, but is this a story better told when Hannah is more mature? Does it paint her grandmother in a negative light? I may not feel close to my mother, but I don't want that affecting Hannah's relationship with her.

"Well, something kind of funny happened," I say. "Do you remember when Daddy's parents mailed you a birthday card last year from Florida with some money in it, but it got lost and you didn't get the card until a few months later?"

She nods.

"Well, sometimes mail gets lost. And it turns out, that's what was in the box on the stoop. Lots and lots of letters from my great-aunt, Alice. Can you believe it? She sent me all these letters and cards many years ago, when I was a kid, and I am just getting them now."

Her eyes widen with intrigue. "Was there money in them?"

I nod. Alice had sent a few dollars here and there, urging me in postscripts to buy myself an ice cream cone or candy bar with the money.

Hannah scans the large pile of letters. "Will you write her back?" she asks.

"That's a very good question." I marvel at my daughter's ability to get to the heart of things. "I actually received another letter from her, a couple of days ago. She invited us to visit her this summer, to stay on her farm in Wisconsin."

Hannah's eyes pop again, and her lips suddenly purse and bulge. "Like a *vacation*?!" she asks.

I nod, and feel a twinge of guilt at Hannah's reaction to the mention of travel. We went to see Sean's parents for Christmas the year after he passed, and we flew to California for my cousin's wedding when

Hannah was two. But those are trips she could not possibly remember. We haven't gone anywhere in recent years. Elena was right; I haven't taken a vacation in the three years she's been my boss.

"Would you like that?" I ask.

"Yes, yes, yes." Hannah clasps her hands and bounces on the couch like a bobble head; it's her *pretty please with a cherry on top* pose.

There is really no reason why we couldn't drive up to Alice's farm, at least for a few days. There are no dentist appointments, no birthday parties on the calendar. And Alice did write *Anytime is fine.*

After dinner, Hannah insists on packing for the trip, even though I tell her I'm not sure we are even going or when. Mostly, she wants to discern which residents of her small stuffed animal village will tag along. It's a moot activity as I know she'll try to cram all of them into the suitcase I gave her. While she's occupied, I grab the letter and my cell and head to the couch to dial Alice. It rings five times before a woman picks up. Her voice is raspy but sweet.

And familiar, like a lullaby.

"Hi, Alice? It's me," I say hesitantly. "Maggie . . . *Magpie*," I add, trying on the new nickname.

"You got my letter?" she asks.

"Yes." I pause, searching for the next words.

"I'm so happy you called," she says. "So, when can you and Hannah come visit?"

The conversation moves at breakneck speed. I'm silent for a beat.

"Well, you have impeccable timing," I finally say. "I'm actually off work this whole next week," I add, not mentioning my recent panic attack or trip to the ER.

"How soon can you come then?"

Out of habit, I check the refrigerator calendar, though I don't need to.

"I guess as early as tomorrow? But I realize that might not be enough notice."

"*Notice?* You don't need to give *notice* with me." She laughs; it's a chuckle, deep and hearty. "You could show up on my doorstep in the middle of the night."

My cheeks flush with the warmth of her affection, her soothing voice resounding deep within me. My eyes suddenly water, because I believe her.

I'm not sure my own mother would say the same.

"I feel like we have so much to catch up on," I start, feeling like I just woke up from a dream, wanting to tell her everything that's happened, my whole life. "How did you even find me?"

"Oh, we'll catch up on everything. I promise," she says. "Call me old-fashioned, but I don't want to spoil our reunion over the phone. It's been too long, and I want to see your beautiful face when you talk. I want to catch every smile and every glint in your eye. Okay?"

"Okay," I agree.

I factor in what I have to do before we leave—at the very least, ask our neighbor, Mrs. Lee, whom I know only from her occasional gifted jars of kimchi but trust enough, to collect our mail for the week—and do some quick math on the driving time to St. John's Ferry.

I tell Alice we should arrive around lunchtime.

"Then I shall see you ladies tomorrow," she confirms. "I love you, my dear," she adds before saying goodbye.

I sit on the couch a moment with my phone in my hands.

While I can't remember the days I spent with Alice in St. John's Ferry, I somehow—instinctually—know I love her too.

5

The next morning—after I tidy up our flat, clean out the small amount of food in the fridge, and toss the garbage—Hannah and I are ready to hit the road. As we leave town, I see the runners, bicyclists, power walkers, and one skateboard enthusiast on the paved path along Lake Michigan. It's a familiar sight.

When I first visited Sean in Eastridge, I was surprised how much the Midwest suited me, considering I grew up out West. There was no ocean, but Lake Michigan seemed an apt replacement, without the salt and massive waves of the Pacific. There was no redwood forest, per se, but there are forest preserves aplenty. In Chicagoland, the trees are so formidable, deep rooted and large, they create a protective canopy over many a neighborhood street, adding an umbrellalike charm I didn't anticipate. The land is mostly flat, but to me, it was far from boring. It felt sturdy. Comfortable. Stable.

Everything I loved about Sean.

The Maps app navigates me west, away from the water toward the interstate. My shoulders relax once I see the lake in my rearview mirror.

While I still appreciate its beauty—expansive blue-green waters dotted with sailboats—I can only look at the water for so long before its splendor fades, replaced by a memory I don't want to revisit.

❖ ❖ ❖

It was early May, and Sean and I sat on a blanket on the beach.

It was unseasonably warm, and I had packed a picnic—cold fried chicken, quinoa salad, cubed gouda cheese, and green grapes—and we sat and ate and talked and silently looked at the turquoise depths of the lake. This massive body of water, at least to the human eye, ends in a horizon. You can't see the other side. Staring at that line of vast possibility is like looking up at a starry sky. What is out there?

Anything and everything.

I was seven months pregnant with Hannah, so much of our conversation was about her, or the idea of her. We knew she was a girl from an ultrasound a few months prior, but we didn't "know" her yet. We did spend a lot of time daydreaming about her, especially whom she would look like.

She was an unopened gift.

Sean and I had decided that, after Hannah was born, I would extend my maternity leave at the museum indefinitely. I wouldn't work full-time. Instead, I'd devote my attention to being a mother, raising a child, creating a home for our growing family. I was going to cook homemade meals and make baby food from scratch, fully immerse myself in the two things I really truly loved: food and family. Maybe I'd start a food blog, write a cookbook, and eventually, once Hannah started school full-time, attend culinary school like I'd always wanted to.

Without a baby at home to care for, all this domestic work would seem like frivolity. A twenty-first-century woman can't quit her job to cook and bake and play house if she doesn't have kids to care for at home. Sean was one hundred percent behind the idea. He was traditional that way. But the existence of the baby also made the idea palatable to my colleagues, to my mother, to the world.

To me.

As we sat there, the weather shifted. Not dramatically at first. But the temperature dropped a few degrees, and the light breeze we enjoyed an hour earlier morphed into a gust. The clouds hid the sun. It was like sitting in a once bustling restaurant that had suddenly grown quiet. Lights dim. Closing time. Pay your bill and leave, please.

We started packing up the remains of our picnic. I shook off and folded the blanket, while Sean tossed the garbage in a nearby bin. We walked back to the car, and by that time, the wind had really picked up. The sky grew black, rolling and ominous above the parking lot. We couldn't get to the car fast enough. But just as we did, we heard a woman scream.

"Help! Somebody save her. Somebody save my baby! She can't swim. She can't swim!"

It took us only a second to ascertain that a little girl—the same little girl we had fondly watched frolicking in the sand and throwing rocks into the waves earlier—had fallen into the water from the cement pier. And it took only one more second for Sean to snap into action. He ran to the pier, dove into the water, and brought that little girl back to the surface. It all happened so quickly and so slowly. I saw the girl's mother lift her onto the pier, and then I expected to see Sean—a muscular man with broad shoulders and remarkable balance and athleticism—climb up too. But the waves, like the clouds and wind, had grown ferocious, and I watched his hand slip on the edge of the pier, saw his temple hit the cement. Witnessed him disappear into the now gray water.

And that's when I started shouting frantically. Because I grew up in coastal California, I'm a decent swimmer. I wanted to jump in and save Sean, but the raging waves kept my feet planted on the pier. I was seven months pregnant, and nowhere near as strong as Sean. What if the waves pummeled me, pushed me off course, tossed me around? The safety of the baby growing inside me superseded everything else.

Soon, two twentysomething guys who'd been out jogging heard my cries and rushed to help. They dove in but couldn't find Sean. A rescue team later pulled Sean's lifeless body from the water.

That day, and in the slow, dreamlike days and weeks after, my mind couldn't unravel what had happened. Everything was fine. Good.

Perfect. And then, Sean had been noble and brave and saved another person's life. And suddenly, my whole world ended.

Not my whole world. Rubbing my swollen belly was my only solace.

Naturally, after Hannah was born and my maternity leave ended, and the bereavement period was supposed to be over by most people's standards, I didn't stay home to care for her as I had originally planned. Sean's life insurance was enough to pay the initial bills and provide a few months' financial security, but it would not last indefinitely. So I went back to work, to a job I mostly enjoyed. Hannah went to a safe, highly rated day care for the first years of her life, and later, April began watching her full-time. We managed. We survived. But maybe I never stopped yearning for that other life.

"Sometimes, Maggie, when you're a mom, you can't be the person you want to be," my mother told me, patting my back.

"You have to be the person you need to be."

6

Once we exit the interstate, the drive to Alice's farm is all country roads.

Hannah and I spot cows and horses, goats and pigs, red barns with weather vanes, gabled houses with deep porches, and green hilly pastures under sprawling oaks just begging for a tire swing. The bucolic scenery puts Hannah to sleep for the last fifteen minutes of the four-hour drive.

When we finally turn into the entrance of Alice's property, a wave of nostalgia bubbles up inside me like a pot overflowing on the stove. I remember. It isn't distinct. It's more like a blurred-edge black-and-white movie, unfocused, reminiscent of a dream.

Alice's farmhouse is a white Queen Anne, with a large spindled porch and grand steps leading up to it. There's a steep roof and a whimsical corner tower called a turret, exuding Victorian charm. A carved wooden sign that reads "Rosehill" hangs to the left of the front door. I see a woman who I assume is Alice raise her hand to shelter her eyes from the midday sun. She's tall with a thick build, muscular and robust. Her long curly silver hair has been wrangled into a braid that hangs down one side. She wears sturdy blue jeans rolled up at the bottom and a blue, billowy cotton flowered blouse.

And Birkenstock sandals.

She's at my car door by the time I unbuckle and exit. She says nothing at first, just embraces me. Tears sting my eyes. I don't fight them, and they fall.

Alice pulls back from our hug and holds me at arm's length and shakes her head, as if she can't believe it's me, that I'm all grown up, that I'm an adult. She then holds my face in her hands and wipes my tears with her thumb.

"You haven't changed a bit," she says.

I look away from her ocean-blue eyes. They seem to peer a bit too deeply into my soul. I gesture to the house. "I remembered it. The minute I saw it."

"Of course you did. We never forget where we belong." She peeks behind me. "Now, where is Hannah Banana?"

I gesture to the back seat. "Asleep."

"Well, that's a good thing," she says, opening the door to remove her from her car seat. "Now she can stay awake to see the stars."

Hannah stirs as Alice lifts her and straddles her on her hip. I can barely carry Hannah anymore, but the load of a five-year-old seems to be light work for Alice.

"Are we there yet?" Hannah asks, still sleepy.

"You are here, my baby girl," Alice says.

My baby girl. The words shoot through me like a bolt of lightning. Alice called me that in her letters.

Now awake, Hannah looks directly into Alice's eyes. "You're my Great-Great-Aunt Alice," Hannah announces.

"Yeah, I'm pretty great." She chuckles. "And you are Hannah Banana."

Hannah smiles at her new nickname.

"Hannah, I have a very important question for you," Alice says in a serious tone. "Do you like grilled cheese?"

Hannah nods wholeheartedly.

"And tomato soup?"

Hannah smiles and nods again.

"Well then, you are in for a treat. Because I make the best grilled cheese and the best tomato soup. With local butterkäse cheese and tomatoes from my very own garden."

"Wow," Hannah says.

"Wow, indeed." Alice lowers Hannah to the ground and takes her hand. "Leave your things here. We'll get them later," she adds, walking hand in hand with Hannah to the rear of the farmhouse.

I'm about to protest and say we should unload the car first, but instead, I follow them to the backyard garden, and I soon feel a wave of heat where there are no trees and no shade. The sun sits high and beams down on the large plots my great-aunt sows.

"We're going to pick some lettuce for a salad," she explains. "But first come see my rhubarb patch."

I notice an area of deep growth, with large, almost tropical-looking green leaves.

"*That's* rhubarb?" I ask.

"Pretty amazing, isn't it?" Alice squats beside the plants, at Hannah's level, and begins her first gardening lesson. "You see these leaves?" she asks Hannah.

"You can't eat them," Hannah replies. "They make your tummy sick."

"Very good. That's right." She glances at me, impressed with Hannah's knowledge, then provides a more scientific explanation. "Oxalic acid." She lifts the large canopy of leaves to reveal beautiful red-hued stalks beneath. "But this right here you can eat to your heart's desire. It's tart like a lemon, but with some sugar? It's pure heaven. Do you like dessert, Hannah?"

Hannah licks her lips. "Yes, please."

Alice lets out a hearty laugh. "Well, then I know exactly what we'll have for dessert tonight. My blueberry-rhubarb crisp with homemade whipped cream. And you can help me make it." She taps Hannah on the tip of her nose.

"Blueberry?" I repeat. "Not strawberry?"

"Honey, you can put just about any fruit with rhubarb. Blueberries aren't in season yet. But lucky for us, I have some frozen from last year, and that's what we're going to use to make the crisp. When it comes to rhubarb, I prefer blueberry over strawberry. You will too."

Her assured tone reminds me of the certainty of her letter. *The time has come.* But I'm not offended. If she's the kind of person who freezes fruit to enjoy peak produce all year long, then I'm apt to believe her.

I probably will prefer the blueberry.

Hannah goes to bed without dessert.

Not as a punishment, but as a mere consequence of running around in the sun too long. When it's time for eating the blueberry-rhubarb crisp, which she prepared with Alice this afternoon, Hannah is fast asleep on the porch wicker sofa. I see her cheeks are pink as salmon, and wince. We didn't apply sunscreen, even though I packed the bottle April bought the other day. That always seems to happen in late May and early June as we adapt to the new weather. I decide to let her sleep on the porch, in the fresh country air, for a little while longer while Alice and I enjoy the crisp. There are no mosquitoes to bother her yet, just the heavenly scent of lilac bushes at the end of their ephemeral bloom.

I join Alice at a wicker café table with two chairs. She sets out two plates of the crisp, dolloped with whipped cream. She's also poured us two cups of decaffeinated coffee.

"She looks just like you," Alice says.

I smile. Hannah has my brown curly hair and blue-green eyes. "Yeah, she does."

"And Sean? Does she look like him too?"

She says his name with such love, such compassion, as if she knew him.

"She has his smile," I say. "I would call it an impish grin. And she has his dry sense of humor."

Alice adds creamer to her coffee and stirs. "You miss him."

I nod.

"It's the hardest part, isn't it? Of loving someone. Saying goodbye. Letting them go."

Somehow, Alice seems to understand my loss better than my own mother, friends, anyone. She takes a sip of her coffee and sets it down with a clink into the saucer.

"That's an old lady's roundabout way of saying it was hard letting you go," she adds, digging her spoon into the crisp. "It was a different kind of goodbye. Not the same as Sean."

I let my dessert and coffee sit. "Alice, I hope you know, my mother never told me about you. I've literally gone my whole life never knowing that I lived with you, that you raised me for three years. And all those letters and cards you sent over the years? My mother never gave them to me. I just read them for the first time yesterday. It was disorienting, almost like finding out I'd been adopted, but not quite." I realize I'm rambling. "My mother kept it a secret because she didn't want me to find out that she outsourced her parenting. And I'm so sorry. Had I known, I would have . . ."

Alice makes a shushing sound, as if consoling a colicky baby. "None of that matters now." She sighs. "Though, I always wondered if you remembered your time here. But you were so young."

"It's coming back to me," I say. "Memories of things I thought took place elsewhere or with my mom. Like, I remember biting into a tomato like an apple and warm juice dripping down my chin."

Alice throws her head back and laughs, flashing all her teeth and a few silver fillings. "You just loved those tomatoes. Your shirt collars were always stained a watercolor orange."

Alice's laughter relaxes my shoulders, and I finally sneak a bite of the crisp. The mild sweetness of the blueberry makes a difference. "Alice, I do prefer the blueberry. It lets the rhubarb shine more than strawberry."

"See? And it's quicker too. With strawberries, you have to remove the tops and slice them. Extra work. The blueberries need no prep."

I sip my coffee and take a deep breath as I hold the warm mug in my hand, soaking in the beauty of this peaceful night on Alice's porch. *If the purpose of this vacation is relaxation, I've come to the right place,* I think.

"Tell me more," I say. "About my time here."

Alice's eyes meet mine. "It was the loveliest three years of my life. We just . . . got along, you and me. Like peanut butter and jelly. It didn't matter whether we were playing a game or reading or cooking or baking. Or if we just sat quiet, staring at the stars. We had a rhythm. Being with each other was the same as being alone. Does that make sense?"

I nod. "I have that with Hannah."

"I can tell."

"But I didn't have it with my mom. I still don't."

Alice shrugs. "We're not all cut from the same cloth."

I think back to all the times in my life I felt different from my mother. Disconnected. Especially about food. "I used to frustrate her a lot," I share. "Other kids would have loved a frozen pizza for dinner, but I took one bite and said it tasted like salty cardboard. And another time, I stained the countertop making blackberry jam, because the cheap stuff she bought 'didn't have real fruit in it.'"

Alice smiles. "You had a sophisticated palate."

"Thank you. Unfortunately, she just thought I was picky. She'd say 'Why can't you eat like a normal kid?' or 'Just eat it. There are starving kids in China!' You know, no one else—my mother, my aunts, my cousins—seemed to have any interest in food except to eat it, and quickly. My mom doesn't cook. Or bake. She basically microwaves things."

"I know. And my brother, Albert Jr., rest his soul, couldn't boil water to save his life."

"Then I must have gotten my love of food and cooking from you," I say.

She smiles. "Maybe you were born that way, honey. Maybe we both got the foodie gene. But I suppose living here with me probably sparked your natural interest even more. We were always in the kitchen or garden or market."

I sense the impact of Alice's vacancy in my life. "I just wish we had stayed in touch all this time," I say. "If only my mother hadn't hidden our past away, hadn't hidden you away."

Alice shrugs. "I suppose she had her reasons."

"Did she?"

"She loves you very much," she says emphatically. "She just had a hard time balancing her love for you with her love for herself."

My mother in a nutshell. Well put.

"Does she know you're here?" Alice asks.

I nod. I texted my mother last night to thank her for the box of letters and to tell her we were going to see Alice after all. She texted back *Have a nice time*, and that was that.

"We don't talk all that often," I tell Alice. "Maybe every few weeks."

Alice nods.

"So how did you find me?" I ask.

"The internet. Turns out it can be useful sometimes. I went to the library in town and looked you up. The librarian had to show me how to do it. I saw some great articles about your exhibit opening at the museum, and I even found your address. Good thing I'm not some crazed psychopath. That internet is scary. Too much information at your fingertips."

It's my turn to laugh. She's right. I suddenly wish I could live as simply as Alice, without internet or a cell phone. I realize now that I haven't looked at my phone all day, and my laptop is still packed away. I debated about bringing it along—Elena would have told me not to— but I decided I should, just in case. And yet, we've been too busy eating and talking and gardening and swimming in the pond. I wonder if I'll even open it this week.

"I looked you up too," I say. "After I got your letter. I didn't find much. Just a recipe for zucchini bread in the town newspaper. Magpie's Zucchini Bread. Do you have more recipes? I'd love to see them."

"More recipes?" She lets out another hearty laugh. "You might regret asking me that question."

$$7$$

Alice carries Hannah from the outside porch to her bedroom upstairs. It's a darling room with white-and-pink flowered curtains and a dormer window seat perfect for reading or daydreaming.

"This used to be your room," Alice whispers as she rests Hannah on the full bed with a white, lacy ruffled pillowcase. My daughter barely wakes and turns her back to us, rocking her body slightly to nestle into the mattress.

I look around the room once more and try to remember it. I don't. But as we tiptoe into the hallway, I see something else familiar. A rope hanging from the ceiling.

Alice catches my glance. "The attic."

"You pull the rope, and the stairs come down," I say as a memory returns. "It's creaky."

"Do you remember what's up there?"

I shake my head, then pause. "Books?"

Alice smiles. "And then some."

She reaches for the rope, and I watch the trapdoor open and the staircase descend out of nowhere. It screeches, a sound I remember, reminiscent of a Halloween sound effects tape. I follow Alice up into the secret room.

It's part library, part reading room, part artist studio, part puzzle room, part antique storage. The ceiling is high, and we walk around without hunching. It's literally a third floor, the square footage equal to that below. This is what lies beyond the turret window of the farmhouse's exterior.

"I've had dreams of finding a secret room like this in my house," I say as we spill into the space.

Alice laughs. "Oh, that dream. I love that dream. Supposed to mean you're feeling hopeful about the future."

I haven't had a dream like that in a while. "Do you come up here often?" I ask.

She frowns. "Not as often as I used to."

"Did I used to come up here? When I was a kid?"

"All the time. We did art projects up here. You read books."

"I read? At three?"

"Well, you weren't really reading, but in a way you were. You thought you were reading, and that's really all that matters. It's the start. You'd sit by the window and flip through books, the ones with pictures but some without. You liked the cookbooks. You'd point at the pictures of food and say 'Me eat!' It was really adorable."

I laugh. "That explains my lifelong obsession with food."

Alice moves toward a shelving unit filled with various bins and boxes, some labeled and some not. "How did you become a food anthropologist?" she asks nonchalantly, shifting boxes and lifting lids, looking for something.

"It was my mom's idea. She wanted me to be an academic like her, a college professor. So we settled on the most scholastic food-related career that interested me. That ended up being food anthropology. Not every school has a program, but it's become more common in recent years."

"But you wanted to be a chef."

I swallow. Alice just seems to inherently know me.

"I wanted to go to Le Cordon Bleu," I finally say.

"Well, who doesn't?"

"Right?" I laugh. And yet, many people, including my mother and school counselor, didn't understand my dream of going to culinary school. They likened it to wanting to be a ballerina or a professional baseball player. Unrealistic. Childlike. Pie in the sky.

"Why didn't you go?" she asks, shifting a box to the left.

I shrug, despite knowing the answer. I think back to high school, to that Foods 2 class. I had fallen in love with the idea of taking that class. But my mother had said no. "Honestly, I felt like I needed a permission slip," I finally say. "And nobody signed it. Not even me."

Alice nods. "I get that." She pulls a bankers box out from the shelf like a Jenga piece. "Do you still cook? Bake? At home?"

"Sometimes. But not as much as I'd like to. I wish I made more from scratch. With fresh, local ingredients. Lately, I've just been so busy," I say, and to my own surprise, I divulge the details of my recent panic attack. "I'm supposed to be taking it easy this week. Relaxing."

Alice smiles, a glint in her narrowed eyes. "Well, you've come to the right place. St. John's Ferry is definitely a chill place. And a great farming community, if you want to reconnect with food and where it comes from." She sets the box on the table beside us. It's dusty and weathered at the corners. "This is for you."

"What's in there?" I ask.

"Recipes. Family recipes."

"*Family* recipes?"

"Your mother and your grandfather may not have been very good cooks. But *my* grandmother—as in your great-great-grandmother—Rose Brodbeck, was a force in the kitchen. This was her house and farm once upon a time."

"I actually just found that out," I divulge. "Something else my mother never told me." I start to sketch a family tree in my mind. "So Rose is my great-great-grandmother and . . . what was her husband's name?"

"Charles," Alice says. "Unfortunately, he passed quite young. So Rose was a widow, left with two boys to raise on her own: my father, Albert Sr., and another son, Hank."

"Right," I say, starting to make sense of the familial connections. I feel a shiver run through me as I realize what Rose and I sadly have in common. And though my father didn't die, my mother raised me alone. Single motherhood seems to be our family rite of passage. "And your father, Albert, married your mother, my great-grandmother, Doris?" I go on. "She was the actress, and they had two kids, my grandfather—Albert Jr.—and you."

"You got it."

I place my hand on the box protectively. "And these are Rose's recipes inside?"

Alice nods. "Like I said, she was an amazing cook. I lived here with Rose when I was a kid," she adds.

I'm suddenly struck by the parallel of our lives. "For how long?"

"A year. I came for the summer after I finished kindergarten—I had just turned six, about the same age as Hannah. It was just my mother who brought me because Albert Jr. was a teenager by then and had a life of his own. Sadly, my dad was in a rehab facility for alcohol. Did you know that he struggled with addiction?"

I shake my head. "Maybe that's why my grandfather never talked about his family, why I grew up not really knowing about any of you."

She frowns. "Well, it was a good thing I came here that summer. I'd been having trouble in school at the time, behavior issues, poor grades, and I was having difficulty learning to read. Today I'd probably be diagnosed with an attention disorder, but at the time they just thought I was overactive. I was a bit of a tomboy, always wanting to play outside and get dirty and climb trees. Couldn't sit still in my chair. Over that summer, I learned to read and became a lot more agreeable."

I sit down at the table beside us, absorbed by her story. "That's amazing."

Alice joins me at the table and continues. "It was. That's why my grand-mother suggested I stay for the school year too. She told my parents that I was thriving here. My parents agreed for me to stay for first grade. It was easier on them, really. You mentioned my mother, Doris, was an actress, but both of my parents were actors, both trying to build their Hollywood careers. With my brother being so much older, I think they were kind of done with parenthood by that point. But after a year, my mother insisted I come back home. My parents were divorcing, and my father's mental health was spi-raling. My mother soon remarried, wedding a man named Stan. We never came back here again. I missed my grandmother immensely. We started writing letters back and forth when I was in college. But by then, her health had declined. And unfortunately, she passed before I could visit again."

"So when did you come back?" I ask.

"After college. When she died, she left me the house and the farm. Everyone thought I should just sell it and pocket the money. Developers even wanted it at one time. But once I came here, I didn't want to leave. I couldn't. I never went back to California."

I nod but don't comment. I don't want to share with Alice how poorly the family spoke of her, the grudges they held against her, how they made her the family misfit. She doesn't need to know. "Are you glad you decided to stay?" I ask instead. "Do you think it was the right decision?"

"Hard to remove an ingredient from an already-baked cake. But I wouldn't dream of being anywhere else." She pauses and shakes her head. "This is home."

I see something in her expression—Sadness? Disappointment? Resignation?—and feel like there is something she isn't telling me.

"Alice, why did you mail me that letter?" I ask pointedly. "After all these years?"

She shrugs. "Life is short. Time is a gift. And you have to use it wisely."

It's an abstract answer, more like an inspirational quote. It doesn't feel like the truth. But I'm not comfortable pressing her. "Well, I look forward to sorting through these," I say instead, gesturing to the box of recipes.

"I thought you might. Maybe you could even organize them? Compile them into a book for me? I've been meaning to but . . . well, you know how quickly time can pass without doing the things you mean to do. And I'll be honest, sometimes, my hands cramp. Arthritis. Come to think of it, you might want to just take these home with you."

I shake my head. "Oh, I wouldn't feel right about that. They belong here, don't they? In Rose's house? They've been here this long. They should stay."

I stand and lift the box, feel its weight on the pads of my fingers. Without opening the lid, I know it's filled to the brim. What treasures sit inside this box? What insights to the past?

What instructions for the future?

8

Spring 1943

Rose woke to the sound of nothing; no footsteps, no floor creaks, no laughter, no breath. The robins chirped and sang outside the window—always the birds, especially in spring—but inside the house, the weight of silence hung heavy like fog. And yet, after two years living alone, Rose had somehow grown used to the sound. It wasn't comfortable, just familiar, like the middle-of-the-night hunger pangs that once woke her as a child. She'd always been able to go back to sleep despite them, somehow lulled by the familiar hum of her rumbling stomach.

That morning, the sun was up, and that seemed reason enough to get out of bed. Like every day, there was work to be done. That was the beauty of maintenance. It was the only constant in life. Today brought a touch of novelty, though, because Rose anticipated planting the first seeds of the season—spinach, parsnips, chard, beets, turnips, peas, and carrots. Nowadays, everyone called them Victory Gardens. But for people like Rose, those who lived on farms in rural areas, they were the same gardens they'd always tended. She'd learned to grow her own food as a child—an essential skill of poverty—and she thought today, planting the first seeds, was perhaps the most hopeful day of the year, a day to believe in the beauty and bounty of the future.

Rose shivered as she lifted the wool blanket. It was chilly in the farmhouse, but that was usual for mid-April—the house wouldn't fully warm up until late May—so she slipped on a robe and slippers and headed downstairs to make coffee. She'd been quite resourceful with her rationed pound. It was enough to enjoy one cup a day for the past six weeks. But because she'd cut it with dried chicory root and reused her grounds every other day, she'd been able to stretch her last rationed amount a whole three weeks longer. It was a small victory, but victory nonetheless, and the achievement brought a smile to her lips. The less coffee she drank, the more the soldiers, including her son Hank, could enjoy, boosting their energy and morale. They simply needed it more.

While Rose waited for the coffee to percolate on the stove, she peeked out the window and saw the work ahead. Half the day would be spent preparing the soil and the other half planting seeds. She let the early-morning light shine on her face through the window, and said a prayer of gratitude for a bright and sunny day to do this important work. She felt her fingers itch to get started, to keep busy. It was her duty as an American to grow as many crops as she could, for her own use, for her community, the county, and the state. Food was a weapon. Food would win the war. That was the message she heard from President Roosevelt on Farm Mobilization Day.

After a cup of strong coffee, she enjoyed a cornmeal muffin, a bit dry since she'd been eating off her most recent batch for five days, but she moistened it with a spread of blackberry jam. The native shrubs of plump, juicy wild blackberries near the pond were perfect for picking early last summer, and she'd preserved them to enjoy all year long. With her stomach satiated, she quickly dressed and headed out to the yard to begin her work.

She had just started raking dead leaves, when her neighbor, Carol, walked up the drive.

"Good morning," Carol sang. "Beautiful weather for gardening."

"Morning," Rose called back. She set her rake down but kept her gloves on as a sign. She enjoyed Carol's company, but sometimes her neighbor talked too much. "What brings you by so early?"

"Good news," Carol said. "They announced the formation of the Women's Land Army."

Rose sighed. "It's about time."

Rose understood the role the Women's Land Army of America played during the Great War—as a teenager, she had worked alongside her own mother on the farm—and she knew the WLA had been back at work in Britain since much earlier in the war. For some reason, there was a resistance to female farm workers in America, especially in the Midwest, where farming was performed by machines like tractors, balers, and tillers. These machines were deemed too large and too difficult for a woman to control. Rose knew it was only a matter of time before the consensus changed, and they'd allow women to do the very important farm work needed to fight this war from the home front. She just hoped they'd change their minds before it was too late.

"They're organizing under the umbrella of the United States Crop Corps," Carol went on. "Apparently, they've already held training camps for women—college students, secretaries, teachers, clerks, homemakers; you just have to be eighteen and in good health to join. More training camps are planned, and otherwise, it'll be on-the-job training. Representatives from Madison, La Crosse, and Eau Claire are looking to place female students as farm workers in our area as soon as the semester ends. And they're looking for places to stay." Carol eyed Rose's farmhouse in the distance. "If they bunk two or three to a room, I figured you've got space for ten to fifteen young women here."

Rose's house had been louder and bustling once upon a time. But in the years after her husband died, her two sons blew away like dandelion seeds. First, Albert to Los Angeles in hopes of becoming the next Cary Grant, and then, after Pearl Harbor, her youngest son, Hank, enlisted and was stationed overseas. She'd always wanted more children to fill the six bedrooms of this large home, but she'd been gifted only two. What she really wanted was a daughter, someone to teach the skills and knowledge she possessed. She'd studied home economics for two years before she got married, and while she didn't finish a degree, she continued to teach herself how to efficiently run a home, a subject her two sons cared nothing about. Her boys had no interest in learning how to truss a chicken or sew curtains, how to stretch a pound of meat or knit a scarf. She had cookbooks to share and a collection of handwritten recipes that she could only hope to pass down to a daughter-in-law someday, once her sons married. Now, at Carol's suggestion, she might have a dozen surrogate daughters under her wing, all at once. The thought of housing that many girls seemed both exhilarating and next to impossible.

How will I feed so many mouths? How will I keep up with the washing? The dishes? The food prep?

"You want me to run a boardinghouse?" she asked.

"Exactly. A safe place to get a good night's rest, with healthy meals for energy to do hard labor. We can house some of these women here and there, but none of the other farms around here have room for that many girls. Plus, it will be more comfortable for them not to have to live with men."

Rose turned to look at her farmhouse, and suddenly, she could already see these nameless, faceless girls Carol spoke of—young women eighteen, nineteen, twenty years old—full of energy. She could already hear their laughter, their boisterous chatting. She sensed their vitality in a wave of goose bumps.

Maybe I haven't grown so used to silence.

She wasn't one to make rash decisions, but this didn't feel like a decision. It was her duty and purpose. Patriotism. It was another small part she could play to help win the war. These girls were going to do the hardest manual labor of their lives—on-the-job training that would make their backs ache, their hands burn with blisters—and they would need a soft place to land each night.

She eyed her Victory Garden and envisioned these women bent over here beside her, picking the very vegetables they'd eat for dinner. The thought alone buoyed her.

"I can have a representative from the WLA and the universities organizing these girls contact you to answer any questions," Carol offered, as if sensing hesitation.

Rose shook her head and took up her rake. "No questions," she said, starting to remove the dead leaves with renewed vigor. She took a full breath of spring air and felt her heart flutter. She noted the earthy scent of spring, of possibility.

"I'll start preparing for their arrival at once."

9

The following morning, I wake to the smell of freshly brewed coffee. I follow it to the kitchen, where sunlight streams through the east-facing windows and saturates everything with a buttery hue. Alice is nowhere to be seen, but it's clear she's been here. Hot coffee rests in a carafe beside a few white coffee cups and a tray of creamer and various sweeteners. A mound of freshly picked rhubarb stalks—already washed and leaves removed—covers the kitchen island.

I see a note on the small easel chalkboard:

Good morning! Gone to farmers market.

I check the large clock hanging above the sink. It's 7:30 a.m. I usually get up much earlier, but I don't feel groggy. Quite the opposite. I feel like I've had the best sleep of my life, or at least the best in a long while. I fell asleep almost as soon as my head hit the pillow; I can't remember the last time that happened.

I grab one of the white mugs and fix myself a coffee. Normally, at home, I have only enough time to pour black coffee into a thermos and drink it on the way to work. But here, I'm pulled toward the small pitcher of what looks to be heavy whipping cream. And I figure a teaspoon or two of sugar can't hurt either. The result is indulgent and comforting. I could get used to this.

I stand in the kitchen, sip my coffee, and listen: Silence. No traffic. No garbage trucks. No sirens. No beeping. No ticking. No ringing. After a few moments, I hear some bird chirps and cow moos in the distance. I walk to the porch barefoot, and finish my coffee on the swing, listening to the birds and cows and otherwise silent morning.

At eight, Hannah is still sleeping, and I decide to let her doze however long she wants. We are on vacation, after all. When I pop inside to refill my mug, my eyes dart to the pile of rhubarb. When I look closer, I see Alice has left another note beside the stalks:

Maggie Brodbeck has my permission to make whatever she wants with this rhubarb.

And below that, her signature and the date.

A permission slip.

I smile and run my fingers over the stalks. They're a brilliant pinky red and firm. I think back to the strawberry-rhubarb pie I never made after the Eastridge farmers market, overwhelmed by the time and attention it would take. But here, my mind explores possibilities. Pies are a default for rhubarb, and we already enjoyed a crisp last night. I want to make breakfast.

Muffins? Maybe. Scones would be better.

Alice's kitchen is well organized, like Julia Child's. Most of the tools and pots are out in plain sight, not hidden in a drawer. Everything is at hand and where it logically should be. I quickly grab a wooden cutting board from the countertop and a sharp knife from the block, and begin to cut the rhubarb stalks. The heaviness of the knife handle, and the rhythmic, blunt sound of the blade comfort me.

And then I am lost to the passage of time. Or rather, time stands still as I measure flour and sugar, sprinkle cinnamon, shred a stick of cold butter with a box grater, pat a pile of dough into a mound, portion out eight craggy triangular-shaped biscuits, brush each with egg wash, and sprinkle a hint of demerara sugar on top. I pop the tray of scones into the freezer for fifteen minutes while I preheat the oven, then bake them on a parchment-lined baking sheet. They come out beautiful, golden brown and studded with red bursts of rhubarb. While they cool, I whisk up a quick glaze using a rasp to add some orange zest to the icing, then drizzle it onto the scones in a zigzag pattern. I pull a white platter off a display shelf and arrange the scones artistically. Except one, which I bite into, still standing at the counter.

Somehow, it's both dense and light, tart and sweet, moist and dry.

I set the platter on the countertop beside the carafe and erase Alice's note on the chalkboard. I playfully replace it with my cursive script, as if it's the daily menu board at my own bakery.

Orange-Rhubarb Scones. And then for dramatic effect:

Bon Appétit!

A scone and another cup of coffee later, I sit on the front porch debating whether to wake Hannah for the day. The serenity—I am truly alone with my thoughts—feels like a guilty pleasure. I should get dressed and get moving, and yet, I don't want this moment to end. The quiet, the peace, the comfort. Those hours in the hospital after my panic attack have faded away. It's been less than twenty-four hours since I arrived at the farmhouse, but it's already worked some kind of magic. Alice has already worked some kind of magic. The ER doctor referred me to a therapist, but I wonder if staying here for the week could be its own form of therapy.

I hear the crunch of tires on the driveway, and assume it's Alice returning from the farmers market. But I soon see it's a red pickup truck. I make out a bearded man through the window; he waves like he knows me. I look down at my pajama shirt and bottoms and sense the remnants of scone icing at the corner of my mouth. But it's too late to run inside to change or grab a napkin. The man is already walking up the porch steps with a huge smile.

At least I put on a bra.

"You must be Maggie," the man says. "I'm Brady," he adds, extending his hand.

Our eyes meet mid-handshake, and I notice the deep chestnut brown of his eyes; they're as warm and soft and strong as his hand.

"Alice isn't here," I say. "Was she expecting you?"

"I come around on Mondays but usually later in the afternoon." He pauses, as if realizing something. "She's at the farmers market, isn't she?"

I nod.

"She probably left some jam for me."

"Jam?"

"Don't you know? Your aunt is the local jam lady. It's all rhubarb jam this month. Vanilla rhubarb, ginger rhubarb, cinnamon rhubarb, orange rhubarb." He counts the list with his fingers, and I see the hint of a tattoo on his upper arm but try not to stare.

He's dressed in jeans and a T-shirt, but I feel self-consciously under-dressed. "You'll have to excuse my attire," I say, gesturing to my pj's.

He doesn't seem to notice. "It's nice to put a face to a name."

I cock my head in confusion.

"Alice told me all about you," he says.

I feel a sudden pang of sadness. Alice has been talking about me? For how long? And I didn't even know enough to think about her.

"I ran into her in town last week," Brady explains. "I was delighted to see her because she missed our last chamber of commerce meeting. That's not like her, but she said she had a doctor's appointment. Anyway, she said you might be visiting soon. She hadn't seen you in a while."

My stomach suddenly sours as I process these bits of information. Alice recently missed a meeting she usually attends. Because she'd *gone to the doctor*. I think back to last night in the attic. She'd said, "Life is short" and "Time is a gift." I had noticed a microexpression, a fleeting look of resignation that crossed her face. And she'd wanted me to take the recipe box home with me. As if, perhaps, she was giving away her belongings. I couldn't shake the suspicion that Alice's letter was not written on a whim.

"We weren't in touch for a long time," I finally say to Brady like some sort of apology.

He smiles. "Now is all that matters."

A silence falls between us, and I quickly search for something to say. "So my aunt is your jam supplier?"

He nods. "Only the best will do. I come by every week and pick up at least a dozen jars."

"You must eat a lot of toast," I jest.

He laughs, and I see his bright, straight teeth through his thick brown beard. "That's true. I do enjoy a good piece of toast with jam," he says. "But I actually use it for work. I'm a pastry chef. I own a bakery in Madison. But over the summer, I run a culinary-arts program here in conjunction with the state university. It's sort of a summer baking boot camp. We use a lot of jam for cake layers, doughnut fillings, glazes."

I take in his muscular biceps and manly but nimble-looking hands and realize both have likely been shaped by working dough.

"I'm surprised you don't run the program in Madison," I say, trying to stay present, though thoughts of Alice's health still run in the back of my mind like a computer program. "Closer to your bakery and the university?"

"That would be more convenient. But to be honest, I come out here for some R & R. It's a working vacation. Plus, we're farm-to-table baking," he points out. "We source everything locally—the milk, the butter, the flour, the fruit, the jam, the honey. Everything is super fresh, from no more than ten miles away. And I have all my suppliers here."

"That sounds amazing."

He raises his eyebrows. "Really? Then you should come by the camp sometime and see what we do. Actually, are you free this afternoon? Around two?"

"What's happening at two?"

"We're making Ebelskivers. They're these delicious—"

"Danish pancake balls," I spit out.

He cocks his head. "Impressive. Not many people have heard of them."

I shrug. "I'm a food anthropologist."

"That's right, Alice mentioned that. Well then, you understand why I need her jam. To fill the Ebelskivers."

"But usually it's lingonberry jam," I note. "Very Scandinavian."

"Exactly, but since we're all about local and seasonal, and no one grows lingonberries around here, we're substituting your aunt's rhubarb jam. The vanilla rhubarb."

"Vanilla-rhubarb jam inside an Ebelskiver? Now that I have to try."

"Good, so you'll come?"

I pause. "Maybe. I'll have to ask Alice if we have plans. And I have my daughter."

"Right. Hannah," he says. "Five years old?"

I'm not sure if I should be flattered or creeped out by his knowledge of the personal details of my life. "What else did my aunt tell you about me?"

"Just your Social Security number and blood type." He delivers this in a monotone.

I can't help but laugh.

He flashes a wide grin. "Seriously, everyone is welcome. You, Alice, Hannah. Whatever works. I run a tight ship, but it's also casual and fun. Kid friendly."

I want to say yes. In another circumstance, I might even say "It's a date." But I'm in no position to flirt. "We'll see," I say instead. "Maybe."

"I'll take *maybe*."

He smiles, and I look down, tucking stray hairs behind my ear.

"Do you mind if I run inside to grab the jam?" he asks. "I know where Alice keeps it. I've got a tab with her and all that."

"Oh, yes, of course. Come in."

He follows me inside, heads to the butler's pantry, and exits with a box of ruby-hued jars.

"Who made these scones?" he asks, pointing to my plate of goodies and setting his box on the counter.

"I did. They're orange rhubarb," I say. "Alice left out a bunch of freshly picked rhubarb, so I decided to get creative. Would you like one?"

He shoots me a look of awe. I'm nervous as he takes a bite. I made them for me, for Hannah, for Alice. I did not make them to be taste-tested by a pastry chef from Madison.

"Wow," he says, after a seemingly long, thoughtful chew and swallow. "Maybe you should be the one teaching my students how to bake this summer."

"Stop," I protest. "That's child's play compared to what you must do every day."

"Look, Maggie, I do not throw out culinary compliments on a whim. You have to earn them with me. And I'm telling you, that is the best scone I've ever had. Truly."

"I don't believe you."

He laughs. "I'm not kidding. There's a really nuanced flavor and texture balance going on with these. Tart. Sweet. They're moist but also dry."

I note how his description mirrors my own.

"If you didn't study professionally, then you've got some mean raw talent," he adds.

I shake my head, unable to take him seriously.

He raises his hands. "Okay, okay, you're not ready to hear the truth just yet. But I'm eating this one now, and taking this one for the road." He grabs another scone from the plate, sets it on top of his jam box, then dusts off his hands and reaches them toward me.

"It was a pleasure, Maggie," he says, shaking my hand again. "I look forward to—possibly—seeing you later today."

We hold hands longer than we should. I'm the first to let go.

"Possibly," I repeat.

He starts for the door, then stops. "Oh, and if you do come, and I really hope you do, bring a pair of knitting needles, metal if you have them."

I give him a look of confusion. "To knit a scarf?"

He shakes his head. "To flip the Ebelskivers."

Upon her return from the farmers market, Alice enters the kitchen with an empty wooden crate. Hannah sits on a stool by the counter eating her breakfast scone, orange glaze glopping in the corners of her mouth.

"Where are the fruits of your labor?" I ask, motioning to the empty crate.

"I sold them," she says, pulling off her floppy straw hat to wipe her brow of sweat.

"Ah, you go to the farmers market to sell, not buy. Jam, right? Rhubarb this month?"

Alice narrows her eyes. "How'd you know?"

"Brady, the pastry chef. He stopped by to pick up his weekly box of jam."

Her lips curl into a smirk. "Oh, shoot. He mentioned that he needed to swing by earlier than usual. I forgot." From her feigned look of surprise and the smile forming at the edge of her mouth, I get the sense that her absence—and my presence—was very much calculated. "Well then, you met Brady, did you?"

I control every muscle in my face not to smile at her.

"Yes, I met him," I say matter-of-factly.

She cocks her head. "And?"

"And he told me about your famous jam." I check the clock. "Hey, you're home early. Don't most farmers markets go until at least noon?"

"Yeah, but I sell out by ten a.m. And in a few weeks, I'll sell out by nine. June is strawberry jam. July is cherry. August is tomato. And September, apple and pear butters." Her eyes land on the plate of scones. "What do we have here?"

"Mommy made scones," Hannah says.

Alice pats Hannah affectionately on the head. "I knew I left the rhubarb in capable hands. But the question is, Miss Hannah: Did you leave any scones for me?"

Hannah grabs one and hands it to her, then watches intently as she takes a bite.

"This is phenomenal." Alice licks her finger of the glaze and crumbs.

I wave her compliment away like a fly. "It's flour and sugar and butter and rhubarb."

"It's a heck of a lot more than that. Really, Maggie. Forget my jam. We should sell these scones at the farmers market next Sunday."

Her comments echo Brady's. "Oh, they're not good enough to sell."

"Like heck they aren't."

I stare at her. "Are you serious? Would people really buy them?"

"Like hot cakes."

"But aren't there rules? Like health department codes? Don't you need a cottage kitchen permit or a commercial kitchen, something like that?"

She points to the barn. "Put one in about five years ago. That's where I can my jam."

I cock my head. "You have a *commercial kitchen* in the *barn*?"

She grabs another scone from the plate, then turns her back side to Hannah. "Hop on, Hannah Banana. I'll give you girls the tour."

Hannah practically leaps onto Alice's back. I walk behind, noting the energy and vitality of this woman twice my age. It's hard to believe she could be sick. Maybe I'm just a worrier.

When we step into her commercial kitchen, I am nearly blinded by the amount of stainless steel. The countertops, the ovens, the stove tops, the backsplash, the sinks. The rows of hanging stainless steel pots and pans, the stock pots stowed beneath. It reminds me of the Foods 2 class I never got to take.

"This is . . ." I start.

"Cool," Hannah fills the silence.

I make my way through the galley. The space is enormous. Too much space for just making jams and jellies.

"I rent it out to local artisans and farmers. They use it to make various goods," Alice explains, answering my question before I ask.

I imagine the amount of rent Alice must charge. My mother and her sisters sold her short. She's a real entrepreneurial businesswoman. They thought she merely sold jam for a couple of bucks on the side of the road.

"It's lovely," I say. I like how the stark, modern kitchen juxtaposes with the farmhouse and the sprawling countryside outside the sink windows. "What is it about a clean open kitchen? I want to put an apron on right now and make something!"

"I know the feeling," Alice says.

Hannah pulls out the pots and pans from underneath the shining stainless counters.

"Hannah, no, let's not touch anything," I scold.

"You go ahead and play," Alice chimes in. "They're stainless steel," she says to me. "She can't break them."

"They'll get dirty," I protest.

"So, I'll wash them."

Hannah clinks and clanks the pots, changing out the lids, banging on them with various wooden spoons Alice hands her.

Once Hannah seems fully immersed in her culinary orchestra, Alice focuses on me.

"He's nice looking, isn't he?" she says.

"Who?"

"You know who."

"Brady?"

She smiles.

I think back to his beard, his soft brown eyes, his muscular arms, and the tattoo under his T-shirt sleeve. "Yes. I guess. He's pleasant."

Alice lets out a snort. "Pleasant? We're talking about a man here. Not a Sunday afternoon drive."

I laugh too, at my word choice. "Yes, he's handsome." I pause. "Actually, he asked me to come to the afternoon baking class at his camp today. I want to go, but . . ."

Alice lowers her voice. "It's okay, you know. To open your heart again."

I think back to my conversation with Brady. There was a moment on the porch when my stomach fluttered. Brady laughed and smiled, and for a moment, my breath caught.

I shake my head. "It doesn't feel that way."

She pats my hand. "Well, sometimes what we feel isn't always the truth."

10

Later that afternoon, Alice and Hannah have conveniently concocted a long list of plans—more fishing at the pond, harvesting turnips in the garden, reading *Stuart Little*.

So I drive into town alone, and realize St. John's Ferry is an adorable Midwest destination. Brady's classes are held at Camp Stockholm, a former religious sleepaway camp for affluent children turned adult conference and retreat center. It's at the northern end of town, so I enjoy the sights and sounds of Main Street as I make my way there—an old post office, train depot, pharmacy, bakery, bookstore, coffee shop, and a park with a gazebo. Even though it's just a Monday afternoon, people are out walking dogs and popping in and out of businesses. I see signs along the way promoting the town's annual Midsommar Festival and wish Hannah and I could have come later in the month so we could attend. We'll be back in Eastridge long before.

Once I park, I follow the signs to the kitchen/mess hall. Freshly painted in a seaside blue, the cabins face each other like boys and girls in a square dance, with a rustic stone pathway as the dividing line. I soon see Brady carrying an assortment of boxes, including the jam he picked up this morning.

"Let me get the door for you," I call out.

"Perfect timing." He looks over my shoulder. "Where are your partners in crime?"

I tell him about Alice and Hannah's laundry list of afternoon activities.

"They seem to have a pretty special relationship," he notes as we enter the kitchen.

"Yeah, they do. Hannah has only spent one day with Alice, but there's something so natural about their connection." I think about how Alice acts like the grandmother I always hoped my mother would be. "I brought the knitting needles," I add, pulling them out of my purse. "And I came early, to see if you needed any help setting up?"

"I appreciate it." He checks his watch. "I actually have an assistant, a sous-chef, but he's better at setting the oven temperature than an alarm clock."

I smile. "I'm at your disposal. What can I do?"

Brady walks me through the prep needed for today: "I have my students do all their own measuring and mise en place before we start. It's part of the job, and they have to learn that by doing it themselves. But to save time, I do take inventory and organize all the ingredients in one spot on the counter so we don't waste time going back and forth to the pantry." He hands me a copy of the recipe for Ebelskivers and a bussing pan. "Can you pull all the bulk dry ingredients, and I'll grab the wet ones?"

The huge pantry—about a third of the kitchen—is pristine, almost a work of geometric art. Jars, canisters, and bottles of every ingredient possible sit perfectly spaced by category on the shelves, each container labeled and filled. It's easy to find everything in the recipe, from the flour to the baking soda to the powdered sugar.

"I'm really impressed you're making Ebelskivers as part of your class," I say, setting the containers neatly on the counter. "They're a very culturally specific dish."

"True. But I usually have at least five international students in my class. There's an exchange program through the university," he explains, unloading eggs, buttermilk, and butter on the counter. "I like to make those students feel welcome by creating dishes from their countries. I've had students from Russia, Japan, Australia, and even India in past years. They're here for six weeks, and they get homesick."

"So I take it you have Danish students this year?"

"Ja," he says in Danish, before translating. "Yes."

I smile.

"Actually, I have only one Danish student. But I have another from Sweden and one from Norway. We've started calling them the *Scandinavian Trio*. I know, that sounds like a folk music group." He laughs. "Anyway, they each have some version of an Ebelskiver in their country's cuisine."

I nod. "Did you know 'Ebelskiver' translates to *apple slices*? Because they used to fill the pancakes with little bits of apple?"

He raises his eyebrows. "I didn't. But I really am starting to think you should be the one teaching this class."

"Me?" I feel a warmth rise from my stomach to my cheeks, and look away in case I'm actually blushing. I realize it's been a long time since a man—and a very nice-looking one—paid me a compliment. Brady praised my scones earlier today, but this feels different. I'm almost embarrassed by my schoolgirl reaction.

We finish preparations, setting the Ebelskiver pans on the stove, and making sure there are enough clean mixing bowls, whisks, et cetera, for his twelve students. We continue making small talk before his class arrives.

"Have you always lived in the Midwest?" I ask him.

He nods. "Born and raised. But not always Wisconsin. I grew up in a suburb just outside Minneapolis. You?"

"West Coast. Los Angeles."

"My sisters would be jealous. They were always infatuated with California. Hollywood."

"You have sisters?"

He grimaces. "*Three* younger sisters. I'm the oldest."

"Poor guy."

"Yeah, poor me." He laughs. "Nah, it wasn't so bad. In fact, if it wasn't for them, I might not be a pastry chef. I baked my very first batch of brownies in their Easy-Bake Oven. And not to brag"—he throws me a coy look and shrugs—"but my turtle cheesecake brownies became a school bake sale legend."

I smile at his bravado. "Oh, I bet."

Brady smiles, and I try to stay in the moment, but I begin to wonder if I should steer the conversation, ask if he's noticed any other unusual changes in Alice, besides her missing the meeting. The timing feels off, though. Plus, I'm truly enjoying our natural back-and-forth, and don't want to veer us off course.

I catch a glimpse of a cabin through the kitchen window. "Do your students stay in these cabins for the six weeks?" I ask.

Brady nods. "The tuition also covers room and board. Lodging and meals. It's immersive in that way. We eat our meals together here in the mess hall, and in the evenings, we often have a fire, stargaze, play board games, listen to music."

"Oh, you stay on the property too?"

"Yep, it's immersive for me as well. I really get to know my students. Plus, it's a breath of fresh air from city life. The cabin is sparse, and the bed isn't all that comfortable. But I don't know, I think I'm happier here than the whole rest of the year in Madison."

I think about the past twenty-four hours in St. John's Ferry at Alice's farmhouse. I've slept better, eaten better, breathed easier. My mind is quiet, calm.

Am I happier here?

Three female students, all tall and fair skinned, arrive first for class.

"God eftermiddag," the tallest sings.

"Good afternoon to you too," Brady replies. "Scandi Trio, this is my friend, Maggie. I was just telling her about you. She's joining us today. Maggie, this is Katrine from Denmark, Nora from Norway, and Johanna from Sweden."

"Hello," I say and give a small wave.

"Hello," they reply in unison.

"How do you like your stay in the US so far?" I ask.

"Very much. It looks a lot like Sweden," says Johanna, who wears her blond hair in a short pixie style.

"But it's hotter," Nora adds.

"Are you all sharing a cabin?" I ask.

Katrine, the tall one, who has bluntly cut shoulder-length brown hair, answers. "Yes, the one right next door. It's small for three people but very hygge."

"Hygge?" I repeat the word just as I heard it, *hyoo-guh*. "I don't know what that is."

"Really?" Katrine laughs. "I thought all Americans were obsessed with hygge."

"Yeah, it's Denmark's biggest cultural export," Nora says in jest.

The three girls share a laugh.

"But what is it?" I ask.

They look at each other and shrug, letting out small, uncomfortable laughs. Finally, Katrine tries to explain it to me. "There is no exact English equivalent," she says. "But the best word is *cozy*."

"And warm and comfortable and safe." Nora adds. "In Norway, we call it *koselig*."

"Koosh-lee?" I repeat.

She nods enthusiastically.

"And we call it *mys* or *mysa* in Sweden, but it means the same thing," Johanna adds.

"I see," I say, stealing a quick glance at Brady. "Like a cozy environment."

Katrine nods. "Yes, but not only the environment. The feeling inside your heart. In your mind."

"It is feeling whole," Nora says, pulling her long blond hair into a ponytail in preparation for food prep. "Content. Sharing good times with people you love."

"Being in nature," Johanna adds. "And lighting candles."

I narrow my eyes. "*One* word means all of *that*?"

They nod in unison.

"I love it," I say.

"You will come see our cabin after class," Katrine commands. "Then you will understand it more. Okay?"

I pause, slightly taken aback by Katrine's directness. "Okay."

"Okay," Katrine repeats, then looks around the kitchen. "Professor Shaw, where is your assistant this morning?"

Brady Shaw.

"Allen is probably still sleeping," Brady answers.

"We'll wake him," Nora says, pulling Johanna's arm.

"And I'll make him some coffee," Katrine announces, heading to the pantry, as the other two rush out of the door on a mission, smiling and laughing as they go.

"Professor?" I whisper to Brady once Katrine leaves the room.

"She insists on calling me that," he whispers back.

"A good strong cup of coffee should do the trick," Katrine says, toting a bag of whole coffee beans from the pantry. "It worked last time."

"Last time?" I say. "Is it time to find a new assistant?"

"Unfortunately, Allen's father, Gerry, owns this camp," Brady explains. "And he rents the facilities out to the university for a reduced price. Allen is an innately creative pastry chef for his age. But definitely unreliable."

"And clumsy," Katrine adds. "He dropped a knife right next to my foot the other day. And Nora said he left the stove burner on last week after making the caramel sauce."

Brady grimaces.

The other students start filing into the room, grabbing stark-white aprons from hooks on the far wall and heading over to the workstations. Brady darts to the hooks and grabs two aprons.

"For you," he says, handing one to me.

"I thought I was just observing," I say.

"You don't help, you don't eat," he quips. "Plus, you're my stand-in Allen until he has a cup of Katrine's wonder coffee."

"Fair enough," I say, enjoying the sensation of slipping the apron over my neck and securing the ties, wrapping them around my waist once fully before tying them in the front. The tight knot against my rib cage feels comforting. Like a seat belt, a uniform, armor. I feel prepared. Ready for anything. Happily playing a part in all this.

Can an apron embody the spirit of hygge?

As soon as Nora and Johanna return, class officially begins. When Brady starts talking, I'm jolted by the strength and timbre of his voice; he's even more eloquent and charismatic with an audience, and I find myself so mesmerized by his delivery, I'm unable to fully take in the content. But I snap into focus when I hear him say my name.

"As my lovely and knowledgeable sous-chef, Maggie, just informed me," he starts, "'Ebelskiver' translates to *apple slices.*"

The class turns their attention to me and I smile, feeling my cheeks grow warm. "Because they were originally filled with pieces of apple," I explain.

I see a few raised eyebrows and nods. When Katrine smiles with approval, my shoulders relax.

"Today, however, we are not filling them with fresh fruit," Brady goes on. "We'll be using a locally made vanilla-rhubarb jam."

As Brady instructs the class through the demo, his ease and flow remind me of a seasoned ringmaster. And as I help him with various tasks—from cracking eggs to handing him a whisk to preheating the cast aluminum pan—I feel less like a sous-chef and more like a magician's assistant.

"This pan is nonstick," Brady says. "But adding butter to the pan and spreading it within the well will help make them golden brown. For this, you can swirl the pan, but I prefer using a pastry brush."

I begin spreading the butter with the pastry brush as he instructed, and then feel Brady's hand cover mine, guiding my movement. He stands close, just behind me, and I can feel his breath on my neck as he talks.

"You'll want to coat the inside of the wells evenly," he says. "Before adding the batter."

If I were to simply turn my head, our mouths would be mere inches from each other. I focus on keeping my head straight, my eyes on the class.

The rest of the demo continues this way; the warmth of Brady beside me as we fill the wells of the pan with batter, top each with a teaspoon of jam, and carefully flip them. He remains professional and courteous the whole time, acting no different than a sports coach correcting a player's form, and yet . . .

I hadn't expected Brady's touch, his close proximity, to stir me so much.

I grab the dirty dishes and bring them to the sink. I start to spray them with hot water and hope the scrubbing motion will loosen the tightly wound knot developing in my chest. It's been a while, but I remember this feeling. It's pain and joy at once—a deep longing for connection.

Vulnerability.

After class, I join the Scandi Trio back in their room to enjoy the Ebelskivers we made and, of course, more coffee. Brady says he has a few business items to handle, but he'll stop over in a bit. I'm relieved to hear this, still reeling from the intensity of working beside him.

Without seeing any of the other cabins on-site, I understand the work the girls have put in to making their accommodations feel comfortable. It's a fairly small space for three girls—maybe twelve by twelve feet—but they've somehow transformed it into something out of HGTV. Their bunk beds have been stacked to one side, leaving a large amount of floor space for a soft fabric couch, two side chairs— one high back and tufted, the other made of some kind of fur—and a coffee table, all on top of a very fluffy shag carpet. It's so soft, I imagine walking on it barefoot must feel like petting a chinchilla with your feet. A large decorative tray tops the coffee table and houses an artfully stacked pile of books, crowned by a jar candle, one of about seven candles I quickly count in the room. Green houseplants dot the windowsill and seem to beckon the sun through the window. I look up and see the girls have covered the overhead fluorescent light with some sort of gauzy material studded with white twinkling lights. Several pieces of art, mostly woodsy nature scenes, hang on the walls.

"Do you see what we mean?" Katrine asks, gesturing to the space.

"Very hygge," I say.

"Please sit down," Nora says, and I sink into the couch. It's made of memory foam.

I watch the girls quickly pull together a proper party. Johanna plates the Ebelskivers—still glistening with oil and snowcapped with a sprinkling of powdered sugar—and lights the candles. Katrine makes more coffee, and Nora pulls out chunks of cheese and grapes and glazed nuts from their makeshift kitchen and pantry. Soon, we're all sitting around a table of food and drink, laughing and talking in their cozy cabin.

After a few minutes, I notice Katrine studying me rather intently, like I'm a portrait in an art museum. "Maggie, are you by chance of Danish heritage? Or Swedish?"

"I don't think so." I tell them that my last name, Brodbeck, means *bread baker* in German. "I think I'm mostly Western European."

Katrine is still staring at me. In fact, all three of them are.

"It's just that you look . . . Scandinavian," Johanna says.

I self-consciously bite into an Ebelskiver. The rhubarb jam zaps my tongue, tart and sweet. "Really? How so?"

"You're quite tall," Johanna states. "Scandinavian women are three inches taller than American women on average."

"But it's more than that," Katrine adds. "You're resilient."

I cock my head. "How do you know I'm resilient?"

Katrine wiggles her fingers in the air. "It's just your aura. You know your own abilities and trust they'll be there when you need them most."

I suddenly feel like I'm having my palm read. "And that's Scandinavian?"

The three girls all nod emphatically.

"My friend in Finland calls it *sisu*," Nora adds.

"*See-soo?*" I repeat.

Nora nods. "There's no exact translation, but you might call it inner strength or tenacity."

I consider this. "Wasn't Finland named the happiest country in the world?" I ask.

"Yes," Johanna says. "But all of our countries are in the top seven."

I study the three young women for a beat. They look like they're in their late teens or early twenties, yet they seem older. There's something assured about all of them.

"So what's the secret to happiness?" I ask.

"I think the key to being truly happy is having a sense of purpose," Katrine says, "If you have that, you know what to do, how to behave, and you feel like you make a difference in the world."

"Yes, purpose is important," Johanna argues. "But I think being true to yourself is even more crucial. You cannot live a lie. You have to be authentic. You have to figure out who you really are, not what other people want you to be, and then have the courage to be that person."

"Well, I think it's dessert," Nora adds, grabbing another Ebelskiver. "And a good cup of coffee. And good company."

"I'll toast to that," I say, and we all clink our coffee mugs. "On the subject of authentic self, and doing what you love and having a purpose, is this what you all want to do? Become pastry chefs?"

Each girl says yes. Katrine says she dreams of someday being the head pastry chef at a famous hotel in Copenhagen. Johanna says she hopes to start a culinary school and teach classes just like "Professor Shaw." Nora shares that she'd like to open her own bakery in Oslo.

"What is your passion, Maggie?" Johanna asks. "What is your dream?"

The question makes me pause.

I love my job. It's interesting, important, and I'm paid well. The research and teaching at the university level certainly feed my brain, my need for cerebral stimulation. But after spending only a day in St. John's Ferry, I wonder if my job is also feeding my heart and soul. I felt so alive and in the moment when I made the rhubarb scones this morning. And earlier today, in Brady's class making the Ebelskivers,

I went deeply into flow and lost all track of time. It feels like there's a creative energy locked inside me here, dying to get out, something I don't feel at work.

"I'm still trying to figure that out," I finally tell them.

We hear a knock at the door, and a second later, Brady pops his head in. "Ladies, I trust you've been taking good care of Maggie," he says.

Katrine winks. "The best."

His eyes dart to mine. "I'd love to walk you to your car when you're ready to go."

"Oh, we're done here," Katrine says, conspiratorially clearing the plates.

"Yes, plenty of time to walk to the car now," Nora adds, quickly assisting her.

We hear the girls giggle as soon as we shut the cabin door. They're extremely eloquent and intelligent young ladies, but their laughter now reminds me of a childhood playground.

Brady must think the same thing. "If they were any younger, or American, they'd be singing 'Brady and Maggie sitting in a tree' right now," he says.

I can't help but blush. There is certainly a spark between us, but neither of us has put words to it. We walk a few steps along the path, then Brady stops.

"Actually, do you have a few more minutes?" he asks. "I could show you my cabin. It's just on the opposite side of the mess hall."

It sounds like he's asking me to his apartment for a nightcap after a date. The logical side of my brain questions his intentions, but my gut says not to be worried. "Great," I say as we head that way, thinking it's also an opportunity to ask him more about Alice.

Brady's cabin is nowhere near as hygge as the Scandi Trio's. But it's simple and tidy. Minimalist. I try not to look around too much. It feels too intimate, seeing where Brady sleeps.

"Bonus, it's the only cabin with a veranda." He gestures to an outdoor space, a small wooden deck filled with potted plants of early-season herbs and flowers. "Check out this view," he says, opening the glass-paned doors.

I step out to see a stunning vista of the Mississippi River through the trees. "This is breathtaking," I say. "I could get used to this."

"Actually, this is nothing," he says. "There's a secret spot overlooking the river that will blow your mind. I could show you sometime before you leave?"

It feels like he's asking me out on a date. I freeze. That's a line I haven't crossed since losing Sean. True, I've enjoyed our playful banter, and find Brady very attractive. And I'm obviously flustered working so close to him. But a date feels like playing with fire. Because of Hannah. Because my time in St. John's Ferry is fleeting. Because I don't know if I'm ready. I don't know how I want to respond, so I just nod.

"Tell me, where did you go to culinary school?" I quickly ask. "Le Cordon Bleu?"

He flashes me a smile. "Oui."

"Of course. Where else?"

"MIT," he spits back. "If you were my father. He wanted me to be an architect."

"He didn't approve of culinary school?"

"'Cooking and baking is women's work.' And that's a direct quote."

"Ouch. Obviously, he doesn't know that it's a male-dominated profession. Aren't the majority of chefs in the US men?"

"Exactly." He shrugs. "He's come around now."

"What changed his mind?"

"The passage of time. That always helps. Doesn't it? And I was nominated for an award a few years back. Accolades can sway the most cynical of hearts."

I raise an eyebrow. "What award?"

He shakes his head as if it doesn't matter. "I didn't win. But I was a finalist."

I can see he's trying to remain humble. And then it hits me.

"Oh my god, you were a James Beard finalist?" I practically shout.

"It's not a big deal," he says.

"It's the biggest of deals," I retort.

He shrugs. "To the world, maybe. But I really don't do any of this for recognition. It's who I am. It's like breathing to me. I would do it for free. That's how much I love it."

I watch his eyes dance as he talks. They sparkle, even in the afternoon light.

"Wow. A James Beard Award," I repeat.

"Finalist," he corrects me, lifting his index finger into the air.

I wave my hand. "Still. I'm really impressed. For the award—finalist for the award—but also for going to culinary school even when your father didn't approve."

I tell him how I allowed my mother to persuade me into a more secure academic career in food.

"Parents mean well," he says. "The world means well. But the only person you really need to please is yourself."

A silence falls between us, and I take the opportunity to ask him about Alice.

"Brady, you mentioned that Alice missed a meeting recently and that was out of character for her," I start. "Have you noticed anything else unusual?"

He narrows his eyes. "Like what?"

I shrug. "It's just that she asked me here very abruptly, and I'm worried maybe she's . . . dealing with something. But hasn't had the courage to tell me about it."

He nods, seeming to understand what I'm hinting at. "Come to think of it, a few weeks ago. I heard that Alice was selling some antiques at the farmers market. Kind of looked like a mini garage sale. Alice usually only sells her jam. That's all I can think of."

Was she selling her belongings because she needs the money? I wonder. To pay her medical bills?

Brady searches my eyes. "You're worried about her," he says.

I nod. "Alice just came back into my life, and I don't want to lose her already," I confide.

Suddenly, I'm aware of the passage of time and check my watch.

"It's getting late," I add. "I should get going."

"Let me walk you," he says.

As we stroll the cobblestone path back to the parking lot, I tell Brady about my conversation with the Scandinavian Trio about happiness.

"Those Nordic countries really have something figured out, huh?" He keeps pace with me on the path. "From what I've heard, when it comes to work-life balance, life seems to win over there. In America, it's all about the work. Taking a break seems lazy."

"Lazy? That's a dirty word to Americans. Maybe even downright scandalous," I say.

He smiles. "I've definitely not been lazy. In fact, I work *too* much. That's according to my mother, who had no issue with me going to culinary school in Paris, but who now thinks I should be further along in the 'life' part of that balance."

"Ah, she thinks you should be married by now?"

"With 2.5 kids," he adds. "I'm thirty-nine, and she says the odds of grandchildren are dwindling every year."

"Are you dating anyone?" The question emerges involuntarily, and I feel embarrassed at being so forthright. I wasn't planning to ask, but I realize I'm holding my breath for his answer.

He holds my gaze.

"No," he finally says. "But I'm working on it."

11

When I return to the farmhouse, Hannah and Alice are still down at the pond, fishing. I seize the opportunity to squeeze in a few moments alone to settle my mind. I want to talk to Alice as soon as possible—to relieve the growing concern about what she might not be telling me—but after dinner seems like a better time. Instead, I head to the attic. I want to start sorting Rose's box of recipes. It's the kind of busy work that has always cleared my thoughts. I leave a box of leftover Ebelskivers on the kitchen counter—Brady insisted I take some to Alice and Hannah—and make myself a cup of Earl Grey. I'm determined to make some headway organizing what's inside the box.

When I step fully into the attic space, I let out an audible sigh. I take in all the books, the comfy chairs, and crafting and art supplies. It really is a haven. Very hygge. No wonder I liked coming up here when I was a toddler. I spot the recipe box on the table. As I lift the lid, my fingers ache with anticipation. What will I find inside?

Being a food anthropologist, I find recipe histories fascinating. Recipes—once called *receipts*—and cookbooks in general are really the gift of widespread literacy. As more and more people learned to read and write, and they became more mobile, the desire to record and duplicate cherished family recipes expanded. Early recipes contained a list of raw ingredients with no instructions. They were meant to merely jump-start the cook's memory of how to make a dish. When instructions were added later on, they were initially vague and comparative in nature, as in "bake until done" or "add a chunk of butter the size of an egg." Eventually, with the influence of cooks like Fannie Farmer, recipes became more detailed, providing exact measurements for all ingredients and precise cooking instructions with indicators, like "bake until golden brown and firm around the edges," that left less room for error.

Inside the box is an assortment of recipes—some handwritten on loose papers and others on cards, some clipped from newspapers, and some typed. Many of the dishes are likely from the Depression and World War II times. They use the words "thrift," "mock," and "economical," usually indicative of a time when people were concerned about food costs and dealing with rations. I see a recipe for porcupine meatballs—meatballs made of ground beef and rice, meant to stretch ingredients when meat was scarce—and one for cabbage stew and applesauce cake. There are recipes for egg salad and asparagus soup. One yellowed paper contains a recipe for something called Lucy's Victory Cake.

Was there a Lucy in the family? I've never heard the name mentioned before.

I also notice something strange about the recipe. The amounts for everything—the flour, sugar, and eggs—are huge, much more than for a typical cake recipe. It's as if the recipe has been designed for catering purposes. I wonder at what occasion this cake made an appearance in my great-great-grandmother's life. Christmas morning for a large family? Women's social group luncheon?

As I slowly remove papers from the box and sort them into piles by type on the table, I soon discover a thin leather-bound notebook. My breath catches. It looks like a diary or journal, and it's quite weathered. Could I have stumbled upon Rose's inner thoughts? Her deepest hopes and dreams?

But when I crack the spine, I see it's not a diary at all. It's some sort of ledger, with a list of names, dates, and room numbers, plus notes in the margin on food and bedding preferences. Inside the front cover, in cursive, I see several dates. The ink is smeared, but I can still make them out: *May 1943–August 1945.*

Thrilled to have found a primary source of this kind, I gently slip the ledger into a manila envelope to protect it—I know from working at the museum how quickly an artifact can get damaged in transit—and dash back downstairs, where I find Alice and Hannah back from fishing. They are now sitting on the porch swing with glasses of lemonade, reading *Stuart Little*.

"She's a bookworm," Alice says, as I join them on the swing, falling in line with their rhythmic swaying. "Just like her mama."

I kiss Hannah's forehead. It's hot and sweaty. She smells like grass and dirt and sunshine. I notice a dusting of powdered sugar on her chin. They must have discovered the Ebelskivers.

Before I have time to mention the ledger, Alice asks, "How did things go today?"

I tell them quickly about the baking class, and the three students from Denmark, Sweden, and Norway.

"Can I dig up more worms for fishing?" Hannah asks when I'm finished. "Alice says the fish will be biting again after dinner."

"Of course," I say. "But stay where we can see you."

Hannah scoops up a metal pail and small garden spade from the edge of the porch, then marches down the steps, heading across the grass to the mud underneath the oak tree. She squats to dig up worms. I realize how my daughter has transformed in the past twenty-four-plus hours. She's come alive here, I think. Just like Alice did while staying with Rose, all those years ago. Were my early years here with Alice filled with equally rich moments?

"You know, she hasn't asked for her iPad since we got here," I note.

"All kids love nature. Before the world teaches them not to." Alice points to the envelope still in my hand. "What have you got there?"

"Something pretty special. I found it upstairs in the box of recipes," I say, slipping the ledger delicately from the envelope. I hand the thin booklet to her. "I think your grandmother Rose ran a boarding-house here."

Alice opens the booklet, then taps her index finger to the dates listed. "This was during World War II. I think a lot of people opened their homes to boarders during that time. People needed affordable lodging, and it was a good source of income." She shakes her head as she flips through the pages, as if she can't believe her eyes. "Rose certainly kept excellent records."

I look over her shoulder, watching Alice study the piece of history in her hands. "See the names of the boarders," I say. "Clara Clark, Esther Monroe, Peggy Kelley, Sarah Rosen . . . and look, their hometowns and universities are listed too. They must have been college students. Women joined the labor movement during the war. I wonder if these women came to this area for work? And needed a safe place to stay? You know, like Rosie the Riveter."

I picture the iconic poster of a woman showing off her bicep under a denim blue work shirt, her brown hair covered by a red and white-polka-dot bandanna, the words *We Can Do It!* above her image.

I can see the wheels in Alice's brain spin as she looks away for a moment.

"A boardinghouse," she repeats. "You know, I've found some items in storage over the years. Two dining room tables, each with six matching chairs; three couches, two loveseats, and three reading chairs; fifteen coffee cups with saucers, fifteen dinner and dessert plates, fifteen sets of white twin sheets; and fifteen white towels. To be exact."

"That's an awful lot of couches and coffee cups and sheets and towels for a woman living by herself," I say. "They must have been from the boardinghouse."

Something clicks. *Lucy's Victory Cake.* I tell Alice about the recipe, how it seemed like the ingredient amounts would result in a huge cake—or three or four smaller ones.

"Obviously, she had to feed a crowd," Alice notes.

"But who is Lucy?" I press. "You said Alice had just the two sons, right? Albert Sr. and Hank? No daughter?"

"That's right. I'm not aware of anyone named Lucy in the family." Alice pauses. "Maybe she was one of the boarders? Maybe she's listed in the ledger?"

We scour the book but can't find the name.

I steal a peek at the carved wooden sign hanging above us beside the farmhouse door. "Rosehill." A tingle runs down my spine. This house possesses such history. The people—Rose and her family but also these girls in the ledger—who once called this farmhouse home. I am overcome by a sense of place and time.

"Alice, I'm so happy Rose left this house to you," I say.

I watch Alice's face crumple. She closes her eyes and tears fall.

"Alice, what is it?" I ask, holding my breath as I prepare for her answer.

She wipes her eyes. "I haven't been totally honest with you, Maggie," she says. "I asked you to come here for a reason."

I was right. Alice invited me here to say goodbye. I quickly check on Hannah in the yard. She seems too far away to hear anything, too absorbed in her worms.

Before I can reply, Alice goes on. "I feel so ashamed. The truth is, I haven't been a very good steward of Rose's home. I'm going to lose the house and the farm come the fall."

My mind quickly tries to make sense of what I just heard. "What? You're going to lose the farm? How?"

She lets out a deep sigh. "I took a home equity loan to pay for the commercial kitchen, and I haven't been able to make my loan payments. If I don't pay back what I owe, plus interest and penalties, by October 31, they're going to default on the loan. And I'll lose all of this."

My mind wrestles with this new information. I thought Alice was financially capable. She draws income from the commercial kitchen and runs a successful jam business. And she seems so assured.

"When were you going to tell me?" I ask.

"I wanted to tell you," she starts, "but it's not easy to admit. It makes me feel weak. Like a failure. I feel irresponsible."

I take her hands and hold them between us. "You have nothing to feel ashamed about. And this does not make you weak. Running an independent business in this very commercial world is hard. You took a financial risk building that kitchen—a space that benefits so many local artisans—and you just need more time to prove it was worth it."

She smiles. "That's the thing. These folks are competing with online conglomerates and grocery superstores and warehouses. Local farms have been hit hard by drought and a terrible storm earlier this spring. To be honest, they can't always make their rent. But if I revoke their leases, they can't make their products, which means they can't sell their products, which means they lose even more income. I thought I could take the financial burden for them, for a little while at least. But with the adjustable rate on the mortgage and the current economy, unfortunately, I've gotten in over my head."

"Is that why you asked me here? To help you financially?"

She shakes her head. "I wanted you to have the chance to come back and experience this place before it was too late. I always dreamed you'd come back. And I wanted you to stay, at least for a little while, and absorb the beauty of this farm as long as it was possible. But I didn't want you to come out of obligation or pity," she explains. "I wanted you to come back here for you, not me."

"I am. You *are* me." I pause. "And I want to help. I have some money put away."

"No."

"Yes."

"No." A dark cloud crosses her face. "Because even if I pay back what I owe, that's really just a Band-Aid. I don't have guaranteed income for future payments."

I immediately think of Elena's husband, Jim. He's a retired financial adviser. My boss is always saying how much her husband misses work, which was one of the reasons she decided to retire as well. Jim is also a huge history buff. If I contact him, explain the situation, I bet he'd let me pick his brain, help me figure out if I can swing investing in Alice's farm.

"We'll figure it out. Together," I promise to Alice, without mentioning my plan.

Alice turns the ledger in her hands, and a moment of silence passes between us. I change the subject for now.

"Who would know more about this boardinghouse?" I look in the distance at the nearby farms. "Is it possible any of your neighbors know why these girls were staying here?"

Alice shakes her head. "I can ask, but it's doubtful. By the time I came to live here in the '70s, it was all new families. The original farmers probably got too old, and their children didn't want to run the family businesses. Farming isn't easy or lucrative."

My fingers instinctively reach for my phone or laptop, anything where I could quickly type into a search engine and produce an immediate answer. At work, I usually do my initial, broad research online, then acquire the necessary books and articles to read more deeply. But as Alice promised in her letter, she has no internet service and her cell reception is spotty. Waiting for answers feels like both a challenge and a reward. It's rare to sit with mystery in the modern world.

Delayed gratification.

For now, I take a deep breath of country air and run my hand along the white wood siding behind the porch swing, my fingertips catching on its weathered texture.

If only these walls could talk.

12

May 1943

The past six weeks had felt ritualistic, almost religious in nature for Rose, laying the groundwork for a magnificent event. Twelve young women—all college students from state universities—were to arrive the last weekend in May to serve their first stint in the Women's Land Army.

They would stay through the late-summer harvest, working at nearby farms doing a multitude of jobs: plowing fields, tending crops, milking cows, collecting eggs, picking fruit, raising chickens, detasseling corn, shocking wheat, topping onions, driving tractors, and baling hay. These "farmerettes" needed a comfortable bed, nutritious meals, and somewhere to call home, a place to restore their bodies and minds before heading out each morning for the rigors of farm work.

Rose knew it was her job to create and maintain this home.

Over the past month and a half, Rose had begun waking before the sun and hopping out of bed as soon as her eyes opened, surprised that she needed less coffee and less food than usual to commence her growing list of daily chores. Her energy felt boundless, and she found herself humming a rhythmic, upbeat melody through her work. She worried less about her sons and spent more time visiting with neighbors—enjoying a cup of tea and a midday chat with Carol on the front porch or a meatloaf dinner at the Jensens'. At night, after a long day of work, she would read and knit and prepare for the next day, falling asleep as soon as her head hit the pillow, without the hours of rumination that often filled the bedroom's darkness. She sometimes tried to put a word to how she was feeling, this constant sense of power and possibility; it seemed foreign and familiar at the same time.

Alive. That was the only word that seemed suitable.

And then the young women finally arrived early on a Saturday afternoon. Rose's heart swelled when she saw all twelve piled into the bed of Joe Jensen's Ford farm truck, the vehicle they would use that summer to drive to their local jobs. It felt like a homecoming to Rose, though she'd never met them before. She noticed each girl had one suitcase, which she'd tucked behind her legs to save space in the truck bed. Once they parked, Rose watched two of the girls hop off the truck and assist the other women to the ground. They were not in work clothes—they wore lightweight cotton frocks in stripes, polka dots, and floral prints and open-toed shoes, impractical for farm work. *They'll need waterproof boots.* She hoped the government would soon issue appropriate uniforms and footwear. They were worthy of them, soldiers of their own kind.

Rose approached the young women, who were lined up beside each other holding their boxy leather suitcases in front of them, as if intuitively coming into formation.

She smiled. "Good afternoon," she said. To her surprise, her voice wavered.

"Good afternoon," they replied, a melodic, collective sound that reminded Rose of wind chimes.

Rose studied each of the girls' faces and noted both thrill and the fear of the unknown in their toothy grins and narrowed brows. A few self-consciously tugged at the hems of their frocks. She saw in them past versions of herself—the Rose she used to be. Rose before marriage, Rose before motherhood.

Rose before loss, before heartache.

She cleared her throat to keep her voice steady. "We'll have a formal meeting later to review the house rules and daily schedules and responsibilities. But for now, I'll read your name and supply your room assignments. You'll have a few minutes to set your belongings. Then it will be time for dinner."

Rose watched the girls' eyes, and noted how the mention of dinner, a full afternoon meal, seemed to unfurrow their brows. *They're hungry.* They'd likely exhausted calories in the adrenaline of embarking on their new adventure that morning. Perhaps a few had woken with nervous, unsettled stomachs and had skipped breakfast altogether. She felt purposeful having prepared a balanced and easy-to-serve midday meal for these young women—egg-salad sandwiches, asparagus soup, and a spring green salad.

Rose thought the girls looked quite similar to each other, perhaps connected by nothing other than the thread of youth. They looked about nineteen or twenty years old, and she noted that they all had long hair, rolled and pinned up in some fashion. Most of the girls also wore red lipstick, a contrast to their porcelain, unwrinkled skin. She noted some girls were quite slim, while others were rounder or muscular. Rose could already differentiate who would be inclined to particular kinds of farm work based on their builds. But despite the overall essence of their youth, Rose soon learned that each girl possessed a unique spirit.

There was Peggy Kelley, one of the two women who helped the others off the back of the truck. Peggy seemed a natural leader, like the girl Rose always wanted to be in school but never quite was, and certainly a girl she would have chosen to befriend. Rose admired how Peggy commanded attention. It was more than her shiny auburn hair and alluring green eyes. Peggy looked Rose directly in the eye, stood up straight, and accepted her room assignment with a boisterous "Thank you!"

Then there was Esther Monroe, a round-faced, stockier girl who stared at her shoes when Rose read her room assignment. Esther's frizzy blond curls and soft blue eyes conveyed a timidity that her body language supported; her shoulders caved as if attempting to fold her body, to become small enough to stow inside her suitcase. Rose asked Esther to stay behind while the last of the other girls climbed the steps of the farmhouse porch.

"Esther, after you settle into your room, I could use some help in the kitchen," Rose said, hoping the girl would welcome the request. "We'll need to set the table and heat the asparagus soup."

A smile crossed the young woman's lips. "Yes, ma'am."

"I'm certain you've helped your mother in the kitchen over the years?" Rose added, trying to make conversation, trying to connect with the girl. Because Rose felt more comfortable in the background too, she had more in common with a girl like Esther than a girl like Peggy.

Esther shook her head. "Unfortunately, no. She died when I was very young."

Rose's heart opened even more for Esther. She placed a hand on her shoulder. "Oh, my dear, I'm so sorry. I'm sure you miss her every day."

"I do." Esther laid her hand on her chest. "But I keep her here, in my heart."

Rose smiled, and thought of her late husband, and her children, so far from home. "There is no better place to keep the people we love," she said.

As Rose watched the young woman head up the porch steps, she wondered how timid Esther, and all the other girls, would grow over the course of the summer.

Maybe I'll change too.

13

The following morning, I wake up determined to find an answer to Alice's money troubles. I need to save her farm, my family's farm. I fib to Alice that I need to quickly check in with the museum summer interns—and leave her happily collecting eggs from the henhouse with Hannah. I head to the St. John's Ferry Library to use the internet, armed with my laptop and cell phone. But work is far from my mind. Instead, I call Elena's husband, Jim.

As I suspected, Jim is more than eager to talk shop. But after reviewing my financials, we come to a fork in the road. I have the money to help Alice, but I'd have to pull the funds from either my 401(k) or Hannah's 529 account. Either way, I'd suffer the consequences, and so would Hannah: taxes and additional penalties, not to mention not having money for retirement or college.

Is Alice's farm worth that risk?

I leave the library with my head spinning. As I open my car door, I hear someone call my name. I look up to see Brady waving at me from down the street, a small paper bag in hand.

We walk toward each other.

"Fancy meeting you here," he says.

"What's in the bag?" I ask.

He lifts it. "Dried lavender. For shortbread cookies. Allen messed up the order from the local farm, so I had to run quick to the spice shop here in town." His eyes land on the library behind me. "Getting caught up on your summer reading?"

I shake my head and gesture to my laptop bag. "Getting some work done."

He nods, then cocks his head, studying me. "Everything okay?"

"Yeah, everything's fine." My gaze falls to the sidewalk.

"Really?" he asks. "'Cause I just so happen to have an hour before I have to be back at the camp. And there just so happens to be a really great coffee shop on the next block." He smiles. "And coincidentally, I'm a really good listener."

I smile back at him. It's hard not to. He really is that charming. "You're right," I say. "I've got something on my mind."

"Let's go then."

He playfully juts out his elbow, and I link my arm through his, holding his upper arm with the opposite hand. As we walk toward the coffee shop, I feel his developed bicep under my fingers and remember what I think I saw there yesterday.

"Do you have a tattoo on this arm?" I ask, trying to keep our conversation light for now.

"Yes."

"Of what?"

He smiles. "Guess."

"A heart? With *Mom* written across it?"

"Oh, you got me pegged. I am definitely a mama's boy. But that's not it."

We stroll a few more steps. "A skull?"

"Nope."

"American flag?"

He shakes his head.

"Dragon? Snake?"

"No and no."

I rack my brain and consider his profession. "Rolling pin?"

"That's fun," he says. "But no."

I sigh. "I give up."

"So soon?"

I stop him on the sidewalk and lift his shirt sleeve. It's the Minnesota Twins logo.

"You're a baseball fan?" I ask.

"Not really," he says, "But I am a twin. Or was. My brother, his name was Bryce, *loved* baseball. He was small and he had a bad heart. He died when we were five."

I pull his sleeve back down but keep my hand there, as if trying to apply pressure to a wound. "Oh, Brady, I'm so sorry. To lose a sibling at such a young age. And your twin."

He nods. "Thanks."

We begin walking again, my arm looped in his. "When did you get the tattoo?" I ask after a beat.

"The summer after I graduated from high school. It's a turbulent time, isn't it? Late teens, trying to figure out who you are. How to be an adult. And I think I started feeling the loss of my brother even more. So I found a way to keep him with me, always by my side, so to speak."

My eyes water. "That's beautiful."

We walk a few more steps in silence. "Alice told me about your husband," Brady says.

I quietly nod.

"So I'm glad you asked about my tattoo because—and we don't have to talk about it—but I wanted you to know that I understand. Not exactly. But . . . I understand loss."

It's only three words, but they make me pause. Because they feel like an absolution. A wave of reprieve rushes through me. The loss of a sibling is so different than a spouse, and yet Brady and I understand each other's pain in a way others cannot.

"Thank you, that means a lot," I say, hugging his arm tighter, letting my head fall onto his shoulder for a beat. It's the closest I've let myself get to him—to anyone since Sean—but I give in to the comfort of his words, the simple message they bring:

You are not alone.

Is that why I haven't dated anyone since Sean? Why connecting to someone else seemed so hard? Because I felt like an alien in my grief? Misunderstood? And here was Brady, getting all my complicated pain without me even explaining it.

At the coffee shop—he orders a dirty chai, and I order a lavender latte—we enjoy our drinks at a window table overlooking the main strip. I spot an old-fashioned hardware store and barber shop across the street. This town is so quaint.

"So is that what's on your mind this morning?" Brady asks. "Your husband? I know it's been a little while, but I also know how grief—or just memories—can creep up, surprise you when you least expect it."

"Yeah, it can." I think back to moments when Sean's death hit me unexpectedly. When a sentimental song popped up in my shuffle playlist, when I discovered his fine-tooth comb at the back of the bathroom drawer. "But this doesn't have anything to do with Sean. It's actually about Alice."

"That's right. You said you were worried about her."

I question whether I should tell Brady about Alice's money troubles. It's personal, and this is a small town. I don't want to embarrass her, make her the subject of gossip.

"Can I ask for your discretion?" I ask.

He gestures zipping his lips.

"Alice is in real jeopardy of losing her farm," I get out. "If she doesn't come up with loan payments and interest by the end of October, the bank is going to foreclose."

He cocks his head. "Wait, what? But isn't the farm paid off?"

"She used it as collateral for a home equity loan—that's how she built the commercial kitchen. It was a five-year loan with extremely high interest. And she really should have been able to make her payments and other expenses with the rent from the artisans. But with recent storms and crop damage, and the economic downturn, some of her renters have struggled to pay. I thought I could help her. That's what I was doing this morning at the library. I called a financial adviser."

"I've got money," Brady chimes in.

His eagerness to help moves me. Brady doesn't seem like the kind of person who throws out hollow promises, but I still wonder if his offer is sincere. I share the details of my earlier conversation with Jim, and the financial risks involved.

"You said the end of October?" Brady repeats. "Then there's still time. It would be a shame to see Alice lose that beautiful historic home."

"It's actually more historic than you think," I say.

I tell him about the ledger and my great-great-grandmother's boarding-house during World War II. "We assume the boarders were here to work during the war," I explain. "But we don't know for certain. I know you're not originally from here, but do you know, are there any manufacturing factories nearby? That might have hired these women back in the 1940s?"

"Nothing comes to mind. But there's a historical museum down the street. I bet you could find some answers there." Brady narrows his eyes in thought. "Do you know when the house was built?"

"It's a Queen Anne," I say. "So somewhere between 1880 and 1910? Why?"

He shrugs. "I was thinking if you could prove its historical significance, maybe you could try getting the house on the National Register of Historic Places."

"Genius," I say. "And I'm the one who works at a museum. Why didn't I think of that?"

He smiles. "My grandmother's house was old—like 1860s—and I remember it was a big deal when she got her plaque. I'm not sure if that helps, though. Does being on the Register keep the bank from taking her farm?"

I hesitate. "Not *exactly*. But it could put pressure on the bank to give her more time, especially if local newspapers and historic preservation groups get involved. Bad press." I start spitballing. "There are also philanthropic groups that provide grants and other funding to preserve and maintain homes like hers. And there may be local historic protections. Some towns and counties have something called a historic overlay. It's basically a city zoning ordinance that maintains historic character. So being on the Register could keep the bank from selling this property to a developer who wants to bulldoze it and build a big-box store."

"Yeah, you're definitely the one who works at a museum," he jokes.

I laugh. "It's worth a try. But the process takes time, so I'll have to find out everything I can about this boardinghouse ASAP."

Brady checks his phone. "Well, if you pretend you're drinking an Italian espresso instead of a latte, then we have time for a little field trip."

The Archer County Historical Museum in downtown St. John's Ferry sits directly across from the gazebo park I saw yesterday. Like many small-town buildings, it's a blend of old and new. The lobby, a small rectangular box made of brick, seems to have once been a library or post office, but they've obviously added on over the years. The back portion boasts a two-story ceiling with timber rafters and large paneled, parallelogram-shaped windows that look out over the Mississippi. Being in this local history museum—the smell of polished floors and old artifacts—naturally reminds me of work. I realize I haven't thought about the museum since we've been here, and now, a part of me misses it.

Another part prays for time to slow before I have to go back.

The gray-haired man at the front desk smiles at us with kind blue eyes. "Good morning," he says. "What's brought you two in today?"

I take in his denim button-down shirt, tucked into blue jeans with a brown leather belt. He exudes Midwestern charm. His skin is the kind of tan that comes from working in the sun, not sunbathing.

"I'm visiting my aunt here in St. John's Ferry, and I discovered a really intriguing artifact in her attic," I explain. "I'm hoping to do a bit of research here to find out more."

"That's exciting. What kind of artifact?"

Brady answers. "A ledger from a World War II boardinghouse."

"A boardinghouse? Here in town?"

"On the outskirts," I say. "Rosehill Farm."

The man's lips curl at the mention of the farm. His eyes dance. "Alice's farm?"

I nod, and Brady and I exchange glances. "You know Alice?"

He shakes his head. "Yes and no. I know her a little. I've bought her jam at the market. I'm newer to town—I'm a widower, retired, and I volunteer here at the museum." He offers me a handshake. "Lenny."

"Maggie," I say, returning the gesture. As he shakes Brady's hand, I make a mental note to ask Alice about him. He seems fond of her. "I work at a museum too, in the Chicago area. Natural history."

"That explains why you're here bright and early. First customer of the day." He laughs, and I notice that his lower teeth are a touch crowded. There's something endearing about it. "What specifically are you looking to find here?"

"Well, it's clear the ledger was from a women's boardinghouse from 1943 to 1945," I say. "But we don't know who these women were, why they were living in St. John's Ferry. We assume they were part of the workforce during the war but want to know more."

Lenny nods. "You've come to the right place. We have a whole exhibit on local involvement in World War II. I bet you'll find something there." He hands us a museum brochure and points out the exhibit map. "Meanwhile, let me do some digging. See if I can find you anything useful."

His eagerness to help is simply charming. Small-town hospitality.

The gallery seems small but organized and user-friendly. Walking through the exhibits, I learn some fascinating facts about the Driftless Area, twenty-four thousand acres encompassing southwestern Wisconsin, northwestern Illinois, northeastern Iowa, and southeastern Minnesota. I also relish the exhibit on local Scandinavian heritage, and how that legacy is kept alive with annual festivals, including Midsommar in June and God Jul in December.

"This makes me think of the Scandi Trio," I say to Brady.

He nods. "I was thinking the same thing. No wonder they feel so at home here."

The World War II exhibit explores the ways Wisconsinites helped the war effort. And just as Lenny promised, there's a special section focusing on the women's labor movement. In addition to the riveters, who placed and fastened the rivets used to construct tanks, and the welders, who built Navy ships, we find out women played a variety of other roles during the war. Many performed farm work through the Women's Land Army from 1943 to 1945, some through 1947 on emergency extensions.

I'm especially drawn to a black-and-white photograph dated 1944. It's of a farmerette wearing coveralls, sturdy boots, and a hat with a floppy brim cinched like a bonnet. She's hoisting a round wooden basket full of apples onto a tractor bed. I notice the band around her right arm has the letters *WLA*. I study her face—her expression is happy, proud. Patriotic.

I check the caption, and a shiver of excitement tickles my neck. I gasp.

"This is Peggy Kelley," I announce.

"Who is Peggy Kelley?" Brady asks.

I study the woman's face. "One of the names listed in the boardinghouse ledger."

Brady walks me back to my car. This time, instead of holding his arm, I hold a list of women who were employed at local farms with the WLA, thanks to my new friend, Lenny. He tracked it down while we were looking at the exhibits. I figure Alice and I can cross-reference this list with the names in Rose's ledger, hopefully proving my hunch: My great-great-grandmother hosted a boardinghouse for WLA farmerettes.

"That was fun," Brady says as we reach my car door. "Like a research treasure hunt."

"Ah, yes, the thrill of history," I say. "I'm really glad we ran into each other. I feel better now about all of this. Hopeful. Thanks."

"You're welcome." He smiles, then cringes. "But I do have a small confession to make . . . I called you at the farmhouse this morning, and Alice said you went to work at the library for a bit. So, we didn't *exactly* run into each other."

I feel my cheeks blush. "So you're stalking me?" I say playfully.

"I prefer to call it *tracking you down*. There's something I want to ask you."

"Okay." I shrug, suddenly disarmed by his directness. "What is it?"

"Well, it's supposed to be clear tonight, a perfect night to watch the sunset. So I thought we could have a picnic at that secret spot I was telling you about?"

Everything inside me says yes. Because being with Brady—at his baking class, the coffee shop, the museum, even for just an hour—makes me feel buoyant and expansive.

But he lives in Madison. And I'm in Chicago. I'm going home in four days, and likely starting as the museum director in the fall. I have Hannah, and he runs a full-time business. And right now, I need to focus on helping Alice save her farm. Besides, what would be the point of spending more time with Brady this week? What if I start to feel more? What happens then?

"Actually, I can't tonight," I say.

His kind eyes fix on me. "What about tomorrow?"

My gaze bores a hole in the pavement. "It's just, I've been here only a short while, and I feel like I haven't spent much time with Alice and Hannah," I say.

He's quiet at first, and when I look up, he averts his eyes.

"Okay," he says. "Well, I really should be getting back. Good luck with your research."

As I watch him walk away, my stomach knots. I want to call after him, because I don't want to say goodbye. Not yet. And I want the knot to go away.

But I let him go.

14

Back at the farmhouse, Hannah naps after lunch while Alice and I sit at the dining room table. I tell her about Brady's brilliant idea to get her farmhouse on the National Register of Historic Places, and the work involved. Fortunately, she loves the idea, though I am careful to tell her it is not a guarantee for keeping the farm. Our first order of business is to prove that something of historical significance occurred here, and we get to work comparing the names in Rose's ledger with those on Lenny's list. Our excitement builds every time we make a connection. We ultimately find twenty-two women reflected in both lists over three summers. Lenny's list even notes the locations where various women worked: the dairy, the orchard, the cannery.

"O'Brien's Dairy," Alice notes. "They're still up and running."

I feel a rush of adrenaline. Maybe the dairy has historical archives.

Alice and I start to wonder about these women. Could any of them still be alive? It's possible but not likely. They would be over one hundred years old now. But maybe they shared stories with their families? Left behind journals or correspondence? Any evidence that could tell us more about living in this farmhouse over eighty years ago would be a plus.

"Well, I already thought my grandmother was amazing, and now, I think she was the coolest woman in the world," Alice announces. "How wonderful the man working at the museum found you this list."

"Lenny," I say, grinning. "He seemed very fond of history . . . and very fond of you."

"Me? I don't even know him."

"Well, *he knows you*. He buys your jam, apparently. I think you have a secret admirer, Alice. Though I guess it isn't a secret anymore."

"Lenny?" Alice repeats, trying to place him.

"Tall and thin, gray hair."

Alice shakes her head.

"Well, I should introduce you. Maybe you two will hit it off?"

Alice laughs and waves the idea away. "I think that ship has sailed."

I wonder about Alice's past relationships. Was there ever a special someone in her life? Before I can ask, Alice stands and moves to the kitchen counter.

"All this history research has worked up my appetite," she says. "Would you like a little something to tide you over until dinner?"

I shake my head. "Maybe just a cup of tea. My stomach is a little off today."

Alice sits back down after putting on the kettle. "Penny for your thoughts?"

Now that we've finished combing through the ledger, my interaction with Brady resurfaces. I finally tell Alice about his invitation for a sunset picnic tonight.

"I said no," I add.

"And you regret that?"

The whole scene—his question, my answer, the expression on his face—keeps replaying on a loop. "I don't know. Maybe."

Alice places a hand on my shoulder. "You like him," she says.

I teeter my head. "If I was in a position to *like* someone, then yes, I might. But I'm not."

"Why not?"

"Because we have all of this going on," I say, gesturing at the work in front of us.

Alice eyes me critically. "Is that really why?"

I shrug. "It's too soon."

"Who says?"

"I say."

"Why?"

"I have Han . . ." Hannah is napping upstairs, but I lower my voice anyway. "I have responsibilities."

Alice matches my volume. "You can't get to know a man because you have responsibilities?"

Hannah never knew her father, just like I never knew mine. It doesn't seem fair to introduce another man to play that role, when Sean desperately wanted to be her dad. It would be different if he left us on purpose. Just ran off. But he didn't leave us. At least, not like that.

Alice and I sit in silence for a beat, her question lingering.

"I read an article about Sean's drowning," Alice finally says, her voice soft, gentle. "I found it when I looked you up online at the library."

Over the past three days, Alice and I had talked about Sean, but not about how he died, not about that day. Alice had been polite in not asking, not bringing it up. Until now.

"I can't imagine how traumatic that was for you," she adds. "But I also wonder if maybe . . . you could still be angry with him?"

I feel my heart pulse. "Angry? I'm not angry," I protest.

She purses her lips.

"Why do you think I'm angry?" I ask in a calmer tone.

She shrugs. "Because Sean didn't stop to think about you and the baby before he jumped into that water. He risked his life, not for you or the baby or himself, but for a stranger, a little girl he didn't know."

"But she was a child," I argue. I feel heat rise in my throat. "And he didn't have time to think. Isn't that what you're supposed to do in a moment of crisis? Not think. Do. That's just who Sean was. He was a Boy Scout, an Eagle Scout. He did what was expected of him. He was brave. He was a good man. A noble man. He went into autopilot." I shake my head. "I can't be angry with him for being selfless. For saving someone."

Alice remains calm, cocks her head. "Can't you?"

"I shouldn't."

"But?"

"But . . ." I repeat. "But it seems as if saving that girl . . . doing the right thing, in that moment, was more important to him than his wife and unborn child."

There it is.

"Shouldn't he have thought of us?" The words come out before I can think. It's as if I've passed the point of no return. I begin to rant. "Shouldn't it have crossed his mind that *we* needed him too? That his responsibility was to us? Couldn't he have helped the girl another way? Maybe found a large branch to offer her? Couldn't he have thrown our cooler into the water to buoy her until someone called 911 and help arrived? I know this is all hindsight. I know. But why? Why did he have to jump into the water? Why did he have to be a hero?"

I start to cry, and Alice wraps her meaty arms around me. Her hug feels like being strapped into a seat on a roller coaster. I may go up and down, left and right, and even upside down.

But I won't fall off the edge.

We all go to bed early, but I can't sleep. I finally drift off, then open my eyes forty-five minutes later, wide awake. I toss and turn for a while, then decide to just get up. Feeling the need for fresh air, I head to the porch. The evening air feels cool and a bit moist; there's an earthy smell of dirt and grass and tree bark and the faint but lingering smell of smoke from what I guess is a neighbor's bonfire. It smells like a Friday night high school football game. It smells like camping.

It smells like adventure.

After my talk with Alice earlier, after saying all the things I never said after Sean died, things I should have said to the therapist I saw that first year, I can't settle my mind. It feels like whiplash, processing emotions

I didn't even know I had so long after the fact. Anger. Disappointment. Abandonment.

I didn't even know I was angry.

Is this why I haven't been able to let go of Sean?

I need to move. It's too dark out to take a walk—the sky is jet black without the light pollution of a big city—so I pace the porch. My fingers wriggle, itching to do something. I don't want to wake Alice and Hannah, but I need to expel this energy. I head back inside, and as soon as I see the kitchen, I know what I need to do.

I need to bake bread.

I think back to that morning, after Hannah's graduation, when I wanted to make her fluffy French toast for breakfast but had just finished the last two end pieces of our bread. I didn't have enough flour on hand for a new loaf, not even enough for pancakes. But I know Alice's canisters are full. The absolute best French toast starts with the absolute best bread. And I figure if I make a loaf of challah now, I can transform it into that perfectly thick, eggy, syrup-drenched French toast Hannah loves come the morning.

I work methodically—quietly grabbing flour, yeast, sugar, and eggs. As I start to dissolve the yeast in water, I think back to sixth grade, to when my mother came home to find me baking bread for the first time. We had flour and sugar in the pantry, but I had to get the yeast from our next-door neighbor, Mrs. Holloway. She was always home and essentially on call to assist me until my mother arrived. When she handed me the yeast, she said she wasn't sure how old it was, and that I should "bloom" it first to see if it was still "alive." I nodded as if I knew exactly what she meant, then immediately looked up the word *bloom* in the dictionary. I followed the definition that made most sense, after many references to flowers, to add the yeast to warm water and a touch of sugar and wait for it to get foamy, to prove its viability. What grew inside the bowl in the next five minutes looked like a fuzzy science experiment. I figured that was a good sign, so I went ahead with the recipe directions. I mixed and stirred and kneaded the sticky glob until I got something that resembled bread dough.

Now, I peek at my yeast, water, and sugar combination and smile at the frothy growth.

Proof of life.

The rest of the steps unfold seamlessly. I mix the dry ingredients and crack eggs, then observe as a shaggy dough forms, then vanishes, as I knead it on the countertop. By the time I braid the dough on its second rise, I notice my heart feels lighter, the tightly coiled rope loosened. As if there's more room in there now.

Space. For something—or someone.

"You like Brady," I say out loud in the quiet kitchen. It's the truth, and I feel no need to retract the statement. "You wanted to go with him tonight."

I did. I imagine now what the night would have been like, had I said yes to Brady. We would have shared a picnic somewhere beautiful—some spot that only he knows—and then lost our breath watching the sunset in magnificent pinks and oranges and purples over the river. We would have talked and laughed. It would have been easy. Natural. Much like that night Sean and I picnicked on the beach, before the storm came. Except instead of ending in tragedy, this could end with promise. Brady would have taken my hand as we walked back to his truck. And when we said goodbye . . .

As I wipe flour from the countertop, I vow to stop by the camp and tell Brady that, if his offer still stands, I'd like to go for that sunset picnic after all.

Suddenly, I hear Alice's house phone ringing. I don't know exactly what time it is. I've been in a baking coma. But it's late, has to be past midnight. Who would be calling at this hour?

Before I can pick up, the rings stop, and I tackle the stairs to find my aunt sitting up in bed, the side lamp on, an old-fashioned pale-yellow phone receiver up to her ear, the cord a long stretch of curlicues.

"What is it?" I ask, assessing the expression on her face.

She holds a finger up.

"Where?" she asks into the phone. And then, "How long do you think that will be?"

Then finally: "Thank you for letting us know."

My heart pounds suddenly as I wait for her to hang up the receiver.

"That was Gerry, the owner of Camp Stockholm," she says. "There was a fire."

I remember the scent outside when I was on the porch, the smell of smoke I assumed was coming from a nearby bonfire. "A fire? Where?"

"It started in the kitchen building, and then spread to the two next-door cabins."

"But that's Brady's cabin. And the girls from Scandinavia."

Alice touches my arm. "The girls are safe. Brady got them out," she assures me.

"And Brady?" I ask.

She sighs. "He was taken by ambulance to the county hospital."

15

I spot Katrine, Nora, and Johanna as soon as I walk into the ER waiting room. They sit huddled in a corner, arms crossed, faces somber.

Katrine sees me first. "Maggie," she calls, waving me over.

"Are you okay?" I ask, embracing each girl.

"Yes, yes, we're fine," Nora answers.

"But Brady cut his hand," Johanna adds. "On the window glass, trying to get us out of the cabin. It's a pretty deep gash."

We exchange knowing glances. This kind of injury could really affect Brady's career. His hands are his livelihood.

"You were trapped inside?" I ask.

"The fire started at the front of the cabin, by the door," Katrine explains. "So we couldn't get out that way. That's why Brady smashed the back window."

"He saved our lives," Nora adds.

"Is he okay?" I ask, my breath caught in my chest.

Katrine nods. "But he inhaled a good amount of smoke too."

"How did this happen?" I ask.

Katrine's nostrils flare. "It was Allen. He admitted to leaving the stove burner on again. He probably didn't clean up well and something fell near the flame and just like that . . ." She snaps her fingers to demonstrate the quick action of the fire's path.

"The kitchen is completely destroyed," Nora adds, tears filling her eyes. "Our cabin and Brady's cabin are in bad shape too. We lost all of our stuff. Our clothes, furniture, all of it."

It's surreal. Just two days ago, the cabins were both there, perfect. And now, they were gone. Just like Sean. Life changes in an instant.

"I'm so sorry," I say.

"What will happen to the program?" Katrine says. "Without a kitchen, without Brady, we're not sure it can continue. And we still have four weeks left."

"Don't worry," I say. "Somehow, it will all work out."

And I know that it will, just not how. After Sean's death, it seemed impossible that life would go on, and yet it did. It had to. I missed him every day, but somehow, life continued. It still does. Here I am, five years later, rushing to the hospital to see Brady. I'm here because we are new friends. But I am also here because I care about him in a way I didn't think I could again after losing Sean.

"Is there another cabin for you girls to stay in?" I ask.

The girls shake their heads. "Gerry said he's going to put some air mattresses in the game room for us, at least for tonight," Katrine explains.

"Why don't you come stay with us?" I quickly offer. "My aunt's farmhouse has plenty of room." I think about Rose, how she took in all those young women during the war.

"Would your aunt be okay with that?" Nora asks. "We wouldn't want to impose."

Though I'm newly reacquainted with Alice, I know her heart is big, open to helping others. And we certainly have the room, considering twelve girls lived there once upon a time.

"It would be our pleasure," I say, thinking of all the things we'll need: toothbrushes, pajamas, more food. "I think you'll be more comfortable with us than on air mattresses in the game room."

The girls all nod in agreement.

"Okay, then it's settled," I say. "Let me take you home."

"Knock, knock," I say, even though there is no door to Brady's ER room. It's just a space with a curtain on a track attached to the ceiling. "Is it okay I'm here?"

Brady lies in bed, his left hand lost in a mass of gauze. He looks a bit woozy, but manages a smile. "More than okay." His voice is huskier than usual, probably from inhaling smoke. "But to be honest, I'm surprised to see you."

"When I heard what happened, there was no other place I wanted to be." I sit on the edge of his bed and take his unbandaged hand. "I wish we had gone on that picnic," I start. "If I had just said yes, then . . ."

"Don't. This would have happened whether we went or not. Allen was a disaster waiting to happen. I should have let him go after the first day, no matter who his father is."

We sit silent for a beat.

"I have some good news," I say. "The Scandinavian Trio is all set up at Alice's for the night. They each have their own room. Gerry was going to make them sleep on air mattresses in the game room."

He squeezes my hand. "Thank you."

"They were here, you know. Keeping vigil in the waiting room." I point toward the lobby. "They were really worried about you. But the nurses said it would be a while, so I decided to take them back to the farmhouse and get them settled. They've had a rough night." I pause, look into his eyes. "I was really worried about you too. I guess what I'm trying to say is, I wanted to go on the picnic with you. But I talked myself out of it. And I shouldn't have." I pause. "I like you."

He caresses the top of my hand with his thumb. "I like you too."

We hold each other's gaze.

"Do you know when you're getting out of here?" I ask.

"A few hours? My oxygen levels are good, but they still want to do a chest x-ray."

"You need a place to stay," I say.

"I need a whole lot more than that. You heard the kitchen is gone, right?"

I nod. "Right now, you need your rest. You can worry about all that tomorrow."

He narrows his eyes. "It *is* tomorrow."

"I meant later today." I smile. "When they discharge you, I'll bring you back to Alice's. We have a room for you too. And a change of clothes and a toothbrush."

"Sounds like you've thought of everything," he says.

I nod. But the truth is, I wasn't thinking tonight.

I let my heart call the shots.

By nine the next morning, Alice, Hannah, and I have put together a buffet breakfast for our last-minute overnight guests. Because they all went to bed late, we figured a relaxed, eat-whenever-you-get-up kind of breakfast seemed appropriate: French toast, scrambled eggs, and sausage links we keep warm in a crockpot, yogurt with granola and berries, biscuits with honey butter and Alice's vanilla-rhubarb jam, fresh squeezed orange juice, and coffee. We've put everything out on her kitchen island with a stack of plates and a Mason jar filled with utensils. The coffee and juice sit in carafes on the counter with mugs and glasses nearby.

I went to bed late too. It was past 3:00 a.m. when Brady and I returned to the farmhouse. I fell asleep at some point, but my eyes shot open only a few hours later, my mind energized by the tasks ahead, including finally making French toast out of the challah I baked last night.

"Are they up yet?" Hannah asks, returning from the yard with a handpicked bouquet of clover and dandelions. When we told her this morning about our guests—Brady and the three Scandinavian girls— she snapped into action to make them feel welcome. She helped squeeze the juice and set out the plates, cutlery, and cups, then thought some fresh flowers would look nice on the buffet.

"Not yet," I say.

Alice and Hannah put the flowers in a small white bud vase. When Hannah places it between the biscuits and the yogurt, I can see her natural talent for aesthetics. It's exactly where I would have put it.

We hear heavy footsteps on the stairs. It must be Brady. My heartbeat quickens. After our talk last night, something changed between us. I feel it before he even enters the room.

"Good morning," Hannah announces.

Brady smiles. "Good morning to you too." He throws me a glance before fixing his eyes back on her. "You must be Hannah." He offers his hand. His other hand is still wrapped in so much gauze it looks like a cast.

Hannah shakes it vigorously, like a bell. "And you must be Brady."

"It's very nice to meet you," he says.

"We made you breakfast." Hannah gestures to the buffet. "There's eggs and sausage and yogurt and biscuits."

"I don't think I can eat any of that," Brady says.

Hannah frowns momentarily.

"It looks too good to eat," he adds.

She smiles, catching on to his joke.

"Hannah, could you do me a favor?" he asks. "Will you grab one of those plates and hold it for me? You hold the plate, and I'll put the food on it, okay?"

"Okay," she says.

"Brady, I can fix your plate," I offer.

"No, no. Hannah and I have it under control. Don't we, Hannah?"

She bobs her head.

"Besides, I need to practice being one-handed," he says.

Hannah watches him fill his plate like it's the culminating sequence of a Rube Goldberg machine demonstration. When the plate is heaping, she takes it to the table, then sits beside him.

"I scrambled the eggs," she says.

He takes a bite. "Oh, yes, perfectly scrambled."

"And she also squeezed the juice," I say, bringing him a glass. Our fingers touch briefly when I hand it off to him. It's like being snapped by static electricity, except instead of wanting to pull my hand away, I want to reach out for more.

"Aren't you gals going to eat?" Brady asks when we sit down.

"We sampled while we were cooking," I say. "This is all for you and the girls. They're still sleeping."

"*Who's* still sleeping?" Katrine asks as the Scandinavian Trio shuffles into the kitchen. They're still in the pajamas I bought last night—from a big-box store two towns away, the only place open past midnight.

"Good morning," I say. "I was hoping you'd sleep late and get your rest."

Nora and Johanna yawn and head straight for the coffee while Katrine introduces herself to Hannah, who smiles at them with starry eyes, like they're the big sisters she always wanted.

As they fill their plates with food, Katrine addresses Brady. "Professor Shaw, we were wondering, is the camp over? Should we start booking flights back home?"

Brady sighs. "I hope not. But I just don't know how we move forward from here. I'm definitely not in top shape for culinary instruction." He lifts his bandaged hand. "I don't want to cancel the camp, but we don't have a working kitchen."

A solution suddenly dawns on me: Alice's commercial kitchen. It's bigger than the camp kitchen, really the perfect space. Are there times when no one is using it? Could the students come to the farmhouse for classes the next few weeks? Could Brady and the girls just stay here during that time?

I'll need to talk to Alice first.

"Well, whatever happens," Katrine starts, "we just want to say thank you—Maggie and Alice—for being so kind to us, for taking us in."

"It was nice having my own room," Johanna adds. "This house is enormous."

"It's like it was meant to be a hotel or a bed-and-breakfast," Nora notes.

I smile. "Well, actually, it was, once upon a time."

I tell them quickly about the ledger, the history of the boardinghouse, and my plan to apply for the National Register of Historic Places.

Katrine's eyes light up. "Could I see the ledger?"

"Of course," I say. "I'm surprised, though. Not everyone your age is into stuff like that."

"Katrine loves anything old and musty," Johanna jokes.

"It's true." Katrine laughs. "That's why I'm studying history next year at the university."

I cock my head. "Really? I just assumed from our conversation the other day, when you said you wanted to be a pastry chef, that you were going into a culinary-arts program."

She smiles and shrugs. "Well, that too. I plan to work in a bakery while I attend school." She throws Brady a look. "I don't want to give up either. I love them both."

I admire her confidence. She seems too young to be so self-assured.

"So when did you graduate from high school?" Alice asks.

"Last year," Nora answers for the group.

"You didn't want to go to college right away?" I ask.

"That is typical in the US," Katrine explains. "To go to university immediately after high school. But for us, it's different. Most of us take a gap year, or even two, after secondary school. In fact, it is encouraged. To take time to travel, explore, figure out what you want to do in life, what you're passionate about. Maybe take up a new hobby. This is our gap year."

A *gap year*. I'd heard the term, but never knew it was so popular in Scandinavia. I wonder how many Americans would take a gap year if offered. It sounds intriguing, like a quintessential backpacking-through-Europe experience. And it also sounds lazy and unmotivated and off task. The ingrained American attitude, I know. We think taking a break of any kind is a sign of weakness. Or maybe that's just my mom's influence.

"That sounds wonderful," Alice says.

I nod. "Right now, I'd settle for a gap month or gap summer."

"But isn't that what you're doing here in St. John's Ferry?" Katrine presses. "Aren't you here to explore? To find your passion?"

My eyes meet Brady's briefly. *I'm going back to work on Monday,* I want to say. This is temporary. Nothing really changes after I leave.

"That wasn't my intention," I say instead.

16

While Hannah gives the Scandi Trio a walking tour of the farmhouse grounds, including the pond, and Brady enjoys a quiet moment on the porch swing, I share my idea with Alice. It doesn't take much prodding. She adores Brady, and agrees that the commercial kitchen is the perfect venue for his camp.

"Why didn't I think of that?" she says.

It does take some phone calls and schedule shuffling. But once Alice tells her vendors about the fire and Brady's predicament, they're eager to help. They're all big fans of Brady and support the work he does. Many of them even provide ingredients for his camp, so it's beneficial for them as well. Some of her vendors are ahead in production and willing to hold off for a few weeks; others agree to reduce their production times by an hour. A few are willing to switch their scheduled day or time slot. In the end, Alice reworks the schedule so Brady's camp can use the kitchen for four hours Monday through Friday for the next four weeks.

I marvel at how quickly she made the impossible possible.

We soon head to the porch to give Brady the news.

"What are you two smiling about?" he says as we approach.

Alice gives me the go-ahead with a nod.

"We have a solution to your problem," I announce. "You can hold the camp in Alice's barn."

"Your commercial kitchen?" His eyes dart to Alice. "But you're fully booked."

"She was," I say. "But Alice worked her magic, shuffled a few things around." I sit beside Brady on the swing, awaiting his response. "So? What do you think?"

"It's an amazing facility," he starts. "Better than the one that burned down. I just don't know . . . How will my students get here each day? Most of them don't have cars."

"Oh, I talked to Gerry," I explain. "He has a shuttle bus for special events. One of his staff members will drive your students out here and take them back each day. He said it's the least he can do to make up for Allen's mess."

"He also said your cabins are uninhabitable," Alice adds. "So he's going to pay me the cost of housing you and the girls for the next four weeks as well. That makes it easier for you. You'll have close access to the kitchen for prep, et cetera."

"We figured you can use the next couple of days to get organized," I go on. "Maybe have your students come out this Friday for a test run, and then start classes again come Monday."

Brady looks at Alice and then back to me several times. "You two are quite the team," he says. "You figured all this out while I was sitting out here feeling sorry for myself?"

Alice and I shrug. It felt natural to us.

"Oh, and there's one more thing." Alice lifts a finger into the air. "By the end of the day, we'll have wireless internet."

My jaw drops open. "Wait. *You're* getting internet?" This is news to me.

"I change when I need to," she explains. "It was time to move into the twenty-first century. And it's a good thing. Now that we'll have these youngsters staying here."

"I don't know what to say except 'thank you,'" Brady says.

He stands and hugs Alice first, before turning to me. I'm careful not to bump his bandage, but let him fully wrap his arms around my back. I feel safe, and I can't resist taking a full breath to pull in the smell of soap on his neck.

"I'll go tell the girls," Alice announces, clearly finding an excuse to leave us alone.

Brady and I linger in our embrace.

"Okay. Wow," he says, still trying to process this turn of events. "Well, if we're doing this, I've got to restock everything," he starts. "We didn't just lose the kitchen facilities. We lost everything in the pantry and refrigerator. So if we want to get this class up and running again quickly, I'm going to have to go out and source all of it. Eggs, milk, butter."

Hearing Brady's shopping list triggers me to run through my own. Alice and I now have a growing list of things to buy too, now that we'll have another four mouths to feed. The thought of gathering supplies for our ad hoc B & B literally makes me giddy. While Alice boasts an early crop of garden greens and vegetables, dozens of fresh eggs, and a well-stocked pantry—many items she canned herself—some products, like meat and cheese, we will need to buy.

"We'll go together," I offer.

Brady holds my gaze and smiles. "Together is good."

My morning with Brady proves to be an agricultural tour of the county. While Alice offered to source the pasture-raised eggs for his camp, he still needs locally produced milk, butter, flour, honey, and maple syrup, and so we set out to acquire everything, toting a large cooler to store the perishables.

Our first stop is the dairy farm, where I meet Tom O'Brien, a fourth-generation dairy farmer who raises Guernsey cows. The breed originated from the island of Guernsey off the coast of France and was imported to the US in 1840. Tom explains that these cows produce a golden-hued milk rich in beta carotene that contains only A2 protein, not the A1 protein found in commercial milk from Jersey cows. Tom says the A2 milk is more easily absorbed and digested, and gentler on the immune system. Brady and I stock up on Tom's whole milk, as well as heavy whipping cream, butter, and aged cheddar.

Since O'Brien's was the only local farm listed on Lenny's printout, I ask Tom if he knows anything about the WLA workers during the war, or if there may be any historical artifacts from those days. He draws a blank, but kindly offers to ask his father, who is more of the historian in the family, and get back to me.

At another, newer farm, Brady introduces me to Sally Halvorsen, a local beekeeper. One taste of her Midwest honey—floral but balanced, with hints of alfalfa and sunflower—and I purchase two glass jars. It would taste wonderful drizzled on homemade biscuits with the local butter. Sally also grows the lavender Brady was in town buying the other day. I pick up a jar of the dried herb to play around with in the kitchen, already dreaming of a lavender simple syrup for lemonade.

Our last stop is Molly's Mill, a purveyor of fine stone-milled flours. Brady says he sources his all-purpose, bread, and pastry flour from Molly. She grows the wheat on her property and grinds it the old-fashioned way, between two granite discs powered by a water wheel.

We meet up with Molly in the farm store, which not only sells her various flours, but also a few other local artisan products like goat-milk soap and pottery.

"I was sorry to hear about the fire," Molly says after Brady introduces us. "And your hand."

Brady raises his mitten of gauze and waves, then explains how he lost the contents of the pantry in the fire too. "I'm hoping I can grab a few sacks of flour this morning to tide us over. And then, can you deliver next week's shipment to Alice's farm instead of the camp? I'm running class out of her commercial kitchen from now on."

She smiles. "I know."

Brady shoots me a glance. "Just so you know, Maggie, there is no such thing as a secret in St. John's Ferry."

"I'm beginning to understand that," I say.

Molly offers us a tour, and we follow her across a quaint bridge over a small brook. I take in the mill. The lower half is limestone, and the top half is constructed of wood. The large wooden waterwheel turns rhythmically with the fall of water from the dammed brook.

"This mill dates back to 1855," Molly says, guiding us through the space. "Truly, not a lot has changed in production since then. We still grow the same wheat, including ancient grains like einkorn, that humans have been growing for thousands of years. We also produce emmer, amaranth, spelt, buckwheat, durum, and rye. None have been genetically modified in any way."

"It's amazing how the right flour can really elevate a dish, don't you think?" Brady says. "Like buckwheat has notes of chocolate, so it's perfect in brownies. Emmer has a nutty taste, so I like to use it when I make something earthy and autumnal like, say, pumpkin scones. What did you use in those orange-rhubarb scones the other day?" Brady turns to Molly. "Maggie is quite the baker."

I can't help but blush and glance away before gathering myself. "It was just good old all-purpose," I say. "But I'd love to experiment more."

Molly points to the mill, where I see two massive circular stones, one on top of the other, and a hopper above it. "The benefit of the stone mill is extraction rate," she explains. "We can grind the grains into flour but still keep the germ, which is what has all the nutrients, vitamins, and minerals. Our all-purpose flour, for example, has an eighty percent extraction rate, higher than commercial flours of its kind."

She scoops some of the flour into her hand to show us a sample.

Brady uses his index finger to rake through it. "There's a hint of brown to it. See?"

I pinch the flour and rub it between my fingers, seeing and feeling the difference.

"You likely used this flour for those scones," Molly tells me. "Alice is a regular customer."

When we head back to the store, Brady and I load up on the other flours he needs for class this week, as well as some smaller bags of buckwheat, emmer, and einkorn, which I plan to use for scones, waffles, and desserts.

"That was so . . . satisfying," I say as we drive back to the farmhouse. "I mean, I just bought flour from the woman who actually grows and mills it. And it's the same wheat people were growing ten thousand years ago. How cool is that?" I lift my hands from the wheel for dramatic effect.

Brady laughs. "The coolest."

We lock eyes for a beat, share a smile, and then I quickly look back to the road ahead. It's moments like this that make me want to be around Brady all the time. Sean and I generally got along; we never really argued. But my deep interest in food—where it comes from, how it's grown and prepared, how it's evolved over time, and most importantly, how dangerously far we've moved away from it as a society—was not something we shared. I never felt like Sean truly understood this guiding principle of my life. And to be honest, I'd forgotten it myself as of late. I think back to those weeks before we came here—the fast food and packaged snacks and soulless calories that had become my new normal. I had forgotten that food is everything to me. I live and breathe it. It's who I am at my core, what I've rediscovered since I've been here. And I don't have to explain that to Brady. He just gets it.

It's like he was born with the foodie gene too.

Brady and I grab a quick bite at a deli in town, then return to Alice's farm with the riches of our travels. After we stock the commercial kitchen's refrigerator and pantry, we walk back to the farmhouse. I see Alice is crouched down in the garden.

Just then, a light-blue sedan comes up the driveaway. It's Lenny from the museum. He waves, and I wave back as Brady and I meet him at his car door.

Once parked, Lenny exits the car and immediately pops open his truck, from which he lifts a brimming brown basket.

"Care package," he announces, handing me the bounty. "I heard about the fire, that you and Alice are housing some of the camp students. Thought I could help."

I look down to see an assortment of goodies: cinnamon raisin bread from the bakery in town, a pound of coffee from a local roaster, toiletries, a fluffy throw blanket, a few books and magazines.

His gesture makes my eyes well. "Lenny, this is so sweet. Thank you."

He just shrugs.

Brady runs the heavy basket inside while Lenny reaches into his car for a large envelope. "I also wanted to give you something I found in the museum archives." He holds the envelope protectively, like it's the Declaration of Independence. "For your research about this farmhouse."

"Follow me," I say, taking the envelope from him.

He follows me to the garden, where Alice is harvesting vibrant bunches of arugula and spinach and strawberries.

I introduce them, though I know Alice is no stranger to Lenny.

"I heard you bought some of my jam at the market recently," Alice says.

"Best I've ever had," Lenny replies.

I tell her about Lenny's gift basket; Alice seems equally touched by the gesture.

"Lenny also brought us something from the museum archives," I say, opening the envelope in front of her. I pull out a black-and-white photo of twelve young women—all in overalls and work clothes—lined up on both sides of a wooden sign that reads "Rosehill Boardinghouse."

Alice points to the woman on the end, wearing an apron. "That's my grandmother, Rose."

"Who's the little girl?" I ask, noting the fair-haired toddler Rose is holding on her hip.

Alice shakes her head. "I don't know."

"Where did you find this?" I ask Lenny.

"Well, after you left the museum, I went looking deeper in the archives. As you know, Maggie, the items in an exhibit are often just a small percentage of the artifacts in a collection. I wanted to see if there was something else related to the Women's Land Army. It took a while, but when I found this, I knew it would be valuable and made a copy for you."

I study the picture again. "Isn't that the same sign that's out front? To the left of the door?"

Alice nods. "They must have cut it down to size after the war and moved it to the porch."

"Was it here?" I ask. "When you visited as a child?"

She looks off as if trying to remember. "I don't recall. But it was here when I inherited the house."

"Do you think there's anything on the back side?" I suggest. "Like a date or inscription?"

"Want to take a look?" Lenny asks.

The three of us head to the porch, where Lenny inspects the wooden sign. "It seems strong and intact," he says. "How would you feel, Alice, if I were to unscrew it so we could check the back side?"

Alice nods. "If you think it's safe."

Lenny unearths a travel tool kit, which contains a Phillips-head screwdriver. The two of us watch him gingerly unscrew the plaque from the siding. The screws are weathered and a tad rusty. Lenny says he will likely need to replace them. Once removed, he flips the plaque over and just as we suspected—engravings. A collection of names carved into the wood.

Linda, *Donna*, *Nancy*, *Brenda*, *Judith*, and *Shirley*.

"Are these the girls from the boardinghouse?" Lenny asks.

Alice and I exchange glances and shake our heads. We've looked at the list enough to know these names aren't in Rose's ledger.

"Then who are they?" he presses.

"Yet another mystery to solve," I say.

17

June 1943

On the first full day of farm duty, Rose's eyes popped open at 4:00 a.m. Her brain darted in the dark, but her mind felt clear. She wanted to guarantee a smooth start for the girls, beginning with a healthy, filling breakfast—oatmeal with stewed apples she'd canned in the fall, raisins, maple syrup, and hard-boiled eggs. She'd serve piping-hot coffee as well, because today of all days they would need the energy.

Rose thought that balancing energy was, at a very basic level, what living life was all about. Too much energy, and impulsivity and capriciousness ensued, but too little birthed apathy and depression. And if such balance of energy was essential to living, then there was nowhere more important than home, the place we begin and end our days. In Rose's opinion, a home's energy—whether it enlivens or exhausts us—requires constant monitoring and adjustments for the right combination of cleanliness, comfort, and creativity. If she could provide a balanced home environment for these girls—through the food she served, the aesthetics of her housekeeping and décor, and the overall sense of community she cultivated—she would also provide the scaffolding they needed to meet this challenge, which would ultimately help win the war.

Put in this light, Rose thought her work, and the work of home-makers throughout the world, was actually quite noble, albeit over-looked and underappreciated.

Rose smiled when she saw Esther was the first down to the kitchen, as had been the trend since she'd assisted Rose on the first day. She helped Rose lay out clean tablecloths on two kitchen tables butted together, enough to seat twelve. They set each spot with napkin, cutlery, mug, and glass. Six girls at each table. Sitting together for meals was of the upmost importance for building community.

It is the rule in my house, no exceptions.

While they finished setting up for breakfast, Esther told Rose about one of her only memories of working with her mother in the kitchen.

"We baked a cake together," Esther said. "For my fifth birthday. It was from the Swans Down flour recipe booklet. Yellow cake with coconut icing."

"That sounds delicious," Rose replied.

"My mom liked sweets. Especially in the afternoon with coffee or tea. She called it *fika*. That's Swedish. It means 'a midday coffee break with sweet treats.'"

Fika didn't sound like something you should embrace during the war, Rose thought. Americans were supposed to sacrifice and work hard all day. Eating sweets didn't fit the wartime mentality. And yet, Rose saw how much Esther's face lit up at the memory of her mother. She wanted to honor that, to make her smile more. She also wanted to commemorate the girls' first day on the job, and dessert seemed the perfect way. It was inherently special.

And nothing is more special than cake.

Eggs were rationed but plentiful on her farm, since she owned her own chickens. But with sugar rationed, treats using less sugar or alternate sweeteners—like maple syrup, corn syrup, or honey—were ideal. She contemplated her options for a cake that met these parameters. A Victory Cake came to mind. She'd first seen the recipe in *Woman's Day*. It was a moist cake, with a unique flavor from a blend of allspice and lemon zest.

"Should we bake a cake together this morning?" Rose asked. "While I don't think we should break for fika during the day, we could have it tonight for dessert. To celebrate your first day working for the WLA."

Esther's face beamed. "Yes, Mrs. Brodbeck, I'd like that very much."

As the two of them measured flour and spices for the Victory Cake, Rose shared her best baking tips with Esther, things she learned from her own mother, her days as a home economics major, and from her cookbook collection. She showed Esther that keeping the flour light as you scoop it was the trick to a fluffy cake. Using fresh eggs was essential too. Esther seemed to hang on her every word. The attention almost made Rose blush. Her sons had never looked at her that way, with such deep respect.

As the two worked side by side, Esther began humming. Rose listened with intrigue. It was beautiful, but she couldn't place the tune.

"What is that song you're humming?" Rose asked.

"Oh." Esther blushed. "It's called 'Happier Here with You.' It's a song my mother made up. She used to sing it when she was rocking me to sleep at night. And it sort of became a family lullaby."

"What was your mother's name?" Rose asked as they slid the cake into the oven. The other girls had yet to come down.

"Lucia," she said. "It means *light*. But everyone called her Lucy."

Rose smiled. "Well then, we shall call this *Lucy's Victory Cake*. In honor of your mom and her fika."

Rose felt bolstered by the power of her budding mentorship. *I could really make a difference in Esther's life. In all of these girls' lives.*

She couldn't help but smile. And just the thought of serving the cake later for Esther and the girls to enjoy—the anticipation of their surprise when she revealed the cake after supper—would likely leave a smirk on her face all day long.

After several days of hard work, Rose sat in the parlor after supper. It had been a successful start to this new adventure. She knew all the girls' names—first and last—by heart, had committed their farm assignments to memory, and had gotten a sense of their unique food tastes. She knew Esther had a sweet tooth like her mother, especially for chocolate, while Peggy disliked radishes and Clara enjoyed mixing her mashed potatoes with her vegetables, instead of keeping them separate on the plate.

Rose thought about the girls as much as she thought of her two sons. Her interest in them could not be satiated, and she worried about their welfare constantly. *Susan's hands are chapped and raw.* She noted how the skin broke in cracks along the girl's knuckles. Rose made sure to procure Woodbury Lanolin Hand Cream from the pharmacy. Meanwhile, Sarah started rubbing her left shoulder after cleaning out the animal stalls, so Rose offered her a bottle of Watkins liniment from the medicine cabinet. It would help soothe her muscles. She noticed Rebecca had trouble sleeping, so she made her chamomile tea in the evening. And it was clear all the girls were homesick, so Rose made a point of asking what kinds of meals their mothers normally made at home. Sarah said she missed her grandmother's kugel, while Peggy hankered for her mother's beef stew. So Rose worked these dishes into her menu planning, bringing them a taste of home, comfort, and familiarity in a foreign place.

That evening, the house sat near silent. Several of the girls had retired for the night, while others congregated in the attic, to read, play board games, and chat. She heard the muffled sound of clanking cups in the kitchen, and assumed a few were helping themselves to an evening snack. She detected a whiff of cinnamon in the air.

The girls' chattering seemed to grow louder and closer, and Rose looked up to see Esther, Peggy, and Clara enter the parlor carrying a tray, their faces beaming with pride and a hint of mischief.

"We made you something," Peggy announced.

"Me?" Rose asked, unable to hide her surprise at the thoughtful gesture. She set her knitting aside. Even on warm summer nights, she liked to knit in preparation for the coming autumn and winter. Rose looked at the tray on the coffee table before her. She saw a tea pot, cups and saucers, and four of her forget-me-not-patterned plates, each holding a hearty scoop of what looked to be bread pudding. She couldn't remember the last time anyone had prepared anything with such care, just for her.

"We found some stale bread," Peggy explained. "And we used only a tablespoon of sugar, so we added the raisins for a little more sweetness."

"We were hoping to join you for a chat here in the parlor," Clara said.

Rose felt the corners of her eyes wet, flattered that they wanted to spend their precious time off with her. "That would be lovely."

She had avoided telling the girls much personal information; she liked to listen to them, to be a sounding board, not to talk about herself. But the girls seemed genuinely interested in spending time with her, having gone through the trouble of preparing her an evening treat. She would make a concession.

"You have such a big, beautiful home," Peggy said after they all took bites of pudding and sipped their tea. "We've been wondering"—she looked to the other girls as if trying to gain consensus—"about your family. Do you have children?"

Rose nodded and told them about her sons: Albert, the oldest, in California, and Hank, stationed overseas.

"You must miss them," Esther noted.

"Every day. Grown children might go days without thinking about their parents. But from my experience, mothers keep their children very close to their hearts. They are never far from my mind."

"It must be hard," Peggy added. "Not knowing when this war will end, or when Hank will come home."

Rose knew that once the war was over, and she hoped it would be soon, there would be a hierarchy to who went home first. Those GIs who'd committed the most time, seen the most battles, sacrificed the most, always returned home first. Servicemen would receive points for every dependent child at home, so Rose knew Hank would be closer to the bottom of the list when the time came. He hadn't had time to marry or have children before enlisting. *His whole life is waiting here for him, ready to begin.*

"What about Albert? Does he visit?" Clara asked.

Her stomach knotted. She told them Albert had not been home for at least four years.

Esther set her teacup into the saucer with a clank. "But what about Christmas?"

The holidays had been a quiet affair the last few years. This past Christmas, after finishing her farm chores, Rose had prepared a simple meal of roast pork, mashed potatoes and gravy, and canned green beans from her pantry, with a homemade fruit cake for dessert. She'd spent the afternoon watching the snow fall outside the window, knitting, listening to a Christmas program on the radio, reading *The Heart Is a Lonely Hunter* by Carson McCullers. She enjoyed the peaceful day, and yet, her usual joy at these activities always felt a bit muted when she wasn't able to share it with others. How she wished she'd had someone to marvel at the fluffy white snowflakes or the comforting creaminess of the pork gravy, a companion with whom to delight in the radio program or discuss McCullers's book. *Everything done alone feels like a secret.* While a small secret can feel like a spark and renew us, too many little secrets, day after day after day, have the opposite effect. They fester.

They consume us.

"Holidays can be a bit . . . lonely," she admitted to the girls, who had been patiently awaiting her answer. "It's funny, there were times in my life when I could never get a moment alone with my thoughts—when I was a kid, growing up in a house full of brothers and sisters, and after my children were born, when I always had a mouth to feed or a baby to soothe. I was surrounded by noise and chaos. I never imagined a day when silence was my only companion."

The girls all fell quiet, and Rose questioned whether she should have revealed so much to these young women, who likely did not yet have the life experience to comprehend.

Esther patted Rose's hand. "That's why this week has meant so much to me," she divulged. "To be honest, being at home this summer with my father, away from school, would have been so isolating. I'm so happy I joined the WLA. I wake up every morning excited to do my job, and be a part of this community. I go to bed looking forward to the next day. I feel like I belong to something, that I've made friends for life."

Peggy reached out for Esther's hand, and Clara hugged her shoulder from the other side. "We feel the same way," Peggy said.

Esther looked to Rose. "Mrs. Brodbeck, you have been so kind to me, to all of us this past week. Like a mother. And I want you to know that means the world to me."

Rose laid her hand on her chest and smiled. She knew having these girls all summer was a gift for all of them. They were willing recipients of her affection.

And she still had so much love to give.

They talked for a good half hour, their conversation cut short only when they heard a firm, startling knock on the farmhouse door. It was probably her neighbor, Carol, Rose thought. She was the only person who ever came by in the evenings, usually to borrow an egg or firewood.

But it wasn't Carol. It was a Western Union messenger.

"I had trouble finding the house, ma'am," the boy said, apologizing for knocking at such a late hour. And then he hesitantly handed her the message.

The bold, black words swirled on the paper, bits and pieces reaching her consciousness.

THE SECRETARY OF WAR . . . HIS DEEPEST REGRET . . .
YOUR SON, PRIVATE HANK BRODBECK . . .
MISSING IN ACTION.

18

After Lenny leaves, Alice and I come back inside and find the others hard at work in the kitchen. It looks and smells like they've been baking for the past hour.

"What's all this?" I ask, surveying the space.

"Fika," Hannah announces, waving her arms over a smorgasbord of sweet treats.

"A coffee break?" I say, recalling the Swedish bakeries in the Andersonville neighborhood of Chicago.

"Oh, but it's so much more than that," Johanna promises.

She goes on to tell us that in Sweden, *fika* is both a noun and a verb. It's a ritual, a midday break for coffee and sweet treats, but also socialization and conversation. Getting together with an old friend to fika is common. She says some employment contracts in Sweden even include a clause guaranteeing workers the right to fika during the business day. The word *fika* comes from an old Swedish word for "coffee," she explains.

"It's therapeutic," Nora adds. "It seems off task, but it actually boosts productivity and well-being."

After listening to the girls' description, I realize fika is something I enjoy often without even realizing it. Around midday, my mind and body usually request it—a subtle headache develops, a tension in my shoulders—and I need a restorative cup of coffee or tea and something sweet before tackling the rest of my day.

"You don't need an excuse for fika, but we certainly have one," Katrine adds. "Brady told us the good news. We're so happy to stay longer and continue the camp. So we're celebrating."

Alice and I help finish the fika preparations by moving everything to the kitchen table. The seven of us move as parts of one unit, an energetic flow working in tandem. The communal vibe overcomes me with a sense of hope.

Anything feels possible.

We talk and laugh over coffee and the delicious Scandinavian treats—almond bars, honey cardamom cake, and lemon elderflower tarts. I find out my daughter has been with them in the kitchen all afternoon, washing dirty bowls, measuring spices, and applying egg wash to the bar dough carefully with a brush.

"So the almonds stick good," Hannah explains.

My daughter's expression—wide eyes and a narrowed brow, the perfect blend of determination and curiosity—gives me pause. What a wonderful experience the Scandi Trio gifted her this afternoon, the opportunity to tinker in the kitchen.

I turn my bar upside down. "Yes, those sliced almonds are very stuck."

After we linger at the table, I feel renewed, inspired. I think of all the new quality ingredients I have from the shopping trip this morning with Brady, and an idea comes to mind.

"We should celebrate more," I announce. "With a special dinner. Tomorrow night."

Brady looks to the Scandinavian Trio, then back at me. "Who told you?" he asks.

"Told me what?"

Katrine clears her throat as she stacks dishes. "Tomorrow is Professor Shaw's birthday."

My eyes dart to his. "It's your *birthday*? *Tomorrow*?"

He nods, sheepishly.

"Why didn't you tell me?"

"There's kind of a lot going on." He shrugs. "When you said 'special dinner' just now, I assumed one of the girls told you."

I shake my head. "I just thought before classes start back up Friday, we should have this really memorable meal together. I had a vision of it just now."

"The power of fika," Johanna says, collecting forks for the dishwasher.

"Maybe." I smile. "I saw it so clearly, all of us, outside on the porch."

"Like in a movie?" Nora asks.

"Oh, like the patio lunch scene in *Chocolat*?" Katrine chimes in.

Brady laughs. "You want to ladle chocolate sauce over roast chicken?"

"Maybe not *exactly* that," I say. "But *like that*. Sumptuous. Decadent. A feast."

"Then I'm in," Brady says. "But let's make it less about my birthday and about all of us spending time together. It could be like the staff meal at the restaurants I used to work at, where we'd all sit down to eat before the start of the shift. It grounded us before the storm."

"How old are you going to be, Brady?" Alice asks as she loads the dishwasher.

He pauses. "Forty."

"Forty?" I exclaim, playfully punching his good arm.

I can think of only one dish: Chicken with Forty Cloves of Garlic.

I mentally run through what I need to make the entrée, which is a kind of *fricassee*, a fancy French word for a stew made of browned chicken in a creamy sauce. Garlic, when raw, can often be bitter and overpowering, but when cooked in this dish, it's surprisingly sweet and buttery. The recipe creates a rich, flavorful sauce that tastes simultaneously light and smooth. I recall what I bought today with Brady— fresh chicken from the farm and a bottle of sauvignon blanc from the gift shop at the mill that I can use to make the sauce. I also bought fresh thyme and garlic—six beautiful heads still attached to the papery husks—from Sally's farm. I realize I bought almost all the ingredients for this dish without even knowing I was going to make it. It seems meant to be. I will need cognac, but Alice has a well-stocked liquor cabinet, and heavy cream, which I know she also keeps on hand.

When I tell the group my menu idea, it's greeted with enthusiasm. Inspired by the developing theme—which seems to be French, specifically Provence—they each take on a component of the meal.

Since it's Brady's birthday and he has only one good hand, we give him the easiest job: purchasing goat cheeses for a predinner cheese board.

Katrine feels inspired to prepare a salad Niçoise, sans tuna, with a mustardy herb vinaigrette, providing a much-needed acidic element to counteract the rich cream sauce.

Nora offers to bake some crusty bread for mopping up the sauce.

Alice suggests that with all the flavor in the chicken and salad, a simple vegetable—like haricots verts—is in order, and Hannah agrees to assist her. I think she may just like saying "haricots verts," which she repeats on a loop.

That leaves dessert. I offer up the dried lavender I purchased earlier, which Johanna eagerly volunteers to use for a strawberry-lavender layer cake.

With tomorrow's dinner plans in place, and the kitchen tidy, the girls ask to run to the market to grab a few more essentials. Alice offers to drive them, and Hannah tags along.

And then, it's just me and Brady.

He looks at me intently.

"What?" I finally ask.

"You. You're bursting at the seams."

I suddenly question whether I showed too much enthusiasm. Sometimes, this happened with Sean. I'd overwhelm him with my energy, my passion.

"I should dial it down a notch?" I say, a question in my tone.

He grips my arm. "Maggie, no. I was going to say it's like you . . . came alive today. Something is different about you. It's in your eyes. In your voice."

I know he's right; I feel it too. This stirring ball of energy, like a bear suddenly waking from hibernation. I'm so hungry. For good food, but also for life, for the days to come. For the potential right in front of me.

I remember my conversation with the Scandi Trio the other day about hygge: cozy comfort, a sense of purpose, following your hopes and dreams, being true to yourself.

"I think I know what it is," I say.

Brady raises his eyebrows.

"I'm happy."

Brady's birthday dinner is everything I imagined.

Every one of my senses engages, feels heightened. The dinner table is beautifully set by Katrine, using Alice's pale-pink linen napkins, white tapered candles, and Mason jar bouquets of flowers crafted by Hannah. I watch the pure pleasure on everyone's faces through the soft glow of late-day sun and candlelight, their mouths delighted by the balanced but robust flavors of the food, their hearts warmed by the laughter and camaraderie of this shared meal.

"Time for 'Happy Birthday,'" Johanna sings, popping up from the table to grab the cake, a stunning lavender-scented masterpiece atop a white cake pedestal. It's worthy of a magazine shoot. Katrine and Nora quickly clear our dinner dishes and set a pretty dessert plate and clean fork before each of us.

"Where did these come from?" I ask, inspecting the forget-me-not floral pattern and golden scrollwork on the plates.

"Rose, my grandmother," Alice says. "These are from the collection I found in storage. I assume she and her boardinghouse residents once enjoyed desserts off these plates, and I thought it only fitting we should too."

Brady, who sits beside me, eyes his cake. "This is gorgeous, Johanna."

"Thank you." She lets out a nervous giggle. "You know, it is very daunting to bake a birthday cake for your pastry instructor. Let's just hope it tastes as good as it looks," she adds.

He stares at the cake a beat longer, his expression wistful. I wonder what he's thinking. Birthdays can be painfully reflective, and the milestone years even more so. They bring up the questions we avoid asking ourselves the rest of the year.

Namely, am I where I should be at this point of my life?

I wonder what Brady wants, deep in his heart.

His expression softens. "Now that's a lot of candles," he says.

"Forty," Katrine notes, as she begins to light them. "We counted every one."

We sing "Happy Birthday" to Brady, and now it's his turn to look around the table and study our faces in appreciation. Mine is the last, and he lingers before blowing out all his candles to our cheers. Johanna and Katrine work together to cut and serve the cake, while Nora returns with a pot of coffee and cups and saucers.

One bite of the cake, and I let out an audible sigh. It's early summer on a plate. The strawberry—freshly picked from local fields—is sweeter than candy and the lavender adds a floral depth to both the filling and the frosting. Meanwhile, the white cake is so light—a sponge cake made with egg whites—that it melts in my mouth.

With our bellies full, it would be easy to sit at the table for a good while. Then Hannah spots a yellow glow in the yard that disappears and reappears. And then another.

"Fireflies," she cries.

"Want to catch them?" Katrine asks.

Hannah is already out of her seat.

Nora and Johanna start to clear the dessert plates, but Alice stops them. "Ladies, go with Hannah and Katrine and catch fireflies. I'll clear the dishes."

The girls smile and laugh as they skip down the porch steps with Hannah.

I reach to collect the dessert forks, but Alice also stops me. "You too. Relax. Enjoy."

Brady shifts in his chair. "Alice, really, let us help."

"Brady, I am an old woman," she asserts. "If I say I want to do it, then I want to do it. Nothing would make me happier than to know you two could enjoy the end of this beautiful meal together on the porch. I'm cleaning up, and that's that."

She heads into the house with a stack of dishes before we can argue.

After a moment of silence, with the girls' distant laughter in the background, Brady speaks first. "I don't want this night to end," he says.

The candlelight seems to glimmer in his brown eyes. They're so captivating, I have to look away. "Me neither," I say.

He takes my hand in his, and playfully caresses my wrist with his thumb.

"So classes start up again here tomorrow," he starts. "Allen may have been clumsy and forgetful, but he still did a lot of prep. I need an assistant."

"I can help," I say.

His eyes widen. "Really?"

"Well, tomorrow at least. But then I'm going home this weekend, so maybe Katrine and the girls can take turns being sous-chef during the week. I'm sure Alice can chip in too."

Brady looks away and slowly nods.

"What's wrong?" I ask.

He sighs. "I don't know why—I guess it was wishful thinking—but when you said you could help, I thought you meant you were staying," he says.

"For the next month?" My heart sinks. "But I have to go back to work on Monday."

His eyes fall to his lap. "Yeah, of course you do."

It's the reality I've been avoiding all week, while I rescued Brady and the girls from the hospital, and shopped at the mill and dairy farm, and made elaborate breakfasts, and even more elaborate dinners. It's been fun, like playing. But I've been living in a fantasy. Because I can't stay. I have to go back to real life. This was a vacation—one I hadn't planned to take—and it's ending. I don't get a gap month or gap summer or gap year. I have a real life, with real responsibilities. A career. A mortgage. A child to rear.

"If I could stay, I would," I add, apologetically.

He doesn't say anything, just nods.

I let go of his hand and get up then, suddenly unable to sit and be in the moment. I can't look at him, can't process his disappointment. There are still dishes on the table, and I start to grab them and stack, scraping off bits of frosting, clattering the forks. I sense that Brady is unsure of what to say or do.

Just as I turn to bring the dishes into the house, he stands, and stops me.

"Maggie."

I look into his eyes even though I'm afraid of what I'll see there.

And then he kisses me. The plates rest in my hands between us, but my clenched shoulders fall, and I lose my breath. The taste of him—sweet, laced with birthday cake frosting—and the woodsy scent of his beard swirl together. I feel intoxicated, the backs of my knees turning into mush.

When he pulls back from the embrace, I look into his eyes again but say nothing. I am certain I have never been kissed like that.

Not even by Sean.

I'm at a loss for words. Fortunately, he does all the talking.

"I imagined you leaving in two days," he says, tucking a stray hair behind my ear. "And I knew I'd regret not kissing you, at least once."

And then he walks away, following the path the girls took earlier. I watch him descend the front steps, and want to call out after him.

Instead, I let him disappear into the darkness.

19

It's past midnight when Alice finds me on the porch swing in my pajamas, staring up at the night sky—clear but freckled with stars.

She holds two mugs of tea.

"Chamomile," she says, handing me a mug. "To help you sleep."

Since it's early June, the temperature at night has dipped to the sixties, so I eagerly take the warm mug in my hands. "How did you know I was out here?" I ask.

She shrugs, as if to say she just knew.

I sip the tea. It's so smooth, and naturally sweet, with hints of apple and honey. "This is chamomile?" I take another sip. "It tastes different."

"It's from my garden. I dry my own flowers and herbs for tea."

No wonder it tastes so good.

"You leave in two days," she says after a beat.

"Yeah."

"But you don't want to."

I shrug. "It doesn't matter what I want. I have to, Alice. I have a job. A home. Responsibilities. That's what happens at the end of a vacation. You always wish you could stay longer, wish you had booked a few more days at the hotel. But you have to go back. You can't stay forever."

Alice sips her tea and nods. "Maggie, no one is asking you to stay here forever."

"But Brady asked me to help him run his baking camp. Be his assistant. Be his new Allen. For the duration of the camp."

"And you said no?"

I shake my head as if to say I didn't have a choice.

"I have to go back to work on Monday," I argue.

"But what if you didn't?"

"What do you mean?"

"I mean, is it possible you don't have to go back to work on Monday? What would happen if you didn't?"

I snicker. "I'd get fired?"

"They can't fire you for needing time off."

"But I don't need time off."

She raises her eyebrows. "You don't?"

I sigh. "I can't permanently be on vacation. I have to go back to work. I'm hoping to get a promotion at the end of summer, and Hannah starts first grade in the fall. Our life is there." I hear how defensive I sound but can't stop. "I can't not go back to work because I'm enjoying living here at your farm, and these wonderful people, and this food, and this land, and how it all makes me feel alive inside for the first time in a very long time."

Alice laughs. "Alive for the first time in a very long time? Gee, that sounds like a horrible reason to stay."

Her sarcasm is thick. Though she does have a point. I smile. "Am I having an amazing time? Yes. Do I love it here? Yes. Does my daughter love it here? Yes. Do I feel a real sense of purpose and connection here? Yes. Did I meet someone I could just maybe fall in love with?"

I pause, remembering Brady's kiss earlier on the porch. I can still feel the weight of his lips on mine, even now. I feel a twinge of guilt. I hadn't allowed myself to think about someone in this way since Sean. But I know he'd want me to be happy, for Hannah to be happy too.

"Yes," I finally say.

"But?"

"But," I repeat. "I don't have the luxury of time or freedom to follow my dreams. I'm a single mother, who has to put my daughter first and foremost over my own happiness."

"You don't have the luxury of being happy?"

"Not when my daughter's livelihood is at stake. She needs stability."

"But Hannah is happier here," Alice argues. "You said it yourself. She's not even asking for her iPad or to watch TV. She's playing outside, catching fish and fireflies, reading, getting her hands dirty. When you talk about her livelihood, there's more to that than whether her mother has a high-paying job."

She's right. I think of Hannah, the smile that's been plastered on her face since we got here. Her eagerness to help—pick flowers, cook with the Scandi Trio. She's come alive here too.

What happens to her when we go back to real life?

"Look, Maggie, this is your choice," Alice says. "But I urge you to stop seeing this in black and white. Open your mind and heart to some gray. No one is asking you to permanently move here. But why not stay longer? Why not stay for the duration of the baking camp? Be Brady's sous-chef. I just don't think you're asking *Why not?*"

Why not? Because I'm afraid of what happens if I stay any longer. How happy will I be? How fulfilled? How attached will Hannah get? And what if we get hurt? What if all this gets taken away from us again in a heartbeat?

Isn't it easier not to find out?

"You know, I was engaged once," Alice says.

I turn toward her, tucking one leg under me. I'd been wondering about her love life, or lack thereof. "You were?"

"To Richard. My college sweetheart."

I lean in. "What happened?"

She looks off into the night sky. "Well, he asked me to marry him at our graduation, and I said yes. We were going to move to New York City. He had a great job lined up in advertising. I was a home economics major—an already dying field, with the women's lib movement— but I had several job opportunities in the test-kitchen field. Around that same time, Rose died and left me this house. And like I told you earlier, once I came here, I didn't want to leave. Richard and I did long distance for a good year. It was hard. He expected me to sell this place and move to New York so we could finally get married. But I just couldn't leave. I didn't have to go all the way to New York to realize this was where I belong. This life, here on this farm, is what I wanted. I felt so connected to St. John's Ferry. It felt wrong to leave, with my grandmother and grandfather buried just miles away. I asked Richard to come here, but he didn't want a small-town life. He wanted adventure, what New York could offer. We wanted different things at that point. And it ended."

I touch her arm. "I'm sorry."

"Oh, please, that was so long ago."

I think of Lenny, how fond he seemed to be of Alice. "And you never met anyone else?"

She shakes her head. "A date here and there. Nothing of substance. Living in a small town doesn't help. Any available bachelor felt like a distant cousin. And then, I just got to a point where I felt content, figured why bother getting entangled with someone now? But you still have so much love to give, Maggie."

I sigh. "But I just don't know how it could work."

"You know, there was a point to my Richard story," she goes on. "But I'm not sure I did a good job making it."

"I thought it was to prove that walking away is sometimes the best choice?"

"Now I know for sure I didn't do a good job." She shakes her head. "My point was that you need to do what you truly want, what you feel deep inside, not what you think you should do." She taps her head with her index finger to make her point. "It made more sense for me to move to New York, to marry Richard, to sell the farm. On paper, it looked like the best life for me. But it's not what I wanted. It's not what that little voice inside of me told me to do, knew was right for me. My point was that often, the best choice is not always the logical one."

I look Alice in the eye. "So you're saying . . . listen to my heart?"

"Exactly." She pats me on the shoulder like a teacher encouraging a student. "Look, I just want what's best for you. So I'm asking you to consider how you could stay longer. Does the museum *really* need you in person come Monday? Could you use more of your vacation time? Could you work from here?"

I think about my usual obligations at the museum during the summer. Most of it is desk work. Emails, phone calls, video calls, documents. Summer interns usually take the physically demanding work, like acquisitions and archiving, which I could oversee remotely. It is possible for me to do my job from here, especially now that there's internet on the farm.

"I'll think about it," I say.

"Good. That's all I wanted." She pats my knee and stands. "Now go to sleep," she adds brusquely, before heading back inside.

I linger on the porch after she leaves, continue looking at the star-studded sky. But I sense Alice's absence, like a child who accidentally let go of a balloon. I imagine how the conversation would have gone had I been speaking with my mother. Practical and sensible, she never would have encouraged me to stay any longer than necessary, or even consider the possibility. To her, what matters is money, and titles, and awards, and moving up in the world. Looking successful to others, exceeding society's standards. But happiness? Real fulfillment? Being your true self, even when the world tells you to be someone else?

These are not my mother's values.

And this is the gift I have in Alice, a woman who feels maternal toward me, but who also wants me to be me, not the version of me that serves her. My whole life I've craved a mentor. I've looked for that mentor in my boyfriends and friends, in my college professors, my boss. Someone who would stand beside me, hold my hand, whisper guidance in my ear, but also trust me to step boldly in the direction of my dreams. I've been here less than a week, and Alice has already played that role too many times to count.

Why not? I hear Alice ask again.

Why not? I ask myself.

I swing on the porch and repeat the words, hoping they'll become my own.

Friday morning comes too quickly.

It's quiet when I come downstairs. I start a pot of coffee and unload the dishwasher while it brews. I'm surprised by how comfortable I feel in Alice's kitchen after such a short time. *How quickly humans adapt to a new normal.* I try to picture my kitchen back in Eastridge, but the image is rudimentary, details missing. It feels like I've cooked more in Alice's kitchen than I ever did back home, though I know that can't possibly be true.

I start thinking about the morning ahead. Brady's students will arrive at ten to tour their new kitchen facility and set up—the pantry, their stations, their aprons, everything they need for classes to fully resume next week. Since Alice and I planned to welcome them with a coffee bar and a hearty late-morning brunch—egg, fennel sausage, and white-cheddar biscuit sandwiches—I decide to throw together an oatmeal bake to tide the rest of us over until then. Oatmeal, often mundane and mushy, transforms into something gourmet when baked in a 9 × 13 and flavored with maple syrup, vanilla, apples, and nuts.

By 7:30 am, everyone is up for the day—Brady fully showered and dressed, Hannah and the Scandi Trio still in pajamas. We enjoy the oatmeal bake and discuss the day's plan. I try to pretend everything is okay, that my mind and heart are not at war. The kiss last night has built a wall of tension between Brady and me. We avoid each other's gaze. It feels wrong. Just when we were getting close, the truth of me leaving has introduced a lethal reality into our fantasy relationship.

After breakfast, we're left alone in the kitchen, and the silence is so awkward, I can't take it. I stand at the sink washing dishes while he sits at the table finishing his coffee.

"I'm going to try to finish the application for the National Register of Historic Places later today," I say, my back to him.

I glance in his direction, but Brady doesn't look at me. He's staring into his coffee. He shrugs. "That's important. Do what you have to do," he says.

I try to engage him in conversation again. "How are things looking for today's class?" I ask. "Anything else I can help prep? I know your hand is still bandaged. It can't be easy."

He brings his empty coffee mug to the counter and sets it down with a thud.

"I've got it," he says.

"Okay," I say back.

Silence.

He's about to walk out of the room. "Brady?" I call after him.

He turns and leans on the door frame. "Yeah?"

"Don't be angry at me."

He sighs. "I'm not angry."

"It feels like you are. You're not really talking to me."

He shrugs. "I just don't know what else to say."

"I took a week off work, not a month," I say. "How can you be upset with me for having to go back to work?"

"It's not work, Maggie. I get that. It's . . . us. This. It seems like you don't even want to try. I think this could work, you and me. Actually, I know it can. Because I've never had this kind of connection with someone. But you're afraid to let me in."

I feel heat rise in my throat. "I'm not afraid."

He doesn't say it, but his expression speaks volumes: *Bullshit.*

"I'm not," I argue again. "It just doesn't make sense. Why start something we can't keep going? How is this going to work?"

"I don't know," Brady exclaims, throwing his arms into the air. "But haven't you heard of something called faith? Trust? When something feels right—and this does, you and me; it's like nothing I've ever experienced—you just follow it and figure it out."

Once upon a time, I might have felt that way. But now, five years after losing Sean, after raising Hannah on my own, it seems childish and irresponsible. Sean was all about math, logic, absolutes, black and white. And I loved all the gray. We evened each other out that way. But after he passed, I became more like him. I had to. But maybe it was also a way of handling my grief, taking on some of his attributes. Now, I don't know how to let go of the black and white, embrace the gray.

Brady and I stand silent, staring at each other, the space between us growing indefinitely.

He purses his lips. "You don't think I'm scared? But I'm willing to take that chance, even though I know you have the potential to shatter my heart into a million little pieces."

I realize how much I don't know about Brady's past. I know he's never been married, and his mother was nudging him about having children, but has he ever been in love? Or has he been in love too many times to count?

Tears fill my eyes. I am afraid. I'm afraid to fall in love again because I'm afraid my heart will be broken again, even worse. I loved Sean. He was my husband, the father of my child. But I had to work at that relationship. What I feel with Brady after only a short time—the way it feels so effortless, so natural, not like work at all—is scary. This could be the greatest love story of my life, and I'm too chicken to turn the next page.

"I just don't know how you can walk away from this," he says.

When I don't say anything, Brady shakes his head as if ridding himself of me.

And then he's gone.

20

When Brady's students arrive and rave about the coffee bar and egg sandwiches, the day seems to be on an upswing. But all the positive vibes dwindle, at least for me, once class resumes.

To ease back in, Brady plans for his students to practice techniques like tempering eggs for lemon curd and whisking a silky ganache. I work alongside him during the lesson, assisting when he needs an extra hand, but I feel out of place. I'm clumsy. Brady still won't really look at me, and our interactions feel cold and clinical, as if I'm Allen and not the woman he kissed on the porch last night.

I don't linger once class ends. I want to throw all my energy at something that feels safe and tangible, like finishing the application for the National Register of Historic Places. It takes ninety days or more for approval, and I want to complete it before I head back home. I realize that with the fire, housing Brady and the Scandinavian Trio, and relaunching the baking camp, Alice and I have had very little time to discuss the financial details of her impending foreclosure. I promised her we'd figure it out, and I want to keep that promise. We need to put a plan together before I leave for home.

I'm in my bedroom, laptop open, for only a few minutes when I hear a knock on the door. I spring to answer it, thinking—hoping—it's Brady. But it's Katrine. I hope I don't look disappointed.

"I tried catching you after class but you left so quickly," she says.

"Yes, sorry, I wanted to finish up that application for the National Register."

"Want some help?" she asks.

"That would be great," I say, realizing I don't really want to be alone after all. "You said you wanted to see the ledger anyway."

We sit on my bed, and I show her the artifacts we've collected so far—the ledger, the WLA list of workers, and the new photograph from Lenny of the girls out front. She studies each with true interest. Over her shoulder, I quickly review the ledger again, scanning for Linda or Brenda or Shirley, the names we found carved into the back of the Rosehill sign. But Alice and I were right. They aren't there.

"Is this all you need for the application?" she asks.

"It's enough," I say. "Ideally, I would find one of these farmerettes. There is a narrative portion of the application, and it would be nice to include a personal account. I'm not sure any of them could still be alive, though. The odds are slim. I was going to comb through obituaries, but I never had time to do the research."

Katrine reaches for my laptop. "Well, we have time now," she says.

The free obituary database through Ancestor Quest includes all published obits starting in 1930. Katrine and I work through the twenty-two names—the women Alice and I cross-referenced, who appear in both Rose's ledger and the WLA master list I received from Lenny. We find obituaries for twenty. While most of the women married and adopted their husbands' surnames, their maiden names are listed in the obituaries. We match these to the names in Rose's ledger. Rose also kept note of her boarders' hometowns and the universities they attended. These details also help us match each obituary to the correct woman.

"So who does that leave?" I ask.

"Esther Monroe and Peggy Kelley," Katrine says, reading the names from the ledger.

"So these two women are either still alive, or they passed away and we just couldn't find their obituaries," I say.

"Let's Google them," Katrine offers, already typing Esther Monroe into the search engine. It doesn't yield anything promising, so she tries Peggy's full name.

We scroll through the results, but the first hits are for business-women obviously too young to be our Peggy Kelley. We don't find a good match until the bottom of the page.

"Okay, here's a newspaper article from two years ago," Katrine says, eyeing the screen. "It's about a high school choir performing Christmas songs at the Walden Center for Senior Living in Green Point, Wisconsin. Where is that?"

"That's about an hour away," I say. "I drove through it on my way here."

Katrine focuses on reading. "Okay, well, there's a quote here from one of the residents, Peggy Gibson, about how much she enjoyed the visit. And she's featured in a photo with her great-niece, Judy Kelley. So maybe her maiden name was Kelley?"

We study the picture. "It really could be her," Katrine exclaims. "Hopefully, she's still alive."

I quickly call the senior facility in Green Point to figure out whether Peggy Gibson is still a resident. The receptionist says, due to privacy restrictions, they can't divulge any information about residents, but they would forward my name and number to Peggy's family.

Unfortunately, if I want to include a personal narrative with the application—a primary source of sorts—all we can do is wait. So I hedge my bets on Peggy and decide to put the application on hold for now. While we tidy up the space, Katrine puts the ledger back into the manila envelope.

"What's this?" she asks, slipping a black-and-white photograph from under the ledger's leather cover.

"That was in there?" I take it from her. "I didn't see it."

"It was tucked in the back here," she says.

Katrine moves closer, and we huddle to inspect the photo. It's of a toddler with light hair, wearing an apron much too big for her, the center pocket filled to the brim with eggs. The girl is smiling, windblown hair in her face.

"That's the same little girl in the group photo," Katrine notes. "The one Rose is holding."

I notice the same thing. I turn the photo over and read a handwritten note:

Lucy at the henhouse, 1945.

"So *this* is Lucy!" I exclaim.

"*Who's* Lucy?" Katrine asks.

"I actually don't know for sure." I quickly tell Katrine about my great-great-grandmother's recipe for Lucy's Victory Cake. "If this is Lucy, who is her mother? It has to be one of these women in the photo, right?"

We stare at the picture again, trying to spot a resemblance in the sea of faces.

Our concentration snaps when my cell phone rings—it's a number I don't recognize. When I answer, a woman introduces herself as Judy Kelley, Peggy Gibson's great-niece.

"The staff said you just called," Judy says. "I'm actually here this afternoon visiting Peggy. Fortunately, it's one of her lucid days."

"She has dementia?" I ask.

"Yes. It comes and goes. Today, she has clarity. I asked her whether she was in the Women's Land Army and lived at the Rosehill Boardinghouse, all the details you left in your message. I had no idea about this time in her life, but she really brightened when I mentioned it. It seems she is the Peggy you're looking for."

My heart leaps. I give Katrine a thumbs-up, and she smiles. "Oh wonderful. She may very well be the last farmerette still alive."

"This was your grandmother's boardinghouse?" Judy asks hesitantly.

"Actually, my great-great-grandmother's boardinghouse. I've been staying here and uncovered quite a history. I would love to talk to Peggy sometime soon, if you think she'd be open to a chat?"

"Yes, but like I said, she has good days and bad days. And they don't run on a schedule, per se. It's hard to plan ahead of time."

"I understand," I say, knowing I'm leaving tomorrow and wondering when I'll even be able to come back.

"How far away are you?" she asks.

"About an hour."

A pause. "Any chance you could come soon, as in this afternoon? I find when she is like this, she stays coherent for a few hours. But as the day progresses, she fades."

Peggy is over one hundred years old. What if she passes away soon, and I miss my chance to talk to quite possibly the only living person who remembers the boardinghouse?

"I'll be there," I say.

On the hilly ride to Green Point, we drive through small towns, much like St. John's Ferry, with obvious European influences. The historian in me wants to stop in each one. One town is Cornish—its early settlers immigrated from Cornwall, England, and the quaint but formidable limestone buildings reflect this heritage. Another was settled by Norwegians and boasts statues of trolls throughout the city streets. Yet another village looks like a mini Switzerland, with gabled roof buildings and restaurants advertising a Swiss potato dish called *rösti*. On this peaceful drive through the Midwest countryside, I realize that it's possible to travel Europe without ever leaving Wisconsin.

When Alice, Hannah, and I arrive at Walden Center for Senior Living, Peggy's great-niece Judy meets us and escorts us to her room. Peggy sits in a wheelchair near the window. Beside her are a cup of tea that has gone cold and a butter cookie with one bite taken. Her hair is short and white, sticking up at the crown. She wears a curler in her bangs.

"Peggy, these women are here to see you," Judy says in a firm but loving tone. "They want to talk to you about the Women's Land Army."

Peggy turns from the window and smiles warmly at us.

"Rose, is that you?" she says to Alice.

"No, I'm Alice. Rose's granddaughter."

I introduce myself, and Hannah too.

"You look so much like Rose," Peggy says, her speech slow and shaky. "Where is she?"

We look to Judy to assess whether we should mention that Rose has long passed away, but she shakes her head.

"She couldn't make it today," Alice says instead.

It is technically the truth.

"Aunt Peggy," Judy says. "Can you tell these ladies about Rosehill Boardinghouse?"

Peggy's eyes light up. "Rosehill," she begins. "Yes, I lived at Rosehill for three summers. In 1943, 1944, and 1945."

As Peggy begins to talk, Judy reaches for a coloring book and crayons and hands them to Hannah, who eagerly opens to an empty page.

"You stayed there while working for the Women's Land Army?" I ask.

She nods. "There were twelve of us. Though not the same twelve every summer."

Alice shows Peggy the photograph of the farmerettes, the one by the sign. We brought it in hopes of jogging her memory. "Is this you in the photo?" Alice asks, pointing to the tall, athletic woman in the back row.

Peggy's eyes narrow, then widen. "Yes, that's me," she says. "And this is Clara, and Sarah," she adds, pointing to other girls with a shaky finger. She rattles the names off by memory, the same names we read in the ledger. And then she goes on to tell us so many vivid details, about arriving in the back of a truck, meeting Rose that first day, eating asparagus soup and egg-salad sandwiches, the hard labor of working the fields and milking cows and picking fruit and driving tractors, going to dances with soldiers and laughing and talking for hours.

"Were any of the farmerettes named Linda or Nancy? Donna, perhaps?" Alice asks. We still haven't solved the mystery of the names inscribed on the Rosehill plaque.

Peggy shakes her head.

"What about Lucy?" I prompt, pointing to the little girl Rose holds in the photo. "Can you tell us anything about this girl?"

She closes her eyes first, and then beams. "Lucy," she says with adoration.

"Who was she?" Alice asks. "Who was Lucy?"

"She was our baby, our little girl. We were all head over heels in love with Lucy."

"*Our* baby?" Alice repeats.

"But Aunt Peggy, who was her *actual* mother?" Judy presses.

"Esther," she says.

"Which one is Esther?" I ask, luring her eyes back to the photo.

Peggy frowns. "She's not in the picture." She crunches her nose and her bottom lip quivers. "Why isn't Esther in the photo?"

"Maybe she's the one taking the photo?" I offer.

Peggy shakes her head, confusion knitting her eyebrows. "No. It was a man from the newspaper. He took the picture." Peggy's left eyelid starts to twitch.

"It's okay. Maybe she was sick that day," Alice offers, trying to calm her sudden anxiety. "It seems like maybe you all helped take care of Lucy?"

Peggy pauses and seems to regroup. "Yes, we took turns watching her, feeding her, diapering her that first summer, and the next year, holding her hand as she walked, playing peekaboo." The woman's eyes begin to tear, and her smile sours. "And then we lost her."

I steal a glance at Hannah. "Lost her?" I ask.

Peggy starts to cry. "She was stolen from us."

"Stolen as in *kidnapped*?" Alice asks.

"He took her," Peggy blurts. "He took her. He took her. He took her," she repeats. Her voice grows deeper, guttural. She begins to tear a tissue into tiny pieces.

"Aunt Peggy," Judy says firmly, rubbing her back. "Take a deep breath." And then to us: "I'm afraid we may have lost her now."

We watch as the woman who, a few moments ago, conveyed energy and strength and mental clarity morphed into a tired, despondent old woman staring out the window. Her distress seemed to have shut off her mental acuity like a light switch.

"Aunt Peggy," Judy says, trying to get her attention.

Peggy turns from the window. "Oh, hello," she says, seemingly startled. "Are you my nurse?"

And just like that, our visit with Peggy is over. We go home with even more questions about Lucy than when we arrived.

Namely, what exactly happened to her?

21

In the weeks after learning that Hank was missing in action, Rose rode waves of emotion, from fear of the worst-case scenario to hope that he would be found. Some days, it was hard to get out of bed, and others, Rose bolted up, ready to diligently work through her sadness. She felt so grateful to have the girls—Esther, mostly, but also Peggy. All of them. They seemed to know just what to say or do to ease her pain, despite the cavernous hole in her heart.

Sometimes, they were her caretakers rather than the other way around.

But the girls were young, too young to stay home every Saturday night. So a month after receiving the news about Hank, Rose allowed them to attend a dance at Fort Green, a military base almost an hour's drive away. For weeks, Peggy had been gently advocating for the outing. There, they would do the foxtrot and flirt with soldiers bound for Europe's front lines. It would be morale boosting for the men, and an adventure for girls who spent their days in barns and fields.

"Are you sure you'll be okay here without us?" Esther asked.

"It's only for the night," Rose said, though she knew it would be an especially quiet, contemplative night. "Now you go on and have fun."

In the hours before the dance, Rose watched the girls flit around each other's bedrooms like bees visiting garden flowers—one pinning a curl back in the mirror, the other tightening the latch of her shoe strap, another applying Victory red lipstick and kissing the excess off on a handkerchief. Clara borrowed a dress from Peggy, while Esther pinned up Susan's hair. They fussed over themselves, and each other, and it made Rose smile.

This is what it is to be young.

Rose prepared herself for a quiet night. The twelve girls would take two cars to the fort and return late, with smeared lipstick, runaway curls, a dress rip, and juicy details about the young men for whom they'd flipped their hair all night. Meanwhile, Rose would knit, read, and plan the coming week's meals. Clara's birthday was this week—she would turn twenty on Wednesday—and Rose wanted to cook her a special dinner and bake a cake, like her own mother would, if she were home.

About forty-five minutes after they left, Rose heard the whir of a car engine. She peered out the window to see one group of girls already back. Peggy was walking with her arm around Esther; the others trailed behind like baby ducks.

Rose met them at the door. "What happened?"

"I don't feel well," Esther announced.

"She got car sick," Peggy explained. "We pulled over, and she threw up in a cornfield. We decided to come back but told the other girls to go ahead."

"I'm sorry," Rose said, rubbing Esther's arm. "I know how much you were looking forward to this."

Esther nodded and held her stomach.

"The rest of you can still go," Rose offered. "I'll take care of Esther."

"Nah." Peggy swatted the air. "Seems too late to go now."

"And we don't want to go without Esther," Clara chimed in. "It wouldn't be right."

Rose saw the discomfort in Esther's eyes. "Would you like to rest upstairs? I can bring you some tea and something for your stomach?"

"Thank you," Esther said weakly.

Rose escorted the girl up to her bedroom, which she shared with Peggy.

"I'd like to change my clothes first," Esther announced. "Can you wait in the hall a minute?"

Rose nodded, and stood outside the girl's door. Once Esther gave the go-ahead, Rose returned and sat at the edge of the bed.

"I feel a lot better now," Esther said.

Rose patted her hand. "That's good. It was probably motion sickness from the car, like Peggy said. I used to get horribly nauseated on car rides, especially when I was pregnant with my boys."

Esther stared intently at Rose for a beat. "Maybe it was the car," she said, before looking away. "But I feel much better now. To be honest, I think it was my girdle." Esther gestured to her lower abdomen. "It was too tight. It made me sick."

"That can happen," Rose said. Then she remembered how Esther had fallen asleep several nights in a row before the sun went down, how she yawned through breakfast the next morning even after a full night's sleep. But she held off asking more questions. She knew from raising her own children that sometimes it was best to say nothing, ask nothing, and wait. The truth would usually bubble up like oil from the ground.

Esther shook her head. "I just wanted to look pretty. Thinner. I thought maybe more boys would dance with me. But now I've ruined everyone's evening."

"No one's night has been ruined."

Esther shrugged as if she wasn't so sure. "If I had just accepted that I am what I am, then I might have had a better time. I'd be out dancing instead of in bed."

"Well, then you learned a lesson you can apply to the rest of your life," Rose said. "And that is a greater gift than one fun night out dancing."

Esther looked back at her with softened eyes. "I didn't think of it like that."

"You are beautiful, Esther, inside and out," Rose added, placing her hand on top of hers. "And the lucky man who falls in love with you will love you whether you wear a girdle or not, because you are the one and only you."

"Thanks." Esther reached out to hug her, holding her tighter and longer than Rose expected. Just as she did with her boys once upon a time, Rose let Esther pull away first.

"You know, I think I'll have that tea now," she said, her cheeks already pinker in hue. "And maybe, I realize I didn't eat much before the dance, a few biscuits or crackers?"

Rose happily took Esther's order and descended to the kitchen, her steps keeping beat with the music emanating from the parlor, The Glenn Miller Orchestra on the record player. She heard the unmistakable sound of foot stomping, heels on wood floors. The girls were dancing after all.

The night was still very much young.

Rose would make tea and gather some biscuits for Esther, and prepare some snacks and drinks for the other girls. They would make the best of the evening.

Maybe she would even dance a bit too.

Hank—wherever he was—would want her to have a few happy, carefree moments, even if her heart ached with worry.

22

On the way home from Green Point, Alice and I speculate about Lucy. Peggy said she was Esther's daughter, yet Esther was not in the picture. Why? Where was she? And what did Peggy mean when she said they "lost" the girl, that she was "stolen from us"?

"Do you think she meant that literally? As in, she was actually kidnapped?" Alice asks. "We could find out. There would be a newspaper article about that, if it happened."

"I'm not sure we can trust what she said," I note. "But she did say 'he took her' a bunch of times. Could the *he* in this case be God? And 'he took her' means she died?"

"That could be." Alice shakes her head. "I hope neither of us is right."

When we return to the farmhouse, Alice heads inside while I offer to bring in the mail. My conversation with Brady this morning, the tension between us during class, has been eating at me. I want a few minutes alone to think.

In Alice's mailbox, there's a catalog and credit card offer, plus a flyer from a new restaurant opening in St. John's Ferry. But the stark-white envelope from First Country Bank & Trust stops me in my tracks. I start to open it, then pause. I shouldn't. It's addressed to Alice. But I have a gut feeling it's not good news, and I have to know what it says. So I gently tear it and unfold the paper with bated breath.

I quickly scan the document, and my heart sinks.

In a nutshell, Alice's local bank sold her loan to a bigger conglomerate bank, who now plans to foreclose on her property by July 31 if the back payments with interest aren't paid.

That's three months sooner than the original date.

They can't do that. I won't let them.

But really, what can I do? We're going home tomorrow. How can I fight this when I'm four hours away, working full-time at the museum, especially if I take that promotion? Already, there weren't enough hours in the day. I was barely holding it together back in Chicago. How could I take on a new position, manage Alice's farm crisis remotely, and still be there for Hannah?

I stand on the gravel driveway, stuck in thought, unable to go back inside with this news. I'm not sure if my poker face will kick in when I see Alice. I need to process. So I start walking.

Instead of the trail around the pond, I head toward the road. The pond path loops, and I already feel like I'm going around in circles.

Fortunately, the country road is lined with majestic oaks and maples, providing pockets of respite from the late-afternoon sun. I inhale and exhale a few counted breaths of clean country air and settle into a rhythmic step. I try to tap into a quiet space.

There are so many reasons to go back home tomorrow as planned. Work. The promise of that promotion. Hannah's budding friendships with kids at school that should be nurtured with at least a few playdates this summer. Bills to pay. Mail to open. The everyday maintenance of our flat. A return to routine. It feels reckless to stay here.

And yet, there are equally valid reasons to stay. Alice. Saving her farm. Brady. The baking camp and the Scandi Trio. The growing wonder I've observed on Hannah's face, in her engagement with the land, the kitchen, and all the wonderful people holding her up. The deep sense of peace I feel being here. St. John's Ferry has definitely worked its small-town charm on me.

Alice told me to listen to my heart. The best choice is not always the logical one, she said. She said not to think, but to feel.

When I think about going home, my fingers clench. My breath tightens like a coil. But when I think about staying here, I have the opposite reaction. My chest expands. I feel like I'm floating. Buoyant. Above the clouds.

I'm right where I'm supposed to be.

An odd sense of calm overcomes me. I turn around and head back toward the farmhouse. It's as if my mind and body spring to action, ready for battle. I now know exactly what to do:

I'm staying here, in St. John's Ferry.

I'm going to save Alice's farm.

And this isn't only about me or my happiness. It's about Hannah. She's blossoming here, and I don't want to stifle that. At least, not yet. It's about Alice, this farmhouse. It's about Rose. It's about the Women's Land Army. It's about my family legacy.

It's about preserving the beauty of a simple life.

It's what feels right.

I haven't always been a champion of my own best interests, but I am a warrior when it comes to the welfare of the people I love.

I don't show the letter to Alice. Not yet. I want to have time to think, to first come up with a clear plan to help her. But I do call Elena at the museum, and after I explain the situation, my boss clears me to work remotely for the next four weeks, essentially the rest of June, instead of coming back on Monday. We talk through the nuances of the next weeks. As long as I have my laptop, phone, and internet, there really is no reason why I can't do my job from here. She also assures me, when I ask, that working remotely will not affect my chances of getting the promotion come fall. I call Hannah's babysitter, April, to explain the change of plans, and assure her that I will pay her for the time she was scheduled to watch Hannah.

Then I make an in-house call for reinforcements.

Brady isn't in the farmhouse, so I head to the commercial kitchen. I find him standing at the stainless steel counter, reviewing printed recipes in preparation for class, an open notebook beside him. We make eye contact, and then he refocuses back on the notebook, jotting something down, likely a supply list. I grab my apron from the hooks and slide it over my neck.

"Professor Shaw, I'm reporting for sous-chef duty," I say, tying the strings.

He doesn't reply.

"For the rest of today." I add. "And Monday, and Tuesday, and Wednesday, and Thursday. Basically every day until the end of this camp."

He snaps to attention. "Wait. You're staying?"

I nod and wag my finger at him. "But please note that I'm working remotely, so I have to bounce between chopping nuts and writing emails."

He cracks a smile, and relief rains over me. "We'll set up an office for you in the dry storage room," he jests.

"Perfect. I've always dreamed of a cardboard-box desk and milk crate stool."

He laughs. "What changed your mind?"

I tell him about the letter from the bank, the new, very constricted, timeline to pay them back.

"I need to save Alice's farm. But I don't want to tell her about this new development until I've had time to come up with some sort of plan. Will you help me figure this out?" I ask. "Brainstorm?"

He lays his hand on mine. "Count me in. I'll do everything I can to help."

"Thanks." I look into his eyes, feel the warmth of his hand pulse through me. "Look, about earlier . . ."

He cuts me off. "Maybe you're right. Maybe if we're going to work together, we should keep this relationship platonic. Or it could get too complicated."

"Oh, but complicated is good." I slide his hand into mine. "I think we want to develop layers of flavor here. In fact, I think it's one hundred percent okay if I'm your assistant and we're . . ."

"We're what?" He inches toward me, so close I can feel his breath on my lips.

This time, I kiss him first. It's like last night's kiss on the porch, times ten. It's so intense I actually feel dizzy afterward and place my hand on the counter to steady myself.

"I want to try," I tell him. "This. You and me."

"Maggie." His voice is soft as he lifts my chin with his finger. "Have dinner with me tonight. Just us. We'll flesh out a plan. Together."

"I'm all yours," I say. "Where?"

He flashes me a mischievous smile. "You still owe me a picnic."

Brady insists he drive to our dinner picnic, despite his bandaged hand, but I start to regret the choice as we climb the narrow, steep gravel road to Jensen Bluff Reserve. The road—if you can even call it that—is full of blind hairpin turns, and navigating them is anxiety producing. Fortunately, we seem to be the only risk-takers—and that's even more apparent when we arrive at the top.

"It's so beautiful," I say, taking in the view, a panorama of green and blue—grass, trees, hills, valleys, the river, the sky.

The corner of Brady's mouth curves impishly. "You ain't seen nothing yet," he says.

We walk toward a rough-hewn path that seems to have been carved by footsteps. Brady adjusts the straps on his backpack, and we fall into step on the trail.

"I come here every other day to walk, to think," he says, as we keep pace. "It's meditative."

I take in my surroundings again. "I can see that."

"Sometimes, I don't want to leave. I guess that's why they close the gates an hour after sundown. Otherwise, people would just set up camp here."

"You love it here, in St. John's Ferry," I say.

"That didn't sound like a question."

I laugh. "It wasn't. More like an observation. You feel connected to this place, in a way you don't to Madison."

He nods.

"So why not live here instead?" I ask, as we simultaneously step over a threatening tree root.

He sighs. "To be honest, I think I'm afraid that if I live here, see this beauty every day, it'll lose its magic. It won't be special anymore. And I'm not willing to give that up."

We walk quietly for a minute, passing a worn wooden bench and several placards denoting various native birds and flower species.

"Where exactly are we going?" I ask.

"My happy place," he says.

The forest around us grows denser; the blend of tall grasses and dirt turns rockier underfoot. We're close to the edge of a bluff, I realize.

Brady stops suddenly, just before two large evergreen trees intertwine their needles, making it unclear where one begins and the other ends.

"I probably should have asked you this before we walked all the way out here," he says.

My heart skips a beat. "Ask me what?"

"You're not by any chance afraid of heights, are you?"

"Are you kidding me?" I laugh out of nervousness. I'm not afraid of heights. But the way he asks, the wild look in his eyes, tells me I might be in for a more adventurous dinner than I thought.

"I'm one hundred percent serious," he repeats. "Are you afraid of heights?"

I stare back at him. "No."

"Good. Let's go."

He ducks to where the tree needles are sparse, and I follow. He holds the branches back on both sides to carve a path. Some of the needles brush my arms and legs, and I'm relieved they're soft on the skin.

Once through, I expect to see something in view, but it's just more trees on both sides and a narrow rock path. Brady goes first, but holds my hand to guide me, pulling me behind him like a wagon. My steps become smaller and timid, as if I'm walking blindfolded. But then I see a flash of light at the end of the path, and something glistening in the sunlight. Finally, we step onto a rock—a tan, veined bluff about twelve feet by twelve feet. The most majestic view.

The Mississippi River.

"Wow," I say.

"Right?"

After that, I'm speechless. We sit a hundred feet above the river—a steely gray-blue vessel—and all that lies beyond, what seems to go on for miles. And while we're not close to the edge, with no rail, or even rope, to delineate earth from sky, it feels risky, like holding your breath.

"Welcome to the best alfresco dining spot in all of the Driftless Area," he says.

It's surreal, like something I've watched on an IMAX screen. I try to put words to the image before me. "This is . . ." I shake my head. I have none.

Brady takes me in his arms and pulls me so close, our noses touch. "I've never brought anyone here before," he says.

"Thank you for trusting me with your secret."

We stay like that, inhaling and exhaling the other's breath, until we give in to the tension and kiss. Again, my knees give way, and I'm thankful his arms lock at the small of my back, keeping me securely in place.

Brady looks deeply into my eyes, and then seems to make his mind up about something. "Okay," he says. "Time to eat."

I help him wrestle out of the backpack, careful not to bump his bandaged hand, but he insists on unloading it. He hands me a thick flannel blanket and asks me to shake it out before laying it on the rocks. After that, I'm instructed to lounge while he sets everything up.

I watch him take out a wooden board and set it between us, placing various local cheeses—a twelve-year cheddar, a lemon Stilton, and a spreadable fig-and-honey chèvre. Then, he pulls out a bottle of chilled sauvignon blanc, a corkscrew, two stemless melamine glasses, and grapes and crackers.

"Is that Mary Poppins's bag?" I laugh. "How did you get all of that in there?"

He smirks. "This is just the first course."

He crosses his legs in front of him and sighs, looking up at the sky. I join him, feel the subtle wind on my face, soak in the beautiful backdrop for our picnic. I sip the wine and let out a breath too. This is the epitome of relaxed luxury.

I break the ice. "So is that really true? You've never brought anyone else here before?"

He smiles and shakes his head. "You're special, Maggie."

My heart flutters at the sound of my name. "But you've been running the camp here for years, right? Certainly, there must have been *someone* you wanted to bring?"

He sees right through my vague question. "You want to know about the skeletons in my dating closet?" he says with a laugh.

"Well, it's only fair, isn't it? You know about me, and my husband."

I don't like how I sound, argumentative and defensive.

"I've got nothing to hide," he says coolly. "What do you want to know?"

I shrug, but go straight there. "Have you ever been in love?"

"Yes. Three times. A girlfriend in high school, another girlfriend in college, and a woman I met on a blind date right around the time I opened my bakery. We ended up dating for several years."

"But?"

"The first two—well, we were young. And the last . . . I always thought that once I got the business figured out, and things settled down, I'd naturally feel ready to go there, pop the question. But it never came. That feeling. To be honest, it just felt . . . empty. Something was missing. I didn't know exactly what, but I grew up watching my parents—they are an anomaly, still crazy about each other after forty-two years of marriage—and I wanted *that*."

"Forty-two years . . . that is really remarkable, especially nowadays," I say. "I didn't get any blueprint for what a marriage should look like. I don't even know who my dad is."

Brady frowns and places his hand on top of mine for a beat. "I'm sorry," he says.

I tell him the story about my parents' short-lived tryst, how I grew up without a father.

"Have you ever tried to find him?" he asks.

I shake my head. "I literally have nothing to go on."

That's not entirely true. It's quite possible that if I took a DNA test, I'd discover him or other family members in the results. I've heard stories of adopted children finding their parents this way, people well into adulthood discovering they have families they never knew. But I've never built up enough nerve to take a test. Maybe I'll be disappointed when the results are inconclusive. Maybe I do find him, but when I reach out, he rejects me. Maybe he won't be everything I've dreamed he'd be. Sometimes, it feels better not to know.

"Well, all I have to say is, he really missed out not getting to know you," Brady says. "Because you're pretty amazing. And I meant what I said this morning. I've never experienced anything like this before. What's happening between us." He pauses. "This feels different. This is different." He sighs and shakes his head. "Sorry, am I being too forward?"

"No," I say. He exhales visibly in relief. He's right. It's palpable, the tension between us. Like magnets being held too close. "I feel it too."

We look into each other's eyes.

He smiles. "So did I pass the test?"

"With flying colors," I say.

He reaches for a grape. "So tell me more," he says, after popping it into his mouth. "About the letter from the bank. You said the deadline changed?"

"Basically, she now owes the money by the end of July or they're going to foreclose on the farmhouse. And while we could probably scrounge up the money, without stable, long-term income, I feel like that's only a temporary fix. She's just going to be in trouble again in a few months."

He nods. "So we need to help her bring in more revenue. And fast."

"Right. I've been wondering what it would take to get our pseudo bed-and-breakfast up and running for real. I assume there are permits from the village and obviously health and building code requirements. I'm not sure how long that would take, how much she can ask for a night, or how that would offset the cost of food and other supplies. It's a huge business proposal. Not something we can just throw together in a few weeks. And then I wonder about whether she would need a business partner, someone to help run it."

He nods. "I think it's doable, long term. But she needs a short-term infusion of cash. As in now." He pauses, then his eyes fill with youthful wonder. "Oh, I have an idea. You've heard of the Midsommar Festival?"

I nibble on some Stilton. The bitter lemon peel zaps my taste buds. "I saw signs about it in town. It's a summer solstice celebration?"

He nods. "Right, June 21, the longest day of the year. But June 24 is also St. John's Day. So here in St. John's Ferry, there are four days of festivities. It's a huge event. It draws people from all over the Midwest. This one festival usually puts this whole town in the black. The hotels, restaurants, and local stores all benefit from the influx of people that one week."

I watch Brady's eyes dance as he talks; his enthusiasm is infectious.

"So my baking camp usually culminates with the festival," he goes on. "It's our final project, so to speak. My students essentially design a mobile bakery and menu and then sell their goods at the festival. The locals love the treats, and my students get real hands-on experience running a bakery. Of course, other groups sell food. This is Wisconsin, so there's a brat tent and a pretzel tent and a beer tent."

"That sounds perfect," I say, wondering how this could benefit Alice and the farmhouse.

"It is. Except I've always thought something was missing from the festival, something really special and sophisticated, something no one has ever tackled."

I hold my breath, awaiting the reveal.

"A farm-to-table dinner," he says. "Imagine this: People seated at long tables, inside and outside the barn, under the lights, under the stars, a bonfire, dancing, beer and wine flowing, and a mouthwatering prix fixe menu, showcasing all of the local artisans from the Driftless Area."

I dream along with him, until logic sets in. "But the festival is in three weeks."

"Yeah, it's definitely tight. But I know all the right people. Everyone in St. John's Ferry loves Alice. And if they heard she needed help, they'd come running. They'll donate goods and food so it's almost all profit. I really think if we hit the ground running, ASAP, this could happen."

"How much could we charge?" I ask.

"Events like these go for one hundred and fifty dollars a person. If enough people attend, that's enough to pay the bank and hold her off until she gets another secure source of income."

"And the event could put Alice's farm on the map for weddings and other events," I note. "That would be a great platform for starting a B & B."

Brady smiles. "Exactly."

I sit with the idea. It sounds like so much work. But it also sounds like so much fun.

"Okay," I say after a beat.

"Really? Because I can't do this without you."

We lock eyes. "Let's do this," I say.

23

Brady and I eat and talk and laugh over our picnic dinner of Swiss chard and feta phyllo pie, watermelon-mint salad, and apricot-pistachio olive oil cake, all while the sun puts on a show, setting in orange, purple, and pink streaks.

Brady kisses me inside his truck before we head up to the farm-house after dark, an unspoken agreement about public displays of affection, especially in front of Hannah.

As we near the house, we see firelight dancing in the yard and head there instead. There's a large tent set up next to a fire and chairs.

"We're camping," Hannah announces as she exits the tent. She's wearing Katrine's sweatshirt over her pajamas to stay warm; the air grew chilly once the sun went down.

I smile at her excitement. "I see that."

Katrine, Nora, and Johanna exit the tent and wave. "We want to sleep out here tonight. With Hannah. Would that be okay?" Katrine asks.

I look to my daughter. She seems like she's having the time of her life, hanging out with these older girls who treat her like a little sister.

"Do you want to sleep out here, Hannah?" I ask.

"Yes, yes, yes. Can I? Please, please, please?"

"She's never slept in a tent before," I explain to the girls.

"I know," Katrine says. "We were talking about camping tonight, and she said she'd never camped. It's a beautiful night for it. And Alice had a tent."

"Are you sure you don't want me to stay out here too?" I ask. "You might get scared."

She shakes her head. "I'm not scared."

I can see how badly she wants to be alone with the girls, a burning autonomy. It's bittersweet. She's growing up, away from me, and yet her strong desire for agency makes me so proud. When I say yes, Hannah squeals and jumps up and down.

I notice Katrine suddenly nudges Hannah in the side and raises her eyebrows. Hannah's eyes light, and she runs back into the tent, returning with a flat box wrapped in Christmas paper. The paper is yellowed and frayed at the edges.

"We found this in the attic," Hannah says, handing it to me.

"Where?" I ask.

"In the floor!" she exclaims.

I turn the gift around in my hands.

"The floor was sticking up," Hannah says. "I dubbed my toe on it."

"*Stubbed* your toe?" I clarify.

Hannah nods. "The board was wiggly. So I pulled on it, and there was a secret hiding spot in the floor. And that was in there!"

"Wow, Hannah. How exciting!"

"Look at the tag," Katrine prods.

I squint to read it. It's faded but still legible. "To Lucy," I read out loud. "Merry Christmas! Love, Rose."

"Should we open it?" Hannah asks, unable to contain her childlike wonder in the midst of an unopened gift.

We contemplate the dilemma at hand.

"It feels a bit wrong," I say.

"Like it isn't ours to open," Katrine adds.

Hannah nods. "Because it's Lucy's."

I study the present in my hands, which must be over eighty years old. Why was it hidden under the floorboard? Why didn't Lucy receive it? Why is it still unopened?

"There was more," Katrine adds. "Under the board. A stack of letters, all sealed, all addressed to Rose's son Hank overseas. Never mailed."

"Where are they?" I ask.

"Hannah wanted to be the one to give you this," she said, gesturing to the gift in my hands. "But we left the letters on the table in the attic. Alice went to bed already, but she said the two of you could look through them tomorrow. Together."

I nod.

Hannah tries to head back into the tent without even saying goodbye.

"Hey," I call after her. "Can I get a good night kiss?"

She rushes to my side, kisses my cheek, then darts back to the tent.

"Good night," I call out again, but she's already distracted.

Brady and I say goodbye to the girls and head inside. It's quiet and most of the lights are either off or dim. I'm eager to talk to Alice about the latest letter from the bank and the farm-to-table dinner idea. I'm also intrigued by the unopened letters Rose wrote to Hank, waiting for us in the attic. But all of that seems like tomorrow's problem, and Alice is asleep anyway. I turn my full attention to Brady.

"Are you tired?" he asks.

"Not really."

"Me either." He grins. "So it's Friday night, you've got three babysitters, and you're not tired. What do you want to do?"

I shrug coquettishly.

"I mean, I know what I want to do," he says.

I hold my breath, unsure of what he's going to say, unsure of my response, especially since Hannah will be sleeping outside. And I'm not sure I'm ready to push our relationship any further. I don't want to spoil it.

"I saw a Scrabble game in the parlor." Brady's voice is a deep whisper.

Relieved at his benign suggestion, I match his tone. "Oh yeah?"

"I'm thinking culinary edition," he says. "Bonus points for any cooking or baking words."

"Oh, you are so going down," I say with a flirtatious smirk.

The following morning, I finally sit Alice down at the kitchen table and tell her about the letter from the bank and the unfortunate new timeline to pay the money back.

Her face collapses. "The end of July? That's only two months from now. What am I going to do?" she asks, looking off to the corner, seemingly for some kind of answer.

In her worry, I see the effect of this financial stress on Alice. She's usually so positive, a glass-half-full kind of person.

"What about the Historic Register?" she asks, suddenly hopeful again.

"That takes at least ninety days," I tell her. "And I haven't even finished the application yet. I was going to add Peggy's narrative before I submit it."

Before she becomes too disheartened, I fill her in on the farm-to-table dinner idea. Brady told me he's ready to move—and call an emergency meeting of the powers that be—but of course, Alice has to sign off on it first.

I describe the dinner to her as a culminating event for the Midsommar Festival and a fundraiser to save the farm.

"But that's in three weeks," Alice argues.

"Brady says it's doable," I explain.

She holds her coffee mug like a steel pole on the L train. Her face turns ashen. "It's not that I don't think it's a wonderful idea, a thoughtful idea, it's just . . ." She emits a weighted breath. "Well, it's just a lot of attention. And I'm not comfortable with that kind of thing."

I place a hand on her shoulder. "But people in this town love you, Alice. You've given them so much. Let them give back. I know that's not your style. You want to lift others and not the other way around. But wonderful things can happen when you let people help you, when you let them love you. Give them a chance to show how much they care about you and this farm."

As the words come out, I realize it's the same speech I need to give myself.

"And you'll promise to come back?" Alice asks, a wrinkle of worry forming at her brow. "For the event?"

"Actually, I'm not leaving this weekend after all," I add. "My boss cleared me to work remotely for the month. There's no way I would leave you with all this. We're a team."

Alice smiles. "Well, I guess it's a good thing I got that internet. *Wi-Fi*, you call it, right?"

I give her an affirming smile.

I head outside to find Brady. He's leaving for Camp Stockholm soon. I don't see him out there, but I do see Hannah and Katrine at the campsite. They sit around a morning fire; Johanna and Nora are presumably still asleep inside the tent.

"Good morning, campers," I call as I near them. "How was it, sleeping in a tent?"

"Fun," Hannah shouts. "I heard crickets."

"I bet you did." I give her a quick peck on the cheek.

"Katrine is going to teach me how to whistle today," my daughter announces.

"Whittle," Katrine corrects.

"Whittle?" I repeat, trying not to let concern cross my face. "As in, carving a piece of wood with a knife?"

"Don't worry, Maggie," Katrine asserts. "We'll be very careful. I started whittling when I was Hannah's age, and I've never cut myself. We'll start with a vegetable peeler and work up to a knife."

This is the kind of parental moment where you know you have to say yes or risk your child's developing autonomy in the process. Worst-case scenario she nicks her hand and it heals. I remind myself that I have to let her get hurt sometimes. It's the only way she'll learn. It dawns on me how much I've changed this past week—a far cry from the panic attack I suffered the day Hannah and April went to the beach.

I see Brady exit the farmhouse. "Well, I can't wait to see what you create," I say, working a smile onto my face as I walk away.

I meet Brady by his truck. "You weren't leaving without saying goodbye?" I ask.

"Of course not," he says.

Because I am his sous-chef, Brady had asked me to go with him to the camp. He's debriefing the rest of his students on next week's plan, which includes French delicacies like madeleines, crème brûlée, and macarons. His hope is that outlining the coursework will facilitate more efficient use of the commercial kitchen. I wanted to go, just be with him, but I said I better take the weekend to organize for work, read those letters with Alice, plus spend some quality time with Hannah. She seems happy and content, but I can't shake the feeling that I'm not doing my job there.

I tell him that Alice has agreed to the farm-to-table dinner.

"That's great news," he says. "I'll get moving on it today."

I search his eyes for something more. "You're not still sore with me, are you?" I pause. "For kicking your butt at Scrabble last night?"

He places a hand to his heart. "Not going to lie. Still stings a little. But you won fair and square with *hazelnut*. Triple-word score, with the *z* tile, a culinary word, and you used every letter you had for the fifty-point Scrabble. I didn't have a chance."

It wasn't the Scrabble loss I was worried about. It was what happened afterward. Brady and I had walked up to the landing outside our bedrooms, and we'd stopped in front of his room to kiss and say good night. Then he opened his door, took my hand, and gently guided me to follow him. But I'd stopped at the threshold.

"I don't think we should. I'm sorry."

"Don't be sorry."

"I'm just not . . ." The word was *ready*. I wasn't ready. I was ready for the physical part. After six years of celibacy after Sean's death, I craved being in a man's arms again. Not just any man, but a man like Brady. But I wasn't ready for what might come afterward. The intimacy. The attachment. The vulnerability.

"Maggie, I'm here. I'm with you." His voice had been a soft whisper. "And I'm not going anywhere. So tonight, tomorrow, next week. Three months from now. A year." He'd squinted and cocked his head, as if maybe he'd gone too far. "Whenever you're ready. Okay?"

I'd nodded. "Okay."

Now, standing by his truck, I survey his face, looking for any hint of lingering rejection.

But all I see is Brady.

I use the rest of Saturday morning to check items off my to-do list. First, I set up a makeshift office in my bedroom so I can actually go back to work Monday, albeit remotely. Alice offered the desk from her room, which will serve my posture much better than the bed.

Then—because I forgot to do it yesterday—I text my neighbor Mrs. Lee to ask her to continue collecting our mail for the next few weeks. She replies with an envelope emoji and a smiley face, and I take that as a yes.

I also check my work email, which I've severely neglected. There are only a few important emails, but it takes me longer to think through how to reply. Getting back into work mode is going to be a struggle come Monday.

Finally, I complete the application for the National Register of Historic Places. While it won't be approved soon enough to make a difference with the bank, I feel certain we will save this farmhouse, and I want to do everything I can to keep it standing for many years to come. I attach digital photos of the Queen Anne–style farmhouse, copies of the ledger, and Lenny's photo. After completing the narrative portion of the application—describing the house's historical significance and many details Peggy shared—I upload everything and say a prayer.

After lunch, while Hannah and the Scandi Trio go fishing at the pond, Alice and I head to the attic to inspect the letters the girls found last night. We deliberate about opening them, Lucy's present as well. After much back-and-forth, we decide to open the letters but leave Lucy's gift as is for now.

As we open and sort the letters, we note that they start in 1943, in the months after Hank went missing. It seems Rose continued to write to her son, perhaps to keep him close or as therapy, a way to sort out her feelings. It's also clear the affection Rose feels for the WLA workers, particularly Esther.

Alice and I sit side by side and read a few of the letters. In the third one, Rose mentions the farmerettes gifting her a wooden sign, erecting it in front of the boardinghouse, and then . . . Esther's pregnancy.

Alice and I hold each other's gaze.

"Lucy," we say in unison.

24

September 1943

It was a perfectly beautiful day—blue skies, plenty of sunshine, temperatures in the upper seventies, a subtle breeze—but Rose had been dreading this day, and now it was here. The mid-September potato harvest would mark the end of the WLA session. The girls were due back at school—the university had shortened the school year by a few weeks to accommodate summer farm work—but it was time for their return. They would come back next year in late spring; they had all promised to do so. And while Rose felt certain some of the girls would in fact return, she knew it was the last time she would see others. *Who knows what the next school year will bring for these young women?* One was bound to get married; one might graduate and begin full-time work, while another might drop out of school to work for the family business. Rose couldn't say which future belonged to which girl, though of course, she had her predictions. But she also knew how surprising life could be, what cards could be dealt to the least suspecting player. You could fight life, but sometimes it was best to just go along for the ride.

The potato harvest was a two-week ordeal, and today would be the end of the laborious job. Every girl in the house—including those who had mainly worked in dairy or animal husbandry over the summer—was on hand to finish the work. In fact, everyone was. Even the local school had been off the past two weeks for a potato break. Children worked alongside their parents in the field. The work—manually digging out potatoes from the cold, brown earth with a fork—began at 7:00 a.m. and ended at 5:00 p.m. It required a strong back and sturdy knees. Fortunately, these young women had trained all summer long, their biceps meaty from hefting bushels of vegetables and milking Guernsey cows by hand, their lower backs strengthened from pitching hay or picking cherries. But despite the physical demands of the farming season, sometimes nothing could prepare the body for the potato harvest. It was that grueling.

The same could be said for Rose. Although she'd been emotionally preparing for the girls' departure, for the house to plummet into a deafening silence, to return to worrying only about her own needs, the change would not be easy. She'd done it before—when Charles died, when Albert headed to Hollywood, when Hank left to fight the war, when the telegram arrived—and she'd likely do it again. But that didn't mean she'd ever get used to saying goodbye.

Today would feel like a loss.

But there was work to do, and she woke earlier than usual to prepare a hearty breakfast of scrambled eggs, sausage, potato pancakes, and applesauce for the final day of the potato harvest. The girls woke earlier as well, as if they, too, were trying to squeeze more minutes from the day. One by one they came downstairs with smiles that masked their own conflicted feelings. Likely, they had missed university and felt ready to return to their studies. They were a family, however—had become a family over the past three and a half months—and she knew the girls would also miss each other.

Rose watched Peggy pull an extra chair from the parlor and squeeze it into the already full table. She set a coffee cup and plate there too.

"Is someone joining us for breakfast?" Rose asked.

"Yes," Peggy answered. "You."

Rose did not usually sit with the girls at meals. Despite the friendships she'd forged with them, she always maintained that division. But

Peggy insisted, and the other girls cheered and clapped. Rose found herself unable to say no.

Like any other morning, the girls buzzed about the kitchen table, passing around the eggs and sausage and pancakes. They all had so much to say, and it was beautiful, the harmony of their voices, each girl providing her unique pitch and timbre to the orchestra of their friendly banter. It rose and fell in volume like a symphony. Rose sat quietly and took it all in. She wanted to remember this moment tomorrow, and through the fall and winter, when the house quietly waited for a return to life.

She was caught off guard when Peggy stood and clanked her coffee cup.

"I'd like to make a toast," she announced.

The girls quieted and sat up in their chairs, grabbing their mugs or glasses.

"To Rose," Peggy said.

Rose blushed at the sound of her name. She smoothed her apron, suddenly self-conscious. She wasn't expecting this attention.

"The best host a girl could ask for," Esther added.

"Thank you, Rose, for everything you've done for us," Clara chimed in.

And then all the girls clanked cups and tipped them back like champagne flutes. Meanwhile, Rose sipped her coffee and held the mug in her hands, prayerlike.

You've done far more for me than I have for you.

After breakfast, Rose was in for yet another surprise. The girls called her outside. When she stepped onto the porch, she saw the group standing huddled in a mass.

"Okay, now," Peggy exclaimed.

When they dispersed, Rose saw the surprise: a carved wooden sign erected in the front yard that read "Rosehill Boardinghouse."

"We thought your farmhouse needed a proper name," Peggy exclaimed.

"Do you like it?" Clara asked.

Rose beamed and stepped closer. "It's beautiful," she said, running her fingers along the grooves. "How did you make this happen?"

"The Jensens have a woodshop," Peggy explained. "We've been planning it all summer. The hard part was agreeing on a name."

"But we kept it simple," Esther said. "Your name is Rose and your farmhouse is on a hill."

"It sounds fancy, doesn't it?" Peggy asked.

"Rosehill Boardinghouse," Rose said, rereading the sign. "It's perfect."

Then the girls hustled away in preparation for the rigors of potato day, and Rose found herself alone with Esther by the sign.

"I'm not sure I'll be back in the spring," Esther said quietly.

Rose knew why. She'd had an inkling since the night of the dance, when Esther came home nauseated from wearing a too-tight girdle. *Morning sickness*, a completely inaccurate name for an all-day ailment. The look on Esther's face when Rose mentioned her own pregnancies with Albert and Hank told her the truth that night. She'd been studying Esther ever since—how much she ate and slept, her energy levels, even the growing roundness of her face.

"What's his name?" Rose asked.

Esther flinched. "Please don't tell the other girls."

Rose nodded solemnly.

"Henry," Esther said. "We met at school back in May, just before the end of semester. He dropped a book, and I picked it up and chased him across the quad to return it. We chatted for a long while," Esther went on, "and then my stomach growled. He said he should buy me a meal as a thank-you, and we went to the local lunch counter and talked all afternoon. And then he asked me to have dinner that night too."

Rose reached for Esther's hand and nodded for her to continue.

Esther kept her eyes on the grass beneath her feet. "It all went very fast." She blushed. "Except then the semester ended, and Henry took an internship back home in New York, and I joined the WLA." She paused and frowned. "He wanted to write, to call, to keep in touch over the summer. I guess I wasn't sure what would happen once school started again. I thought it would be easier for him to end things with me," she said, "if we weren't in touch to begin with."

Hearing Esther's story, Rose reminisced about her husband, Charles. They'd met at a boxed-lunch social, a fundraiser for the local school to purchase a bell. Young women from town prepared a lunch for two, packed it with their name on a slip of paper inside, then decorated the outside with bows and ribbon. Eligible men bid on the boxes, not knowing who had prepared them. Once all the boxes were spoken for, they'd learn the identity of the girl who'd prepared the meal, and the two would enjoy the contents together.

Rose had made curried egg-salad sandwiches on homemade rye bread and oatmeal cookies. She'd decorated her wooden lunch box plainly, with a single blue ribbon tied in a bow, and hoped whoever bid would appreciate simplicity. Because she was a simple-looking girl. She'd noticed Charles Brodbeck as soon as he came into the schoolhouse—he had a chiseled jaw and intense brown eyes—and she secretly hoped he would bid on her box when the time came. To her surprise, he did. And later, when the two sat on a picnic blanket, she asked why he had bid on her box.

"Was it because it was different from the others?" she'd asked, pointing to the now untied blue ribbon. "Because it was so simple?"

"It was because it was yours."

She crinkled her nose. "But how did you know?"

He'd swallowed a final bite of egg salad. "I followed you here. And I memorized the box in your hands."

It was the first time any man had shown such interest in her, ordinary girl that she was. And he had won her heart forever.

Her thoughts returned to Esther. She cataloged the timeline of Esther's love affair. *May.* "You're due in February then?" she asked.

"I counted," Esther said. "February 14."

This child will be full of love. "Are you planning to tell him, when you go back to school?" she asked.

Esther nodded, bit her lip. "I'm scared."

"But remember, he wanted to stay in touch with you all summer," Rose reminded her. "It was *you* who rejected *him*."

Esther's eye grew wide with hope. "That's true."

"He loves you, Esther. And he'll want to marry you. If that's what you want."

Esther met Rose's gaze. "Do you really think so?"

Rose didn't know the young man, could not vouch for him. But he had fallen for Esther—plain, sweet, shy Esther—and a man attracted to a girl like her, a young woman of subtle, beautiful, and remarkable substance, was likely a very good man.

"I really do," Rose told her.

As Esther walked away, Rose thought about writing Hank again. Ever since the telegram arrived, she'd been writing him whenever she missed him, whenever she couldn't sleep and her thoughts swirled, whenever she felt like it.

She missed his letters, even though the sight of his penmanship used to make her cry at times. She swore the paper even smelled like him. Sometimes, she could tell from his tight, left-slanted cursive that he was holding back, that there was so much more he was feeling and thinking but couldn't put into words. Hank had never wanted to burden her. He'd been like that as a small child too. He'd go with a hole in the big toe of his sock, so as not to add to her mending. When he enlisted, he said the only downside was the worry it would inevitably cause her. His letters had always detailed the mundane aspects of war—the food they ate, the games they played off duty, the names of his bunkmates. They read more like letters from summer camp than from enemy lines. Hank never mentioned death, though thousands had lost their lives, and thousands more had lost their limbs. There was never a sign of despair, of fear or fatigue, though she knew there was plenty of that.

Although her son had been missing for several months, Rose held on to the belief that Hank was still alive. *The war did not take him. He is somewhere.* That was the hope of any mother. That her child had a future.

The letters she wrote Hank now were different than the ones she'd actually mailed in the past. Those letters had been about Hank, how he was doing, and how she could support him while stationed overseas. But these letters, the ones she addressed but didn't mail, were about her, her thoughts and feelings and ramblings, things she normally wouldn't have told him. The letters had helped her survive, to keep going.

Once, when Hank was a child, he'd hidden his toy planes and trucks under a loose floorboard in the attic after his father had threatened to take them away for bad behavior. So Rose had been putting her letters to Hank there too, for safe keeping.

Dear Hank, she began.

It seems my suspicions about Esther were correct . . .

25

Our time reading Rose's letters in the attic is cut short when Alice and I hear car doors slam and loud voices downstairs. I peek out the turret window and see a number of cars in the driveway.

"Are we having a party?" I ask.

"Looks like it." Alice points to a white sedan. "That's the mayor's car."

Downstairs we find a large group talking and laughing in the parlor—Brady, the Scandi Trio, Molly from the mill, Tom O'Brien from the dairy farm, and Sally the beekeeper, plus more than a handful of other people I don't recognize. I also spot Lenny. He smiles and waves from the corner, and I wave back.

"Alice and Maggie," Brady says, spotting us. "Perfect timing. I was just about to come find you." He gestures toward the group assembled before us. "Welcome to the first official meeting of the St. John's Ferry Midsommar Farm-to-Table Dinner Committee."

I smile at their eager faces, their open expressions. Wow. I'm beside myself. These are people who care enough about a cause to actually do something. I give a little wave.

"We just came up with this idea last night," I whisper to Brady. "And you've already formed a committee?"

"We've got three weeks," he says. "Every day counts. Every hour."

Alice and I take seats near Brady, and I scan the room. Hannah isn't here. But my alarm bell doesn't sound. I trust the Scandi Trio. I know the girls wouldn't leave Hannah fishing by herself. Before I can ask her whereabouts, Katrine taps my hand.

"In her room reading," she explains, and I nod.

We begin with introductions; it's a who's who list of sorts. In addition to the people I recognize, there's Bob Nielsen, mayor of St. John's Ferry; Pamela McFarland, Midsommar Festival Committee president; Miles Hardy of the St. John's Ferry Chamber of Commerce; Mary Cooper of the county Farm Bureau; Fred Collins of Collins's Country Meats; and Meghan Dahl of Bluff Orchards and Farmstand.

The group makes decisions quickly, including the date and time of the dinner. Pamela will handle publicity, with Katrine assisting, as a subset of the Midsommar Festival Committee. Ticketing procedures will be managed by the Farm Bureau, and Bob will handle permitting through the village office. Alice, Nora, and Johanna will run production design with the baking-camp students—basically setting up the site, the tables, parking.

I can't believe how much this group accomplishes in twenty minutes' time.

Lenny raises his hand. "How can I help?" he asks.

Before anyone has a suggestion, I give my own. "Maybe you should work with Alice and the others on setting up the site. There's going to be a lot of footwork there. We should have one more person on that."

The groups agrees, and Lenny flashes a grin—my hunch is at the mention of working with Alice. Nothing wrong with fundraising *and* playing matchmaker.

Alice and I exchange glances; she knows what I'm trying to do, but I look away before she can give me a talking to with her eyes.

"Maggie, you and I are in charge of the menu," Brady finally says. "Obviously, we want to feature the local food and artisans, but it's also Midsommar. Scandinavian heritage should be reflected in the menu as well. So Scandi Trio, you're on deck for consultation."

"Not to pressure you," Pamela says to Brady and me as the others start to disperse, "but the menu is the first order of business. Once we have that, we can start publicizing. The good news is I already secured Art Cavanaugh, the food editor of the *Madison Gazette*, as a special guest. He's the one on the *Wisconsin Eats* PBS show. That should increase ticket sales. But we also need to procure goods, et cetera. Do you think you two could put the menu together by end of day tomorrow?"

Brady and I smile at each other.

"I guess we know what we're doing the rest of this weekend," he says.

Brady and I thought developing the menu would be easy. Our shared love of food, and his expertise in the food business paired with my research and planning skills, seemed like the perfect marriage in this endeavor.

But after sitting at the kitchen table for a good twenty minutes, all we have to show for our time and energy is a blank notepad. We toss around some ideas—an entire menu featuring one in-season ingredient, like strawberries, kale, or dill, or an old-fashioned fish boil—but nothing sticks long enough to jot down.

"You know what the problem is," Brady says. "I'm a visual person."

"We're in here," I say. "When we should be out there?"

He smiles. "Precisely."

We quickly pack up and head to the barn for inspiration. On the way, I try to get our creative juices flowing.

"If you could sum up your goal for this dinner in one word, what would it be?" I ask.

"Memorable," Brady says after a beat.

"Okay. What's the most memorable meal you've ever eaten?" I ask.

Even though we're only walking from the house to the barn, Brady takes my hand, and the sensation of his fingers laced with mine surprises me, as if a ladybug has just landed on my shoulder.

"Off the cuff?" he says. He shakes his head as if deciding not to tell me after all. "It's going to sound weird."

"What?" I ask.

"My great-grandfather's funeral."

"A *funeral?*"

"You should have seen the smorgasbord," he exclaims. "What is it about death that makes people want to cook their hearts out? I guess food is the only practical thing anyone needs after someone dies. There is nothing you can say or do to diminish loss. You have to go through it, not around it. And meanwhile, you still have to eat."

I nod, thinking back to when Sean passed. My kitchen had never been so full of food. From Sean's family, my family, Sean's coworkers, my coworkers, our Pakistani neighbors in the flat above, and Mrs. Lee below. Some of it homemade, some store-bought, but all of it oozing with love. My appetite was small; I ate only enough to get through the day, to keep my heart beating and my knees from buckling, and, of course, to sustain the baby quickly growing in my belly. I donated some to a local shelter. Other items, I froze and ate later, a month after, when the pain was worse and fewer people were around.

"So what was on the smorgasbord?" I ask.

He closes his eyes as if watching a movie in his mind. "Roast beef. Mashed potatoes and gravy. Fried chicken. Sliced glazed ham. Potato salad—it was salty and sweet; it had chopped bread and butter pickles in it. And dill. There was a bean salad too—with green and yellow wax beans and kidney beans and garbanzo beans—but this one didn't have mayonnaise. It was a sweet vinaigrette. There were rolls, warm from the oven, and butter. And other salads made of Jell-O and cream cheese, plus sauerkraut and other pickled vegetables. And the desserts. Bars and cookies and cakes and pies. Oatmeal-date bars and quick breads: zucchini bread and lemon poppy seed and date nut. Iced tea and lemonade and coffee."

I squeeze his hand. "Sounds a lot like our family picnics."

"It was sad," he says. "Everyone was sad. My great-grandfather—his name was William, but everyone called him Bud—was a really gregarious guy. Everybody loved him. I was about nine. But it was different than when Bryce passed. This time, I guess because we'd already lost Bryce and my great-grandfather was in his nineties, there was something almost comforting in the sadness. Kind of like a rainy day or a sappy song playing on a record player. I think it was all the people and all the food. It was a reminder of all we still had—the food, each other—even though we'd lost so much."

And this is what I love about you, Brady, I want to say. *How deeply you feel and how openly you share those feelings.*

"That's beautiful," I say instead.

He smiles. "It's funny, considering I've eaten at some of the most decorated restaurants on the planet. And my most memorable meal was essentially a Midwest potluck held at a VFW."

I laugh. I can picture the atmosphere, including dark wood-paneled walls and linoleum floors. "Yeah, but sometimes it's the simplest meals that we remember most," I say.

We step inside the barn and take in the space—the high-pitched ceiling, the wooden beams. "So what about you?" Brady asks, pulling the barn doors fully open to let in the light.

"I was in college," I say, helping him with the door. "I'd gone back early to train as an orientation leader. A thunderstorm came through in the late afternoon and the power went out, and those of us there—most of the school still hadn't returned to campus—congregated in the lounge. We had flashlights and lit candles and listened to the radio for alerts. This was just before smartphones took over the world. It got to be dinnertime, and we were all starving. So we went back to our rooms to scour for supplies, and we made a meal out of what we had. There were food combinations I never would have dreamed of—a chutney of canned peaches and pickles—on top of rye crisp crackers with cream cheese. It was surprisingly good. When I look back, I remember the novelty of it all, the *we're all in this together* mentality. It forced us to bond."

We stand in the doorway, between the barn and the green space outside. Brady studies me for a beat.

"We're overthinking things," he finally says.

The realization moves through my body in goose bumps. "You're right, because what do our most memorable meals have in common?"

"That it really wasn't about the food," he says.

"It was about the moment and the people. The emotion," I say.

"The food was good," he argues.

"It *was* good. Great. Amazing, even. But it was secondary to the experience. And in the end, it was simple."

"It was simple," Brady repeats. "So I guess it's back to basics," he adds, heading back into the barn. "Let the ingredients speak for themselves. Meats, starches, vegetables."

"Open-faced sandwiches and hearty salads," I add, visualizing people gathered around tables, chitchatting while taking hearty bites of our fare. "With bursts of flavor from sauces and dressings and pickled condiments."

"And desserts," he adds. "Simple desserts but lots of them. I see those on a buffet here." He waves his hand to signal the location of the dessert bar.

"Handheld desserts," I add. "Like brownies. Frosted, cakey ones you can hold."

"Exactly. Nothing that requires a fork or even a plate. Just a napkin. Chunky blocks of layered fruit bars and cookies the size of your hand." He stares at the fictitious table as if he can really see it. "We should ask the Scandi Trio for help, to bring the Nordic flair. They're all about cookies and pastries."

As we lock up the barn again, we share a smile. We've unblocked the obstacle. Our momentum pulses with every step back toward the farmhouse, where we find Alice on the porch swing. She's holding a piece of paper, and her eyes are red rimmed and watery.

"What is it?" I ask, hoping it's not another letter from the bank.

She hands me the paper. It's one of Rose's letters to Hank. Alice must have resumed reading without me.

"This explains why Esther wasn't in the photograph," she says.

26

Christmas Eve 1943

A light snow began early Christmas Eve morning, setting a lovely backdrop for the holiday. Rose felt thankful that it was not enough to accumulate, or inhibit travel by car—just enough to dust the trees.

She woke early to prepare for the arrival of her guests later that afternoon. A few weeks ago, she received a letter from Esther, who was now almost seven months pregnant. She and Henry had married and were living in an apartment near campus. Because of the baby, Esther decided to leave school, and her days felt quiet and lonely while Henry attended classes. _I miss you, Rose. Terribly,_ she wrote. _Henry and I would like to spend Christmas with you at Rosehill, if you'll have us._

It was wonderful news, considering that Albert would not be home again this holiday. His letter arrived only days before Esther's. Due to the war, long-distance travel proved difficult, and money was tight. Acting roles were hard to come by in Hollywood, so he'd taken a job at a factory in the meantime. He'd met a woman, an actress named Doris, and they were in love. In fact, they'd gotten married. Doris was pregnant, due in spring. If it was a boy, they planned to name him Albert Jr.

Rose desperately wanted to see her son, and meet her new daughter-in-law and see her round belly, but still, she really just cared that her son was happy. And California—with its ocean and beaches and mountains and deserts—seemed to help fill a bottomless thirst in Albert's heart the

Midwest could never quite quench. Maybe being a husband and a father would do that for him too. Maybe, if Albert cared for others as much as himself, it would extinguish the emptiness that had always seemed to plague him.

With Esther and Henry's visit, there was quite a lot of work to do, and Rose now relished the fullness of her schedule. There would be no time to miss Hank or Albert or her late husband. She was most excited about Christmas dinner. She was roasting a duck. There were no turkeys to come by—the few available were reserved for the soldiers to enjoy overseas—but she had procured a duck from Carol's husband, who hunted game. She would serve the duck with an orange sauce, accompanied by a celery-and-sage dressing, mashed potatoes and gravy, carrots, peas, and cranberry sauce. For dessert, they would enjoy an assortment of candies, seafoam—a light honeycomb type of candy made from brown sugar and corn syrup—and cereal squares made with butter and marshmallow.

The day passed quickly but with intent. By the time Esther and Henry arrived, Rose felt a small sense of peace. While times were tough, food rationed, a country at war, she took comfort in preparing a simple but full meal, in company and conversation.

The moment Rose saw Esther's round, cheery face and swollen belly, she felt a stinging in the corners of her eyes. Tears fell freely as she hugged the young girl.

"Oh, Rose, now you've gone and made me cry," Esther said.

Henry quickly produced a handkerchief and handed it to his wife.

"This is my Henry. Henry, this is Rose."

"A pleasure to meet you," the man said, hugging her as well. He wore spectacles, and his brown hair was combed over neatly. "I've heard so much about you, and about Esther's time here at your farm."

"How wonderful," Rose said, taking their coats. "But I know so little about you, Henry. Please leave your bags here in the foyer, and let's warm up with some tea and cookies in the parlor." Rose escorted them into the front room. "It's toasty in here with the wood stove. And your room is directly above it, so you'll stay warm as you sleep."

"You have a beautiful home," Henry said, smoothing his hair over nervously.

Rose smiled. She could already tell he was a good man worthy of Esther's love.

She poured tea as they selected cookies from the platter. She'd made two kinds—molasses and orange drop.

"I want to know more about you, Henry," Rose prompted.

Esther and Henry looked at each other and smiled. A nervous laughter escaped Esther's lips. "Henry is studying to be a doctor," she said.

"A veterinarian," he corrected, adjusting his glasses on his nose.

Esther placed her hand on his. "He was 4-F on account of his eyesight."

"I'm practically blind without my glasses," Henry added. "I'm colorblind too."

"It's a good thing he can't see, or else he'd be off fighting the war, and I never would have met him." Esther laughed. "Although it's probably also good he can't see so well, or he wouldn't have fallen for me in the first place."

"Dear, you mustn't say things like that." Henry patted Esther's knee. "You're the most beautiful woman in the world."

Esther beamed. "That's the baby," she said, rubbing her stomach. "I just know she's a girl, and her beauty is radiating through me."

"Oh, Esther. I'm so very happy for you," Rose said.

Esther looked down at her shoes. "My father is not so thrilled," she went on. "He said I worked hard to become an educated woman, and I've thrown it all away."

Rose sighed. Disappointment comes easy to parents. *Because our children are reflections of ourselves.* "And what about your parents, Henry?" she asked.

"They're deceased, ma'am." Henry put his arm around Esther. "I'm an only child, so Esther and the baby are my only family." His lips grew tight, his eyes narrowed. "I want you to know, Rose, that I was planning to marry Esther all along," he explained. "The baby just pushed us to do it sooner."

Rose appreciated Henry's effort to earn her favor. She nodded in understanding. "Your father is still sour with you, Esther?" she asked. "Is that why you're spending Christmas here and not at home?"

Esther nodded hesitantly. "He'll come around."

"Of course, he will," Rose assured. "He won't be able to deny a beautiful baby. Once the baby comes, none of it will matter, the when and the how."

Esther turned to Henry. "Do you see why I adore her so? She loves so unconditionally."

Henry nodded and kissed Esther's hand.

"It's too bad you weren't able to be with your family this holiday," Rose said.

Esther smiled. "Oh, but I am. You're my family, Rose. You've been like a mother to me. Your children are very lucky to have you."

The women shared a knowing look about Hank.

It was the kindest compliment—that Esther felt she'd treated her with the love and care of a mother. And yet, it stung. Because sometimes she wasn't so sure her children—specifically Albert—felt all that lucky to have her. If he did, wouldn't he have tried to come home for Christmas, write more, call more? Throughout her mothering years, she felt like she had so much love to give, so much knowledge and wisdom to teach her boys, and sometimes, her children, even Hank, had been unwilling students of her guidance, of her life experiences.

"Well, this is a true celebration," Rose said. "Not only is it Christmas, but this beautiful child will be here very soon."

Esther frowned. "I'm going to miss working at the dairy this spring," she noted.

"Yes, you'll be sorely missed. But you will come visit," Rose assured her. "And the girls will fall in love with your baby girl."

"Do you really think so?" Esther asked.

Rose smiled. "I just know it."

Only ten days later, a heavy, thudding knock—like shutters in a storm—woke Rose from a sound sleep. She threw on her robe and slippers and, armed with a lantern, descended the stairs into the foyer, where the knocking had grown into a bang.

She opened the door to see Henry standing there, his face white, his eyes sunken, the fear of a wounded animal in his eyes. He held a tightly wrapped blanket in his arms; something wriggled under the cotton.

"Rose," he said—it was all he could say.

Rose tried to swallow the lump in her throat, which had bubbled up from her stomach the moment she saw Henry. "What happened?" she asked, instinctually taking the blanket from his twitching arms.

Henry stumbled farther into the foyer and collapsed onto the bottom step of the long staircase, where he put his head in his hands. In the glow of lantern light, Rose could see the tearstains on his cheeks.

"She's gone," he said.

No. No, no, no, no.

"The baby came early," Henry stammered. "Six weeks. There was so much blood. It wouldn't stop. The doctor couldn't make it stop. I couldn't make it stop."

Rose noticed a ring of blood on Henry's shirtsleeves, as if he'd dipped his hands in it. The truth was hard to take in, but she let it: Esther died in childbirth.

My dear, sweet Esther is gone.

And just as devastation ravaged Rose's body—first, the freefall drop of her stomach, followed by a dull, heavy tugging on her heart—it was almost immediately counteracted by restraint. Esther—the young girl she'd grown so close to, who'd brought joy to her world when she needed it—was gone. But Rose did not have time to process her pain.

Maybe she couldn't, not now. She would put that aside for another day. Emotional triage. Today, she would help those who needed her the most.

"How is the baby?" Rose quickly asked, even though she held the child, warm and wriggly, in her own arms.

"She's okay," Henry said.

She. Rose peeked under the blanket to see an angelic face—full cherubic cheeks, alert eyes, a dusting of sandy-blond hair. She brought the child closer to her bosom and held her tightly, rocking her back and forth, up and down. While the baby wasn't crying, and seemed perfectly content, Rose rocked her anyway, as if to say the pain is coming.

"I can't take care of her," Henry said bluntly. "I need you to take her."

Rose felt certain he meant he couldn't take care of her now, not indefinitely. Yes, now he was distraught, a man who had just lost his wife. But later, a few weeks from now, when some of the pain subsided, he would raise this girl. He would honor Esther by caring for the life they created together.

"Yes, I will take care of her," Rose said. "Until you can."

"I don't think I ever can."

"You feel that way now."

"But I don't know how to care for a baby. I don't even know if I can live without Esther."

"It's the baby that will help you live without her," Rose explained to him, knowing she was also trying to explain this to herself. "She's going to keep you going. She's going to give your life purpose."

He shrugged, and then shook his head and sobbed into his hands.

There was no reason to argue with him in this state. He would come to realize the truth in time. What mattered was the baby. She would need to be fed and bathed and loved. And Henry would need to be nursed back into a man who could take on this challenge. He was broken, but Rose could fix him.

"Did you give her a name?" Rose asked.

Henry looked up from his hands, his eyes red and swollen. "What?"

"The baby? Did you give her a name?"

He shook his head.

"What were Esther's wishes?"

He swallowed back tears to speak. "I don't know."

Rose looked down again at the bright, beaming face, the only beacon in this very dark, stormy night.

Light. Lucia. Esther's mother.

"We'll call her Lucy," Rose announced.

For Rose, caring for an infant was like riding a bicycle. Once you learn how to do it, you never truly forget. You may feel a bit rusty, and the rules about what to feed a baby and how to put a baby to sleep change with the times, but it all comes back so quickly. Rose was in her element.

Henry had come to see his daughter, but only for a few hours at a time. After months of caring for Lucy full-time, things became second nature to Rose. How quickly her left arm grew stronger as she held Lucy, stirring the pot at the stove with her right. How lightly she slept, awaking to attend Lucy's every whimper in the night. How many times had she smelled the top of Lucy's head, a scent that seemed to hold the very essence of the child? Rose tried to enjoy every moment because she hoped one day Henry would feel strong enough to take her back, to be her father. But he was still so fixated on losing Esther. Rose suspected he even blamed Lucy for her mother's death. *Time heals wounds,* she repeated, trying to believe the adage herself. The truth was, despite time's passing, she missed Esther every day. Hank's disappearance had already left a hole in her heart, and losing Esther had only deepened it. Rose actually felt it—a tender, dull aching—in her sternum. She often placed her hand there to stifle the pain. One day, Henry would raise Lucy. But meanwhile, Rose processed the loss by giving Lucy as much love and attention as she could.

It's the only way I can truly honor Esther.

During the day, when Lucy was awake and in need of attention, it was easier, as Rose's task-focused mind never wandered toward Esther. But evening was another story. Once Lucy fell fast asleep in her bassinet, Rose would retire to the parlor to read or knit. And in the silence of night, alone with her thoughts, the tears would inevitably come. She'd fall apart in a sudden, heavy sob. She cried for Esther, for Hank, for Charles. The tender spot in her heart never felt so raw.

As time passed, Rose debated about how to tell the other farmerettes about Esther. She imagined them showing up for the first day of WLA work, and their shock at learning of her passing. It would be better for them to know before the summer, to give them time to process. So that winter, she sent them all letters.

It was a wise choice. Because when the girls arrived, while saddened about Esther, they'd had months to mourn, which meant they were able to give Lucy the love and attention she deserved.

Rose met the girls on the front porch with the baby in her arms, but she didn't hold her for long. The moment one woman held Lucy, another eagerly awaited her turn. She was passed around like a plate of hors d'oeuvres, from one set of arms to another, from one smiling face to the next. The baby talk ensued: "You're so beautiful, yes you are" and "Who's so precious?" and "Oh, she has Esther's eyes." Lucy's cheeks and forehead, freckled with kiss marks, displayed the affection of a roomful of women.

Lucy may not have her mother. But she has all of us.

Once everyone came inside, the discussion soon turned to how Rose would manage running the farm and cooking meals, while also caring for an infant.

Rose swatted the problem away. "I did it when I had my own."

"Yes, but it's still a lot of work," Clara said.

"One of us should stay back to help you each day," Peggy added.

Before Rose could say anything, Peggy had retrieved a pencil and paper and begun creating a schedule.

"A full day is too long," Peggy proposed. "We should do half days. That way, we still get some farm work done each day. And the rotations will be more frequent. Once a week."

Within minutes, a schedule was made and each young woman had signed up for a shift. Rose watched how quickly and easily the women agreed to the task, and filled in where they were needed. The organization of life—of caring for others, of meeting their needs—was effortless.

Rose had fared well caring for Lucy alone the past months, but having the girls' help for the summer would be a blessing. And as she watched the girls still fuss about, she knew Lucy would never be starved for attention.

She will be surrounded by love.

27

In the weeks before the farm-to-table dinner, time moves both swiftly and slowly. The days are long, the nights short. We juggle the demands of putting on the event with running Brady's baking camp. And the two often intersect as his students take on challenges from sourcing food to prepping ingredients.

I balance it all while also working remotely, often rushing back to the farmhouse after a session so I can clock back in. By the end of the day, my brain feels mushy; working on a computer for so long makes my eyes bleary and my head feel like it's filled with helium. But reading with Hannah helps counteract the sensation. Of course, her skills have improved so much this summer; she's the one reading to me. Before the exhibit opened, I was so busy, I didn't have the bandwidth to even sit down with her most nights. But now, our daily thirty minutes of story time is what restores me. And fortunately, I don't have to raise Hannah alone anymore. Without Sean, I was the center of Hannah's universe, the parent who cleaned and bandaged her skinned knee one day, and the next, taught her how to do magic tricks with a deck of cards; I was the parent who reviewed her math homework packets and enforced tooth brushing, but who also slept in twenty-minute intervals by her side when she had a tummy virus. Now, while I'm playing sous-chef, Alice runs her own version of a summer camp, blending activities to keep both Hannah's brain and body healthy, from nature hikes focused on animal habitats and leaf recognition to hand-eye hobbies like crocheting and puzzles. After baking class, the Scandi Trio takes over, enriching Hannah's afternoon with baking tutorials, hair braiding, and watercolor painting. By dinnertime—we don't eat lunch together most days, but a family meal is the rule every night—Hannah is bursting at the seams to share her day. And I revel in the joy and comfort of these other adults also positively influencing her life.

It takes a village.

During all this, when we have time, Alice and I also continue reading Rose's letters, each drawing a clearer picture of her pain at the loss of Hank and Esther, her growing attachment to Lucy, the camaraderie of the WLA farmerettes, and ultimately, Rose's courage to persevere. There are many letters, and because we are reading them in chronological order, we still haven't figured out what happened to Lucy, what Peggy meant that day when she said *He took her*. And we still can't bring ourselves to open Lucy's Christmas gift. Not yet. Every time I think about ripping the paper off, something stops me. It never feels right.

Often, during these chaotic weeks, when I'm in the throes of kitchen work, from Brady's camp to organizing details of the farm-to-table dinner, I think back to Alice's suggestion of selling my scones at the farmers market. I can't help but smile.

We had no idea how immersed in food my life would soon become.

As the dinner date nears, I try to stay calm. I know it's normal to panic before a major event—especially one requiring people to show up in large numbers, especially with Alice's farm on the line. The enthusiasm of the early brainstorming days, always full of possibilities, is replaced with "What if?" worries. I'd been through this many times at the museum; the day an exhibit opens is one of the most nail-biting occasions for a curator. It's a point of no return. Will people come? Will they like it?

It's the epitome of vulnerability.

While everything seems to be going according to plan, there's a lot left to chance. The weather is fine today, but in five days' time, a summer storm could pummel the Midwest, causing people to cancel on the dinner or have to remain in the barn. It could ruin the outdoorsy atmosphere of our event. Or our refrigerators and freezers could putter out and leave us without safe food storage to feed hundreds of people.

While I thought I'd panic-planned for all scenarios, something else surprises us.

"Art Cavanaugh isn't coming on Saturday," Brady announces at breakfast.

"But he's our celebrity guest," Alice notes from her post at the stove, where she prepares a Dutch baby pancake to serve the crowd.

"And we've advertised that he'll be here," Katrine chimes in.

"Why can't he come?" I ask.

Brady shrugs. "Something about another last-minute opportunity he couldn't refuse."

"But he committed to our event," Katrine argues. "He gave his word."

"He said one of the other food editors would come," Brady offers.

"But none of them are as famous," Katrine asserts. "None of them have a cookbook. None of them have a TV show about food." She begins pacing the kitchen floor.

"Who else could we get?" Brady asks, throwing his hands in the air. His hand has healed and the bandage is now gone. "Especially on such short notice?"

The room falls silent as we pull out drawers in our mental file cabinets, frantically searching for a person, a name, as big as Art Cavanaugh. Or better yet, bigger. And not just someone, but someone one of us has a connection to, an association worthy of a short-notice favor of this kind. Being a museum curator, almost everyone I exhibit is dead. They are literally history. Except one.

Ruth Rivers.

Would she do it?

My heart says yes. This event is everything Ruth Rivers is about. While she enjoys international fame and is based in Los Angeles, her Midwest roots run strong. It's part of her appeal: her Minnesotan "dontchaknow" accent, even after twenty-five years in California; her humble ways, despite being the premiere chef and baker of Hollywood, catering award-show events and the Instagram-worthy birthday parties of movie stars' children.

But *can* she do it?

Probably not. She lives thousands of miles away and follows an impossible schedule, between cookbook events, TV show tapings, and running her own whole grain–based bakery in LA. I remember there was only one night we could book her for the museum exhibit, and we scheduled that a year in advance. How could she possibly come to St. John's Ferry, Wisconsin, in five days' time?

Impossible.

But shouldn't I at least try?

Katrine is right. It's a bit embarrassing to promise Art Cavanaugh and then not deliver. But guests would understand if we got someone even better. And Ruth Rivers is that someone. She blows Art Cavanaugh out of the water.

"What about Ruth Rivers?" I say into the silence.

Katrine's eyes bulge. "You know *Ruth Rivers*?"

"Kind of. I interviewed her for a museum exhibit and met her last month at the opening. She is so down-to-earth."

"I know. I love her. I follow her on social media," Katrine says with newfound energy. "Oh my god! Wait a minute! She's here."

The three of us look at her quizzically.

"What do you mean?" Brady asks.

"She's *here*." Katrine points to the floor. "In the Midwest." She grabs her phone and scurries to pull information up on the screen. "She just posted yesterday that she was taking a much-needed break back home. And there was a picture of some old flour mill in Minneapolis."

"The Mill City Museum," Brady blurts.

"Right, so she isn't far away," Katrine notes. "A couple hours' drive. She's on vacation, I think."

A chill runs down my spine. What are the odds that Ruth Rivers is only a two-hour drive away and on a break from her rigorous schedule just when we need her most? It's almost too good to be true. I try to keep my expectations in check. I still have to ask her, and she still has to say yes.

"Do you have her publicist's contact info?" Brady asks me.

"Better," I say. "I have her cell phone number. She called me when I interviewed her. I was never planning on using it again. But . . ."

The three of them stare at me, willing me to move.

"Well, what are you doing sitting here talking to us?" Alice asks.

In the hours after my phone call with Ruth Rivers, I move about in a sort of dreamlike daze. I can't believe I had the nerve to call *the* Ruth Rivers and ask her to attend the event at Alice's farm, in the tiny nobody's-ever-heard-of-it town of St. John's Ferry. And more so, I can't believe she said yes. Quickly, and without much begging on my part.

"Maggie, I'll be there," she said.

And while this was supposed to defuse our anxiety, instead it upped the ante and tripled the pressure. Now we aren't just putting on a dinner to save a farm. We're putting on a dinner worthy of Ruth Rivers, worthy of people's expectations of a Ruth Rivers event. My exhibit opening had been catered by a renowned chef in Chicago. I hadn't had to worry about the food at all that night.

This time, the food is everything.

On the other hand, Katrine's job, working with members of the village council on publicizing the event, couldn't be easier. All they have to do is inform the media of Ruth Rivers's appearance. Her name would do the rest.

And that's exactly what happens. Soon, the Chicago, Minneapolis, and Milwaukee news stations commit to covering our dinner. And in just a day, the remaining tickets sell out, with a waiting list of hundreds, prompting us to develop an online donation site.

This small-town event—to celebrate Midsommar, to highlight the hard work of local food artisans, to honor the dying breed of Midwestern farms, specifically Alice's farm—is now bigger than anyone could have imagined.

The news even travels to California, to my mother, who calls my cell the very next day.

"When were you going to tell me about this event you've been planning?" she asks.

"I already did," I say. We talked about it two weeks ago when I called to check in. But I remember hearing computer keys clicking in the background. She was only half listening while answering emails.

"No, you said you were putting on a *dinner*," she retorts. "I thought it was some Midwest-community-potluck-in-the-church-basement kind of thing. But this is a *major event*. I mean, Ruth Rivers! That's amazing!"

My mother obviously did not remember that Ruth Rivers was featured in my museum exhibit, or that she actually attended the opening.

"I heard your event is already sold out," she goes on. "Otherwise, I'd be there."

A twinge of guilt zaps my stomach. I hadn't considered asking my mother to attend. I didn't think she'd want to travel all the way to Wisconsin. I didn't think she'd enjoy it. To her, eating was just something you had to do each day. She didn't seem to derive much pleasure from food and, therefore, got no delight from looking at food, talking about food, or preparing it. I thought she'd be too busy. But people can surprise you.

"Oh, well, Mom, you're family," I quickly say. "If you want to come, I can still get you a ticket. No problem."

"Really? Oh, that's nice of you." A pause. "Though really, I shouldn't. My schedule is tight, and I have my summer school classes. It's such short notice. Had I known about it earlier."

You did know about it earlier. I bite my tongue.

"Anyway, congratulations. I'm so proud of you. Making the news!"

There is more I could tell her. I could explain how the past few weeks have felt more like a real summer than I've had in decades, the kind of summer I used to have when I was a kid. Summers of great physical and emotional and spiritual change, summers that marked the end of one school year and the beginning of the next. Transformational.

I could tell her that of all the jobs I've ever had, this one—simultaneously putting on this event and serving as Brady's camp sous-chef—has been my favorite, and I don't want it to end. The work is constant and encompassing and challenging, but I love it. Even after a long day, when I go to bed with a sore back and achy feet, I wake the next morning ready to tackle it all again. I have never felt this engaged with my work before.

I could tell her about Brady, that I am falling in love with him, and that it is the most exhilarating and scary feeling, all at once.

I could tell her that sometimes, a lot of the time lately, I fantasize about not going back to Chicago at all, about staying here, living this life every day.

But I don't tell her any of these things. They feel like secrets, meant only for someone who can understand them. And while my mother fed me, clothed me, and paid for my education, something always seemed to be missing from our conversations.

A bad connection, garbled with static.

28

By early evening, the night before the event, everything that can be done is done. I've triple-checked the timeline and checklists. With so many people involved, every task has been accounted for. So Friday evening is a time to unwind and have fun.

Brady and I head to the festival grounds in town. Katrine, Johanna, and Nora took Hannah earlier to enjoy face-painting, games, and carnival rides, and Alice is also there, selling her jam at the artisanal booths.

Brady and I hold hands as we walk through the gazebo park in the middle of town. A band plays folksy, polka-style music across the clearing—near large white tents, where festivalgoers lounge at long tables enjoying beer and wine, cheese, sausages, and pretzels; others mill about, chatting. There's an air of relaxation and joy to the whole scene.

I almost don't recognize Hannah when she flits over. She's transformed—thanks to the high school girls running the face-painting booth—into a sequined butterfly, her hair adorned by a crown of yellow and white flowers, matching ribbons cascading down her back.

Brady and I naturally drop hands when we see her. It still feels too soon.

"Mom, can we have a sleepover tonight?" Hannah asks, before I can even comment on her festive new look. "In the attic?"

Nora, Johanna, and Katrine stand beside her, their eyes wide with anticipation.

I consider tomorrow's timeline, which requires a bright-eyed and bushy-tailed start. "Do you think you'll get a good night's sleep up there?"

"To be honest, I don't think we'll sleep well anywhere," Nora explains.

"We're too excited about tomorrow," Johanna adds.

"It was a long week," Katrine says. "We want to go back to the house and order pizza and just kind of, what do you call it? Veg?"

"We need to decompress," Hannah adds as if on cue.

I try not to smirk at my almost six-year-old daughter using the word *decompress*. She pronounces every syllable, as if she memorized the word for a school play.

I consider the benefit of having Hannah upstairs with the girls tonight. It will give me time and space to gear myself up for tomorrow. We were planning to sleep in the same room tonight; my room is already cleaned—new sheets on the bed—in preparation for Ruth Rivers's arrival tomorrow afternoon. But to be honest, I might sleep better without Hannah in the room.

"Did you check with Alice?" I ask.

"She said it's fine, but we had to ask you," Katrine replies.

"Sounds like fun," I say.

The girls share smiles. "Come on, ladies," Katrine commands, leading her crew back to the parking lot.

"Bye, Mom," Hannah says, throwing her arms around me and hugging me harder than expected.

"Have the best time, honey," I say in a half whisper, then let her go, watching the ribbons fly behind her as she catches up to the others.

"What kind of pizza do you want?" I hear Katrine ask as they walk away.

I hear Hannah answer "Pepperoni" with true conviction.

"She's having the best night of her life," I say to Brady.

"And what about you?" he asks.

I smile. "The night's not over yet."

That evening, after soaking in the festival and talking until our throats hurt, we decide to go to bed early. Alice has already called it a night, and Hannah and the Scandinavian Trio are tucked in the attic with enough cookies and popcorn to last until morning. Brady and I walk upstairs holding hands, and again pause outside his bedroom. He kisses me as we lean against the door frame, pressing me with his body.

He pauses to look at me, then lets his knuckles graze my cheek.

"Have I told you how amazing you are?" he asks, his face mere inches from mine.

"No, tell me."

"You really knocked this out of the park. This whole event."

"Well, don't speak too soon. It hasn't happened yet."

"But it will, and it's all because of you."

I shake my head. "Me? More like *we*. All of us. I haven't done this alone."

"But you're the heart. You know that, right?"

"I am?"

He nods. "It's you at the center of this. The energy. You're what keeps all of this moving. We each do our part, but you hold the vision, the dream."

I run my fingers along his beard, just as he grazed my cheek. I get lost in his brown eyes. I feel a double-edged pit in my stomach, a simultaneous ache for him and a fear of needing him too much.

Brady presses his nose to mine, our lips an inch apart. So close, I can taste his breath.

"I'm falling in love with you, Maggie," he says. "No. Let me correct that. I love you."

His words surprise, exhilarate, and frighten me, all at once. I want to get fully swept up in this moment. The words *I love you too* rest on the tip of my tongue. And yet, I stop right at the edge of that cliff. It's like a threshold I want desperately to cross, but hesitate, afraid of free-falling.

Instead, I hold his gaze.

We should go to bed, I think. *Get a good night's sleep. We should focus on tomorrow.*

But instead, I take his hand and lead him into his bedroom.

My eyes pop open, and while my mind seems sharp and alert, for a moment, I question where I am. And then it comes back to me. Brady's room.

I feel the warmth of his body beside me, the heaviness of his arm over me. I forgot how good it feels to wake up in a man's arms, and I lie there enjoying the weight of him. I can see from the nightstand clock that it's 3:15 a.m., too early to get up for the day. And yet, it feels like my brain has already gotten its morning dose of caffeine.

I've overlooked a detail. About today, about the dinner. That must be it, I think, because there's my nagging intuition—how you feel if you forget to blow out a candle or close a garage door—and I rack my brain. What have I ignored? We've painstakingly planned, organized, and prepped for this event. We've run through it all—Brady, me, the whole event team—over and over again.

And then it hits me, the reason I woke so abruptly.

I've been so busy working remotely, planning the dinner, playing sous-chef to Brady, and watching over Hannah, that I avoided an inevitable truth. After today, after the dinner, I'm supposed to go back home to Eastridge.

Back to my old life. Leave St. John's Ferry. Leave Alice.

Leave Brady.

This season will soon be over. So while today is a glorious day, it's also bittersweet. When the camp and the dinner end, this new lifestyle ceases too. Like Cinderella's coach, I turn back into a pumpkin.

I can't fall asleep again, so I stealthily lift Brady's arm to slip out of bed. I pad my way to the kitchen to make a cup of Alice's chamomile tea.

I'm going to miss this kitchen.

I think back to all I've enjoyed in this space—making the rhubarb scones, meeting Brady for the first time, sitting at the kitchen table having heart-to-hearts with Alice. Fika with the Trio, preparing Brady's birthday dinner, making breakfast sandwiches for his students. It seems like a lifetime of memories crammed into the span of a month.

Suddenly, I'm overcome with doubt. What if we don't make enough money to keep the farm? What if Alice loses this legacy?

This farmhouse, this kitchen, has been a haven for so many—for Rose and her family, for the boarders of the Women's Land Army, for Alice, for me and Hannah, Brady and the Trio. It's been a source of strength, a foundation.

In planning this event, we included gourmet, locally sourced, and Scandinavian food, as well as early summer bounty. But we have nothing on the menu to honor Rose, her legacy, the role she played during a very difficult time for our country. While men were fighting overseas, the women were here giving their best, pushing themselves physically and mentally to help win the war.

I think back to the recipes from the attic, the dishes that aimed to satiate Americans despite hardship and rations. Unfortunately, I've only sorted through half the box. Once I found the ledger, and started the application for the National Register, I neglected sorting them, organizing them into a book for Alice. I vow to go back into that box, once the dinner is over, and finish the job before I leave. For now, I decide to pull one recipe out and replicate it for the farm-to-table event. Coincidentally, it's one that Rose adjusted to serve a crowd, once upon a time.

If we want this event to be a success, and if we want to honor the past, truly respect American farms and farmhouses, I can't think of a better dessert:

Lucy's Victory Cake.

29

August 1945

On the evening of August 14, most of the girls crouched in the berry fields at Jensen's farm next door. Conditions had been so favorable, there were simply too many raspberries to pick. It was an all-hands-on-deck kind of day, where everyone pitched in to get the work done before the sun went down. These were autumn raspberries—a bit smaller but less susceptible to insects—and the first harvest was abundant. Even though so many of the WLA farmerettes had put in a full day at their respective posts, they lent a hand. It was hard to resist the delicious, delicate raspberries. They'd turned a vibrant magenta overnight.

Meanwhile, Rose and Lucy worked hard in the farmhouse kitchen preparing a late supper for the girls to enjoy upon their return. The August heat had squelched everyone's appetites and cold dishes seemed the only cure. Rose stood at the kitchen counter slicing cucumbers for a creamy side salad—she would mix the cukes with onions, dill, and sour cream—and Lucy perched beside her on a chair, placing each slice into a colander to be topped with salt and drained. The radio played lightly in the background, but Rose and Lucy sang their own tune. The song Esther taught Rose, and Rose taught Lucy.

"Been around the world, a time or two," Rose sang to Lucy. "But I'm just . . ."

Lucy's eyes lit up in preparation for her part. "Happy here you," she sang, her voice high and sweet, toddler honey.

The line was "happier here with you," but Rose preferred Lucy's version.

It was moments like these—when the two of them worked side by side at the counter or in the garden or at the kitchen table or on the front porch—when Rose felt most alive. True to her name, Lucy's presence illuminated everything. When she was with Lucy, Rose saw everything in Technicolor and heard everything at a clearer frequency. Lilacs smelled sweeter and blankets felt softer. This was the gift of youth—the ability to note and appreciate the simple details—and this was the blessing of having Lucy in Rose's life.

Rose was so caught up in the moment, she jolted when the background music on the radio suddenly stopped and blunt, urgent voices echoed from the radio.

"We interrupt this broadcast . . ." was followed by Harry Truman's voice and the words *surrender of Japan*.

"It's over," Rose cried, wiping her hands on her apron and turning to Lucy. "The war is over!"

"War over!" Lucy repeated.

Rose grabbed her white kitchen towel and handed Lucy a silver metal pot and wooden spoon. "Bang on this like a drum," she instructed, tapping the pot. Then the two went hand in hand to the farmhouse porch. Lucy banged the drum as only an eighteen-month-old could, while Rose waved her white kitchen towel back and forth, up and down, in the pattern of an infinity symbol.

"The war is over," they sang, over and over again, until their voices felt hoarse. "Peace, peace! The war is over!"

Soon, the girls ran from Jensen's field. Despite the labor—their achy muscles and sore feet—they were renewed by this news, running fast, smiles stretched to their limits.

Rose lifted Lucy to her hip, but still Lucy banged her drum, and Rose waved the flag in one hand above her head.

"Japan surrendered," Rose screamed as soon as the girls were close enough. "It's over. It's finally over."

Peggy reached for Lucy and took her from Rose's hip, swinging her in circles on the farmhouse porch. The girls untied their handkerchiefs from their necks and waved them in the air. Some girls linked arms and swung each other around, square-dance style. They hugged and screamed and wept and cheered. Rose's cheeks began to ache from all the smiling.

As a farm truck and several automobiles drove by, honking horns like alarms, it seemed only fitting that they go to town. Without changing their dusty, sweat-stained clothes or freshening up, without eating, they piled into the back of the farm truck, and drove to where they knew the others would gather. The townspeople and the farm folk—everyone within a ten-mile radius—had flocked to Main Street, and Rose marveled at the sight.

Confetti and streamers floated through the air. American flags hung high and flapped in the wind. Music blared from radios, cheers erupted. Lovers kissed. People danced in the street. Restaurants started handing out free food. Rose wondered what the rest of the world, the rest of the country, was doing at this moment. If such a big celebration occurred here, in small-town Wisconsin, what was happening elsewhere?

What were they doing in, say, New York? Times Square?

It was euphoric, this new sense of peace and freedom and relief. The pain and suffering of the last four years were over. Our soldiers would come home soon.

Maybe, just maybe, Hank would come home.

But the end of the war brought the end of other things, Rose realized. The girls would go. The men would eventually return and take back the farm work, the dairy work, the fields. The WLA would disband. Rose tried not to think about this fact, the underbelly of the joyous news.

It dawned on Rose—as she watched ecstasy spread through downtown St. John's Ferry—that the cold, simple supper she planned for tonight would go uneaten, as food and drink and good cheer seemed to flow out into the street from local establishments and from the kitchens of nearby homes.

They returned to the farmhouse late, and Rose thought about the following day. The president had declared today and tomorrow holidays. While the animals still needed to be fed—even on holidays—the farm work would be minimal and the celebratory mood would certainly continue. The girls and her neighbors had danced and sang and socialized in the streets downtown, but Rose still felt the need to put together a meal, to signify this historic day with a worthy feast. Rations were still in place—those wouldn't be lifted quite yet—but she knew she had an abundance of eggs. And she had sausage. While large cuts of meat, like steaks and roasts, were rationed, the more processed meats were not. They had raspberries, of course, freshly picked. And her summer Victory Garden had produced a large yield; she had vegetables to pick tomorrow, and she and Lucy had canned others earlier in the summer. She knew the girls would sleep longer, having been up so late celebrating. As she sat at her kitchen table, she quickly developed a menu for what she was calling "Victory Brunch." It would be a mid-morning feast. She would invite her neighbors and local farmers and farm workers. But that meant at least twenty-five to thirty people, maybe more. Could she fit that many people in the house? Not at the same table. She would need to host the brunch somewhere else.

The barn, she thought.

She envisioned it now. Long tables and tablecloths. Fresh flowers. Platters of colorful food. Laughter. Community. Cake.

Yes, every celebration deserves a cake.

She knew her recipe for Victory Cake by heart. But she would need to make three cakes to feed this size group. So she took out a piece of paper, and began jotting the recipe down again, tripling it this time, counting up the ingredients and the number of eggs Lucy would need to help her gather in the morning.

Lucy's Victory Cake, she wrote at the top of the page.

It was a Victory indeed.

30

The morning of the dinner is full of sunshine and blue skies. My fears of inclement weather dissipate, and I start to believe everything will work out as planned.

Maybe even better than planned.

Brady and I start prepping in the commercial kitchen. I tell him about my idea of adding Lucy's Victory Cake to the dessert table—an homage to my great-great-grandmother and the history of the farmhouse. He loves the idea of highlighting a recipe from the farmhouse's past. Plus, the ingredients are so simple, no last-minute trips to the store required.

There's a knock at the door and Brady's hands are full. I answer, thinking it's one of the girls with an armful of supplies.

I'm surprised to see a man I don't know. He's quite tall and slender, and his long, silver hair is pulled back in a low ponytail. His eyes are soft, contrasting with stark black-rimmed glasses.

He stares at me a beat before saying anything.

"Is this the site of the Midsommar dinner?" he finally asks.

"Yes."

I watch his shoulders relax. "Good. Because I just unloaded fifty chairs and five tables without checking if this was the right place."

I laugh. His delivery is deadpan, but sweet. I step outside, shutting the door behind me, so as not to bother Brady. "Are you from the rental company?" I ask.

He shakes his head. "I'm a guest at the hotel in town."

"The Ferry Inn?"

He nods.

I cock my head in confusion. "And you delivered the tables and chairs?"

He smiles. "I volunteered. Sam, the owner, was supposed to bring them. But he twisted his ankle loading them onto the truck, so I offered to help."

Poor Sam. "That was nice of you."

He places a hand to his heart. "My pleasure. I'm in town for the event. Sounds like it's going to be quite the party."

"Thank you. It's been a lot of hard work, but hopefully, it will all pay off." I look into his eyes. They're a beautiful, brilliant blue. "I'm Maggie," I say, holding out my hand.

He meets my handshake but almost seems stunned, as if he's forgotten his own name. "Christian," he finally says.

I detect an accent but am unsure of its origin. "You said you're here for the event?" I ask. "Did you travel far?"

"A few hours," he says. "Minneapolis."

"That's great. We were hoping to pull people from all over the Midwest. I guess I should be thanking our publicity team for a job well done."

"You really should. I wasn't planning to attend. But when I saw the newspaper article, I felt compelled to come. Drawn to it, actually."

"Really? What was so compelling? Let me guess, was it Ruth Rivers?"

He smiles. "I think it was more than her. This whole event. Everything about it." He shrugs, as if to say the feeling was too complex for words. "Spoke to me."

I feel a warmth radiate from my chest to my cheeks. "Oh, I love that. Thank you."

He nods, as if to say *you're welcome*, then looks around. "Is there anything else I can do?" he asks. "To assist?"

My mind reels with tasks. "Well, most of the work is food prep, cooking and baking. I don't know how comfortable you are working with food. But yes, we can put you to work," I say. "First, let me introduce you to my partner in crime."

I open the door to the kitchen, and he follows me inside.

"Hey, Brady, we have an extra volunteer this morning," I call. "This is Christian. He's—"

"Knudsen," Brady says, cutting me off. His eyes are open and bright. "Oh my god, I can't believe this. You're Christian Knudsen!"

The man looks at me sheepishly, his cover blown.

"Maggie, this is the owner of *The Cookie Tin* in Minneapolis." He enunciates every syllable to illustrate the magnitude of this man's presence. "It's the most revered Scandinavian bakery in the country."

I watch Christian bow his head in humility.

"I'm sorry, I had no idea," I say, cringing at my words: *I don't know how comfortable you are working with food.*

"Please, Maggie," he says. "Do not be sorry. I'm not a celebrity."

Brady laughs. "Don't listen to him. This guy is a *god*. I feel like I'm dreaming," he jests. "Sir, what brings us the pleasure of your company today?"

"The farm-to-table dinner," he says.

"He felt compelled to come," I try to explain. "Drawn to it for some reason."

Christian and I make eye contact. He gives me a small nod, as if to say I got it right.

Brady crosses his arms and smiles. "Now I'm sure this is a dream."

"I want to help," Christian says, seemingly embarrassed by the sudden attention. "Please. Put me to work."

Brady gives an affirmative nod. "Yes, sir." His eyes dart around the kitchen. "Well, if Christian Knudsen is here, I'm not going to have you pickle vegetables. We're making a boatload of cookies and cakes today, a number of them Scandinavian in origin. I'd be honored if you helped with those."

"Of course," Christian says.

I watch the tall, lean man walk to the other side of the room and grab an apron from the hooks. He's so unassuming, so down-to-earth as he ties the apron strings and smooths out the front. A man of great skill and even greater modesty.

There is something serendipitous about his unexpected arrival. It's a sign, I think. We are on a path budding with potential.

Everything is going to be more than okay.

The news of Christian Knudsen's appearance travels quickly, and the Scandinavian Trio buzz around the barn like honeybees.

"I guess I'm the only one who doesn't know who he is," I say once I realize they revere him as much as Brady does.

"Well, he was born and raised in Denmark," Katrine says.

"Sweden," Johanna corrects.

"Yes, fine, technically *southern* Sweden," Katrine admits. "But basically, right across the water from Copenhagen, so we like to claim him as our own. He's well known back home and here in the States. But he's not TV-cooking-show famous."

"He's kind of private and mysterious," Johanna adds.

"Confident but not arrogant," Nora chimes in.

"And unbelievably talented," Katrine notes. "Maggie, this is really good for publicity. With Ruth Rivers here, the event was already going to be widely covered by the media. And if Christian Knudsen is also in our pictures, this could really blow up on social media."

"Which means more donations to save Alice's farmhouse," I say. I can't help but smile. You can plan for the best, and sometimes, things turn out even better.

I leave the girls, Brady, and Christian to work and go back to the farmhouse to check on Hannah and Alice. As I head that way, I spot Ruth Rivers driving up in a beige four-door sedan. It's a new car, shiny and recently buffed, but an average, middle-class automobile. She may be food royalty, but she certainly doesn't wear a crown. I rush to greet her.

"Ruth!" I call out.

"Hello," she says, then immediately hugs me. Her embrace is heartfelt; she even pats the space between my shoulder blades, the way a grandmother hugs. She reminds me a little of Alice.

"How was the drive?" I ask.

"Contemplative," she says.

"Well, I am just so grateful you're here. It seems like a dream."

She smiles; the wrinkles at the corners of her eyes reflect years of laughter. "And I am so grateful to stay in this beautiful, historic farmhouse for the night. I saw the turret. It's a Queen Anne, isn't it?"

I nod. "Like I told you on the phone, it's been in my family a long time, and we're trying to keep it that way."

Ruth takes my hands and squeezes them. "And that's why I'm here. When you said it used to be a boardinghouse for the Women's Land Army, I knew I had to come. There is nothing more important to me than preserving history."

"And food?" I say.

"Oh, yes, and food."

We share a laugh, then she seems to study me. "You look different," she says.

"I do?" I glance down at myself. "How so?"

She squints. "Lighter. Brighter. Did you do something different with your hair?"

I nervously run my fingers through it. "No, in fact, I need a haircut and some color, but I've been so busy, I haven't made time."

"You've been here awhile?" she asks.

"About four weeks."

"That explains it."

"It does?"

"Nothing like spending time in the countryside to clear your mind and open your heart."

I relish this conversation with Ruth. While I could be starstruck, chitchatting with *the* Ruth Rivers, it feels more like my conversations with Alice. Easy. Familiar.

We head inside and I show her the downstairs—dining room, parlor, kitchen. We find Alice and Hannah hard at work at the kitchen table. They're in charge of the centerpieces—colorful but simple bouquets of local wildflowers in Mason jars with raffia bows.

"Wow, these are beautiful," I say, after making introductions.

"Only thirty more to go," Hannah announces, her eyes set in concentration as she plucks the lower leaves from a daisy. I love watching my daughter's face when she's deep in concentration. She crinkles her nose a bit, and her lips curl.

"Looks like the table decorations are very much under control," Ruth says. "How about dinner preparations?"

"So far, so good," I say. "And we've had some unexpected good fortune. A famous baker showed up out of the blue this morning with some chairs from the Ferry Inn. He's over in the kitchen baking goodies for tonight. I'd never heard of him, but everyone else here is starstruck."

Alice looks up curiously from her flower work. "Really? Who is it?"

"Christian Knudsen?"

Ruth's mouth visibly gapes. "He's here?"

"You know him?"

She shakes her head. "We're acquaintances. I've met him at events over the years. He's a bit reserved. Mysterious."

"Isn't he? I got that same idea when I met him."

"Well, now I'm intrigued," Alice chimes in. "I haven't heard of him either."

"I'm not surprised," Ruth explains. "I've gathered he doesn't like attention, the media. I don't either. But he's been able to stay out of it better than me. I feel obligated to participate in all that—mostly for my fans, my publicists are pretty persistent too—but he doesn't seem to have that same hang-up. With Christian, it's about the food. Plain and simple. No fanfare. He could really be in the spotlight. His lack of fame—for instance, you not having heard of him—is his doing. If he'd let the foodie world control his popularity, he'd be one step down from James Beard."

We leave Hannah and Alice to finish up the vases and head upstairs, where I show Ruth her room. "There's fresh linens," I say. "And a basket of snacks and water next to your bed here and some toiletries in the bathroom. Some books and magazines. A candle."

"This is simply darling, Maggie," she says, gesturing to the bedside table, where I also placed a vase of fresh flowers, similar to the bouquets Alice and Hannah are making. "I feel like I'm in a fine B & B."

I smile. "So about tonight," I start, "I'll run through a quick outline with you now, and then give you some time to settle in, have some tea, relax."

"Sounds perfect."

I detail the night's events, culminating with the bonfire.

"A bonfire? How lovely," she says.

"It's tradition. The major festivals in Scandinavia all have them. They believed the fire warded off evil spirits. But it's really all about celebrating life and love."

"Life and love." Ruth seems to ponder this. "Two of my favorite things."

I want to pry—to ask her if she's dating, has someone special in her life—but it doesn't feel like the right moment.

"Me too," I say instead.

When I return, the commercial kitchen is in a state of organized chaos, like any back-of-the-house before a major event. Lots of moving parts, a sense of urgency, a rhythmic hum, pivoting action. All hands on deck.

I'm surprised to see Christian making what look to be raspberry caves. It's a simple thumbprint, jam-filled cookie—a popular Swedish treat—and so it somehow feels like watching Julia Child make a box of mac and cheese. Brady should have assigned him something more complicated. But when I look at Christian's face—the concentrated joy evident in his relaxed smile and soft, focused eyes—I realize I may be the only one who thinks his talents are being underutilized.

Christian looks up and meets my eye, then waves me over.

Grabbing an apron on my way, I meet him at the bench.

"Would you like to help me with the hallongrottor?" he asks.

"Hallongrottor," I repeat. "Raspberry caves. Absolutely. Looks like you already made the dough. Did you use the industrial mixer?" I ask, pointing to the other side of the kitchen.

He raises his hands. "These are the only mixers I need."

"Really? You mixed the dough by hand? Doesn't that melt the butter too much? From the heat of your hands?"

"That's exactly why I use my hands." He raises a finger into the air. "We don't want cold butter like we might for pie dough or biscuits or scones. We want room temperature, even warm, spreadable butter. We want this dough soft and pliable. We want to be able to shape it, and we don't want it to crack."

And this is why we have Christian Knudsen making the raspberry caves.

"That's amazing," I say. "A small detail that makes a huge difference. We're lucky to have you."

He shrugs, unable to fully receive the compliment. "I'm not any smarter or more skilled than other bakers. I just have a lot of experience. And most importantly, I've learned from that experience."

I nod. "What can I do?"

"We're going to scoop and roll the cookies into balls, then put them into these muffin tins."

I see the muffin tins, each lined with adorable paper cupcake liners boasting a raspberry design. "Do the muffin tins keep them from spreading too much?"

"That's right. They keep their shape when baking."

"So we'll roll them all out and then go back and place the indentation?"

He shakes his head. "Normally, that would be the most efficient way. Keep doing the same action instead of switching between actions. But in this case, it's really important that we make the thumbprint immediately. Otherwise, the dough will dry and the cookies could crack."

"That makes sense. So roll, then imprint?"

"Exactly. I'll roll, and you make the indentation with your thumb."

"Should I use a tool instead?" I ask, considering how the cookies will look on the display table. "So they look uniform?"

"To be honest, I find uniform a bit boring. I like the oblong shape of the thumb. These are thumbprint cookies, after all."

I find his relaxed approach refreshing. "You're the boss," I say.

We work side by side in rhythm. It's easy but meditative. We must look so productive, Katrine comes by with her phone and snaps a few action shots.

"For social media," she explains. "To hype the event."

I notice Katrine seems to pause and stare at her phone screen.

"Did they come out alright?" I ask. "Are my eyes closed?"

She looks up at the two of us and smiles. "Nope. They're perfect," she says, before moving on to the next station.

After a few minutes, Christian and I resume chatting as we work. He asks me about why I came to St. John's Ferry, how I came to put on this fundraising event. He even asks about Brady.

"He seems very fond of you," Christian says.

I smile, but act surprised. "Why do you say that?"

"He's looked over this way a number of times since you walked into the kitchen," he notes. "I doubt he's looking at me."

I laugh. "He could be. He thinks the world of your work."

Christian shakes his head. "No, no. I can tell. It's you he's watching. He really cares for you. You've grown close recently?"

Close. Yes, we are close. I think back to last night. How natural it felt being in his arms. I always imagined the first night with a man after Sean would feel off, like the first time using your arm after getting a cast removed. I thought it would be clumsy, clunky. But it felt normal, as if I'd been resting my head on his shoulder my whole life.

"I really like him," I say, surprised to be telling this man I just met about my feelings for Brady.

"Good. Life's too short to spend time with someone you don't like."

Alice and Hannah peek their heads in to check on preparations. Hannah rushes to me, throwing her arms around my waist. Alice follows behind.

"She said she missed you," Alice explains.

Moments like this remind me that every time Hannah fights for her autonomy, there is an opposite reaction, a reattachment. She often wants to venture out on her own, but always comes back to ground herself again. It's the push and pull of the parent-child relationship that I assume will continue through her high school years, and maybe even college. We haven't spent much time together the last few days because of the dinner. After all this is over, we need to reconnect. We should do something special.

"Who is this young lady?" Christian asks.

"This is my daughter, Hannah," I say.

Hannah still has her arms around me but looks over at him. He crouches down to her level—he's easily six four, so not an easy feat.

"Hello, Hannah. I'm Christian."

"Are you a chef?" she asks, as ignorant of his fame as I had been.

"I'd like to think so. But, to be honest, more of a baker."

Hannah spots the cookies we've begun making. "What are those?"

"Raspberry caves," he tells her. "Would you like to help?"

She releases her grip from my waist. "Yes, please."

"Good. You see those little holes we're putting in the center of the cookies? Those are the caves. They'll be filled with the most delicious raspberry jam—jam your Aunt Alice made. You can help make those holes with your thumb."

I watch Hannah lift her thumb.

But her thumb is too small, I think. Her imprint won't match the others in size or depth or shape. And these aren't just cookies for a family holiday. These are for display purposes too. They have to taste good, but they also have to look good.

Before I can say anything, Christian puts his thumb next to hers. "Your thumb is smaller than mine," he notes. "So you'll need to use your thumb twice."

"Twice?" she asks quizzically.

He takes her hand and shows her the movement. "Yes, this way." He pushes her thumb into the cookie. "And then this way," he adds, turning her finger forty-five degrees in the other direction before pressing it into the dough.

Hannah pulls her thumb back and smiles. "It's a heart!" she says.

"And think how pretty that will be when filled with raspberry jam," he says.

"A *red* heart!" she exclaims.

"That's right. These will be the extra-special cookies on the table. Not everyone will get one. They will be rare. In fact, only the people who notice the heart will take one. And that's why you're here. To make the special cookies for people who need a little love in their lives."

She smiles. "Okay, but first I have to wash my hands," she announces before running to the sink, with Alice in tow.

"You've trained her well," he says to me.

"Thank you," I say. "For including her. It's hard to have important work to do and also be flexible with kids."

"Parenthood is hard," he says.

"Do you have children?" I ask.

He pauses. "Yes," he says hesitantly.

"I'm sorry. I didn't mean to pry."

He shakes his head. "Please don't apologize."

We work silently for a beat.

"I wasn't a good father to her," he finally says. "But I'm trying to be now."

I think back to what Brady said to me, when I told him Alice and I hadn't been in touch until recently.

"Well, now is all that matters," I say.

31

Later, when Hannah and I walk back to the farmhouse to finally get ready for the night—freshen up and change our clothes—I hear Alice talking to someone in the parlor, a woman.

I freeze and listen more closely to the timbre of their voices.

It can't be.

"Grandma," Hannah exclaims after we round the corner, running to my mother's side. They haven't seen each other since the holidays, and I feel a twinge of guilt at Hannah's emphatic response.

"Surprise," Alice blurts, making eye contact to gauge my response.

I narrow my eyes, wondering how this all came about. "Surprise is right," I say, reaching for my mother once Hannah lets go.

"You're so thin," my mother notes as she embraces me.

I don't respond. I've actually gained weight but have never felt healthier.

"What are you doing here?" I ask instead.

"The dinner."

I turn to Alice. "And you knew?"

"She's the one who called and convinced me to fly out," my mother explains.

Alice lays a hand on my arm. "I'm just so proud of you, Maggie. You've worked so hard. And I really thought your mother should be here to see you shine."

I would have expected a touch of anger or resentment to bubble up at my mother's sudden appearance, but it doesn't. She has somehow lost her power. Or maybe I'm the one who's changed? Maybe it's like Ruth said: Nothing like spending time in the countryside to clear your mind and open your heart.

"I was very happy when Alice called." My mother pauses. "Because I owed her a long overdue apology. I shouldn't have kept you two apart all these years."

I check in with Alice, and she nods, indicating her forgiveness. It's water under the bridge. I'm not sure I could absolve my mother so easily. I still have much to learn from Alice's grace.

"Grandma, want to stay in my room?" Hannah chimes in.

I look for my mother's luggage. "Yes, Mom, are you staying here?"

She shakes her head. "Alice offered. But it sounded like you had a very full house—with the culinary students and Ruth Rivers staying here as well—so I booked something in town. You know I'm a very light sleeper. But thank you for asking, Hannah. I'll tuck you in before bed. How about that?"

Hannah smiles.

This news lightens something in my chest. I think I can handle her unannounced visit, but having my mother here overnight feels like too much amid everything else I have going on. Baby steps.

"I'm really happy you're here, Mom," I say.

And I realize that I do actually mean it.

The evening begins with a cocktail.

I pause for a moment on the farmhouse porch to watch the spectacle unfold. Attendees stop first at the outdoor bar, where a few of Brady's students serve our signature drink: Nordic June, a blend of aquavit, citrus-herb syrup, cucumber juice, lime, and local honey on ice with a sprig of rosemary. It's herbal, thanks to the aquavit—a

Scandinavian liquor that evokes dill, fennel, and caraway—but it's also mellow and a little sweet from the cucumber and honey. Served in an old-fashioned glass, on loan from a downtown bar, it's a stunner of a drink. I see several guests photograph the cocktail in just the right light to post on social media.

This is happening.

The appetizer course—served off silver platters handled by more of Brady's students—includes three open-faced mini sandwiches, some topped with the freshest locally made goat cheese and pepper jelly, others with smoked salmon and cucumber, and others with ham and Jarlsberg. I'm offered one as I pass by, and the spicy-sweet jam, combined with the smooth, tangy cheese, is heaven in my mouth. I scan the sea of people—in flowered sundresses, wide-brimmed straw hats, suit jackets paired with jeans, sandals—and let out a sigh. People mingle and chat, simultaneously indulging their senses. The feeling is light and playful, but also elegant. Everyone seems to be having a really great time, and dinner is still to come.

I find Brady near the oversize grill, where we'll cook the salmon. He spots me and flashes me his biggest smile.

"Well, good evening, gorgeous." He reaches around my waist and looks like he wants to kiss me. Because of Hannah, we've been careful not to openly display affection. But this time, I fall into his embrace and kiss a spot on his neck, just under his ear.

"Where's Hannah?" he asks, surprised by the kiss, eyes darting around the crowd.

"She's still at the house, visiting with my mother," I say. "But they'll be over soon."

"Your *mother*?"

I fill him in on her surprise visit, including the conversation I overheard an hour ago, which is why I've let my guard down.

To my surprise, Hannah asked my mother to style her hair. They sat on her bed, where my mom wove her curly brown hair into a French braid, like she once did for me.

I didn't mean to eavesdrop, but I was walking right by the room. The door was ajar.

"Tell me what you've been up to this summer," I heard my mother ask.

Hannah mentioned reading and fishing in the pond, catching fireflies and camping, baking and whittling. The Scandinavian Trio. "And Brady taught me how to tie my shoes," she added.

"Who's *Brady?*" my mother inquired.

"He's Mommy's best friend."

I smiled at her answer. I couldn't see my mother's face but could imagine raised eyebrows.

"Best friend?" my mother repeated.

Hannah giggled. "They're in love."

"Really? Why do you say that?"

More giggles. "Because they smile at each other funny."

My relationship with Brady—which I'd struggled over how to broach with Hannah these past weeks—was obviously a nonissue to my daughter. She already knew.

"Well, she was right," Brady says now, flashing me a grin. "We do smile at each other funny."

I take him in. His broad shoulders look strong enough to bear the weight of anything. I think back to last night, how safe and secure I felt lying in his arms. And I remember what he said just before that, and what I didn't say.

I reach for his face now and cradle his beard in my hands.

"For the record," I say. "I love you too."

I expect to feel vulnerable, to crumble inside, because the last man I said that to was Sean. But I don't. Instead, a peace washes over me.

Brady's smile says it all.

"Now, that's enough of that." I quickly let go of his face. "We have a dinner to put on."

The next thirty minutes pass quickly. It's filled with glass clinking and small bites, quick hellos and elbow squeezes. Katrine rings a bell to signify the beginning of the dinner, and people find their seats at the long, beautifully set tables inside the barn—white tablecloths and linens, local wildflowers, white lights strewn through the rafters. Relish trays dot the tablescape—each filled with pickled herring, cottage cheese, cheddar cheese spread, crackers, rye breads, pickles, and olives. It's both elegant and rustic, an homage to Wisconsin supper clubs. At one end, closest to the kitchen, I sit with Brady, Alice, Lenny, Hannah, Ruth Rivers, and the other members of the committee. My mother sits with us too, fawning over Brady. With his culinary students and local restaurant servers hard at work plating and serving, we receive the gift of simply enjoying the meal.

"Where's Christian?" I ask, realizing he isn't seated by us, as I had requested.

"In the kitchen," Brady answers. "He said he'd rather oversee things there."

"So that's why you're so relaxed."

"I do believe in my students," Brady says. "But yeah, having Christian Knudsen in the kitchen tonight totally helps."

Once everyone is seated, the mayor of St. John's Ferry, Bob Nielsen, stands and gives a formal welcome on behalf of the committee, then hands the mic over to Pamela McFarland, Midsommar Festival Committee president, who gives a few words of gratitude. Then it's our turn. Brady and I offer an overview of the menu thus far—the cocktail, the hors d'oeuvres—and where the items were sourced, from O'Brien's Dairy to Bluff Orchards and beyond.

Brady goes on to describe the upcoming courses: The salad made with local spring greens, strawberries, goat cheese, and roasted and dehydrated beets, followed by milk-soaked fried chicken, biscuits with lavender honey, and braised ruby-red Swiss chard, followed by honey mustard–glazed grilled salmon, nutty wild rice, and grilled asparagus. And for dessert, overflowing platters of every sweet treat imaginable—from brownies to raspberry caves, from slices of almond kringle to mini strawberry-rhubarb pies, not to mention Lucy's Victory Cake.

And of course, after-dinner coffee and spirits.

I see everyone's eyes grow wide with anticipation. And then, the moment we've all been waiting for arrives. Brady hands the mic over to Ruth Rivers. She stands at the foot of the table, wearing a breezy lavender linen sundress, herbal cocktail in hand, and looks out at all of us. She is so poised; there is so much thought behind her soft hazel eyes.

"My grandparents owned a farm much like Rosehill, about an hour outside Minneapolis," she says, making eye contact with a few members of the audience. "And good thing. Because it was the constant of my childhood. Life changed; my father lost his job, my parents moved, I switched schools, friends came and went, but the farm remained the same. Like time, their farm seemed as if it had always been and would always be. Of course, I didn't realize this then. It's with the gift of hindsight that I understand the role the farm played in my life. It was the floor beneath my feet whenever the rug was pulled out from under me.

"We live in an ever-changing world. And we've come far. Medical advancements. Technology. Bigger and better. And that's inevitable. But in the midst of all of that change, we need something to hold on to, something to ground us. To call us home. For me, beyond my grandparents' farm, that's always been food. It's how I count my days. After decades working in this industry, I can tell you it's not an industry without change, without struggle. Sometimes, it's downright challenging. But I believe it will always endure. Because food is both a basic need and a luxury. It fills our stomachs but also feeds our souls.

"Yes, tonight is about Rosehill. It's about saving one of America's farms, a slice of history. It's also about food. I don't know about you, but I can't wait to enjoy that delectable menu just described to us. But as I stand here tonight, I see in all of your faces what tonight is really about."

She pauses, and I feel everyone hanging on her words.

"Hope," she finally says. "We promise to be *formidable* in the face of challenge and change. Tonight is about having the courage to think better times are ahead. It's about doing something to assure that outcome. And every single one of you has helped make that happen. In coming here tonight, you've chosen to contribute to your community, to maintain history, to make connections with others, and yes, to eat some absolutely amazing food. So let's pat ourselves on the back for a job well done and feast!"

The applause is cacophonous in the high-roofed barn and doesn't die down quickly. Finally, as the salads are brought to the tables—the bright red of the berries and beets contrasting with the creamy goat cheese—the diners begin to make small talk. As the noise dies down to murmurs, I sit quietly, pondering Ruth Rivers's speech. It was, in some respects, a prayer before eating. And perhaps a mantra for this entire trip to St. John's Ferry, which turned out to be so much more than I could have ever imagined.

As I clink glasses with Brady, Alice, and Hannah, I feel Ruth's sentiment in my bones.

Things are good now.

But even better times are ahead.

As the evening dies down, I find my mother at the dessert table, a brownie and several hallongrottor in hand.

"Maggie, everything is absolutely delicious," she says. "I can't stop myself."

I smile. "Thanks. I just can't believe you're here, Mom. I know it's not an easy trip from LA." The closest major airport is in Minneapolis, two hours away. Coming here likely required a layover and a rental car.

"It wasn't, but I'm glad I came," she says, taking a bite of a raspberry cave.

"So the dinner was worth the trip?"

"Yes. But I didn't mean the food. Seeing you, this." She gestures all around. "It's remarkable what you've accomplished. You have a real gift for all this. For cooking, hosting, bringing people together. You always have." She pauses. "I didn't understand when you were a kid, and I know I wasn't supportive when I should have been. I regret that. I guess what I'm trying to say is . . . I'm sorry. Truth is, I've never seen you happier."

While I didn't think I needed it, her apology and approval of my current lifestyle—everything I've put my heart and soul into in the past month—feels like a blessing. Permission.

"These are to die for," she adds, raising one of the raspberry cookies from her plate.

"Hannah actually helped make those," I tell her. "This Scandinavian baker came to help us at the last minute, and those were one of his contributions."

I look for Christian in the crowd, hoping he's finally come out of the kitchen to enjoy the event, but I don't spot him. Instead, the Scandi Trio approaches; their huge grins signal they have some kind of news to share.

"Maggie, Diane, you won't believe it!" Johanna blurts. "We're going viral!"

"Katrine posted the pictures online," Nora adds. "And the social media world is oohing and aahing about the food. They're also donating to save Alice's farm."

"Here, see for yourself," Katrine insists, handing me her phone. My mother looks over my shoulder as I scroll through the photos. They're stunning. Katrine is a natural photographer, capturing just the right angle, the best lighting. In some photos, the food is in focus, while the background is blurred. In others, everything seems saturated in sunshine. It's all a feast for the eyes, the kinds of images I've seen posted by food celebrities.

"Great job, Katrine," I tell her, still swiping through the photos.

I land on the picture of Christian and me in matching aprons. Our hands are deeply engaged in the work. But for just that moment, we looked up at Katrine. We have the same expression on our faces, like we're caught off guard but embracing the distraction. It's a delightful photograph, playful and raw.

"Oh, I love this one," I say.

"Who is *that*?" my mother asks, pointing at the photo. Her blunt tone harkens back to my childhood, the *I'm not in the mood for games* voice.

"Christian Knudsen," I explain. "He's the Scandinavian baker I was just telling you about, the one who made the raspberry caves." I look for him again in the crowd. "I was going to introduce you."

My mother takes Katrine's phone from me and stares at the photo; her eyes freeze, then flit. She looks visibly deflated, her wrinkles piled like a shar-pei.

"Are you okay, Mom?"

"Yes, yes, fine." She pushes the phone back into my hands. "But I do think I've had one too many of these sweets. So, if you'll excuse me, I'm going to head back to the house for a little bit."

She hurries away, practically stuffing her half-full dessert plate into Nora's empty hands. I just stand there, shell-shocked.

"What was that about?" Katrine asks.

I still hold Katrine's phone and look back at the screen, at the photo of me with Christian.

"She looked like she'd seen a ghost," Johanna says.

I study the photo, taking in each of our features. Christian's eyes, my eyes. His nose, my nose. His lips, my lips. His chin and jawline, mine. We look alike. Eerily alike, actually. Is it just the photo? The way the light hits us?

"I saw it too," Katrine says.

"What?" I ask.

"The resemblance."

Yes, Katrine had paused to look at the photo right after she took it.

"Wow. Yeah," Nora says, also eyeing the photo. "You could be father and daughter."

We could. And yet, that's absurd. Christian couldn't possibly be my father. But as soon as that thought lands, my brain refires.

He's the right age, about the same age as my mother.

He's European.

Christian.

Chris.

"I wasn't a good father to her," he'd told me earlier. "But I'm trying to be now."

But the most obvious clue? The way my mother just behaved. Johanna was right. She did look like she'd seen a ghost.

A ghost from her past.

32

I spot Christian sitting alone by the fire. Other people might look out of place or antisocial sitting so removed at an event, but with his calm, monk-like demeanor, it seems natural, expected. He looks contemplative as he stares at the fire, and I see in his relaxed jaw a kind of inner peace.

"Mind if I join you?" I say.

"Maggie. Hello. Yes, of course." He pulls the closest chair even closer. "Please."

I sit, and we both stare at the fire for a beat. Maybe it should feel awkward, quietly sitting next to each other, but it doesn't. I let the fire's warmth hit my cheeks. It feels like lying in the sun on a hot summer day.

I speak first. "I wanted to thank you again for everything you did this morning, today, tonight. You were a godsend. I don't know what we would have done without you."

He smiles. "It was truly my pleasure."

"It feels like a miracle," I say. "Someone like you, with your background and experience, just showing up out of the blue, ready to help."

"You put on a great event. Don't be surprised that people wanted to play a part in it."

"I know. It just seems . . . serendipitous."

He doesn't say anything. We sit again quietly, and this time, it's uncomfortable. There is so much I want to say, to ask him. My mother was gone by the time I got back to the farmhouse. She left a note, saying she felt ill and was heading back to her hotel. She would call tomorrow. I wasn't surprised. She always needs space, distance, when she feels threatened, and facing my father after all these years likely felt like a tsunami.

"What's on your mind, Maggie?" Christian asks. "Something is weighing on you."

I look at him, but remain quiet. This means so much to me; there aren't enough words.

"You can tell me." His voice is gentle and authoritative at the same time.

So fatherly, it brings tears to my eyes.

"It's just that I never knew my father," I finally say. And to avoid looking at his reaction, my eyes focus on the orange flames. "My whole life. I never knew him. And I recently found out . . . I was recently given hope that maybe we had somehow, miraculously, found each other. After all this time. On one hand, it seems hard to believe. And on the other, it feels, at least in my heart . . ."

"True," he says.

I nod.

"I'm sorry, Maggie," he adds.

I look into his eyes to see what he means by this. Is he apologizing out of politeness—as in, *I'm sorry that happened to you*—or is he actually apologizing, for not being in my life all this time?

He turns toward me. "I didn't know you existed until five days ago."

And there it is. A sudden, warm gush of heat rises from my throat to my eyes. A wave of relief and joy so powerful, I stop breathing for a second.

Christian Knudsen is my father.

I shake my head, unable to believe it, even though I desperately want to.

"How did you find me?" I manage to ask.

He exhales. "There was an article in the Twin Cities newspaper. I saw a photo of the event team working on preparations at the farm, and there you were in the background, carrying a basket of fresh-picked strawberries. To be honest, I was mesmerized when I saw you. You looked so familiar, like a woman I spent time with many years ago, and I quickly read the caption, saw your name. Maggie Brodbeck. And of course, I kept digging until I figured out your mother was that woman."

The tears fall, and I wipe them with my wrist. "My mom told me you didn't know each other's names," I explain. "Only first names. You were Chris. And she was Diane."

He nods. "That was the rather silly arrangement we agreed on at the time. We were young and wanted to focus on our careers. Had I known about you, I would have been there, all this time. I can't change the past, but I decided I had to come here to at least meet you."

I let his story sink in. "Were you going to tell me?"

"When the time felt right."

"And that was now?"

"It was clear to me you already figured it out." He pauses. "How?"

"Well, this may be hard to believe, but my mother is here tonight."

His eyes dart to the lingering crowd. "Where?"

"Well, she *was*," I correct.

I tell him about the photo Katrine took of us, my mother's reaction, and what I saw when I really looked at the picture. What I felt when I met him. What I observed when he worked with Hannah, the grace and patience of a grandfather.

"I'd like to see your mother," he says. "Talk to her. When she's ready, of course."

I nod. "I just can't believe you found me," I say, trying to keep my tears at bay. "It's kind of lucky, isn't it?"

He narrows his eyes. "Is it luck? Or did you bring me to you?"

I shrug. "How could that be?"

"Maggie, you created the scenario for me to find you. You came to the farm with Hannah, you made all of these new friends, you found out about Alice's financial troubles, you planned this fundraiser, and then this event was publicized in the newspaper I read."

I shake my head. "But I didn't *intend* to find you."

"You listened to your inner voice, didn't you? The one that said *yes*. The one that said *I like that, I want that*. You followed what called to you, what spoke to you. And in doing that, you created a possibility for me to one day simply read the newspaper, like I do every day, and find you."

He's right. I was following my heart, doing what felt true, what made me happy each day. And that string of events ultimately brought my father into my life.

I dab my eyes. "Well, I'm so happy you're here now."

He takes my hand. "Not just now, Maggie. Forever."

He reaches over to hug me, and I rest my cheek on his shoulder, and we sit there a good minute, holding on to each other, and everything we haven't shared, and everything we hope to share in the future.

The morning after the farm-to-table dinner feels like so many before—the morning after high school prom, the morning after my wedding, the morning after I gave birth to Hannah. Something magnificent happened, and it's reflected in the afterglow.

Everyone sleeps late, but as they trickle down to the kitchen for coffee and breakfast, the house feels full. I'm up first to make coffee, and Alice soon follows. Then Brady. And then Hannah and the girls, who slept in the attic again to make room for Christian. I insisted he stay the night instead of going back to the Ferry Inn. The afterparty lasted into the wee hours of the morning.

Alice had the forethought to know none of us would feel up to cooking in the morning, so she'd made cinnamon rolls the day before. She serves them this morning with simple scrambled eggs. As we all sit in the kitchen—some at the table, some at island stools—it feels like being wrapped in a blanket. I'm surrounded by my family and friends.

These are my people.

And then there's a knock at the door. Alice runs to answer it, then returns a moment later.

"It's your mother," she tells me. "She's waiting for you on the porch."

I steal a glance at Christian—*my father*—and then at Brady. I take a deep breath and quickly head outside, where I find her sitting on the swing.

"I know about Christian," I say, sitting beside her.

She nods. "I'm not surprised. I didn't exactly hide my shock. I knew you'd figure it out."

"He's here. Inside. He spent the night."

She nods. "I'm not proud of my behavior, Maggie. It's just . . ."

I take her hand. "I get it. I can't imagine how overwhelmed you must have felt seeing a photo of him after all these years, and then knowing he was here. I don't fault you for needing space, needing time."

"Thank you." She sighs. "I just never thought I would have to face him. The odds were just so slim. It was statistically possible, but not probable."

My mother, the math teacher.

"How did he even track you down?" she asks.

I explain how Christian found me, why he came to the event.

"He wants to talk to you," I say. "Would you be open to that?"

She shakes her head. "I don't know. What would be the point?"

"Me," I say. "*I'm* the point. He's my father, and I want to have him in my life. I mean, he never knew about me. He never had the chance to *be* my father."

"I told you, I didn't know how to find him," she argues.

"I know. But he found me. After all these years. You don't think you owe him something? Not even a hello?"

My mother holds her jaw tight. "Okay," she says. "Send him out."

Somehow, in their twenty minutes on the porch, Christian charms my mother into joining us inside. I have no idea what was said—I hope to get a play-by-play from one of them later—but I'm just so happy their conversation didn't end with my mom flying home early. The group conversation feels awkward at first, stilted. But once Alice brings my mom a cup of coffee, and Hannah serves her a cinnamon roll, the mood shifts. Comfort food. The fix for all that ails.

The banter continues, and our conversation quickly turns to last night.

We each share highlights and our favorite moments, and all the complimentary feedback from the guests. It was such a success, the mayor and festival committee want to make it an annual event, which will only further help the St. John's Ferry tourism industry.

"Oh my god, you won't believe this," Katrine squeals, looking at her phone.

"What?" everyone seems to reply, our eyes laser-focused on her.

"We made the news," she says.

It is exciting information, but not all that shocking. The event had already been written up in newspapers in major Midwest cities like Minneapolis and Chicago, and had made the local news segments there as well.

Katrine detects that we don't quite understand what she means and tries again.

"The *national* news," she says. "That big morning show. *Today's American.*"

Now, we erupt in cheers.

"That's amazing," Brady says.

"Are you serious?" I ask.

Katrine nods and points at her phone. "I'm watching the clip right now."

"Now I regret not owning a TV," Alice says like an apology.

"We can watch it on my phone," Katrine offers, and we all crowd in behind her.

The clip is short, but the farm and the food shine in every shot. The morning-show hosts even comment about the allure of the event, the importance of small farms, and of course, Ruth Rivers and Christian Knudsen.

"They certainly make a dynamic duo," one of the morning-show hosts comments.

I steal a peek at my father and Ruth, who stand next to each other in the huddle, and see them lock eyes for a beat before turning their heads back to the screen.

A dynamic duo indeed.

We all watch the clip again, each on our own phones, unable to believe this brush with the national media. It buoys us the whole morning, as we return to real life.

"This just keeps getting better," Katrine announces a few hours later. She's been dealing with the aftermath of the media frenzy all morning. "We just got a huge donation online."

"How huge?" I ask.

"Fifteen thousand dollars," she says.

My eyes bulge. "*Who* donated that kind of money?"

"Must have been a corporation," Brady adds.

She shakes her head. "It came from a woman in New York, Lucia Penderglass. And all she asks for in return is a tour of the house and farm."

"Lucia?" Alice repeats.

I lock eyes with Alice, then we both turn to Katrine.

She grins. "Well, I think we found our Lucy."

33

Christmas Eve 1946

Rose looked at her Christmas tree, a spruce from Jensen's farm, decorated with homemade ornaments and strands of pine cone garland. She couldn't fathom how a whole year had passed. Last Christmas seemed fresh in her memory. Had it been only a year since President Truman lit the national Christmas tree for the first time since 1941? Despite the passage of a year, Hank was still missing. Rose felt the familiar ache in her chest as she watched other soldiers return home, and prayed every night that, one day, Hank would too.

Meanwhile, Lucy helped her pass the time. Lucy turned two in January, and the next month, they made valentines together. Rose delighted in wiping Lucy's hands of red paint, laughing along with her sweet giggle as the cloth tickled her skin. In March, they helped a neighbor tap trees for maple syrup, and in April they hunted for Easter eggs under the oaks. How gently Lucy placed her eggs in the basket, Rose thought, as if putting a baby doll to sleep. Rose fondly observed Lucy picking lilacs when they bloomed in May, and gobbling up the strawberries that ripened in June. Rose fed her sandwiches, juicy with the tomatoes that swelled in August, and together, they played in the first leaves that fell at the end of September. The October chill brought vibrant-red leaves, keepsakes of the season, that they pressed into books, and November gifted oversize squash for Lucy's small hands to pick.

Now it was December, and Rose could hardly believe Lucy was almost three. While Lucy took her afternoon nap this Christmas Eve, Rose prepared for the arrival of Peggy and her husband, Robert Gibson. The end of the war brought an end to most rations, and Rose eagerly prepared the food they would enjoy this evening. Peggy and Robert, who lived in Minneapolis, would spend Christmas Eve at the farmhouse, a stopover on their drive to Peggy's parents' home in Milwaukee. For the first time in a long while, they would eat beef. She'd considered a roast, but decided instead to make Swedish meatballs with gravy over egg noodles, with a side of braised red cabbage and glazed carrots. They'd enjoy a salad, cheese, and sausages beforehand. It would all feel indulgent after so many years of sacrifice.

When Rose opened the door to greet Peggy and Robert, a dusting of snow speckled their shoulders and hats. She couldn't help but recall this same day three years ago, when Esther and Henry arrived in a similar fashion, full of hope and expectation of being with child. So much had happened in the past three years—the loss of Esther, the gift of Lucy—and for a moment, a wave of nostalgia threatened to steal the joy from this special day. But Rose tried to remember how important it was to live in the moment, as we never know what the future holds, good or bad.

"Where is my Lucy?" Peggy asked, looking behind Rose. "Where is my big girl?"

Rose took Peggy's coat. "Napping upstairs. She'll be awake in a few minutes."

Peggy's shoulders sagged. "I bet she's grown. I hope she remembers me."

"Of course, she will." Rose turned to Peggy's husband. "You must be Robert."

"Yes, ma'am." He reached for her hand, but Rose hugged him instead.

"Peggy mentioned you were warm and friendly," he noted, pulling back from her embrace. "She's very fond of you."

"As I am of her," Rose said.

Just then, as if on cue, they heard a gentle singsong from upstairs, a high-pitched collection of babbles and notes, like birds chirping in the early morning. It was the most beautiful sound to Rose's ears, a child happily waking from slumber.

"May I get her from her nap?" Peggy asked.

"Let's go together," Rose said, thinking Lucy might be frightened if someone other than Rose came in. Most days, it was just the two of them.

Rose followed Peggy into the room to find Lucy sitting up in her bed, playing with her baby doll. Her blond hair laid flat on her head, and her eyes appeared swollen with sleep, but she seemed in good spirits.

Lucy looked at Peggy and raised her arms out to her, as if she'd seen her every day.

"Hello, my darling," Peggy said, scooping her up. Lucy immediately hooked her arms around Peggy's neck, like a chimpanzee might cling to a zookeeper. She snuggled her head onto Peggy's shoulder.

"Well, if that doesn't prove it," Rose declared. "She remembers you."

Peggy closed her eyes and soaked in the moment, the comfort of holding a child whose arms and legs were still anesthetized by slumber. Rose watched Peggy as she smelled the top of Lucy's head, as Rose had so many times.

"Oh, I've missed you," Peggy said, swaying back and forth, a dancing hug. Then her face suddenly fell, and her eyes filled with tears.

"What is it?" Rose clutched Peggy's arm. She assumed it was how much Lucy looked like Esther. Sometimes, the likeness was too much for Rose too. She often felt a wave of sadness at the realization that Lucy would never know her mother.

"I won't have children," Peggy said instead.

"Of course, you will. You said you and Robert have been trying. It will happen."

"The doctor said I am unable to get pregnant or birth a child."

"Oh, Peggy, I'm so sorry. Are they sure?"

She nodded. "They did many tests."

Rose thought about Albert and Hank, from pregnancy to birth to childhood. She would never regret the time and attention she invested in them. Motherhood is a job of cultivation. You don't necessarily reap what you sow. The world is often the receiver of that gift.

"I'm so sorry," Rose repeated.

Peggy wiped a tear away with her free hand; the other hand and arm secured Lucy to her hip. "There are options, Robert said. Adoption. We have so much love to give. It will all work out." She snuggled up to Lucy again. "And I have you, little Lucy."

Rose watched Peggy and Lucy touch noses and foreheads and stare into each other's eyes, just as she and Lucy did in the quiet moments, after sitting in the chair and reading, after her bath. It was remark-able, how comfortable Lucy seemed to be with Peggy, even though she hadn't seen her since the summer. They had a connection, an unex-plainable bond.

Rose followed the two of them down the stairs to greet Robert, who was still seated in the foyer. She paused halfway and watched the scene unfold before her. Robert stood and rushed to them, and Lucy smiled and giggled and played patty-cake with him, still on Peggy's hip. A happy family, Rose thought, as she took in the sight. It was beautiful. Precious. It could have been an advertisement.

As Rose continued down the steps, watching the three of them connect in such a genuine way, a wave of simultaneous comfort and loss overcame her. Lucy had no mother, and a father who rarely came to visit as of late. Meanwhile, Peggy and Robert desperately wanted a child but could not have one. They each possessed what the other needed. And though it would pain her to let Lucy go, she knew Peggy and Robert could give her so much more. They were younger, more energetic, with even more room in their hearts, having no children of their own. She would miss Lucy greatly—terribly, really, it was almost hard to fathom—and yet she had always held back a part of herself from the young girl, hoping her father would someday take her home. She'd hoped all along their arrangement was temporary.

By the time she reached the bottom of the steps, it was clear what she needed to do. She would talk to Henry, ask if they could work out a plan. Perhaps by next Christmas, he would agree to give Lucy the greatest gift of all.

A family.

Rose woke on Christmas morning feeling a great sense of purpose to work with her hands. With Henry arriving this morning, there were so many food preparations for Christmas brunch. Cinnamon rolls, scrambled eggs, sausage, ham steaks, biscuits with jam, and fresh fruit. A strong cup of coffee was her first order of business, and while she sipped her fully leaded brew, she thought about what she would say to Henry, how to convince him to let Peggy and Robert adopt Lucy. She was almost three now, and her memory was just beginning to form. This was the right time for Lucy to begin a new life with Peggy and Robert, before she could remember being too attached to anyone else. Rose wondered how Henry would react to the idea. Would he be angry? Offended? Perhaps he would be relieved? He'd come to see Lucy less and less in the past months. And when he did, Rose noted how preoccupied he seemed; he held her on his lap but his mind and heart were somewhere else entirely. Maybe he knew he wouldn't be able to give Lucy the home life she deserved and would put aside his attachment in exchange for her long-term happiness.

As Rose finished her coffee, she said a prayer of gratitude for Lucy, then set herself to work before she could think too much about how full Lucy's life would be with two young parents—and how empty hers might feel once she was gone.

Soon, Peggy, Robert, and Lucy woke and filled the house with chatter and laughter and life. Everyone was dressed in their holiday best;

Lucy wore her green velvet dress. They played Christmas music and "Let It Snow" echoed through the house while the earthy, spiced smell of cinnamon rolls and the smoky scent of sausages searing in the cast iron pan perfumed the air. It was Christmas morning, Hank was still missing, and yet somehow, her house was filled with love—not with her own children or grandchildren, but with angels who had come into her life.

A knock on the door signified the official start of Christmas morning—Henry.

"Lucy, your daddy's here," Rose announced, nearing the farmhouse door.

She opened it to see a woman with an aquiline nose, harshly arched eyebrows, and a sour purse of the lips. She was holding a basket of fruit and shelled nuts wrapped in red ribbon.

"Rose, I presume?" the woman said, before shoving the basket into Rose's hands. "Henry's still in the car getting the presents. I'm Angelica." Her gloved hand shot out like a jack-in-the-box.

Rose narrowed her eyes, but shifted the basket into the crook of her elbow so she could return the handshake. "Angelica?"

"Henry's fiancée," she spat, as if the fact was as commonly known as the alphabet.

"Fiancée?" Rose repeated, and watched Henry scurry up with an armload of presents.

"Merry Christmas, Rose," Henry cheered. "I see you've met Angelica."

Rose nodded but no words came. "I didn't know you were engaged, Henry," she finally said. Now she understood why he had not come to see his daughter, where his mind had been when he had.

"It all happened so quickly," Henry explained. "You see, Angelica is the daughter of my boss, Fred Penderglass. I'm sure you've heard of him. Penderglass Auto?"

Rose nodded. In other words, she was rich. How she wished Henry had been able to continue his studies in veterinary medicine.

"Well, aren't you going to invite us in?" the fiancée commanded.

Rose stepped back and opened the door fully to allow the woman inside, her large stature made grander by the oversize fur collar of her coat. The woman seemed immediately out of place in the farmhouse. Where she was sharp and edgy, it was curved and comfortable. Rose wanted to sweep the woman up and out the door like debris, but it wasn't in her to be mean.

"Angelica is from New York," Henry announced.

"Are you?" Rose asked. She had so many questions. How did you meet? When are you getting married? Why didn't you tell me sooner? Instead, she just watched Angelica throw off her coat and glide into the parlor singing, "Lucyyy? Oh Lucyyy?"

Rose quickly tossed Angelica's coat on the rack and set the fruit basket on a side table so she could follow the woman. It felt like a raccoon had suddenly busted through her front door, and she was chasing it to curb the destruction of its path. Lucy sat on Peggy's lap, content and smiling, but Angelica lifted the girl from Peggy's arms with the force of a hungry shopper.

"Hello, Lucyyy," she sang. "Hello, you beautiful girl."

Lucy's face compressed, her nose and eyes pinched, her lips pursed. She looked like she'd sucked on a lemon. And then she exploded into tears, kicking her arms and legs to wriggle out of the woman's grip.

"Henry, do something," Angelica commanded.

Henry scooped the girl from Angelica's arms, and Lucy's flailing movements ceased, but her tears remained as she rested her head on her father's shoulder.

"My word. What a tantrum," Angelica said.

"You startled her," Peggy argued, a disapproving look clear on her face.

But this didn't stop Angelica. "Lucy," she shouted. "We brought you presents. Don't you want to open your presents?"

"We were planning to eat breakfast first," Rose said, thinking of her own handmade present for Lucy. She'd hidden it in the attic for her to find, in the same place Hank used to hide his toys.

Angelica waved the idea away. "But children can't wait to open presents. Let's have Lucy open hers right now."

Lucy hid in the folds of her father's neck.

"Well, she's hungry," Rose tried again. "And she has opened some gifts already this morning. Like that rocking horse."

"Oh dear, it's rather large," Angelica noted, looking down her nose like it was just a pile of wood. "That was awfully kind of you, but I don't think we have room for it in the car, along with all of Lucy's other belongings."

"Lucy's belongings?" Rose inquired, her eyes darting to Henry for an explanation.

He remained quiet, and Angelica filled the silence.

"Oh, didn't Henry tell you? We're taking Lucy to New York with us tomorrow," she announced. She reached over and pinched Lucy's cheek. "That's right. I'm going to be your new mommy."

Rose couldn't look at Henry or Lucy or Peggy or Robert, who all remained quiet in the storm of Angelica's wake. As she felt her cheeks grow hot, her breath heavy, she abruptly left the room and retreated out the front door. The sudden cold air helped her breathe again.

She had already prepared to say goodbye to Lucy. But she had not prepared to hand her off to Henry and that wretched Angelica, a woman she felt certain would never love Lucy like a real mother. Rose also knew if she let Henry and Angelica take Lucy today, she would likely never see her again.

Within a matter of minutes, everything was gone.

The dream—of Peggy and Robert raising Lucy, of loving her and protecting her—was over before it even began.

34

For being over eighty years old with a full head of snow-white hair, Lucia Penderglass is sprite. She walks with a skip in her step, a bounce of the knees. We meet her and her daughter, Lynn, on the gravel driveway, where she stands with her eyes closed for a moment, breathing the country air. Then she opens them and turns in circles for a 360 view of the farm.

By the time we get close enough to hug her or shake her hand, her eyes are full of tears. She blinks. The tears fall.

"I had all but given up on finding this place," she says.

"You remember it?" Alice asks.

Lucy narrows her eyes and nods.

"It has haunted her," her daughter interrupts. "The memory of this place."

"Oh, I don't care for that word," Lucy argues. "*Haunted.* It sounds like a nightmare. And that wasn't it. Not at all."

Her daughter remains silent.

"How would you describe it?" I ask.

"Lured. Enticed. Called by it. Like a fairy tale. Like a melody. I could see it—this place—so clearly in my mind, and yet I could never find it. I had started to think I had dreamt it, my memories of being a child on this farm. Maybe I'd had a high fever one day and made the whole thing up. But it was so real. In my mind. So clear. The porch.

The stairs. The barn there." She points a curved, knobby finger at the outbuilding. "That oak tree. The maples. The gravel."

I'd had a similar experience when I arrived, prompted by the memory of biting into that juicy tomato on a hot August day. My memory of the farmhouse and my years with Alice had been buried, but that juicy tomato was always there.

"She's drawn pictures of it," Lynn chimes in. "Painted it many times. I've been looking at this farmhouse my whole life. That's why I recognized it, when I saw it on *Today's American*. Of course, I thought, it couldn't be. But I had to show her. It was so close to what she'd always described."

"Did you know right away?" Alice asks. "When Lynn showed the news clip to you?"

"Oh, yes. I knew. I couldn't believe it. This figment of my imagination was real." Her eyes dance. "Here in Wisconsin."

Alice reaches for Lucy's hand. "Would you like to come inside now?"

Lucy remembers the inside of the house too. The parlor, the location of each room and bedroom, and of course, the attic steps that pull down from the ceiling. She touches everything, her fingers curled with arthritis, as if she doesn't believe it's real.

After the tour, we retire to the kitchen table to enjoy tea and cookies. The Scandi Trio has baked assorted kinds for the occasion—oatmeal chocolate chip, lemon drop, and snickerdoodle.

Alice hands Lucy the photograph of the farmerettes posed by the boardinghouse sign and points to Rose. "Do you remember her?" she asks.

Lucy closes her eyes and holds in another round of tears. "She smelled like sweat and onion and cinnamon, all at once," she says. "And I can feel her arm around my waist, my legs straddled on her hip. Her face." She pauses, take a breath. "She was magic."

Alice smiles and nods.

"I never knew who this woman was," Lucy goes on, "this woman I saw when I closed my eyes. I knew she wasn't my mother or my grandmother. They looked quite different. When I was about five or six, I asked my mother who she was, certain she must have been an aunt or cousin or a family friend. But my mother said she couldn't fathom who I was talking about. When I pressed the issue, and described the farmhouse, she said she'd read me Laura Ingalls Wilder's *Little House in the Big Woods*, and that I must be remembering Ma from the book. The farmhouse must have been the cabin in the woods. I was so young, she said I'd dreamt up my own characters and setting as I listened to her read." She pauses. "I believed her at first. But after I read *Little House in the Big Woods* again when I was older, I knew my memories had nothing to do with that book. It's a wonderful story, but quite dissimilar. Over the years, I came to learn my mother could be cruel and manipulative and selfish. And she could lie." Lucy clears her throat. "So now, I want to know, who was Rose Brodbeck? I mean, who was she to me?"

Alice, Katrine, and I exchange glances. We know the full truth, because we continued reading the letters Rose wrote to Hank, and the very last one, dated Christmas 1946, explained that Henry and his fiancée, Angelica, took Lucy, just when Rose was going to ask Henry if Peggy and Robert could adopt her. This is what Peggy must have meant when she claimed *He took her*. Sadly, after that day, Rose never saw Lucy again.

We pause to consider who will be brave enough to set the record straight, to tell Lucy, a woman in her eighties, that her mother was not really her mother.

"Please," Lucy begs. "I want to know the truth."

I decide to deliver the news, mostly so Alice and Katrine don't have to.

"Apparently, Rose took care of you after your mother, Esther, died in childbirth," I say as plainly as I can. "Your father was too distraught to care for you, so Rose took you in."

Lucy stares off for a beat. "So my mother was not really my mother," she says. "She was my stepmother."

"You didn't know," Alice states.

She shrugs. "Not consciously. But I always suspected. My father died just before I turned five. And like I said, she was cruel. Crueler than I thought a mother could be to her own child. But it's a terrible truth to bear, and I never fully looked for it. I may have grown up wealthy, gotten anything that money could buy, but I was poor when it came to the things that really mattered, like love."

"Okay, I'm confused," Lynn inserts. "How did Esther come to know Rose?"

And we go on to tell them about the Women's Land Army, about the Rosehill Boardinghouse, about the friendships forged between Rose and the girls, and in particular, with Esther. About Esther's father disowning her for getting pregnant, about the night Henry came pounding on the door with a baby in his arms. We show Lucy the photograph of herself with an apron full of eggs and the recipe for Lucy's Victory Cake. We also show her a photograph of Esther, her mother. After some looking, the O'Briens finally located a few photos taken at the dairy during the war, and one was of Esther milking a cow, with "Esther Monroe, WLA" written on the back. Finally, we give her the Christmas present the girls found in the attic, still wrapped, though yellow and worn and torn at the edges, the tag with her name lovingly written by Rose.

Lucy stares at the package, stunned to receive such a gift decades after the fact. Her fingers glide against the paper seams, the ribbon curves, her name on the tag.

"I'm going to open it," she says.

"Are you sure, Mom?" Lynn asks. "Maybe you should do it later. Or maybe not at all. Maybe it's too much right now."

Lucy shakes her head. "These kind women didn't open it when they found it," she explains, tugging at the ribbon. "They saved it for me. And so, they will get the pleasure of watching me open it now."

The silence is heavy, less the sound of ripping paper, as we watch her remove the ribbon and wrap, revealing a plain brown craft-paper box. She lifts the lid, and we all gasp when we see ruffles of a colorful vintage fabric. Lucy lifts the cloth and holds it up.

A child's apron.

We all gawk at the relic. I'm surprised it isn't more yellowed, but it's been protected from sunlight and air, under the floorboard. It's a classic 1940s farmhouse apron design, simple but with some frills, a ruffled hem. Rose had obviously sewn it specifically for Lucy to grow into over the years.

"This tells me a lot." Lucy rubs her fingers over the stitched seams, then places the apron against her body and hugs it like a blanket.

"She's buried at the cemetery in town," Alice offers. "If you'd like to pay your respects."

"I would," Lucy says.

I see a corner of white inside the box.

"There's a note," I say, knowing a written sentiment from Rose would mean one hundred times more to Lucy than the apron itself.

Lucy's curled fingers shake as she slips a finger under the flap and pulls the letter open, the glue barely sticking after so many years. We watch with bated breath as she slides a folded card from inside the envelope and opens it.

I watch her eyes fill with tears as she reads the card.

"What does it say, Mom?" Lynn asks.

Lucy takes a breath before reading:

> *Been around the world, a time or two,*
> *But I'm just happier here with you.*
> *Why does the sky seem ever so blue?*
> *'Cause I'm just happier here with you.*
> *Love, Rose*

"It sounds like a song," Alice notes. "But I don't recognize it."

Lynn and I both shrug, unable to place the lyrics either.

"I do," Lucy says. "My father used to sing it to me. I never heard it again, on the radio, so I always assumed he made it up. But if Rose knew it too, then it must have come from Esther."

Lynn reaches for her mother's hand. "You see, Mom? Rose loved you."

Lucy holds the letter to her chest as she did the apron.

"And I loved her," she says.

After Lucy and Lynn have gone, Alice and I sit alone on the front porch, rehashing all that happened. Alice stares at the groove of her tea-mug handle, and I can tell she's contemplating something.

"Penny for your thoughts?" I ask.

Alice snaps out of her introspection. "It's just, after talking with Lucy today, I can't help but think about how much Rose lost in her lifetime. Her husband, her sons, Lucy."

"You?" I add.

"Me," she says with a sigh. "Did I break her heart too?"

35

June 1961

Rose peered out the farmhouse window, and watched her daughter-in-law, Doris, and granddaughter, Alice, exit the vehicle for a moment before greeting them. Sadly, she hadn't seen her son or daughter-in-law or grandson Albert Jr. for almost seven years—one summer, they stayed two nights before driving to Wisconsin Dells—and she'd never even met her granddaughter. She knew Alice only from photographs. And yet, she loved her deeply and unconditionally. Her farmhouse door and her heart had always been open to all of them.

Doris stuck out like a sore thumb against the backdrop of the farm. Her perfectly coiffed platinum blond hair—twisted up in the front like a cinnamon bun, with large rolls of curls on both sides—hinted at her career in Hollywood, as did her oversize sunglasses and bronzed arms and legs. She was a California girl. Meanwhile, Rose noticed how Alice, despite having lived on the West Coast her entire six years, blended in with the trees and grasses and flowers, as if from the same color palette. She wore blue jeans and a tan T-shirt, and the golden flecks in her hair resembled strands of wheat.

It was during a phone call a few weeks ago that Doris agreed to bring Alice to visit. According to Doris, Alice had been struggling at school this past year. She couldn't read yet, and she misbehaved. She was often out of her seat and talked back to the teacher. Doris assumed it had something to do with her parents' ongoing marital issues—and her father's ongoing absence while in rehab from alcohol addiction. Doris spoke of Alice's school troubles in a detached way, as if detailing the antics of a naughty puppy. "I don't have time for this," she said that day. Her career was really taking off, and she needed Alice to fall in line. Alice was rough around the edges, a tomboy, she said. She was happier playing in dirt than with dolls.

A change in setting is what the girl needs, Rose thought, and offered to take the girl for the summer.

"Good afternoon," Rose called to them from the farmhouse porch.

"Hello." Doris offered a half-hearted hug, then grabbed her daughter's hand and pulled her forward. "Alice, this is your grandmother."

"Hello, Alice," Rose said, holding back her desire to smother the girl in hugs and kisses. She sensed apprehension.

"Hello." Alice paused and crinkled her nose. "Do you have a name? Besides Grandma?"

"My name is Rose. But when I was your age, my friends called me Rosey Posey. You can call me that if you'd like."

Alice's eyes lit up. "Rosey Posey," she repeated.

Doris placed a hand on her daughter's shoulder. "No, no, Alice, she's joking with you. It's not appropriate for you to call her that. Call her Grandma."

Alice dropped her mother's hand. "But she said . . ."

"Who's hungry?" Rose asked, attempting to defuse the impending argument.

"Not me," Doris announced. "Just a glass of water for now."

"Well then, Alice, guess it's just you and me for lunch. Do you like picnics?"

Alice nodded.

"I have a pond, you know." She pointed to the other end of the property. "We can have our lunch down there. Do you like to fish?"

Alice scrunched her lips. "I don't like fish. Mommy eats tuna, and it's stinky."

Rose laughed. "I said do you like *to fish*? Do you like to throw a line in the water and catch a fish?"

"I don't know. I've never done that before."

"Well, I think you'll love it. There will be lots of fun things to do here, things you never did before. You're going to have the time of your life this summer."

Alice looked up at her with large, inquisitive eyes. "Promise?"

Rose grabbed the girl's hand and led her up the porch steps. Her granddaughter's palm was moist and a bit sticky, as if she'd just eaten a popsicle.

It reminded her of Lucy.

"Cross my heart," Rose said. "I promise you're going to grow like wild."

After lunch, Rose and Alice sat cuddled on the porch swing reading *Stuart Little*. Rose smelled her granddaughter's hair, full of sweat and sun and dirt. Midwest summer.

A car pulled up the drive.

"That's your mom," Rose said.

"I don't want to go home," Alice cried.

"I know. I don't want you to go home either."

When the summer had ended, Rose had convinced Doris to let Alice stay even longer, to attend school nearby. The past year with Alice had been full of comfort and wonder and hope. They'd developed their own routines—treats like pineapple upside-down cake and baked Alaska in the afternoons and hours of reading out loud in the evenings. It had been a true gift of time. She'd known all along that one day, this day, would come. Alice would leave. She thought she'd be better prepared when the time came. She'd lost so many people in her life—her husband, her son, Esther, Lucy. In some ways, she'd lost Albert too, many years ago, not physically but mentally and emotionally. Loss was the downside of love. Rose knew that. But it hurt so much more now, in this moment, than she'd ever imagined. Her heart had broken and mended so many times over. Was she a fool to think she would heal every time, no matter how many times it was cut in half?

Tears flooded Alice's eyes. "Why can't I stay?"

Rose wiped her tears away with her thumb. "Because your mother thinks it's best if you go back to California. She misses you. She loves you. And that's where your family is."

"But not you. You're my family too."

"Yes, I am. And I am always here for you."

Rose and Alice turned to see Doris park in front of the farmhouse, their conversation now constrained by seconds.

"When will I see you again?" Alice asked.

Rose smiled. "Probably Christmas."

"But that's a long time away."

"It seems long," Rose explained. "But all of a sudden, Christmas will come. It always does."

Doris made her way up the porch steps to greet them. "Did I hear Christmas?" she repeated, instead of rushing to hug her daughter. "Why are we talking about Christmas?"

"Because that's when I will see Grandma again," Alice announced.

Doris narrowed her eyes and cocked her head; not one blond hair moved. "Oh, Rose, you're coming out to California for Christmas?"

Rose shook her head. "I thought you'd come here."

Doris pursed her lips. "I can't commit to that. I just auditioned for a part. The secretary on a TV show. If I get it, well, I really don't know that I can take time off to come all the way out here." She folded her arms. "Besides, you've never come to California."

Because you've never invited me. Because I don't feel welcome.

"Come to think of it, have you *ever* left Wisconsin?" Doris asked pointedly.

She hadn't.

Some people enjoyed adventure, needed to explore distant lands. But Rose was content here. Her everyday world in St. John's Ferry always felt like enough. She felt tethered to the ground, but not chained or imprisoned. It was more like a security feature; she was tied down so she wouldn't blow away.

But she knew it was more than that. Hank had been missing now almost twenty years, and still Rose expected him back any minute. She might hear the porch steps creak and the doorknob rattle and then his voice spiral up through the rafters.

Mom, I'm home, she could hear him say clear as day.

The truth was, this home, their home, was the last place she'd seen Hank alive, and she felt called to stay here until he came back. Leaving would mean giving up on that dream.

Someday, Hank might come home, and she wanted to be here when he did.

"Do you *really* want me to come visit you in California?" Rose asked.

"Of course," Doris said. "I mean, you'll have to let me know exactly when you'll be coming. There will be a number of Hollywood holiday parties that I hope to be invited to. My spare room is a bit of a mess. We'll have to clean it up, of course." Doris looked off in confusion, as if the future lacked any sort of structure or order. She waved it all away with a flutter of her hands. "But we'll work it out."

Alice took Rose's hand and squeezed it. "Will you come, Grandma?" she asked. "Will you come see me at Christmas?"

Rose took both of Alice's hands in her own, and they locked eyes. "I will be there," Rose said.

Two weeks before Christmas, Rose's bag was packed and waiting by the door, her train ticket to LA secured in her purse. Her neighbor Carol would arrive any minute to drive her to the station.

As she pulled down the stairs to the attic, she thought about the apron she'd sewn for Lucy. It was still stowed under the floor plank with the letters to Hank. She knew it might seem odd to give Alice a gift she made for another child, and yet Rose didn't see it that way. Rose viewed the apron as more of a family heirloom, something to be passed down from one generation to another. She hadn't seen Lucy since the day Angelica and Henry took her away. She'd tried to write, but her letters were always returned. Lucy would be almost nineteen years old now. Even if Rose could find her, Lucy would have no use for the apron. It wouldn't fit her. Besides, keeping the apron under the floorboards like some sort of shrine was living in the past. And Rose wanted to live in the present, and in the future.

Alice is the future, she thought.

As she began to climb the stairs, the telephone rang—bleating from its post in the kitchen—and she ran back down to answer it.

It was Doris. "Oh, good, you haven't left yet," she said.

Rose noted the panic in her daughter-in-law's voice. "What's wrong?"

"Oh, nothing. Actually, everything is quite wonderful. I was going to tell you when I saw you, but I met a wonderful man. Stan. We've only known each other two weeks, but he's the one. And well, he's invited Alice and me to his parents' home in Sacramento. So we'll be going there for the holiday. They have snowcapped mountains. And a swimming pool. And all sorts of cousins and kids for Alice to play with. I'm sure you understand. I know you didn't really want to come out all this way anyway."

Rose had no words.

"I do have to say goodbye now, Rose. Stan has the car packed and running. Maybe we'll come see you in the spring. For Easter. Wouldn't that be nice?"

"Easter," Rose repeated; it was all she could say.

She felt like she'd swallowed her heart.

"Oh great, then it's settled. Look, we'll try to call from Sacramento, but just in case, merry Christmas."

"Merry Christmas," Rose said.

And then, when Doris seemed ready to hang up, Rose called out, "Wait. Can I please speak to Alice?"

But Doris was already gone.

Rose set the phone back on its receiver and just stood there, staring at it. Eventually, a knock at the door stirred her from her trance. It was Carol, on time to take her to the train station.

"I'm sorry, Carol. I'm not going," Rose said. "Doris just called."

Carol cocked her head. "Is everything okay?"

"Something came up."

Her neighbor nodded. Nothing more needed to be said.

"Christmas dinner will be at three p.m. as always," Carol offered. "You can bring a pie."

"Thanks," Rose said, not sure if she would go. She'd been to Carol's once before and regretted it; sitting around with Carol's family only made Rose miss her own even more.

After Carol left, Rose climbed the stairs and saw the attic steps where she left them. She could mail Alice the apron or wait until they came at Easter and give it to her then. She chastised herself.

They weren't coming for Easter either.

A sudden fatigue washed over her; her legs felt full, heavy with lead. She placed the apron back in its spot under the floorboard, then returned downstairs to make a cup of tea, which she drank in front of the wood stove.

She looked around the room and thought, for the first time that holiday season, that it looked so bare. She hadn't put up a Christmas tree or decorations because she assumed she'd be in California for two weeks. Now, in the plain space, she saw the ghosts of Christmases past—faint outlines of a tree, ornaments, tinsel, garland. Family. Friends. Her husband and Hank and Albert. Esther and Henry. Lucy and Peggy.

Alice.

Rose felt that horrible ache in her chest, a pang deep in the center, and placed her hand there as she always did, but the pressure did not seem to work this time.

She didn't want to feel like this ever again.

36

The day after Lucy's visit to the farm, Alice and I sit in the attic sorting and organizing the rest of the box of Rose's recipes. I'm supposed
to go home in a few days, back to Eastridge and back to work, and I
don't want to leave the project unfinished. This time, we find many
recipes from the late 1950s and early '60s, like Beef Wellington, which
I know Julia Child helped make famous. There's also one for cheese fon-
due, clipped from a woman's magazine, and a newspaper print version
of Baked Alaska. Chicken à la King. Pineapple Upside-Down Cake.
Ambrosia Salad. We even find a stained copy of Julia Child's *Mastering
the Art of French Cooking*, with several recipes earmarked, including the
one for Beef Bourguignon.

"This cookbook had just come out when I came here in 1961,"
Alice exclaims. "Rose and I cooked from it together. I helped her make
a lot of these dishes, and others from that time period. My favorite was
pineapple upside-down cake."

I watch Alice stare off.

"What is it?" I ask.

She sighs. "I just wonder what my grandmother's life was like after I
left. Do you think, at some point, she gave up on loving people, needing
them? Do you suppose it was just too painful? I'm not sure what she
did in those years. Did loneliness eventually kill her? Would she have
lived longer if I had come to see her before I graduated from college?"

I consider this, then shake my head. "I think never seeing you again must have hurt her, but if we've learned anything about Rose, it's that she was a survivor. She loved, and she lost. But it seems she never closed her heart. She always had the courage to be vulnerable, to love again." I hold Alice's gaze. "Like you. I can imagine how vulnerable you must have felt mailing me that letter."

Alice nods. "I'd sent you so many cards over the years, for birthdays and Christmases, but year after year, I never heard back, and so one day, I stopped sending them. It hurt less that way. I didn't know if you would even receive the letter I typed, or reply, or want to see me again. But I was going to lose my home, the farm, everything I've ever known and loved. I knew I couldn't do this alone. Or rather, I didn't want to. I needed you."

I reach out and hug her, and we hold each other for a beat.

"Well, I can guarantee you *alone* is not something you're going to be now or in the near future," I say, pulling back to look her in the eyes. "In fact, with the number of people in this house, you must be begging for a few moments of silence."

We share a laugh.

"Speaking of not being *alone*," she starts, "Lenny asked me out last night."

I try to contain my enthusiasm. "Oh really?" I hold my expression in. "That's nice."

"Go ahead and celebrate. You know you want to."

I silently clap my hands. "I think he's *so nice*," I say.

"It's only dinner and a movie. They're showing *Casablanca* at the downtown theater." Alice shrugs. "We'll see."

The fact that Alice said yes is enough for me to let the topic go—for now.

We continue our work. Just as we pull the very last recipe from the box, we spot a cassette tape underneath. Alice grabs it and reads the inscription on the black-and-white label.

"Tunnel of Fudge Cake," she reads.

"Do you have a cassette player?" I ask.

As Alice pulls out the relic of technology, I cross my fingers that the tape is still in working condition. Alice presses play and we hear my great-great-grandmother Rose's voice. And from what she says, we gather she's conducting a cooking class at the farmhouse for some local teens. At the beginning of the recording, Rose gives a sort of introduction and mentions it's 1966, and she's been teaching the classes for three years. She's recording for one of her students, Linda, who is sick and can't attend. During the class, Rose shows the girls how to make a Tunnel of Fudge cake, which she says just won second place at the Pillsbury Bake-Off. They bake the cake in a Nordic Ware bundt pan, because that's the kind of pan the winner, Ella Helfrich of Texas, used.

Listening closely, we hear the names of a few of her students—Judith, Nancy, Donna—and realize these, along with Linda, are some of the names we found inscribed on the back of the Rosehill sign. The new sign—cut down from the original and placed to the left of the door—must be a symbol of a new chapter in Rose's life, a testament to Rosehill Farm's endurance.

When we finish listening to the tape, we sit in silent awe. What a gift, a keyhole peek into Rose's life after Alice left.

"See?" I say. "Rose didn't give up after you left. She kept finding ways to connect with other people, by sharing her gifts, by sharing the things she loved."

37

Spring 1963

On the first sunny spring Saturday, when the ice and snow melted and the air through the cracked window started to smell like grass, Rose decided to head to the new grocery store one town over to buy some ingredients she didn't have on hand. She was going to make Beef Bourguignon from her favorite cookbook. It highlighted authentic French cooking for American kitchens. It was a hearty dish, and she would take some next door to Carol and her husband, James, who'd been under the weather for quite some time. She'd dropped off chicken soup earlier in the week and a cinnamon coffee cake two days ago. But somehow, it didn't seem like enough, perhaps because she sensed in Carol's vacant stare when she answered the door that James's illness had turned grave. Preparing food was the least Rose could do. Sometimes it's the only way to show someone you care. *I'll make dessert too.* Pineapple upside-down cake, Alice's favorite.

As Rose moved about the new grocery store, collecting the items she needed—beef, garlic, bacon, fresh mushrooms, and red wine—she started to feel her mood lift. She'd been a bit sad the last few months, ever since Doris canceled her visit to California. She missed Alice. But today seemed different. She felt buoyant as she maneuvered her cart through the gleaming store, taking in the brilliant displays of fruits and vegetables, and she found herself making eye contact with and smiling at the other shoppers, as if they were all in on a secret.

Today, spring had sprung.

Today, I'm making beef Bourguignon and pineapple upside-down cake.

After she returned home, she neatly set out the ingredients on the countertop and pulled the other items she needed from the pantry. Cooking always felt easier when everything she needed was at her fingertips. Before starting, she set the mood by putting on a Skeeter Davis record in the parlor. She delighted in the woman's syrupy voice as the song "The End of the World" wafted through the air. She then opened her cookbook and began reviewing the recipe, but startled when she saw a teenage girl standing in the doorway. She was holding an empty Mason jar and one of Rose's dinner plates.

"I'm sorry," the girl pleaded over the record player in the next room. "I knocked, but no one answered. I'm Judith. Carol's niece. Well, great-niece. I've come to return your dishes." She held the items out like a peace offering.

"Of course. I remember. I met you at Christmas one year," Rose replied, rushing to take the items from the girl's hands. "I told Carol it was no rush at all," she added. "I didn't need them back anytime soon."

Judith tucked a strand of her blond bob behind her ear. "I think it gave her something to do—washing and drying them to give back to you."

Rose nodded. "Your uncle has been sick for some time."

"Yes, ma'am, he has."

A silence fell between them, and in that quiet, Rose knew her suspicions about James's health were true.

"Well, how fortunate Carol is to have your help," Rose said, putting the dishes back where they belonged. "Are you staying with them?"

"Right now, just on weekends. But when school lets out, I'll stay longer. I live in Green Point. My mother thought Carol could use some help in the house. But I don't know why she sent me. I don't think I'm much help to Carol. My sisters are both much better cooks. I can't even sew."

Rose smiled. "Maybe that's why your mother sent you, so you could learn. Nothing teaches you better than experience."

Judith shrugged. "I told her I'd try my best. You know, I was supposed to take a home economics class in the fall, but we have a new superintendent. He's from Chicago, and he's got very different ideas about how a high school should be run. He says they don't have the budget for that class anymore. He called it *antiquated*. Some of my classmates think it has something to do with that new book by Betty Friedan. They're letting the teacher go at the end of semester."

Rose noted the girl's disappointment. "Oh, that's too bad. That was what I studied in college, home economics," she explained. "What most people don't know is that it was actually designed to keep women *out* of the kitchen. As in, teach them to run a household so efficiently, like a science, so they could have more time for other endeavors."

Judith cocked her head. "That's interesting. I didn't know that."

Rose studied the girl's doe eyes and gentle disposition. "You really wanted to take that class, didn't you?"

Judith nodded. "My mom started working when I was ten. And I think that's wonderful. She really loves her job, and she's really good at it. But that's also why my sisters know how to do things—like cook and sew—and I don't. No one taught me."

Judith's eyes landed on Rose's French cookbook, the items on the counter. "What are you making?"

"One of Julia Child's recipes," Rose said, showing her the page. "And my granddaughter's favorite cake."

Judith looked to the corners of the kitchen, as if she could see beyond to the rooms upstairs, and sized up the home. "You have a big family to feed?"

"Actually, no. But at one time, I did." Rose traveled the twenty years in her mind, when twelve girls arrived in the back of Fred Jensen's truck and called this farmhouse home. "My children are grown and live far away. I live alone. This meal was just for me. But I like to eat well, alone or not. Of course, I was planning to send some over to Carol and James as well." Rose paused. "You know, if you really want to learn how to cook and sew, I'd be happy to teach you. I can teach you how to bake bread, can vegetables and jam, bake and frost cakes, roast a chicken, all sorts of things."

"Really?" Judith's eyes lit up.

"Yes, you could come for an hour or two each weekend when you visit Carol and more in the summer when school is out."

"Oh, and maybe some of my friends from school could come too?" Judith's eyes danced. "They're really great girls. Nancy, Donna, Shirley. They're disappointed about the class cancellation too."

Rose imagined this group of teenage girls crowded around her farmhouse kitchen, notebooks in hand, hanging on her every word. The thought tugged at her heart. "Well, sure, I don't see why not. We'll see how it goes with just us first. You'll have to make sure it's alright with your parents and Carol."

"Yes, ma'am." Judith beamed. "Could I help you now? Make the beef and the cake?"

Rose felt her cheeks warm. "I suppose. But I think you should call Carol first to check," she added, pointing to the telephone.

While Rose waited for Judith to make the call, she ran through the steps of the beef recipe in the book, as well as the ones for the pineapple upside-down cake, though she did know them by heart. Her process would be different and a tad slower if she had to stop and teach Judith along the way, and she considered how to manage the various tasks and timing. Thinking ahead, she cracked the kitchen window open a few inches, knowing the heat from both the stove and oven, plus the rising spring temperatures outside, would surely make the kitchen warmer than usual.

Rose took a long, deep breath of fresh spring air, then smiled.

Summer was on the horizon.

38

Christmas Eve

I close the door to our apartment as softly as possible, not wanting to wake Brady or Hannah quite yet, and step out into a dark, crisp morning. It's early, the sun has yet to rise, but I'm full of energy for what the day holds. I pull my wool cardigan tight as I walk the worn path from the barn to the farmhouse, anticipating a cup of coffee with Alice. Adding an apartment to the back side of the commercial kitchen had been Alice's idea, a way for Brady, Hannah, and me to live here, a way to co-run the Rosehill Farm B & B and Cooking School with Alice, while maintaining our own family residence. Of course, it was a good business decision as well. The fewer rooms we occupy in the main house, the more rooms we can rent out to travelers and cooking enthusiasts.

The B & B and school, both inspired by Rose, are closed for the next two weeks, but the house is anything but empty.

Katrine is here; she flew in two days ago for the holiday and will stay until New Year's. Nora and Johanna stayed home to be with family, but plan to visit in the summer.

Lucy and her daughter, Lynn, are also here for a few days. We've grown quite close to them in the past months. In addition to her hefty donation that helped saved the farm, Lucy also used her financial and business resources to locate Rose's son Hank, who had gone missing in action. Because of Lucy's efforts, Hank's remains were finally located in a common grave in Germany, and then brought back here for a proper burial. He now rests beside Rose and Charles in the St. John's Ferry cemetery. Lucy said it was the least she could do to thank Rose for the love and care she'd given her, all those years ago. Although we'd planned to bring Lucy to visit Peggy, Peggy unfortunately passed peacefully in her sleep before we made the trip.

My father and Ruth Rivers occupy the other two rooms. They drove in together from Minneapolis and seem to be getting along in a way that makes me giddy with hope. The thought that Ruth Rivers could one day be my stepmom is surreal, but I try not to get ahead of myself. With the five of them, plus Lenny, whom Alice goes out with every week but still calls her "friend," we are a total of ten for Christmas Eve dinner, Christmas morning brunch, and Christmas dinner. That's why Alice and I are meeting this morning, to run through the game plan for the holiday cooking. And to connect over a morning cup of coffee before the day's work unfolds.

I step onto the farmhouse porch. So much has changed. I see the Rosehill sign beside the door next to the bronze National Register of Historic Places plaque Lenny installed. We learned of the farmhouse's inclusion in the fall, after we'd already saved the farm with funds from the farm-to-table dinner and donations from Lucy and other donors, but I still count it as a win. It's a tribute to Rose, to the Women's Land Army farmerettes, and to the students in Rose's cooking class in the 1960s.

As I open and shut the farmhouse door, I catch a glimpse of the diamond ring on my left hand. A few weeks ago, on Thanksgiving, Brady asked me to marry him. He told me he left the recipe for his pumpkin-pecan pie in the pocket of my apron. I had slipped my hand there to find not a piece of paper but something hard and velvety. A ring box. I opened it to see a group of diamonds set like a rosette. It was vintage, ornate, and delicate. It had been his great-grandmother's ring; his mother had given it to him the last time he was back in Minneapolis.

"When did you know I was going to marry Maggie?" he asked her.

"I'm your mother," she said. "I knew the first time I met her."

"Really? What was it about her?" he asked.

"Oh, it wasn't her," she explained. "It was you. The look on your face when you introduced her. The way you act around her. She brings out the very best in you, Brady. And that is all I ever wanted for you."

Although I wasn't expecting the ring that particular morning, his proposal did not come as a surprise. After the farm-to-table dinner, I went home to Chicago and he to Madison. We tried long distance but soon found out we really couldn't stand being apart. Living without seeing him every day felt like walking around without the other half of my body. And we both deeply missed St. John's Ferry. So we began building our life together over the phone one night, dreaming up the idea of moving here, running a full-time cooking school in conjunction with the B & B. On paper, it seemed like a plan full of obstacles—quitting jobs, selling property, packing and moving, enrolling Hannah in first grade at the local school, the same school Alice attended as a child—but it all felt effortless. I'm not sure why. Maybe it was because I felt certain I was on the right path.

I just kept saying yes to that little voice inside me.

The power of that voice felt evident when we attended Hannah's first-grade holiday concert last week. As I watched her sing and dance to "Let It Snow," I couldn't help but remember the night of her kindergarten graduation seven months ago, when I felt like my brain and body were at odds with each other, in two different places. But as I sat between Brady and Alice in the St. John's Ferry Elementary School auditorium and watched Hannah onstage, my mind and heart had never felt more in sync.

When I make my way to the farmhouse kitchen, I find Alice at the counter, pouring us two mugs of coffee.

"Good morning," she sings. "Merry Christmas Eve."

"Merry Christmas Eve," I say back to her, and we hug. It's a firm, all-encompassing embrace.

"How did you sleep?" She hands me my mug, already fixed the way I like it.

I sip my coffee before answering. "I had a hard time falling asleep," I finally say.

"Me too." She laughs. "Too excited."

We lean against the counter, talking. "To be honest, I'm rethinking the brisket," I divulge. "I found a recipe from the 1950s that uses cola in the braise. It makes it really tender. I think I want to do that instead."

Alice nods her approval. "I'll add cola to the shopping list," she says. "I was tinkering with the kringle recipe. I think I want to do half whole wheat in place of the high-protein flour."

"Oh, that sounds good," I tell her. "It will add a deeper flavor. A nuttiness."

"I think it will still turn out okay. Don't you?"

"I don't see why not. But you can always ask Brady, or my dad."

"I don't want to bother him. He's our guest this week."

I smirk. "You know he's not going to sit back and let us wait on him, right? He will have his hands in everything. That's just what he does."

Alice smiles. "True."

Having my father in my life—at Christmas or anytime—has been the most unexpected blessing of the past months. We talk on the phone several times a week and text daily. And while he still lives in Minneapolis, he and Brady are actually talking about opening a bakery together in downtown St. John's Ferry. It's hard to believe that someone I never knew could become such an integral part of my life. But he is my father, and we have found so much in common beyond our love of food. We can talk for hours. Our discussions run deep—we tackle big ideas and abstract concepts and never reach a conclusion, which is just fodder for our next conversation. Our talks are ongoing and complex. Brady and I have great conversations too. And I adore my chats with Alice. After what went down at the farm-to-table dinner, even my relationship with my mother has improved—I now try to focus our conversations on what we do have in common. But my relationship with my father is most unique; being with him is a lot like being with myself, in the least lonely way possible.

Next Christmas, we're even planning to go to Sweden to meet my aunts, uncles, and cousins. It's hard to believe I have a whole family I've never met. In another country, no less. Looking back, the Scandi Trio was right when they told me I *looked* Scandinavian. Little did we know it was close to 50 percent.

"Well, should we get started?" I ask Alice, grabbing a yellow steno pad and pen and heading to the kitchen table.

"There's something I want you to open first," she says.

I see her reach under the table and grab a wrapped present. It must have been sitting on the chair out of sight. She hands it to me.

"But aren't we opening presents tomorrow?" I protest, unwrapping the box anyway.

"Yes, but by then, it will be too late."

I peel back the paper and uncover a white box. I lift the lid to see a familiar pattern. It's almost identical to the fabric Rose used to make Lucy an apron all those years ago. I reach for the fabric and shake it out to reveal an adult-size apron just like the one Rose made Lucy, ruffles and all.

"You didn't!"

"I did."

"I love it!"

"I knew you would. I thought you and Hannah could be twins."

I steal a peek at the side of the cabinet, where the matching child-size apron hangs on a hook. That day Lucy came to the farmhouse back in June, she'd taken the letter from Rose with her but gifted the apron to Hannah.

"This looks about your size," she told my daughter, who immediately put the apron on and twirled around as if it were a taffeta gown.

"Fits like a glove," Alice said. "Like it was made for her."

"It was." Lucy smiled and let her eyes flit around the room. "It was made for a girl destined to learn and grow in this kitchen."

Now, I slip the apron Alice made over my neck and tie the strings tight around my waist, that familiar sense of duty rushing over me as I don my new uniform. Then I reach for Alice and pull her in for a long hug.

Alice quickly steals the pen and paper from the table. "So, what's first?" she asks, taking on the stenographer role now that her arthritis has improved. She does this almost every time we plan a meal together.

And I let her.

Because while she writes, I get to talk. And ask questions. And let my eyes dance around to all the intricate nooks of this kitchen, where I seem to find more than just the inspiration to cook, but a recipe for life.

ACKNOWLEDGMENTS

Human connection is a core theme of this novel, and in my opinion, the secret to finding happiness. It is also the secret to my success as a writer, as I could not do this dream job without the love, support, and guidance of some truly amazing people.

I will be forever grateful to my literary agent, Kevan Lyon, who not only opened her heart to this book via a cold query, but continued to champion it every step of the way. Kevan, you always seemed to know what I needed to hear and how to say it—nudging me when to let go and when to hold firm—and I continue to pinch myself at being one of the clients on your who's who list of authors. A special thanks to the staff at Marsal Lyon Literary Agency, especially Lexie Krauss, for supporting this book early on, and to Ashley Hayes, of Uplit Marketing, for promoting my work in the social media realm.

A heartfelt thank you to my editor at Lake Union, Emily Freidenrich, who understood this story on so many levels and who never seemed to waver in her enthusiasm for it. Emily, working with you has been an absolute godsend. The time, attention, and care you have given me and this manuscript is everything an author hopes for. Also at Lake Union, a shout-out to Carmen Johnson for forwarding this manuscript to Emily, somehow knowing we'd be a perfect match. I'd also like to thank my editors Brittany Dowdle, Jenna Justice, and Phyllis DeBlanche. And I can't forget to thank Emily Mahon for her beautiful cover design.

When it comes to developmental editors, Laura Chasen is one of a kind. I could not have asked for a more experienced, talented, and thoughtful editor to whip this manuscript into shape. Laura, I have never felt so seen. You seemed to inherently understand this story and its characters almost as much as me, and I felt I had a true partner in the editorial process. You pushed me past my comfort zone time and time again, asking me to go deeper and write scenes I'd avoided writing in the past. Your ability to get inside my characters' minds was uncanny at times, and your personal knowledge of Scandinavian lifestyle proved invaluable. I am truly honored and blessed to have worked with you.

To my first readers—Gail Angell, Laura Biela, Katie Colfer, Laura Dutzi, and Neil Hansen—for providing thoughtful and helpful feedback in the development of this book. Each of you gifted me with insights that made this book so much better.

I was fortunate to acquire and read books that inspired and informed some of the plot, historical details, and themes of this book. These include *On the Farm Front: The Women's Land Army in World War II* by Stephanie A. Carpenter; *The Year of Living Danishly: Uncovering the Secrets of the World's Happiest Country* by Helen Russell; *The Little Book of Hygge* by Meik Wiking; *Old Farm Country Cookbook: Recipes, Menus, and Memories* by Jerry Apps and Susan Apps-Bodilly; and *Women in the Kitchen: Twelve Essential Cookbook Writers Who Defined the Way We Eat, from 1661 to Today* by Ann Willan.

In addition to these books, I found this *Prologue Magazine* article extremely helpful: "To the Rescue of the Crops: The Women's Land Army During World War II" (Winter 1993, vol. 25, no. 4) by Judy Barrett Litoff and David C. Smith. Special thanks to the Smithsonian National Museum of American History's Behring Center for their depiction and descriptions of Julia Child's kitchen and to Michigan State University's "Spud Harvest" depictions of potato harvesting in the 1940s. I also found the hallongrottor tips and tricks on scandinavian-cookbook.com especially helpful.

A warm thank-you to Nicole Bujewski of The Book Kitchen in Mineral Point, Wisconsin, for her support for and enthusiasm of this book, and her expertise in helping me develop the recipe in the appendix. I also thank the Elawa Farm Foundation in Lake Forest, Illinois, where I attended a gorgeous farm-to-table event, which inspired the writing of specific scenes in this book.

To my fellow author friends, including Kate Quinn, Renee Rosen, Aimee K. Runyan, and the other "Lyonesses" for their ongoing support and encouragement, providing insights on everything from book titles to social media promotion. You inspire and educate me, and I am so lucky to have been welcomed into this elite group. Also thank you to author Mary Kubica for her continued friendship, support, and inspiration.

There are so many talented women I admire in the food world, and they have inspired me not only in the kitchen but in these pages. These include Giada De Laurentiis, Zoë François, Erin French, Joanna Gaines, Ina Garten, Dorie Greenspan, Sophie Hansen, Elizabeth Poett, Jessie Sheehan, Nancy Silverton, Ruth Reichl, and Alice Waters. I also thank Kerry Diamond and Diana Yen at *Cherry Bombe Magazine*, and the members of the Cherry Bombe Bombesquad for inspiring me and for educating me about the culinary world.

A sincere thank-you to author Sasha Martin and her book *Life from Scratch*, the book that marks the beginning of my renewed passion for food and my love of food memoirs.

I am indebted to the wonderful independent bookstore owners who support authors by recommending books and hosting events. I am especially thankful for Arlene Lynes, of Read Between the Lynes in Woodstock, Illinois, for never giving up on me. Arlene, every time I saw you, you asked about my next writing project, never ceasing to believe that I would indeed finish and publish another manuscript. I always left our visits with renewed confidence in myself.

Thank you to the wonderful libraries of Chicagoland, which provided a peaceful, inspiring setting for writing this book and quiet contemplation. I also thank Panera Bread and their sip club for providing a "home office" too many times to count during the writing of this book.

To my readers, thank you for championing my first book and the wonderful reviews you shared. Please know, I went back and read those positive reviews when I needed encouragement along the way, when I needed a reminder that I am in fact a good writer and can do this. I hope you love this book as much as the last, and it inspires you on your own path to happiness, whatever that looks like for you.

To my family and friends who supported me along the way, cheered me on, or provided feedback on book titles.

I am fortunate to have a very loving and supportive family that encourages my goals. Specifically, thank you to my mother, Gail, for her unwavering support of my dreams. Mom, you always told me I could do whatever I put my mind to, and I believed you. Thanks to my sister, Lisa, for always being my number one cheerleader. You are the most fun person I know, and I have to remind myself to be more like you. Thanks to my father, George, for his continued enthusiasm and always being ready to tell people about me and my books.

I am forever grateful to my children, who have taught me as much about life as I have tried to teach them and inspire me to be the best version of myself. To Luke and Amelia, who endured two full years of homeschooling during the pandemic, a life-changing experience that helped me rediscover my love of food and history and breathed life back into my career. And to Andy, my fellow "foodie," who not only shares my passion for good food but also helped me test recipes for the back of the book.

And finally, to the love of my life, my husband, Neil, the rock beneath me. Neil, you have always gifted me the space and time to do what I love. You are always there for me—whether it's to develop cocktail recipes or serve as a sounding board for my ideas—and I could not do what I do or do it well without your support. I love you and the beautiful life we've created.

I am always happier here with you.

BOOK CLUB DISCUSSION PROMPTS

1. Memory plays an important role in this novel, especially early childhood memories. For example, Maggie and Lucy both remember moments from when they are only three years old. What is your earliest memory? Upon reflection, is there anything remarkable or telling about this memory?

2. Maggie's mother, Diane, asked Alice to care for Maggie for several years while she finished school. While Maggie understands the struggle of balancing motherhood and career, she also judges her mother for "outsourcing" her role as a parent. How would you feel if you were Maggie? Can you understand the situation from Diane's point of view? When is it acceptable for a parent to hand off the care of a child? Are fathers held to the same standard as mothers in this regard?

3. At first, Maggie is wary of going to Alice's farm because cell phone service is spotty and there is no internet access. Once there, she is surprised when her desire to connect to technology is suppressed. In what ways do you rely on modern technology? To what extent could you live without a cell phone, internet, and social media? What are the benefits and drawbacks of technology?

4. Maggie reflects on occasions in her early childhood that illustrate her natural ability and curiosity with food. Looking back on your own childhood, what were your innate interests and

skills? As you matured, did you follow these instincts or chart a different path? Why do you think you made this decision? To what extent should we put stock in our early childhood interests?

5. World War II and the Women's Land Army provide plot background for the flashback chapters from Rose's point of view. While the British WLA has been featured in television and film, the American WLA is lesser known. How much did you know about the WLA before reading this book? Did anything about the program surprise you? What impact do you think this program had on women's changing roles in society?

6. The Scandi Trio introduces Maggie to the concept of *hygge*, which essentially translates to "cozy comfort." What brings you comfort? In what ways could you incorporate more cozy contentment every day?

7. Maggie feels closer to Brady once he reveals his understanding of loss and shares details about the death of his twin brother. How has a shared experience connected you to other people? Is it a prerequisite for connection or can a relationship grow from difference?

8. The role of motherhood is prominent in this book. Many women—Rose, Alice, and Maggie—play a motherly role to young women in their lives. Thinking back on your life, which women helped shape you? What roles can grandmothers, aunts, or family friends play in our lives? In what ways can motherhood be exemplified without biological ties?

9. Near the end of the novel, after a home economics class is canceled, Rose begins teaching a culinary class for young girls. Home economics has seen great decline in high school, often replaced by electives like culinary arts and fashion design. In your opinion, should home economics still be taught? What are the benefits and drawbacks of a course like this?

10. The two storylines—present day and the 1940s—focus on two characters, Maggie and Rose, respectively. What do these two women's stories have in common? How do their experiences differ? Which character did you identify with more? Why?

11. Happiness is an overarching theme of this book. In your opinion, is happiness the ultimate pursuit of life? What benefits or drawbacks could this pursuit create? How do you know if you're happy? What does happiness look or feel like to you?

12. By the end of the book, Maggie's life has changed dramatically, but the journey required courage and the choice to step outside her comfort zone. If you had the means—money, time, energy, freedom, courage, et cetera—to chase a dream, what would that dream be? Are there any small steps you could take now to pursue this dream?

RECIPES

RASPBERRY CAVES (HALLONGROTTOR)

MAKES TWENTY COOKIES

Ingredients

20 paper muffin liners
1½ cups all-purpose flour
1 cup (two sticks) unsalted butter, room temperature
½ cup sugar
¼ teaspoon salt
1 teaspoon vanilla
1 teaspoon lemon zest (from about 1 lemon)
1 egg yolk
½ cup raspberry preserves
powdered sugar for dusting

Directions

1. Preheat oven to 350 degrees F. Set out twenty paper muffin liners on a double sheet pan. (Liners are essential for cookies to keep shape and minimize spread.)
2. Sift the all-purpose flour into a mixing bowl and set aside.

3. To the bowl of a stand mixer fitted with the paddle attachment (or a separate mixing bowl and electric hand mixer), add the butter, sugar, salt, vanilla, and lemon zest and mix on medium speed for five minutes until pale yellow, light, and fluffy, scraping down sides of bowl with a rubber spatula several times as needed. Add the egg yolk and mix again on medium until just combined.

4. Using a rubber spatula, fold half of the flour into the butter mixture until incorporated. Then fold in the remaining half until fully incorporated and dough is uniform in color.

5. Wrap the dough in plastic wrap, flatten into a disk, and chill in refrigerator for 15 minutes.

6. Working quickly, scoop about one tablespoon of dough, roll into a ball, place in muffin liner, and repeat process with remaining dough, lightly dusting hands with flour if dough becomes too sticky. Using your thumb in a downward motion, make an indentation in the center of each ball. (Tip: Dip your thumb in flour, shaking off excess, before making each indentation to prevent it from sticking to the dough.)

7. Place a dollop (scant ¾ teaspoon) of preserves in the center of each cookie.

8. Bake for 15–20 minutes, until edges are just starting to brown and the preserves are starting to bubble.

9. Cool for 5 minutes on pan before removing to fully cool/set on wire rack.

10. Dust with powdered sugar, if desired. Remove liners and serve.

Recipe developed by Nicole Bujewski of The Book Kitchen and Amy Gail Hansen

Nordic June

Makes 1 Cocktail

Ingredients

1 ounce lime juice

2 ounces cucumber juice (see note*)

1½ ounces aquavit liquor

2½ ounces citrus-herb syrup (see recipe below)

½ cup of ice

2 ounces premium club soda

1 rosemary sprig (optional for garnish)

Directions

1. Add lime juice, cucumber juice, aquavit, and citrus-herb syrup to a glass and stir.
2. Add ice, then top off with club soda. Garnish with rosemary sprig.

Note:

* To prepare cucumber juice without a juicing machine, peel then chop one medium-size cucumber. Puree the chopped cucumber with an immersion blender or in a blender. Strain the pulp through a piece of cheesecloth or by pressing it through a fine sieve/strainer. Collect the juices and discard or reuse the pulp for another purpose. One medium cucumber will make about one cup of juice.

Citrus-Herb Syrup

Ingredients

2 rosemary sprigs
2 teaspoons dried fennel seeds
2 teaspoons dried caraway seeds
½ lemon peel (cut off in ½-inch to 1-inch pieces)
½ orange peel (cut off in ½-inch to 1-inch pieces)
1¼ cup water
1 tablespoon sugar
1 tablespoon honey

Directions

1. Combine all ingredients into a small saucepan and bring to a boil.
2. Decrease heat to low and lightly simmer 5 minutes, stirring occasionally.
3. Remove from heat and cool completely.
4. Strain and chill until ready for use.

Note:

To prepare a nonalcoholic version, omit aquavit and increase citrus-herb syrup to 4 ounces.

Cocktail recipes developed by Amy Gail Hansen, Andrew Hansen, and Neil Hansen

ABOUT THE AUTHOR

© 2024 Neil Hansen

Amy Gail Hansen is the author of *The Butterfly Sister*. A former English teacher and journalist, Amy is also a professional food-history lecturer on topics ranging from Midwest sweets to New Orleans cuisine. She is an avid cook, baker, and reader, and never ceases to be amazed by the story of food and the remarkable ways it shapes our lives. She lives in the Chicago suburbs with her husband and three children. For more information, visit www.amygailhansen.com.